THE
CRASH

Robert Peston is ITV's political editor, presenter of the politics show *Peston*, founder of the education charity, Speakers for Schools (www.speakers4schools.org), and vice president of Hospice UK. He has written four critically acclaimed non-fiction books, *How Do We Fix This Mess?*, *Who Runs Britain?*, *Brown's Britain* and his latest, *WTF?*, which was described by the *Financial Times* as 'mandatory reading' for anyone seeking to understand Brexit, Trump and the collapse of confidence in western liberalism. His first thriller, *The Whistleblower*, published by Zaffre, was 'brilliant' according to the *Guardian* and called 'a rollicking read' by the *Evening Standard. The Crash* is its sequel.

For a decade until the end of 2015, he was at the BBC, as economics editor and business editor, and in the 1990s he was at the *Financial Times*, as political editor, financial editor and head of investigations. At the BBC he played a prominent role in exposing the causes and consequences of the credit crunch, banking crisis and Great Recession. Peston has won more than thirty awards for his journalism, including Journalist of the Year and Scoop of the Year (twice) from the Royal Television Society.

Find him on his blog at itv.com/robertpeston, on Facebook at facebook.com/pestonITV, and on Twitter @peston. He hosts a podcast with Steph McGovern, *The Rest is Money*.

ROBERT PESTON

THE CRASH

ZAFFRE

First published in the UK in 2023 by
ZAFFRE
An imprint of Zaffre Publishing Group
A Bonnier Books UK Company
4th Floor, Victoria House, Bloomsbury Square, London, WC1B 4DA
Owned by Bonnier Books
Sveavägen 56, Stockholm, Sweden

A CIP catalogue record for this book is
available from the British Library.

Hardback ISBN: 978-1-83877-778-4
Trade paperback ISBN: 978-1-83877-779-1

Also available as an ebook and an audiobook

1 3 5 7 9 10 8 6 4 2

Typeset by IDSUK (Data Connection) Ltd
Printed and bound in Great Britain by Clays Ltd, Elcograf S.p.A.

Zaffre is an imprint of Zaffre Publishing Group
A Bonnier Books UK company
www.bonnierbooks.co.uk

For Jul and Ed

Prologue

WHO KNEW THAT HAVING MY little finger cut off with a pair of secateurs would feel like injecting a speedball? I feel high and low, pinging and woozy. I suppose this makes some kind of sense. I never had reason to think about what happens when a limb, even a small one, is severed without anaesthetic. Why would I? My kind of journalism is a relatively low-contact sport. But the acute pain has induced an adrenaline rush and now, what with the blood oozing through the gauze, my oxygen levels are on the low side. Presumably.

As a scoop-getting reporter, I am adept at assessing risk. I don't say that to show off. Just to insist that I'm not being melodramatic. There is no point lying to myself. I can exclusively reveal that the odds of me passing out and dying here, on the top floor of this monstrous architectural tribute to financial globalisation, are greater than evens. But I don't feel especially anxious or scared. Maybe it's the shock-induced speedball. Or perhaps the deaths of people I love have given me perspective.

There are worse things than it ending now. Like having to listen to more of their self-important bollocks, their instructions to write a blog asserting that what they've done is in the national interest. They want me to be their reputational launderette. But the last laugh is on them. I inserted a coded message into the blog, which my colleagues at the BBC will instantly translate, and any minute now they'll be picked up by a squad of armed and uniformed Metropolitan Police officers.

Except I didn't do that. I wouldn't know how. And even if I did, it would have put Amy and Jess in too much danger.

They've won. I'm done. It's over. Probably for the last time, I am alone again, not counting Bill and his special forces mate, who are chatting and smiling as they monitor my final minutes. Bless 'em. Thank God that Bill, unlike his employers, doesn't feel compelled to go on and on about how it's my duty, for once in my life, to rescue a bank, rather than bring it down. They say I should think about what's good for the people. They mean for themselves. Cunts.

Through the wall-to-ceiling windows, two hundred and fifty metres below, is the capital, spread out like a geometric carpet. London is my town. Always has been. If I shout loud enough in my head, it will be like a BBC broadcast. They'll hear me down there and I'll be saved.

'You all right, mate?' Bill says. 'Soon be over. Don't you worry.'

I shoot him a winning smile. Or at least I hope that's what it was. Who knows anymore?

I remember my lost finger, my darling little finger. We've been through so much together. Did they put it in the front pocket of my Lacroix jacket? I think so. Not much use it being there. What am I going to use to scratch the right side of my nose? If that's impossible, I might as well give up, pack it all in. I'm tired. So tired. What's that wetness on my face? Oh no. I'm crying. I can't stop myself. *Kill me now, kill me now, kill me now.* Bill is walking over, with his colleague. If I die here, at least I've done the right thing.

For once.

Chapter 1

'**M**um. Please. You are not going to die.'
'You don't know that. You're not a doctor.'
'I've spoken to the doctors.'

Not for the first or last time, I wonder why my mother, Ginger Peck, needs me when things go wrong but argues with me about everything. We are in the Royal Marsden Hospital in fashionable Fulham Road. Its design is supposed to dispel the inevitable dread that accompanies a cancer diagnosis. All around us are plate-glass windows, with panoramic views of West London. We're a stone's throw from somewhere Mum and I would rather be, the art nouveau jewel of Michelin House and Terence Conran's exquisite Bibendum restaurant, where we could be anaesthetising ourselves with champagne. Instead the poison of choice here is actual poison, toxic compounds manufactured to kill cancerous cells. This is a factory farm of patients with assorted malignant tumours, hooked up to clear plastic bags, hanging from IV poles, whose thin tubes drip the lethal chemotherapy fluid through cannulas and into the bloodstream.

'Mum, the operation was a great success. They cut everything out. The chemo is just an extra protection. Adjuvant Chemotherapy. You're having it to wipe out any stray cells they couldn't see.'

'Doctors lie.'

'Mum, they don't.' I screw up my eyes tight. She's right, of course. Doctors are often economical with the truth, especially when they fear the patient can't handle it, and when they do that very human thing of talking up the slim odds that a horse called 'remission' will finish first. But I have spoken at length to Dr Khan, and I am persuaded Mum's doing as well as we could have hoped.

I've been parenting my parents in crises for as long as I can remember. Actually, that's me building my part, which some would say is typical. In fact I've been parenting them for ten years, since my big sister Clare was murdered. Till then, she was always the grown-up in the family, the one who comforted our child-like parents. Since she died, I've used my work addiction to keep a distance from them, except when there's a crisis and they can't cope – which happens too often. Their conceit, especially dad's, is the two of them live by the rules of pure reason. It's largely a fiction. Much of the time they are scared and emotionally stunted children, the Ashkenazi Jewish legacy, perhaps. Whenever they're ill, it's both the end of the world and denial like you've never seen. Here's the pathology: Mum assumes she's about to die, Dad says doctors (or dentists, or psychiatrists) are charlatans licensed to do harm and refuses to accept she's in trouble. Which is why I am here, mothering my mum, while Dad's at home doing *The Times* crossword.

The lady in the blue leatherette armchair next to Mum turns to her. She might be my age, though life's not been kind to her. Her skin is too pale and white, and her warm, deep brown eyes are exhausted. She's smiling, though.

'Is this your first time?' Mum nods. 'My third. It's not so bad, once you get used to it.'

'That's good to hear,' I say. 'Did you hear that, Mum?'

'I can't pretend it's not tiring,' the lady continues, 'especially when you get home and the chemo starts killing all the cells. You won't want to get out of bed for a day or two.' I can see the anxiety

2

in Mum's eyes. 'The thing I hate most is the steroids. They make me feel very anxious, and they fizz up my brain, if you know what I mean – which isn't great when I'm worried anyway.'

Mum tries to be brave and smiles invitingly. 'I'm Ginger.'

'Nice to meet you. Liz. I'm Liz. Hope I didn't worry you. I didn't mean to. This is definitely the best place to be for people like us.'

There's a buzzing in the pocket of my black pinstripe Ozwald Boateng trousers. It's one of the two BlackBerries I carry everywhere. I try to ignore it, but the itch of not knowing who's trying to reach me is unbearable. It's the bat phone, the BlackBerry whose number I share with just a tiny number of the most important people in my life. I don't mean friends, but rather the well-connected contacts who might be able to help me with a story. I've always been too negligent with those who may have thought of themselves as friends, but it's not something over which I lose sleep. Work is the thing.

Although the buzzing stops, I have to look at the screen or I'll go mad. My hand's already tugging it out of my pocket.

'Sorry, Mum.'

'It's fine, Gil. Your work is important.' She pauses. 'Though I honestly don't know why you came with me today. You fuss too much. I would have managed perfectly well on my own.'

'Mum!'

'Is this your son?' says Liz. 'Don't I recognise you from somewhere?'

'You probably saw him on the news. He works for the BBC.'

I half register my mum showing off about me. My attention is on my BlackBerry. The text is from Tracy, the PA to Downing Street's director of communications, who I've been sort of dating. Which means we've been having secret, late-night, after-work sex. We'd both be in the shit if our bosses knew, but she's decided she doesn't care, and wants to normalise the relationship. In a moment of weakness, I agreed to go on a

3

double date with her best friend, a Number 10 press officer who has a stockbroker boyfriend.

8, says the message. *The Wolseley. Don't be late.*

I don't reply. Giving Mum a side glance, I see she has unfolded the *Guardian*, so I take the opportunity to look at emails. Seventy-four new messages. I scroll through the subject summaries, which are the usual mix of BBC corporate directives, PR flacks urging me to big up their clients – *they can all fuck off* – and analysts who obviously never watch the BBC, because they think we'll care that they've changed their recommendation on the shares of this or that multinational.

Revised expenses limits for BBC entertaining
NewGate recommendation upgraded from neutral to buy
Temporary fund freeze

I pause at the last subject line, and click. It's a press release, which I would normally delete without reading. The sender is a French bank, Banque de Maghreb, or BM, which in recent years has built a substantial investment management arm in the City of London. What do they mean by a 'fund freeze'? That's novel. I read.

BM Capital Bank temporarily suspends the calculation of the net asset value of the following funds. What follows is a list of investment funds, all managed by BM, that contain hundreds of millions of dollars harvested by BM from professional investors. The bank says:

It has become impossible to value certain assets accurately, irrespective of their quality, because of the evaporation of liquidity in important segments of the US securitisation market. In particular, it is not possible to value the assets underlying US ABS in our funds. This means we cannot provide a reliable net asset value for the funds. In order to protect the interests of our investors, and to make sure they are treated equally, BM Capital Bank is suspending redemptions from and subscriptions to the funds until further notice.

I read this twice, bewildered. BM is saying it will no longer allow its investors to withdraw their money from a fund made up entirely of so-called asset-backed bonds. The bank says it is incapable of valuing them so it dare not allow its investors to cash in, just in case it gives investors too much money, or – I suppose – too little. This is extraordinary in so many ways, but most of all because the bank is telling its customers they can't withdraw their money. *They can't have their money!*

Surely this is a huge story. I bite my thumb and think hard. As usual when I think, I start pacing and nodding my head back and forth. When I was a child, this mannerism drove Mum mad, she said I looked as though I was *shuckling*, or rocking like an ultra-Orthodox Jew at prayer. 'We're not in the *shtetl* anymore,' she would say, long before I knew what she meant. I am trying to remember when a bank last refused to give customers their money, drawing on twenty years of professional interest in these things.

'This never happens,' I mutter under my breath, as I get that familiar and addictive rush of excitement from spotting a story and wanting to nail it before anyone else.

This one will be a challenge. At the BBC, everything has to be explained simply enough to make sense to the whole nation. I tried to do that, even when at the *Financial Chronicle*. But since moving to the BBC I've learned that my obsession with finance and numbers is not shared by everyone. We did a survey and discovered that a third of our audience had no idea that high interest rates were bad for them if they had debts on their credit cards. So what on earth will they make of 'asset-backed securities'? I am not even sure I understand them, having filed them in my head under the category of the boring gubbins of financial capitalism. They're like sewage and water pipes. We don't need to understand precisely how they work or where they are, so long as when we turn on the tap the water comes out. Only when the loo won't flush do we wish we had an inkling how to fix it.

I need to talk to someone who lives and breathes this stuff. Jess? My erstwhile protégé at the *Financial Chronicle* is cleverer and more diligent than me, and inevitably she's now higher up the food chain, as the *FC*'s deputy editor. But on a story like this, she's a competitor; I'll wait before ringing her. Marilyn? She'd be my best bet: these days she's paid to spot accidents like BM's before they happen and stop them. But ringing is a bit dodgy. As director of financial stability at the Bank of England she's not supposed to talk with media reptiles like me. And what's also probably relevant is we've been on-off-on lovers for much of my adult life. If you've heard about the problem of conflicts of interest in the City of London, and the so-called Chinese walls that are attempts to limit them, well my relationship with Marilyn is not so much a coach and horses through them but a wrecking ball.

Mum has her eyes closed and is nodding over her paper. I can't tell if she's asleep, but I won't disturb her. I text Marilyn.

Chat?

What about? pings back instantly.

BM.

There's a pause. Finally: *5 mins.*

Mum opens her eyes. 'You don't have to stay, darling. You've got work to do.'

'I want to stay. But I have got to make a quick call.'

I walk to the stairwell and wait. Exactly five minutes later, a call comes in from 'number withheld'.

'Hi lover boy.'

'Hi beautiful.' I can hear the sound of traffic. She's gone for a walk, and I picture her in Throgmorton Street just behind the Bank of England, and despite myself, the two of us in her bed. She's naked, except for her stupidly expensive black French lace bra, her indulgence. She's on my face. Moaning. 'I shouldn't be talking to you, but I miss you,' she says.

That's a bit different. She doesn't normally proffer endearments.

'Miss you too.'

My emotional antennae are worst in class, but I wonder why the affection. 'All OK? You sound a bit down.'

'Just a bit overworked. How's your mum?'

I'd forgotten I'd told her about Ginger's cancer. 'Making progress. It is hard though.'

'You clocked the BM press release. I thought you would.'

Straight to the point, as usual.

'What do you need to know?'

'What's gone wrong? Why doesn't BM know how much its funds are worth? Does this have implications for other banks?'

She breathes out heavily. 'You said a quick chat. I'll tell you as much as I can, but I haven't got long.'

'I owe you.'

'Yes.' The traffic noise recedes. She must have turned off the main road. 'I'm going to go back to basics, and forgive me if you know some of this. Do you know what an asset-backed security is?'

'Pretend I don't.'

She laughs. 'They're investments, bonds. They pay a coupon, in effect an interest rate. Typically they're manufactured and sold by banks, but they don't have to be.'

She really does think I'm an idiot. But I won't interrupt.

'Now the thing about these ABS bonds is that they're fashioned out of the loans the bank has made to its customers.'

'Like mortgages.'

'Exactly. Loads of mortgages. So the kind of ABS bonds called mortgage-backed securities, or MBS bonds, are a mixture of tiny slices of thousands and thousands of mortgages. In other words, the owner of one MBS bond would receive slivers of the interest paid by an army of people who've borrowed from the banks to buy their homes.'

I'm beginning to panic about how on earth I can tell this story on air. At this point, I am working hard to keep up. What will the BBC's viewers and listeners make of it?

'That's sort of amazing.'

'Don't be too amazed, because there are securities that are even more extraordinary. Banque de Maghreb's funds own a more rarified form of ABS, called CDOs, or collateralised debt obligations.'

This is never getting on air.

'Going back to why this is a problem, home owners are still paying their mortgages, aren't they?'

She snorts. 'In the UK, yeah, pretty much. But do you know what a subprime loan is?'

'Obviously.' I regret the impatience in my tone. I need as much from her as I can get. 'It's a home loan provided to a riskier borrower, probably in the US, and someone who might be in an insecure job or on a low income.'

'Yes, but believe it or not, those aren't the highest-risk ones. We've recently learned that the American banks have been giving mortgages to people who haven't got *any* job or source of income at all.'

'You're joking.'

'I wish. It's been going on for years.'

'How is that even possible?'

'It became attractive for banks, because these subprime borrowers are charged a higher rate of interest, at a time when interest rates in general are pretty low. So superficially they could be more profitable than other loans.'

'Not if the interest is never actually paid.'

'Exactly.'

The BlackBerry vibrates with an incoming message; I ignore it. All my attention is on what Marilyn is telling me.

'So – to state what you already know – anyone without a job, or who loses their job, will struggle to pay the interest. And that's where the CDOs come in. Think of them as financial sausages. Into the grinder you put in some proper beef, but you also mix in some offal and maybe even fat and gristle and bits that nobody wants to think about. Out the end comes something you can fry and eat. The idea of CDOs is pretty much the same. The bankers mince together risky loans with less risky loans, and then slice and dice them into bonds. The idea is to turn something poisonous into something edible. You could see it as modern-day alchemy. It's been brilliant business for the banks.'

'But?'

'Yeah, there's definitely a *but*. A few months ago, there was a housing downturn in the US. And not just any downturn. One that led to borrowers all over America failing to repay loans. And at that point the claim made for CDOs, that they are secure investments, was – to put it mildly – tested.'

'And?'

'We can safely say the BM Capital statement shows there's a problem. BM is admitting it doesn't have a clue how to value these CDO bonds, what price to put on them.'

I close my eyes to concentrate. 'I see. So each of these different CDOs contain thousands and thousands of different home loans, and BM is saying it can't be sure which of the bonds contain half-decent loans, that will ultimately be repaid, and which are made out of garbage. So it can't give investors their money because it doesn't know how much of that money has been lost. Is that right?'

'Yup. BM, which bought these CDOs from American banks, is calling out the banks that created these bonds. It's the little boy shouting the emperor has no clothes.'

'And does the nakedness of the emperor matter only to BM's customers or is it more important than that?'

'It's definitely important. Without anyone noticing, this bond market has exploded in size. There are different types of CDOs, and also insurance policies for the CDOs. The investors who buy them borrow more money using the bonds as collateral. And then they borrow again to reinvest again and again and again. It's a market in total worth trillions of dollars.'

Trillions. I pause.

'You said "trillions"?'

'Lots of trillions. And the market is a vital source of finance for banks because when banks sell the loans they've made to investors, they use the proceeds to lend more to households and businesses. So if there is a problem in the ABS market it turns into a problem for the whole economy. It's like turning off a mains pipe feeding the system. It could lead to a shortage of loans for all of us.'

'Jesus.'

'Quite. Got to go.' The line goes dead.

Fucking Marilyn. She's always doing that. Disappearing just when she has my undivided attention.

My ear is aching from pressing the BlackBerry against it so long. I lower the phone, and notice the message that came through while I was on the call. Tracy has texted again.

Why haven't you replied?

I continue to ignore her. Without being conscious of it, I've gone back into the chemo room and am still pacing.

'Sir. Would you mind?' A senior nurse comes up to me. 'We work hard to create a calming environment. It's important.'

'Oh God, I'm so sorry.'

'If you can't keep still, perhaps go outside?'

It's my ADHD. When I have a big thought in my head, I can't keep still. I used to self-medicate with cocaine, but I gave up after I overdosed on my fortieth. No sleep that night and at dawn I tried to read a piece in *The Economist* on private equity funding. I couldn't understand a word. I tried three times! In a state of panic, I took myself to A&E, and when I explained that my brain was fried, that I could no longer understand *The Economist*, the nurse laughed, gave me sedatives and sent me home to sleep it off. From that day, my preferred drugs are the endorphins I generate on the treadmill and the adrenaline of deadline-driven work.

Mum opens her eyes.

'Dear, is everything all right?'

Shit. I've probably embarrassed her. 'It's a story thing, Mum. I'm just thinking.' Decision made. 'I've got to file a blog. I'm going to sit in a cafe for an hour to write it. I'll be back after that.'

*

Between the whitewashed walls of Carluccio's restaurant, nursing a skinny cappuccino, I compose a piece for Peckonomics, my widely followed blog. I have the ability to self-publish from my BlackBerry, having persuaded the BBC's bosses that time is of the essence when it comes to price-sensitive reporting and analysis. I've assured them I would never bring the BBC into disrepute. They trust me because they're not remotely interested in what I write about – they don't think it really matters – and they have no expertise in it. I tap away on the tiny keyboard, oblivious to everything around me. I talk about how America's 'subprime poison' has been repackaged by clever Wall Street bankers to look like precious metal. It remains poison, and it is wonderfully apt that the costs of this failed experiment in alchemy are being borne by banks in the European Union, whose governments are so hostile to America's testosterone-fuelled model of financial capitalism.

Before I file, I get a text from Jess at the *Financial Chronicle*. *Bond markets paralysed. European Central Bank intervening. Huge.*

I reply. *I know! Publishing now.*

Bastard.

I start to write my final paragraph. 'Banks rely on being able to sell their mortgages to investors in the form of asset-backed bonds. They raise hundreds of billions of dollars from these markets. If that money disappears, banks won't be able to lend. And if banks can't lend we're all in deep trouble.'

Tracy texts again. *Gil!!!* I close the message and go back to the blog. I reread the last line. 'And if banks can't lend we're all in deep trouble.'

I feel pleased, press send and pick up my almost untouched cup of coffee. It's stone cold.

Mum! With a stab of guilt, I remember I promised I'd go back. Leaving the coffee, I hurry back towards the hospital. As I walk, I ring my boss, the BBC's director of news Janice Oldham.

'Janice, we need to get this story about the closure of bond markets onto the *Ten*.' The '*Ten*' is what we call our flagship news bulletin, watched by millions every night. 'We're heading for recession. Everyone's going to be poorer. This stuff is important to our viewers.'

'When is this recession going to happen?'

'I can't be certain. These things aren't a precise science.'

'We can wait then, can't we?'

'Have you read the blog I just posted?'

I hear mouse clicks in the background. 'It's very provocative.'

'Janice, for the first time since Labour took power – longer than that – boom and bust has returned. We're going broke.'

She gives an indulgent sigh, like the parent of an annoying child. 'I like this line in your blog about this being "the end of the end of history". Let's have a think about how you can tell our viewers that history is back.'

'Tonight?'

'Once we've done a bit more work on it.'

I'm blocked and fuming. Best not to express what I am feeling. 'I've got to go.'

The BlackBerry is still in my hand as I return to the treatment room. Mum's there, deep in conversation with Liz. She hears the buzz of the phone as I enter and looks up.

'Who keeps texting you?' she asks.

I shrug. 'No one, Mum.' I've already glanced at the screen and read the message that's just come through.

If you can't be bothered to text back, don't bother to turn up tonight. And don't ring me again. We're over.

Oh well. I wonder if she means it this time. I'm not sure I care. But my blog is out there. And this story is going to change the world. If Janice doesn't get it, she will soon enough.

Chapter 2

I HAVE A RECURRING DREAM OF my sister Clare and me. It's summer; she's nine and I'm seven. We're in the New Forest in Hampshire, at a holiday camp for middle-class lefties. Mum and Dad have left us in the chalet for a night of long-kaftan and wide-lapelled dancing in the resort's disco. It's late. Clare wakes me, and dares me to follow her into the woods, to look for monsters. I always do what my sister says. We walk into the forest, a narrow path surrounded by tangles of brambles and spiky-branched trees. The muffled beat of T Rex's 'Hot Love' thuds from far away. 'Come on,' Clare says. 'We're nearly there.'

And then I'm all alone. Surrounded by the eyes of beasts, like motorway cats-eyes in the headlight glare. This has happened before, I think. When? How? I hear a whisper, from miles away and then close in my ear. 'Find me, Gil.'

I'm not scared, just overwhelmed by misery. I've lost her. She's lost me. 'Find me, Gil.' And then the smell of carrion breath assaults me. I exert every muscle to wake myself, and am welcomed by Dog nuzzling and pawing me.

It was Jess who insisted I get a mutt, after Clare died. She said the responsibility might socialise me. So when my former companion, Cat with No Name, abandoned me for an indulgent old lady who lives upstairs, the border terrier moved in.

'Morning, Dog. Enough.'

I lift the duvet to propel him off the bed and we stretch. His is the more elegant, upward-facing yogic pose. I embark on my short routine of downward facing dog, upward facing dog, tree pose and a handful of warrior poses, to calm my habitual morning jumble of anxious thoughts. It's ten years since Clare was murdered, but the aftershocks still judder. During fitful, restless sleep I too often see her in dreams that can feel more real than my life. This only started happening a few months ago. I have no idea why. For years, I was so anaesthetised that much of life was erased.

I need viscose black coffee, just a little less thick than tar. Caffeine has always calmed me and helped me focus. I ate whole beans as an eight-year-old. In the kitchen, Dog scoffs the mush spooned from a silver foil tray. I open my HP laptop and make my morning assessment of the financial weather via the data supplied by Bloomberg and Reuters: LIBOR, OIS swap rate, 10-year Treasuries. All are measurements of the demand for money and debt, and are a proxy for the health of the economy. Unlike most of my business journalist peers and rivals, I am not so gripped by price movements in stocks and shares. Compared to capital and money markets, stock markets are tiny. Trading in the capital and derivative markets – orders of magnitude bigger than transactions in the so-called 'real' economy – is an obsession. I love it, in the way a sailor loves the ocean. The seemingly chaotic gyrations in markets – the green flickering ticker light for price rises, the red warnings for down – are compelling patterns to me that make perfect sense. Humans are treacherous; markets don't lie.

A month has passed since Banque de Maghreb told its investors it had no idea whether it had sold them fillet steak or dog meat. Ever since, the markets in which banks and investors trade asset-backed bonds – the ABSs and MBSs and

CDOs of my tutorial with Marilyn – have been shut. No one will buy the bonds, so banks can't sell the loans they've made and can't raise money. My alma mater, the *FC*, is all over it, and there's the occasional story on the business pages of the broadsheets. But for most media and most people, it's a war in a faraway country. Almost everyone ignores the rumble of bombs being dropped. Even the prime minister, Neville Tudor, retains his sunny optimism. In my blog, Peckonomics, I've been sounding the alarm day after day, shouting as loudly as I can that we all need to get into our bunkers, because the day of financial and economic reckoning is nigh. But try as I might, I can't get the story onto the *Ten O'Clock News*.

A text buzzes from Jez, one of the *Today Programme*'s producers.

Hi Gil. Could you do a hit at 8.20 on last night's comments from the Chair of the Federal Reserve?

It's the splash on the *Financial Chronicle*'s front page: I've got it open on my laptop. Private remarks Chairman Philpot made at the annual meeting of central bankers at Jackson Hole in Wyoming, capturing the dilemma facing all central bankers. Should the US Federal Reserve and the Bank of England and the European Central Bank provide emergency credit to commercial banks, to tide them over till bond markets reopen and the banks can again raise the gazillions they need? Or should the banks be left to face the painful consequences of their own reckless mistakes? There is a resonant term-of-art that captures the choice: 'moral hazard'. It's all about the pernicious consequences of bailing out bankers when they fuck up, the fear that they'll just do it again if they never face the music.

I scratch Dog's ears. Ecstasy is written in his adoring gaze. 'I agree with you, Dog. It's great that the *Today Programme* has woken up to this story. Better late than never.' I've got forty-five minutes to get my thoughts in order. Quick shower, where

17

I rehearse out loud roughly what I am planning to say. Clumsy shave, par for the course. I don't suffer much from jealousy, but I envy men whose fathers taught them how to shave without mutilating themselves. Back in the bedroom in front of the floor-length mirror, I tweak my hair – one hundred and fifty quid of Nicky Clarke's scissor work, floppy on top, shaped at the back, creative tension between chaos and precision – with just a trace of 'product'. I take pains with the knot of my electric blue psychedelic Duchamp tie at the neck of a laundered-and-pressed white Charvet shirt. A few millimetres of slack. If there's too much pressure at my throat, my neural pathways go haywire.

A couple of years ago, my obsessive compulsive vanity became practical when I finally swapped the relative anonymity of the newspaper byline for speaking my journalism directly to television viewers and radio listeners. After fifteen years, I quit the *Financial Chronicle* and became the BBC's business editor. It is now my job to climb the watchtower and call the direction of markets for millions of viewers and listeners, and no longer just the elite who read the *FC*. And from this watchtower what I am seeing and feeling in this moment are the forces of pessimism building and swelling. The bears, those who expect prices to fall, are amassing, like a dark army on a high encampment. They are poised to swoop down and lay waste to all the phoney, naive optimists. Day after day, the excitable believers in ever-rising bond or share prices reveal themselves as irrational prophets, maniacs, eccentrics. Their numbers are thinning. Soon the remorseless army of bears will roll over them, crush them, slaughter them. The day of capitulation, the reckoning, is nigh.

There's something exhilarating about the prospect of the old, stale and corrupt being swept away. It's scary, but destruction also brings the hope of a new and better beginning. This is a sensation I often have at this season. I associate it with the new school year, the pungent memory of resinous floor wax in a state school cleaned and spruced for the new term. And there's atavism.

For millennia, my ancestors have been celebrating the Jewish new year at this time. Even if I don't celebrate, I'm programmed to welcome the death that foreshadows life.

I put on the headphones, click the metal switch, and press the auto-dial button on the ISDN box installed by BBC engineers. It's like having a private radio studio in my bedroom. 'Traffic,' says the operator. 'Hi, Gil. Just transferring you through to *Today*.' The *Today Programme* has more listeners than any other radio news show in the UK, and its host – John Humphrys – is Britain's most famous and influential presenter. The producer scolds me for dialling in late, and just a few seconds afterwards a familiar Welsh accent is booming through the headphones.

'I've read your blogs and you've been telling us that this closure of bond markets is momentous, that it's starving our banks of cash.'

'That's right.'

'But the chairman of the Federal Reserve, no less, has said he and the Bank of England and the other central banks can sort it out, by lending a bit more to the banks. Your critics are right, Gil. You've been sensationalising, alarming us, for no reason.'

Humphrys wants to get a rise out of me. It's better radio. 'Far be it from me to correct you, John—'

'Well you've done it many times before.'

Ha ha ha. 'Philpot is very clearly *not* saying the central banks will bail out the banks. He's saying they're aware of the problem, they're monitoring it, and they're concerned about what they call "moral hazard". He's worried that if he provides money to the banks to replace what they can no longer raise on bond markets, the banks will never learn to be more cautious and prudent. Banks allowed themselves to become hooked on bond markets to maximise profits and bonuses. That dependency was all about greed. So why should the banks and bankers be rescued?'

Humphrys makes one of his trademark harrumphs, and digresses. 'The chairman of the Federal Reserve made another point, didn't he, Gil? He's hopeful this bond market closure will be temporary.'

Humphrys knows how to wind me up. 'Why on earth should we give weight to anything these central bankers and regulators say to pacify us?' I say. 'For years they argued that all the financial innovations, the CDOs, the credit derivatives, were making us better off, though anyone who took even a passing interest could see it was mainly the bankers getting rich beyond their wildest dreams. Till the thing they all said could never happen actually happened: bond markets closed down.

'So I literally have no idea why Philpot would be so hopeful.' I am speaking with perhaps a bit more urgency in my voice than is strictly in keeping with the BBC code of impartiality. 'And given that the Fed said this kind of crisis was impossible, how can we trust him now? Why believe him that everything is suddenly going to get better again? This is a mess. And not just for the banks. For all of us.'

I switch off the metal box covered in utilitarian black vinyl, which some BBC boffin designed years ago. I tell Dog I'll see him tonight, and that Jackie from upstairs will take him for a walk round Highbury Fields. Then I carry my black Brompton cycle to the street and unfold it. The leaves are crisping; the breeze off the Fields hasn't turned chill yet, but it contains a warning of what's to come. I am thrilled by the romance of incipient autumn.

*

I pedal furiously to the Royal Marsden to join Mum for her meeting with the oncologist. Mum is early, of course, standing in front of the hospital main door.

'I'm on time, Mum,' I say, my habitual guilt making its predictable appearance.

20

'Yes, I know, darling. Well done.'

We walk round to the side entrance, to the consulting rooms. This time we're seeing Dr Costas on Dad's BUPA private health insurance. My parents are socialists, except when it might mean they can't see a doctor in a hurry.

'It's a privilege to meet you, Mr Peck,' Dr Costas enthuses. 'My wife loves you.'

I'd be chuffed. I normally am. But not when he's supposed to be curing Mum of cancer. I murmur something self-deprecating, and Dr Costas explains Mum is tolerating the chemo well and the latest scans confirm what they hoped, that they removed all the visible cancer, and they can't see it anywhere else. 'You'll need to keep coming for regular check-ups, for at least the next year, but so far so good.'

I wish I could give Mum a hug, but she and I are separated by the wooden armrests of our functional chairs. I can feel her relief. It's my relief too.

'Thank you so much, doctor,' she says. 'Thank you, thank you.'

*

Outside, I hail a black cab. 'Mecklenburgh Square.'

The driver lowers his window and squints at me. 'You're that bloke with the funny voice on the news. My missus thinks you're great. Personally I can't see what the fuss is about.'

This is getting boring. I help Mum into the cab, then hoist in the folded cycle. As I sit on the bench next to Mum, there's a buzzing in the side pocket of my Tom Ford jacket. It's the bat phone.

'Gil. Muller here.'

Not what I expected. Robin Muller almost never calls. He's managing director of Schon, the world's most powerful investment bank, whose tentacles reach wherever there's power to be stroked or squeezed to extract profit. At university we were in business together, buying and selling cannabis resin, red Leb, for the captive market within the walls of Chichele College, Oxford.

'Gil. Are you somewhere we can talk, where you won't be overheard?'

'I can be, in about twenty minutes.'

'Ring me back. It's urgent.'

I certainly will. He's perhaps the best-connected banker in London: if a foreign multinational is trying to buy a rival – frequently depleting Britain's stock of truly British businesses – he'll either be driving it, for a massive fee, or trying to frustrate it, for another potentially huge fee. But if we were ever mates, we haven't been for years, in part because our professional interests are so diametrically opposed. Muller and Schon want total secrecy when negotiating huge money-making deals, unless and until they want to harness investor pressure through a leak; my job is to expose these deals, at my convenience, not his. I can't remember the last time he deigned to return a call from me.

I give Mum a guilty look. 'Is it OK if I rush off after I've dropped you home?'

'Of course, darling.'

The taxi is passing Harrods. I stare out the window. 'Remember when you used to take Clare and me there, to see the puppies and parrots in the pet department?'

'I do. Seems cruel now, all those animals in cages. But you loved it.'

'And then that huge restaurant. I still remember the chopped-up Frankfurters in the Russian salad. It seemed so sophisticated.'

She gives me a smile. 'You are funny, darling.'

After handing Mum over to Dad at their flat, I cross the square into Coram Fields and ring Muller. When he answers, his voice is a whisper.

'Things are moving faster than I thought. Call me in an hour.'

'What about?'

'Can't say now. It's to do with what you've been blogging about all summer.'

Makes sense. In the weeks since Banque de Maghreb, my blog has established itself as a sort of unofficial clearing house for the arcana of the bond market crisis. The City's cognoscenti – everyone from financial traders to Treasury officials – read it, and feed me both news and views.

The newshound in me wants the info now. 'Come on, Robin, cough up. You called me.'

'Just give me an hour. You won't be disappointed.'

*

An hour later, I'm staring at the wall in the glass-doored cupboard that passes for my office. I'm on the second floor of the doughnut, Television Centre, that glorious monument from the 1950s, which was when in a cultural sense the Beeb was Great Britain. Through my window I can see row after row of utilitarian, plastic-finished long desks, like refectory tables except each is populated by clunking personal computers. This is the business unit, probably the least glamorous of all the BBC's journalism departments, because the corporation covers business and economics out of necessity, never love.

Muller hasn't rung back. Nothing after two hours, nor five. Annoying. But I don't text him. If I leave any kind of trace or evidence of our encounter, he'll worry about how to explain it to Schon's unforgiving compliance officers, and then he'll change his mind and not leak to me. What I mustn't lose sight of, if he rings, is that Muller never provides a free lunch. If he's giving me a story, he either wants something in return, or it serves his interest in some hard-to-fathom way. Altruism is neither the Muller nor the Schon way.

Finally, at 19.46, just as I am about to surrender to a craving for a large glass of white Burgundy and head to the Groucho, he telephones.

'I'm about to tell you something that I want on air as soon as possible. Can you do that?'

'That depends on what you tell me.'

'Believe me, you'll be interested. NewGate is in deep trouble.'

I am interested. NewGate – Newcastle & Gateshead – is an institution that in the last ten years has transformed itself from a sleepy building society into the UK's fastest-growing bank – darling of investors, a stock-market superstar. Only a few weeks ago, brokers were sending me research papers recommending that investors buy its shares. If it's in trouble now, that's a story.

'How deep?'

'As deep as it gets.'

'Bust?'

'Unless the Bank of England bails it out, yes.'

'How come?'

'Don't be thick. If anyone can work it out, you can.'

I can. NewGate financed its rapid growth by raising much of the money it needs from asset-backed bond markets. Instead of doing banking largely in the time-honoured fashion, that is by taking savers' deposits and lending only that money out, it was at the forefront of parcelling up mortgages into bonds and selling them to investors, using the proceeds to make yet more loans, which again it sold to investors, and so on and so on and so on. Which allowed it to grow from a small building society into a multi-billion-pound bank. Until bond markets seized up. Muller is telling me that the closure of those markets means NewGate has not just run out of money to make loans, but that it has run out of money to repay its own debts. Or at least that's what I deduce.

24

'You're telling me NewGate can't pay its creditors?'

'Your words.'

'Am I adding two and two and making five?'

'I've never known you do that.'

I breathe out heavily. 'Thank you. So the only thing that matters is whether the Bank of England will lend it enough money to stay alive. Will it?'

'Ask your own sources. As I understand it, NewGate's request for an emergency loan is being considered right now.'

My mind races to think who at the Bank of England would make that kind of decision. There's no modern precedent. This would be the Bank acting as what's called 'lender of last resort'. In practice, it's in the gift of the Governor, but I assume it would have to be approved by the full Court of Directors, the board of the Bank.

Who do I know on the Court?

'Why are you telling me this, Robin?'

'I haven't told you anything. We're not having this conversation, are we?'

'Of course not. Not now. Not ever.'

'Good. Don't land me in it.'

*

How does Muller know about NewGate, and why does he want it out? Something smells funny, but not enough to put me off. A story's a story, and this is a cracker.

I can't take him at his word. I text Marilyn: *NewGate?* Just that. I wait. There's no reply. Of course, if the Court is meeting right now, then she may be in the room. She's not a member, but they'd want her expert view. It would be awkward, to say the least, for her to ring me from there.

Who else? Merlyn Whipplington, head of financial regulation at HM Treasury, would be in the loop, because the Treasury would probably have to underwrite any Bank of England rescue. He doesn't pick up, but he obviously sees my missed call because I get a text back a minute later.

What's up?

Talk? Sensitive story.

My thumb's barely pressed the 'send' button when the BlackBerry starts ringing. 'I can't help,' Whipplington says without preamble.

'So you know what I'm calling about? NewGate.'

'As I said, I can't help.'

'You know I will take that as a confirmation.'

'Your prerogative, I simply can't talk about it.'

He hangs up. A second later, the phone vibrates again. I think for a hopeful instant that he's had second thoughts and he's rung me back, but it's a text message. From Marilyn.

Ring Maureen.

Maureen Lynton is press secretary to the Governor of the Bank of England, and she answers straightaway. 'I'm not going to say you're wrong,' she says, when I pitch her my theory about NewGate, 'but give me a few minutes.'

She calls back ten minutes later, I assume after taking advice, presumably from the Governor.

'Look, Gil. No quotes, no fingerprints, no "according to Bank of England sources".'

'Sure.' This is as thrilling as any drug, and I've tried a few.

'As you may know, NewGate has had a serious funding problem since bond markets shut down, a liquidity problem.'

'You mean it's run out of cash?'

Her voice goes into press-release mode. 'We don't have any reason at present to believe that savers are at risk of losing their money. A liquidity crisis is not the same thing as the bank's assets being worth less than its liabilities.'

'But if it can't fund itself, by definition it is insolvent.'

'We have no reason to believe depositors will end up losing money.' She repeats it like a mantra. 'That all depends on whether NewGate eventually incurs losses on the loans it's made, on the mortgages it has provided.'

'OK. But NewGate is famous for being one of the most aggressive lenders in the market. It gives mortgages worth more than a hundred per cent of the value of properties. Surely there's a non-negligible risk that some of those loans won't be paid back. That's why investors are wary of lending to it now.'

'Seriously, Gil, it's important we don't cause unnecessary anxiety to people who have their money in the bank. We have been looking at its books for days, and as I said we have no reason to believe that the value of its assets is worth less than the value of its liabilities. I can't tell you what to say on air, obviously, but it would be incredibly helpful if you could stress that savers' money is probably safe.'

No reason to believe. Probably safe. She's hedging like mad. 'That's fine, I don't want to alarm people. But aren't savers covered by the deposit protection scheme?'

'Only two thousand pounds are protected in full, and then ninety per cent up to thirty-three thousand pounds.'

'Ah.' Now I understand why she's so worried. 'I'll make the point that if the Bank of England is stepping in to provide funding, that should be a reassurance to savers. *Are* you stepping in, though? Will you provide funds as lender of last resort?'

'The Court is meeting as we speak.'

'To provide funding?' No answer. 'My assumption is the Court would not have been convened if you weren't.'

Still nothing. 'I'm taking your silence as confirmation.'

She breathes heavily through her nose.

'Thanks, Maureen.'

'Just remember what I said about the position of depositors.'

'Of course.'

I check my watch. With all the waiting for calls to be returned, it's now 9.20. Was I the only person that Muller called? I flatter myself I was. But maybe others are leaking. I have an uneasy feeling that financial journalists all over London are frantically trying to stand up this story. I have to get it on air. Now.

The bulletins studio is two floors below. No point taking the lift. I walk fast down the stone stairs, calling Janice en route.

'You sure you've got all the corroboration you need?'

'You know me. I wouldn't be bothering you if I didn't.'

'I'll talk to the editor of the *Ten*. We need to get you on air.'

Half an hour later, having been given a dusting of powder by Sarah in the makeup room while swapping our dog news – she has three Labradors – I walk into the studio and sit next to Huw Edwards at the presenter's desk. We are surrounded by the bulky Dalek-looking cameras. There's only one operator. We're in a cocoon of BBC lettering and branding.

'Five minutes to air,' says the floor manager, Mary, as Huw rehearses the headlines he's about to retail to six million viewers on the *Ten O'Clock News*.

'Gil, do you want talkback?' she asks, as she hands me the portable lapel mic. I slip its pack under my jacket and then clip on my belt.

I turn down her offer of an earpiece that would connect me to the raucous gallery. If I wear talkback the PA can count me down to the end of my allotted time, and that might mean I finish on time, breaking the habits of a professional lifetime. Huw can and will signal to me by flapping his fingers, with growing intensity, if he needs to move on to the next item.

The programme editor, Toby, walks in. 'What are you going to say, Gil? That the Bank of England is going to rescue NewGate?'

'That's right. The Bank of England has decided to provide liquidity, cash to NewGate, so that it can keep going. Without the money, NewGate would have to shut its doors. It would be unable to repay its creditors, and they include ordinary savers. I imagine there'll be people here who have money in NewGate.'

Toby frowns. He learned his trade as a producer in Westminster, where stories of success and failure are more nuanced and conditional than the solvent-or-bust of banking. 'So if the Bank has stepped in, and NewGate is all right, are you sure this is a story?'

'It's a *huge* story. Banks are not supposed to run out of cash. It's without precedent in modern times for the Bank of England to exercise its power as lender of last resort.'

I can see Mary getting agitated. 'Boss. It's two minutes to air.'

'Shit.' Toby runs back to the gallery. Huw turns to me.

'It's a great story. Don't worry about Toby. He always panics.'

I raise my eyebrows, and mouth 'Thank you,' as the percussive news theme tune assaults us. It's Huw's cue to say: 'On tonight's *News at Ten*, the Bank of England steps in to rescue NewGate Bank.'

Crash, bang, wallop, goes the musical punctuation. Huw runs through the other headlines, stories that to me sound like noise – about an outbreak of foot and mouth disease in Surrey, and some huge building in the Gulf breaking records for the world's tallest structure. I'm trying to get into the zone, so that I don't muck up my single, unrehearsed opportunity to explain what's happened to NewGate and why it matters.

Huw turns to me. 'I'm joined in the studio by the BBC's business editor, Gil Peck. Gil, I understand you have some breaking news for us about the Newcastle and Gateshead Bank needing emergency support from the Bank of England.'

I look directly at Huw, knowing that the camera is in turn staring directly at me. 'That's right, Huw. I can reveal that the court of the Bank of England is meeting right now, to approve an emergency loan to NewGate.'

'And tell us why it matters.'

'Fear has been stalking the markets for weeks. Important debt markets, which NewGate tapped to raise tens of billions of pounds, have completely shut down. That is why NewGate has run out of cash to pay its own creditors, and has had to turn to the Bank of England for money. I have spoken to the Bank of England, and there is no suggestion that NewGate is insolvent in the fundamental sense of facing overwhelming losses on the loans it has made. But simply for a bank to run out of money is extraordinarily serious.'

Huw gives the viewers his grave face. 'For those with savings in NewGate, what should they make of this news?'

'Well, the Bank of England's official position is that if it believed a bank was no longer viable, if a bank faced unsustainable losses on loans, it would not be providing credit as a lender of last resort. Instead it would be winding the bank down. So as I said, it's plain that the Governor of the Bank of England believes NewGate can keep going.' I remember the line I promised Maureen I'd say. 'To be clear, my sources say the Bank and FSA have looked at NewGate's books and that depositors' money is probably safe.'

I check that I am looking directly at Huw, and I am suddenly conscious of the barrel of the camera staring at my eyes and mouth. Every word is being relayed to millions. I have a nagging doubt that I've missed something or said something wrong. But what? My voice catches, almost imperceptibly, a moment before I deliver my closing line.

'There's no reason to panic.'

Chapter 3

I SLEEP BADLY, TOO MUCH ADRENALINE in my system after the intensity of the scoop. After the *Ten*, I went straight from the studio to my desk to update my blog, and didn't get home until 1 a.m. Then I felt too wide awake. I hadn't had any time to eat and made the mistake of stuffing my face with pita and houmous. I turned on Sky, thought about having a wank, briefly looked at the Babestation channel, thought better of it, scrolled through two hundred others until I found a thirty-year-old episode of *The Sweeney* and drifted into a fitful doze.

I am thrashing around, brushing away what I think are buzzing wasps, when I work out it's the buzzing of BlackBerries on the bedside table. *Shit*. It's after nine. Dog is at the end of the bed, where he always sneaks after I fall asleep, even though he's been told time and again he's to stay in his own bed. I fumble for the BlackBerries.

There are tons of texts, some congratulating me on my scoop, others less happy. One, from Jess, stands out. *TURN ON THE TV. WHAT ON EARTH HAVE YOU DONE?*

I switch on the News Channel and see pictures of customers queuing outside a NewGate branch. There seem to be hundreds of them: the line snakes around the block.

'We've never seen scenes like this in Britain,' the presenter says. 'These customers are alarmed by the Bank of England

31

rescue and they are demanding NewGate gives them their savings. It is a run on the bank.'

Christ. A bank run. Did I do this?

A professor of economic history comes on to talk to the presenter over a crackling telephone line. He says there has never been a bank run in the UK since it became a mature, developed economy. Bank runs are only supposed to happen in fragile nations, not well-run democracies, and definitely not in the country that ruled the waves and the world. There wasn't a run on a UK bank even in the Great Depression of the 1930s, when bank after bank in America was forced to shut its doors. Perhaps the last proper run was of Overend Gurney in 1866.

The bat phone rings. *Number withheld.* Should I pick up? Stupid question.

'Gil, what the fuck have you done?'

It's Marilyn. 'Not you too. Jess just texted the same thing.'

'Of course she did. Unlike you, she's not a total wanker.'

Is she genuinely upset, or is she just winding me up? 'It was a story, Marilyn. What was I supposed to do, not tell NewGate savers that their bank is in serious trouble?'

'I watched you last night. "*Don't panic.*" What were you thinking?'

'Maureen – *your* press officer told me to say that. But I couldn't pretend that what's happened at NewGate isn't serious, and I can't do PR for the Bank of England. NewGate broke the most basic rule of the trade: always have enough liquid funds for an emergency. I probably should have said "Do panic."'

'Well its customers have, in case you haven't noticed.'

'What happens now?'

'God knows. This is a full-on run. We've never seen anything like it. Cash is pouring out of the bank. We'll end up lending way more to them than we thought we'd have to.' She trails off. 'Look, Gil, I know you're just doing your job. But this is massive. Much bigger than you think.'

'I'm not sure I understand.'

She goes quiet again. Finally, slower than before, she says, 'There's a lot at stake. Please take care.'

There's a lot at stake. Bloody obvious. Before I can ask why she said it, she's hung up.

I'm still thinking about it when my news producer, Emma Talbot, texts.

They want you to package for the Six and Ten. There's a long queue at a branch just off Regent St. Are you coming in to TVC?

I tap out my reply. *I'll go straight to the branch. 10.30? See you there.*

There's no time to shower. I look at my hair in the mirror: just scruffy enough. Does it need a wash? Nah. Grey serge Paul Smith suit with faint pinstripe. Pink Lacroix shirt. Wide jacquard silk Kenzo tie, spring flowers on a mauve background. I adjust the knot, so it's snug but not choking, when the bat phone rings again. This time the caller is revealed on the screen: Patrick Munis. Is he going to berate me too?

'Congratulations, old chap,' he says, in his silky Edinburgh drawl. I can hear traffic in the background; he must be driving somewhere. 'You're the most famous person in Britain, the hack who broke the bank. What a crowning achievement to your glittering career.'

'Fuck off, Patrick.' Munis is now the shadow chancellor, but I've known him for twenty years. We were at Oxford together. 'I didn't cause the run. The board of NewGate did that with their idiotic decision to become so dependent on wholesale funding. I'm just the messenger.'

'If you knew your Plutarch better, you'd realise you were always going to be decapitated. More embarrassing for your friend Neville, I'd say.'

'I know you Tories think that everyone at the BBC is in bed with Labour, but he's not my friend.' Neville Tudor is the former Labour chancellor, now prime minister.

'Don't be so self-deprecating. You know him better than anyone. How will he respond? Will he nationalise?'

I haven't had a chance to think about next steps. 'I'm not sure.'

I hear the sound of a car door slamming, and I guess Munis has reached wherever he's going. 'Got to go, late for a meeting. We should have lunch. Soon.'

'OK.'

'On you.'

'Isn't it always?'

We hang up. I need to take stock, work out where this story is going, but it's hard to think with messages and information assaulting me like gunfire in the trenches. And I should have left the house ages ago.

*

Twenty minutes later, I cycle past the Apple Store on Regent Street, turn right, and can immediately see a long queue of middle-aged people, snaking past the plate-glass windows of modish clothing stores, all waiting patiently to get into the bank on the corner. NewGate. Two women are going along the line, one with a hefty camera balanced on her shoulder and the other checking with the queuers that they're happy to be filmed.

'Hope you don't mind, we're filming a piece for the BBC,' Emma Talbot, my producer, says in her flat Manc accent. Those who don't want to be on the news turn their backs or put hands in front of faces.

I dismount, fold the Brompton and join my crew. Emma's in a denim jacket over crisp white cotton shirt. She runs the show when I'm making a short film or package for news bulletins. She sorts the logistics, screens me from the more idiotic questions posed by news producers and tries – usually unsuccessfully – to get me where I'm needed on time. 'I am

34

trying to make you look good,' is her normal refrain. 'You don't have to work against me.'

The camera operator, Petra, is taller, lean, black cropped hair, black sweatshirt with a fading picture of Debbie Harry in her luscious prime on it. We bond over our shared love of the post-punk heyday. Both Petra and Emma are younger than me. Neither takes any shit. Petra is more private, but Emma usually spends at least part of every day regaling me with her misadventures cruising Soho clubs for women.

'Good night last night?' I greet her.

'Amazing. Met this gorgeous girl. She could be the one.'

'You say that every time. You look terrible.'

'Don't worry. Nurofen, Alka-Seltzer, treble espresso. I'll be fine.' She gives me a handheld mic that's wired to Petra's camera. 'Tidy yourself up by the way. Your hair's in a right state.'

I give it a crude comb with my fingers, flatten the sticking up clumps and turn to Emma for approval.

'We need a few vox pops,' she instructs. 'We've got almost no time before lunchtime news.' As I mentioned, she's my time-keeper, among so much else. 'Petra, can you start on a two-shot and then zoom in on the person Gil's interviewing?'

'I'll do my best.'

'We need a few singles too, with Gil not in shot, for the midday package.'

I walk down the line with the microphone. When they see the camera, most people suddenly find themselves in heated conversation that is hard for me to interrupt. Or they conspicuously turn away. I struggle to find anyone willing to be interviewed, until I meet a couple who return my smile. A balding, paunchy man, in a brown suit and suede Hush Puppies, and a woman – his wife? – in a navy Guernsey jumper and black jeans. They look as though they're in their late fifties.

'Gil, from the BBC,' I introduce myself.

'We know who you are,' says the man.

'Could I ask you a couple of questions? For the news?'

He turns to his wife, who is lean, a good inch taller than him.

'Will we be on the *Ten O'Clock News*?' she asks.

'Probably.'

'That's exciting. I'm not sure we have very much to tell you. But fire away.'

Petra positions me at a diagonal to the couple, and stands to my right. I begin by asking, 'Would you mind telling me your names?'

'Jack and Julie Adams,' says the man.

'What do you do?'

'We're retired university lecturers. I'm politics, she's geography,' says Jack.

'And why are you here today?'

'Well we saw you on the news last night,' says Julie. 'We wanted to know what's going on. We have all our savings in the NewGate, you see.'

'We do most of our banking online, for the convenience mostly,' Jack adds. 'We tried to go to the website, but it kept crashing. We couldn't get into our account.'

'There was no access to any information,' Julie clarifies.

'So we decided to come down to the branch.'

This is the cutting edge of twenty-first-century retail banking. Or at least, that was the PR bollocks of NewGate and their ilk. Presumably, NewGate's management failed to invest in enough server capacity to cope with the surge in traffic generated by my story. So when customers couldn't get the information they needed online, they had no choice but to visit a branch. And one thing is plainly leading to another. Television images of people queuing have been a magnet for other customers to come down. The cutting-edge twenty-first-century retail bank is experiencing a very old-fashioned run. So it goes. First there was a run on NewGate's internet bandwidth, now there's a run on cash.

'What do you think you'll do when you get to the till?'

Jack glances at his wife. 'We haven't completely decided. But we'll probably take our money, or at least ask for it to be transferred to another bank.'

'Better to be safe than sorry,' says Julie.

Bingo. Julie has delivered the line I need as the glue of my TV explainer. *Better to be safe than sorry.*

Even so, I record four more conversations – all with people who either couldn't access the website, or who were frightened by the TV pictures. We try to film inside the bank itself, but staff block us, saying we need permission from head office. Emma puts in the calls and sends emails, but no one responds.

'You've caused total mayhem, Gil,' she says, grinning. 'They're never going to forgive you. Are you ready to do your piece to camera?'

Pretty much every news package contains a so-called 'piece to camera', or PTC. It is a BBC convention, and is where I as reporter look at the camera and try to say something in twenty or thirty seconds that somehow sums up the importance of the story. The PTC acts as a bridge between different elements of a film that is unlikely to be longer than three minutes in toto. I stand under NewGate's logo, an orange stylised lit torch against a black background, neo-classical iconography, with the bank's slogan 'Your brighter future' stamped under it. Petra pans the camera down to me from the signage, as I start walking, gesturing and talking.

'In rich countries like Britain, bank runs aren't supposed to happen. But behind me you can see that just hours after NewGate went to the Bank of England for emergency funding, its customers want to take their money out. I asked them why.'

We do the PTC three times, to give us options in the edit. 'See you in the suite at three,' I say to Emma. 'And please tell the *Six* and *Ten* editors what we're planning. Let's not get sucked into the nightmare of letting them negotiate the contents of the package an hour before going to air.'

'OK, boss.'

I unfold the Brompton and cycle west to Television Centre. When I arrive, a text lands from the director of news, Janice Oldham. *Come to my office when you're in.* I wonder how I've messed up. Five minutes later, having manoeuvred TVC's labyrinth of corridors and lifts, I'm on Janice's red sixties-style G Plan sofa. It obliges me to sit up straighter than my normal slouch, while Janice leans back in her office chair behind her glass-topped desk. She's only a bit older than me, but – in half-moon glasses and cream silk blouse, tied at the neck with a wide silk bow – she leaves no doubt about the hierarchy.

'You've caused a stir. Well done.'

'Er, thanks. I think.'

A pause. Janice peers at me. 'Did we cause the bank run?'

Oh – that. 'No. *We* didn't. All we did was reveal the incompetence of NewGate's management. That's our job. How customers would react to the news is not something we could have predicted, and shouldn't have entered into our calculations.'

'Yes. Maybe. Not everyone agrees with *you*.' She considers the tips of her manicured, unvarnished nails. 'Has the DG spoken to you?'

This sounds ominous. The DG, the director general, is the big boss of the BBC.

'Were you expecting him to contact me?'

'He's had some interesting calls since you broke the story last night.' When she says 'interesting' she means 'annoying'. 'The head of the British Bankers' Association, senior Tory MPs, a couple of the DG's City mates. They are unhappy. Very unhappy. They say we should not be reporting when a bank gets into difficulties. One of them actually said it's like a war, we're endangering the prosperity of the country.'

I snort. 'Who said that?'

'Sir Giles Pimlott.' Conservative MP for Mid Dorset, chair of the Treasury select committee, and pompous arse. 'He started talking about D-notices.'

'You're joking.' D-notices are official requests from the government to editors not to publish sensitive information. They are normally associated with matters of national security, spies, terrorists and suchlike.

'I am afraid not. The point, Gil, is that this is a delicate story. You are upsetting a lot of people.' I've been feeling uncomfortable, but now I look directly in her eyes, which are grey and emotionless. 'We're right behind you,' she adds hastily. 'We think the work you're doing is important. But you are going to feel a lot of pressure from powerful vested interests who want you to keep quiet. Don't cut corners, and for goodness' sake choose your words carefully.'

'You know I always do.' For that, I earn myself the kind of stern, quizzical look my form teacher gave me at school, usually when I could not sit still and ended up tipping my chair back and crashing to the floor. 'Janice, I do understand the sensitivity of all this. Surely you know that I don't broadcast or write anything that I haven't properly sourced and contextualised?'

'As I said, we have great confidence in you and we're here to support you.'

Something about the way she enunciates each word makes me think I've just had a warning that's more official and serious than her words would suggest. *This is massive, much bigger than you think*, Marilyn said to me. What have I started?

*

In the edit suite, a dark box of a room glowing with the light of multiple screens, I ask Emma if she thinks I was wrong to do the story about NewGate's funding crisis.

'Not like you to have self-doubts, boss.'

I tell her about my meeting with Janice.

'They're just covering their arses. Don't worry about it.' Emma usually gets to the nub. 'By the way, the editor says you need to voice up the statements from the Bank of England and the chancellor. Which bits should we put in the graphic?'

'Well they don't say very much, either of them, just that they are keeping a close eye on the bank and will make further announcements in due course.'

'That's hardly likely to reassure anyone, is it?'

'Nope.'

The BlackBerry hums. 'Give me a minute, Emma.' I step into the corridor, check there's no one in earshot and answer.

'Jess?'

'You caused a fucking bank run! We're not supposed to do that.'

'What would you have done differently?' I squeeze my right earlobe tight with my right hand, BlackBerry pressed to my ear with my left. I am suddenly anxious. I can deal with Janice's jobsworth lecture – it's the BBC way – but Jess is my friend. I trust her. Does she think I did something wrong?

'It was a proper story,' I insist.

'It is now.'

'Was it a mistake to report that NewGate had run out of money? Its customers surely had a right to know.' Painful silence. 'We're not members of the establishment. We can't baby our viewers and listeners. If a bank is bust, we need to tell them.'

She bursts out laughing. 'I'm messing with you. You should have heard Geoff this morning: furious that we missed the story. Raving.' Geoff Althorpe is the *FC*'s editor.

'It never occurred to me there would be queues outside the branches,' I say. 'I made it clear their money was safe.'

'You said their money was "probably" safe. Important difference. No one in their right minds would leave their money in a bank when there is even a faint possibility they'll lose it. Especially after the website crashed.'

The disruption to the bank's online service, which undermined the confidence of customers. I must not forget to mention it on air. 'I'll call you back. Got to finish my package and do a couple of lives.'

Before going back to the suite, I ring NewGate's corporate affairs director, Sam Barnabus. The first time I ring, the number is engaged. I redial immediately and he picks up.

'Hi Sam, Gil Peck here.'

'I'm not sure I should be talking to you after what you've done.'

'Sam, you know I was just doing my job.'

He grunts. I can hear phones ringing off the hook in the office behind him; they must be going into meltdown. 'What do you want?'

'Why did your website crash last night?'

It wasn't the question he was expecting. 'Why do you care?'

'Because it contributed to the hysteria that caused the bank run.'

'*You* caused the hysteria,' he says. Then, grudgingly, 'But it was certainly inconvenient that customers couldn't log in to find out what was happening.'

'So what went wrong?'

'Off the record? No attribution, not even to "bank sources"?'

I sigh. 'Sure.'

'No idea. We increased server capacity just a few weeks ago, and stress-tested the site against a surge in customer activity. So we don't know what caused the shutdown. We're looking into it.'

'Can you let me know when you have an answer?' Sam's response is a noncommittal exhalation. 'Look, I know I am not your favourite person, but I want to tell this story fairly and accurately.'

41

'Better late than never.'

It's one of those days when I seem to be on air more or less every minute. An hour and a half later, after the *Six O'Clock News* has broadcast my package and I've done a live with George Alagiah, I am in the News Channel studio, being grilled by the anchor, Brian Radford, about whether NewGate's problems are a one-off or whether we can expect other banks to get into trouble. I am trying to convey that NewGate's overreliance on bond markets made it more vulnerable to collapse than other banks, while also making clear that what's happened today is the beginning of a story, not the end.

'So you are saying that we may see other banks get into difficulties,' says Brian, in his clipped public-school English.

Janice's warning repeats in my head. *Don't cut corners and choose your words carefully.* 'The closure of the bond markets is hugely important, Brian. But most banks have other sources of finance.' *What can I say that isn't going to set hares running?* As usual, I am not wearing an earpiece and am therefore not hearing the gallery. But I can see Brian taking in information from the programme editor, through talkback, and reading a screen set underneath the tinted glass table at which we're sitting.

'We're briefly going to the weather,' Brian tells viewers, 'and then we'll have more on the NewGate crisis from our business editor, Gil Peck.'

The programme cuts to the weather studio. Brian turns to me. 'Gil, the editor has asked if you can stay to talk about a breaking news story.'

'What is it?'

'Death of a director of the Bank of England. Apparently police have found a body in West London.'

What has he just told me? No time to think.

'Welcome back. Our business editor Gil Peck is here. But first, let's go to our reporter Dan Hillman, who is outside the Bank of England with some breaking news.'

Hillman is where I've stood and recorded lives and pieces to cameras innumerable times, on the pedestrianised triangle between Threadneedle Street and Cornhill, to the right of Royal Exchange. The white, prison-like facade of the Bank is immediately behind him.

'Thanks, Brian. I'm here because the Bank of England has just announced what, in its words, is shocking and upsetting news, the death of a director, and one of its rising stars.'

His words are daggers of ice.

'Marilyn Krol, who was director of financial stability, has been found dead in her home.'

Chapter 4

ARILYN KROL, WHO WAS DIRECTOR *of financial stability, has been found dead in her home.*

I know what the words mean and yet I don't understand them. It's as though I am listening to a language both familiar and incomprehensible. Each individual word – *Marilyn, dead, home* – is one I recognise. But as a collection they make no sense.

'This is a developing story and not much more is known about the circumstances of her death,' says Hillman. 'We've asked the Met Police for more information and will keep you updated. In its statement, the Bank said, "Marilyn Krol was an outstanding public servant. Her death is a tragedy for her family, friends and colleagues."'

She didn't have family, you arsehole.

Brian picks up and turns to me. 'Gil, you would have known Marilyn Krol, I assume?'

I spoke to her this morning. We had sex a few days ago.

I've lost the power to articulate thoughts. Brian has seen many reporters freeze over the years, it's just one of those things that happens. He covers up my silence. 'As Dan has just told us, this is profoundly shocking news. As business editor, what is your assessment?'

Finally I can speak, but I hear myself as though I am listening to a stranger. 'Yes, Brian. Marilyn Krol was a high-flyer at the

Bank of England, tipped by some as a future Governor, potentially the first ever female Governor. I did know her, had known her for many years. Her death will send shockwaves beyond the City. She was a close advisor to the former prime minister Johnny Todd, both when he was leader of the opposition and after he entered Number 10. She was widely credited with a central role, alongside Todd, in transforming the Labour Party of the mid-1990s into Modern Labour, which of course won that landslide ten years ago.'

Marilyn is dead. She's dead. Kill me now, kill me now, kill me now. I should have chanted my spell before the news was announced, and maybe they'd have said somebody else had died. It's too late for Marilyn. It's too late for me.

In his treacly Old Harrovian accent, Brian is wrapping up this segment of the news hour, and is handing over to the sports presenter. At last. This will give me space to escape. The studio manager signals for me to make a swift exit. Brian takes off his spectacles and turns to me. 'You OK, Gil? I've never known you dry up like that.'

I am in a kind of trance, barely registering what's happening. 'Truthfully, I was taken aback by the Marilyn Krol news. I'd known her for a while. Wasn't expecting it.'

'It's awful,' says Mary, the studio manager. 'You take care of yourself, Gil.'

The sports presenter is saying something about Manchester United's slow start to the season as I take off my lapel mic and hand it to her. I fetch the Brompton from my office. I know where I have to go.

As I leave Television Centre, the lights in the doughnut flicker on behind me. As if triggered by the same switch, there's an urgent vibration in my pocket. On autopilot I pull out the phone, though I don't want to speak to anyone. Well, just one person.

'Jess?'

'I've seen about Marilyn. You OK?'

46

'Yes. No. Don't know. Am processing.' *What happened? I have to know.* 'I'm going to the apartment.'

'What do you mean?'

'I'm going to the apartment.'

'You mean *her* apartment? You can't. The police will be there. No one will be allowed anywhere near.'

'I don't care.'

I disconnect and climb on my bike. In a brain fog, I pedal south-east down Wood Lane, past unremarkable Victorian terraced houses, then left onto the Uxbridge Road. A bus pulls out. The driver sees me at the last moment, and lets me pass. Out of the corner of my eye I see his enraged swearing face. *Why didn't you just flatten me?* The air is choked with car fumes, uncleansed by Shepherd's Bush Green on my right. Drunks and tramps sprawl on benches, as though they've been swept down here by the plutocrats who live yards away in Holland Park's mansions.

Across the roundabout, I am gripped by the idea that if I power up Holland Park Road to Notting Hill Gate I can still save her. I know it's crazy, but I pedal with demonic fury. As I reach the row of unremarkable supermarkets and cafe chains, which seem anomalous surrounded by so much wealth, a left turn takes me into bankers' paradise, new money's invasion of what was – not so long ago – one of the most bohemian and multicultural communities. Marilyn shrewdly bought her first flat here, at a time when someone on a civil servant's salary could afford the prices. She never left. God knows what her place is worth now, although there's no one to care or suffer unworthy thoughts about whether they are in line to inherit – because there is no close family. Although there must be someone? Funny that I could know every inch of someone's body, know every book she'd ever read, know what those books meant to her, and not have a clue about her closest relatives.

Her place is on the top floor of a generously proportioned, white stucco, mid-nineteenth-century townhouse, not quite large enough to be a mansion, though only a few feet shy. You probably know the ones I mean; they look like white-iced wedding cakes. From fifty yards away, I see all the furniture of an official investigation into a tragic incident: a police van, two police saloon cars and an estate, all in their yellow and blue liveries, uniformed and plain-clothes officers milling around. So many cops. No passerby can doubt something bad has happened.

The key to Marilyn's apartment is in my rucksack, where I always keep it. I've had it for years: for the convenience of letting myself in, and because she had a phobia that if she left a key with the neighbours that might mean she'd have to talk to them. Helmeted, I carry my bicycle towards the portico.

From between its classical columns, a chunky uniformed constable raises his palm and directs me to stop.

'Sorry, sir. This is a crime scene.'

'What do you mean, a crime scene? What happened?'

'I'm sorry, sir. I'm not at liberty to say.'

'Marilyn Krol was my best friend. Please can I go in?'

I feel such an idiot. I should have had a better plan. 'I'm sorry, sir. We're not even letting the other residents in for now. It's forensics, you see.'

Behind me, a car pulls up. I turn to see a large BMW double-parking. The driver gets out. She runs round to the front passenger seat to open the door for a stocky, brunette, female officer, silver brocade on the navy collar, royal insignia on the epaulettes, black and white checked neckerchief. Top brass.

And, as chance would have it, someone I know.

'Assistant commissioner Jansen,' I say. 'Kim.' We were at university together, not exactly close though friendly enough. Our careers have been diverging lines, investigators whose aims only rarely align. We've had sporadic contact since Oxford, though not much at all since I implored her for information after my sister died.

48

Her stare freezes the air. 'Peck. I should have guessed you would be here.'

She may have been in the Met for more than twenty years, but she's as posh as ever she was. 'I am sure you've already been told there's nothing more we can tell you.' She walks straight past me towards the front door, assuming I am trawling for tawdry facts about a tragedy.

'Kim, I am not here as a reporter.' I turn towards her and blurt: 'Marilyn and I were friends. Good friends. I might be able to help you.'

I have her attention. 'OK. I naturally assumed ...' She tails off. 'The press office has been inundated with prurient calls from your colleagues.'

'I get it. Don't worry.'

'There is one thing. We are struggling to find next of kin. Mum and dad. Brothers, sisters.'

'I'm not surprised.'

Marilyn and I kept our family lives very separate from our capsuled relationship. But too drunk one night, years after we'd started sleeping together, she slurred why she found it even harder than me to forge ties with others.

'She's an only child, an orphan,' I tell Kim. 'Her parents both died when she was nineteen. Car accident. In all the years I knew her, she never mentioned relations.'

Jansen purses her lips and looks at the air above my head, for what feels an age. 'OK. That's a problem. You and she were close?'

I nod.

'Can we chat off the record, not for reporting in any way? This is sensitive, and we're still establishing the facts.'

'That's fine. I can't really report on it anyway. As I've told you, I have a personal interest.'

'And you won't repeat any of this to a colleague?'

I mouth 'No' and shake my head.

49

She orders her thoughts. 'All the evidence suggests Marilyn Krol killed herself, and obviously we want to know why.'

That horrifying idea has been going round and round my head, taunting me. I've been refusing to acknowledge it. 'That's impossible. She would never do that.'

'Friends, loved ones, often say that in these circumstances. Lots of people commit suicide seemingly out of the blue, with no hint in advance, even to those closest to them. Sometimes it's only afterwards you see the warning signs.'

I try to remember. Marilyn had been telling me for weeks that she was feeling overworked. But that was the whole of it. 'We spoke first thing this morning. She had a lot on her plate. You'll have been aware of the crisis at NewGate?'

Kim Jansen shows the hint of a smile.

'But she was dealing with it,' I say. 'It was the job.' And then something occurs to me. 'If I'm honest, she seemed more worried about me than herself. You must have got this wrong.'

Kim is blunt. 'You can't hang yourself without meaning to.'

I'm caught off guard, no space to ward off a nightmare image of Marilyn's distended neck, her face in agony. I powered here on my bike with the insane hope of cutting the rope and rescuing her. I automatically squeeze my right earlobe, harder and harder until the pain supplants the nightmare.

'Isn't it relatively rare for women to hang themselves?' Jess is next to me. I don't know when she got here – she stole up unnoticed – but she's beside me and articulating my thoughts.

Kim's eyes narrow. 'Who are you?'

'Jess Neeskens. I'm Gil's friend. He needs support – obviously.'

I mouth 'Thank you' to her.

'I'll repeat what I said to Gil,' says Kim. 'I am talking to you on the basis that none of this is ever repeated. Do you agree?' We both nod. 'So, yes, it is more common for men to hang

50

themselves than it is for women. But it does happen. And it certainly looks like that's what happened in this case.'

'Is there a note?' I ask.

'No.'

'So it is possible she was murdered, that it was staged to look like suicide?'

Jess shoots me a pained look. Kim's voice softens. 'Gil, I know this will be very hard for you. Of course I remember all our conversations about your sister. But I've seen too many of these. I am pretty clear this was suicide.'

I'm not convinced. I clutch my right side and inwardly chant: *Murder me now, murder me now, murder me now.*

'I am really sorry to ask. But if we can't find close family, would you be able to help us with the formal identification of the body?'

Shit. Shit. 'Oh God. Really? I guess so. When?'

'Tomorrow morning. Can you do that?'

I screw up my eyes. 'OK.'

'One of the team will be in touch.'

There is nothing to be gained from staying longer. Yet I can't move. I am rooted to the spot, as if I can still undo Marilyn's death. No one says anything. I look at my shoes.

'I should have said this earlier. I am sorry for your loss,' she says, nodding to an unseen officer over my shoulder. 'If you'll excuse me.'

Jess finds my hand and squeezes it. 'Come on, Gil. We need a drink.'

*

The Ladbroke Arms decks itself out as though it's in a prosperous country market town, rather than a part of London where the collective net worth is equivalent to that of a small African country. It's wall-to-wall Sloanes, braying hedgies, barking investment bankers, chirruping consumer public relations executives. The scuffed wood tables, pews and cottage-style wooden chairs are rammed.

'I'll buy,' I say. 'See if there's anywhere to sit.'

'Sauvignon Blanc,' she says. 'Large.'

At the polished dark wood bar, the steward is doing his best to show he is not one of the clientele, two small golden hoops dangling from nose cartilage, 'fuck da police' tattooed on his left forearm.

'I don't suppose you have a New Zealand Sauvignon Blanc?'

'Rhetorical question?'

'Two glasses, please.'

'Medium or large?'

I turn around to see Jess has procured a table in the corner. 'How large is large?' He shows me. It's not far off half a bottle. I have to broadcast later. But. 'Large, please. And two bags of nuts. Not dry roasted.'

I carry the glasses to the table, retrieve the nuts from the pocket of my Paul Smith jacket, and sit. I'm crumpled, outside and in.

Jess gives me a minute to take a few gulps of wine in silence before she asks, 'Do you want to talk about it?'

'Maybe. Yes.' Not the answer I was expecting to give.

'Were you still seeing her?'

'We never stopped. Though maybe we never started.'

The sluice gate lifts and out it all comes. 'For a whole variety of reasons – personal, professional – we never had what the outside world would have called a proper relationship. But the attraction, the physical attraction, was intense. It never waned.' Jess was looking straight at me, but now her eyes move to the table. Have I embarrassed her? I can't stop though. 'We talked all the time. About politics. About our work. But never about the two of us. We never talked about a future together. But we were together. In our own way.'

Jess tears the corner of the bag of nuts with meticulous precision. She shakes out three. 'In all the years you two were not committing to each other, I married, had a kid, divorced, and now have a toxic relationship with my ex. And my attempts to date are a comedy classic.'

'Well at least you tried to be normal.'

She gives a rueful half-assent.

'Would it be wrong to smoke?' I ask.

'Yes. But I'm gagging.'

We've both given up, many times over many years. But it's an emergency. Not the first, probably not the last. Jess goes to the bar to buy twenty Marlboro Lights, while I carry our drinks outside. There's nowhere to sit, so we put our drinks on the window ledge and light up.

'I don't believe she killed herself.' I can't believe it. 'I spoke to her first thing today. She was stressed about the run at NewGate. Said it was part of something much bigger. She was trying to help me. But she was rational, there was no sign of, well, despair . . .' I tail off. I sound as though I am trying to let myself off the hook.

'It's not your fault.'

'Of course it is.' I suck in tobacco smoke too fast and too deep, and splutter. 'If Kim is right, I should have heard Marilyn's cry for help. But what if that is what we're supposed to think? Obviously nobody stumbles head first into a noose attached to a steel beam. What if someone hanged her?'

Jess looks at me with concern and says, 'Gil, I'm so sorry.' I want to cry. I can't. Instead, I half whistle, softly and slowly.

She taps ash off her cigarette. 'I know I shouldn't ask, but it wasn't Marilyn who gave you the NewGate story, was it? If that had ever come out, it would have been curtains for her career.'

'It wasn't her. But even if it was, you can't honestly believe she'd kill herself for that?'

53

'Is there nothing else you can think of?'

'Nothing.' *This is much bigger than you think.* I need to put the pieces together. 'This sounds mad, but I know this is linked to the bond market shutdown. I am certain.'

'Really? I can't see it myself.'

'The sums of money at stake are huge, off the charts,' I say. Through her exhaled smoke, Jess examines me sceptically.

'Do you remember that time you came round to mine after the Schon summer party? You'd seen Marilyn there, apparently with some hedge-fund wanker.'

'I'd had too much to drink.'

'You were furious.'

'I was drunk. Marilyn and I were never exclusive. We were ... Well I don't know what we were.'

Jess retrieves her wine glass from the ledge and sips. 'Maybe I shouldn't say this, but all those years, knowing you were still with her, I could never work out what was in it for either of you.'

'It's not that deep. Two drunks propping up the bar.'

'But after what she did to Clare ...'

Ah, the knife, and my wound.

Ten years ago, my sister Clare was knocked off her bike in a hit and run. She died. Everyone thought it was a tragic accident, robbing public service of one of its brightest rising stars. Only it wasn't an accident. The then leader of Her Majesty's opposition, Johnny Todd, was having a secret love affair with Clare. Each was in an ostensibly happy and stable marriage, each had children. I have never properly understood why Clare became enmeshed. She became pregnant with his child. And she became annoying, because she expected him to put probity before electoral ambition, and help her expose a gigantic fraud by the world's most powerful media mogul, Jimmy Breitner. If Todd wouldn't, she'd reveal their affair to the world, she warned him. His saintly reputation would be soiled, his popularity savaged.

She was murdered. He won a landslide election and became prime minister, for almost a decade. And throughout all this, Marilyn worked for Todd and hero-worshipped him.

'How could you be with Marilyn, knowing what we know? She never even acknowledged what Todd did.' Jess was my deputy at the time; we investigated the story together. She's the other person who knows the truth of it, that I've never won justice for Clare. Only Jess understands.

I take a drag on the cigarette, waiting for calm, order. For months after Clare died, I hated Marilyn. She knew. We didn't call, never spoke. If we found ourselves in the same room, in Downing Street, at party conferences, we'd walk around each other, no eye contact. But then a mutual friend, the now-shadow chancellor Patrick Munis, had a party. A big one. Dry Martinis. Negronis. Bagfuls of coke. We were on a sofa. My thigh pressed against hers. She ran her finger down my face, as she did. From there, inevitably, to her bed. Time after time.

'She promised me she knew nothing about Clare. She insisted Todd had nothing to do with Clare's death either. She believed it was all Breitner.'

Jimmy Breitner. Kingpin of global media, a South African-born tycoon who owns the newspapers and TV stations that make or break governments. He and Todd had a powerful mutual interest in silencing Clare and in Todd winning the election. He wouldn't allow Clare to sabotage it all.

'I trusted Marilyn,' I say. 'I had to.'

Jess stares into an empty glass. We both want another – but not yet. I am feeling sick. I can't face squeezing through the braying bankers in the pub.

'You've lived with the horror of what happened to Clare for too long. And you've never been able to tell the story. I can't imagine how you've coped.'

'I didn't have libel-proof evidence. No newspaper in the world would have published it.'

'Gil.' Jess looks me in the eye, gently takes my right hand. 'What happened to Clare was awful. Same about Marilyn. I can feel your hurt and sadness. But you mustn't make the mistake of assuming history repeats.'

I gulp, and shut my eyes.

'When Clare died, I was too quick to accept the official cause of death, that she was accidentally knocked off her bike. I'm not going to make the same mistake. I understand why the police are going with the obvious explanation. But the last thing Marilyn said to me was that I wasn't seeing the whole picture. I have to listen to her.'

Jess hesitates. She doesn't want conflict, but she's not someone who backs down for an easy life. 'Maybe she was trying to tell you something else.'

The hurt and anger won't be suppressed any longer. 'Marilyn was murdered,' I almost shout. Jess winces. 'It's just like Clare. I'm going to find who did it, and make sure they pay.'

Jess rubs the cigarette tip against the pub wall and then flicks it into the gutter. 'Home time,' she sighs.

I look at the time on my BlackBerry: 9.35.

'Fuck.'

'What's up?'

'I'm due on air, on the *Ten O'Clock News*, in precisely thirty-two minutes.'

She looks concerned. 'You can't go on TV and talk about Marilyn's death in this state.'

'I'll be fine.'

She knows that I keep work and trauma in very different boxes in my brain. Compartmentalisation is my superpower. It's how I kept going back to Marilyn, after everything that had happened. I unfold the Brompton and wheel it to the kerb. Only a ten-minute ride to Television Centre.

A VW Golf, branded with the name of one of the big estate chains, reverses to park a few yards ahead. A young man with

56

backcombed, blow-dried hair gets out. He has razor-sharp pleats in his trousers, a crisp white shirt and a Gucci logo tie. He stares at me. I try to avoid his gaze, but he walks straight towards me, jabbing his finger. 'You're that jerk who wants to bankrupt the economy. Just shut the fuck up before you ruin it for everyone.'

I'm not going to engage. Since moving to the BBC I've discovered that much of the public think they're my boss. They pay the licence fee so they have the right to tell me I'm wrong. There's no point in arguing.

'I am very sorry you feel that.' I try to get on my bike and cycle off, but Jess has come up beside me. She's not having any of it.

'What gives you the right to pass judgement?' She jabs her finger right back. 'You should be grateful that my friend cares enough about this country to tell arseholes like you what's going on. You should say "Thank you" to him, rather than whining that your parasitic job may be in jeopardy. Go home and do what you do best: stand in front of the mirror and pull yourself off, you wanker.'

Not for the first time or last, I am in awe. The estate agent scuttles into the pub, glancing around anxiously to see if anyone noticed his humiliation.

'Bye, Jess.' I give her a kiss on the cheek. 'Thanks for being my friend.'

'Don't you be a wanker too.' She hugs me.

I cycle west, away from Marilyn's flat and back to the light brown brick and glaring lights of Television Centre. In minutes, millions of viewers will hear me spout impersonal clichés about Marilyn's legacy, her commitment to making sure the financial system is stable and her history of fighting for social justice. Huw Edwards will say that police are not looking for anyone in connection with her death, and I'll nod as if I believe they're doing the right thing.

A white van speeds past me on Holland Park Avenue and turns left without indicating. Jess is right. Clare's and Marilyn's tragedies are different. But this time I won't naively accept the version of events that suits the rich and powerful. I *will* find whoever is responsible for Marilyn's death.

Chapter 5

CHARING CROSS HOSPITAL. NINE THIRTY in the morning. I am in a small antiseptic room with strip lighting. In front of me is a body covered in a white sheet on a hospital trolley.

'I'm sorry to ask you to do this,' says the uniformed police officer. DC Clarkson, she tells me. Starched white shirt, coal black trousers. 'Procedure, you know.'

I can't do this. I need to get out. The DC pulls back the sheet at the head end and I stare, stupidly. I had prepared myself for horror. This is worse. It is the contrast between the attempt by the technicians to make Marilyn look as normal as possible – as if she's in gentle sleep, eyes closed – and the violence of the blackened ligature marks.

'Her name is Marilyn Krol,' I say, both necessarily and pointlessly. All the air is squeezed from me. I struggle to get the words out.

'Can I get you a glass of water, sir?'

'I'm OK. Could I be alone with Marilyn, for just a moment or two?'

'It's not procedure.'

'Of course.' I can't take my eyes off Marilyn. I try to sculpt her face into my brain: her angular cheekbones, sharp symmetrical nose, dimpled chin. I want a permanent image of her. So I won't forget.

'I'll stretch my legs outside for a couple of minutes,' says DC Clarkson. 'Don't touch anything, sir. Evidence, you know.'

'Thank you.'

The door clunks shut. I walk to the side of the trolley. I need physical contact, for the last time.

We were commitment-phobes; innocents, in a way, who would hold hands when no one was looking. I fumble under the sheet. Her fingers are icy, but I won't let them go. *I should have heard you. I should have seen you. Why didn't you tell me you were in such trouble? Don't go, don't go, don't go.*

Still gripping her hand, I summon up all my courage. I don't want to do this but I must. I pull back the sheet and examine her body for any signs of violence. If someone tried to put her head in a noose, she would have fought like hell. There should be grazes, bruises on her arms, maybe someone's skin under her fingernails where she scratched him.

What am I thinking? I'm not a coroner or a pathologist; I'm not in an episode of some cheesy cop drama. Leaving aside the horrible welts around her neck, I can't see anything that looks like violence. But maybe in real life, the signs of a struggle wouldn't be easy to detect.

There's a gentle knock on the door. I jerk my hand back. DC Clarkson will think I'm mad. *I love you Marilyn, I love you Marilyn, I love you Marilyn.*

*

Only half conscious of what I'm doing, I navigate the maze of the hospital. Disinfected anonymous lino floors, the signs directing to blood tests, audiology, cardiac, the murmur of businesslike professionals and anxious patients. I escape to the Fulham Palace Road. A procession of buses roars past, but the clamour in my head means I barely notice. Calls to make, contacts to chase, leads to follow up. Loud practical thoughts drown out the rest. Time to focus on what matters. The job is everything.

NewGate can't be the only bank in trouble. When a market shuts down, the pain spreads everywhere. I've got to find the next bank that will go bust, and the next one, and the next one. This is my story. I've got to hold on to it. No one else can own it.

I'm outside a red-brick block of council flats, built in the fifties when it was government policy that everyone should be part of a monogamous family of two point four children and have an affordable roof over their heads and an inside lav. The ideal of the perfect family. Nothing like mine.

Buzz buzz buzz buzz buzz. The BlackBerry had no signal in the hospital. Now I'm outside, it's catching up with a vengeance.

A text from Jess: *The Daily Mail really doesn't like you.*

Another from Janice: *We should talk about the Mail.*

A third from Kim Jansen: *Can we meet outside New Scotland Yard, 12.15?*

I call Jess, and shout, 'What's up?' over the mid-morning traffic.

'What did you ever do to Matt Sharpe?' she asks. Matt is the *Mail*'s assassin, a working-class boy turned hit-man of the nasty right.

'What do you mean?'

'He's written a double-page spread under the headline "Is BBC man trying to destroy Britain?" It's a masterpiece of smear and innuendo. It says your best friends are well-known users of coke, that your dad was a member of the Communist Party at university, and it implies you are somehow at the centre of an unpatriotic elitist cabal that infects Whitehall and the City.'

'Really? Well maybe the last bit is right.'

I instantly regret my stupid joke. The *Mail* is trying to destroy my credibility.

61

'This is my favourite bit. "Peck is widely seen by colleagues as ruthlessly ambitious. *He puts his own glory above everything else*, said one. *All he cares about is getting his name on the lead story, no matter the havoc he wreaks.*"'

'For fuck's sake, that's obviously a made-up quote.'

'Uncomfortably close to the truth, even for fiction.'

'You could be a bit more sympathetic. I've just identified Marilyn.

'Sorry.' She recalibrates. 'How are you?'

'I feel sick. And confused.'

'What do you mean?'

'As Jansen said, Marilyn was hanged. I've seen it with my own eyes.'

'Oh God. I am so sorry.'

I squeeze my right earlobe with all my strength to make the horror go away. 'But I still don't believe she did it to herself.'

Jess sighs. 'We discussed this last night. This is about your guilt at being too quick to accept your sister died in an accident.'

'It's not,' I reply, too quickly, talking over her. 'The bond market, NewGate, Marilyn's death. They're connected.'

'Gil, this is coincidence, or rather correlation. It's not cause and effect.' She's losing patience.

'We have the first run on a British bank in a hundred and fifty years, and the same day a director of the Bank of England is found dead. There must be a link.'

'Be careful where you're going with this, Gil.'

'What do you mean?'

'Don't try to make this all about you.'

'I don't . . .'

'You broke the NewGate story. Whether you caused the bank run or triggered it, you are right in the thick of it.' She hesitates, choosing her words with care. 'I fear that in some deep unconscious way you fear that you, your scoop, tipped her . . .'

'No I fucking don't,' I shout. An old lady wheeling a shopping trolley gives me a disapproving look. 'Marilyn was the regulator – the guardian of the system – not the supervisor of that bank or any bank. She didn't have line responsibility for NewGate. There are a lot of people who should be checking their consciences about the run, but she's not one of them. Nor am I.'

'So what on earth are you implying?'

True to our relationship, Jess has run a blinding highlighter through my wilder allegations, marking where I'm over-reaching.

'I'm trying to work it out. It's complicated. Can we meet? I need your expertise.'

I know Jess will be staring at the ceiling in exasperation. She doesn't want to humour my madness, but she doesn't want to hurt me either. 'Yes, of course. Amy's been asking after you. Come over later. We'll be home.'

Lovely Amy, Jess's seven-year-old. The one good thing that came from Jess's disastrous marriage to an investment banker – who's worth a fortune, moved to New York and forgets to pay child support every single month.

'I'll text when I'm coming.'

I work through the messages. Can't ignore Janice. I'm worried I'll be in trouble over the *Mail* article, that someone will claim it's my fault and I've brought the corporation into disrepute. It turns out, though, that Matt Sharpe has done me a favour. His hatchet job has brought Janice decisively into my corner.

'Ignore the *Mail*,' she says. 'They're jealous we're getting the scoops and they are trying to close you down. Don't you dare let them.'

She's right. *Fuck 'em.*

The *Mail* isn't alone in trying to silence me. But its motives are competitive, and very different from those of the Right Honourable Sir Giles Pimlott, who wants me taken off air with

D-notices, and the chair of the British Bankers' Association, who told the DG I was blowing up Britain's only world-class industry, banking. They have a vested interest in protecting their banker friends. The City gravy train has been spewing cash, on them and their cronies, and they're desperate not to lose it.

Desperate people do desperate things.

*

An hour later, Kim Jansen and I are walking along the Embankment, towards Cleopatra's Needle. Away from the corner with Westminster Bridge Road where my sister was murdered.

'We've got the toxicology back,' Kim says.

'You tested her blood?' There's an unmistakable eagerness in my voice. Testing blood means an investigation, that they're not necessarily treating it as a suicide.

Kim gives me a pitying look. 'We always do in these cases.'

'And?'

'Was Marilyn a heavy drug user?'

This is unexpected, tricky. 'I don't think so.'

'You don't sound sure.'

'Off the record?'

'OK.'

'Well, look, you remember the nineties. You were there. We all did Class A drugs.'

'Not all of us,' she says primly.

'Really? It's me you're talking to.' At college, I sold her cannabis. 'In Old Buildings, you were one of my best clients.' Old Buildings is the Georgian block of Chichele College's main quadrangle.

There's a heavy silence. 'That was a long time ago.'

'The point I'm making is: yes, Marilyn did the things we all did. But I don't think she was still a user.'

64

'There were traces of cocaine all over her apartment, and ketamine in her system. Quite a lot of it.'

'Really?' The neurons in my brain are sparking. 'So she could have been drugged and then hanged by a third party.'

Light rain flecks our faces. A Thames gossamer envelops us. The vapour from our breath mingles with the mist.

'I asked the pathologist that question,' says Kim.

'So you *are* treating it as a possible murder.'

What we are doing is standard procedure. We look at all possibilities. I want to know if she was a regular heavy user because that would condition whether she could have tolerated that much ket in her system.'

'We both were – once. But I stopped. My addictions now are legal ones. I think the same was true of Marilyn.'

'I'm not sure about that, Gil.'

Oh Christ. Is this something else I didn't know about her? 'But surely the ket shows she could have been drugged and killed?'

'Or she took it to numb the terror of killing herself.'

'She wouldn't have been capable of hanging herself with all the tranquilliser in her bloodstream.'

'Not necessarily.'

I have to rethink the Marilyn I thought I knew. When she was nineteen, an articulated lorry crashed through the central reservation on the M1 and hit her parents' car. Marilyn was in the car behind and saw the whole thing. She almost never spoke about it. I suppose there is a chance that after all these years the buried nightmare caught up with her. But I don't – won't – accept it.

'She could have been the first female Governor,' I hear myself saying, simultaneously proud and sad. Her career trajectory was rocket-fuelled: from think-tank wonk, to the leader of the opposition's advisor, then head of the Downing Street policy unit after Johnny Todd became PM in 1997. After five years defining Modern Labour for Todd – devising plans to incentivise the unemployed to come off benefits, to shorten the waiting time for cancer treatment, to remake schools for the internet age – she moved to the Bank of England. She was the most senior woman at the Bank, a brilliant career ahead. No chance she killed herself.

'Any sign of a note?' I ask. There's an aggressive, accusatory tone in my voice.

'Still nothing. But honestly that doesn't mean much.'

'I disagree. I *knew* her.' Or at least I think I did.

There's a loud beeping and shouting. It's a grimy white van coming towards us, with the passenger window wound down. A bald head is hanging out. I imagine the Fred Perry stretched over a beer belly inside.

'Peck,' the driver shouts. 'You legend.'

Kim struggles to suppress her amusement. 'How does it feel to be famous?'

'I'm not.'

'You are. Everyone noticed your NewGate story. Everyone is talking about how you broke the bank.'

'I didn't.'

'You don't have to convince me. I just wondered if you like all the attention?'

I hate the question, because I know she sees my narcissism. Being on television is very different from being at a newspaper, where my stories were noticed, though I wasn't – or, rather, my readers didn't know what I looked like. Don't get me wrong: there was an egotistic hit from writing the splash for the *FC*. But the noise I can generate at the BBC is so much louder. The moment I broadcast or even blog a scoop, knowing my rivals will be obliged to follow up and that important people will be forced to put out exculpatory statements, is better than the rush of the purest, whitest drugs.

The rain is picking up. I wipe my forehead with my hand. 'We should head back,' Kim says. 'We'll get soaked.'

We turn around and retrace our steps. Rain speckles the brown river; on the far bank, the London Eye's capsules on the big wheel are slowly tracking us and watching us through the mist.

'We've found a next of kin,' Kim says suddenly. 'An aunt.'

'What?' I think I must have misheard. 'Who?'

Kim grins. 'The Countess Woolard.'

'A countess? Are you sure? How extraordinary.' Marilyn always implied to me that she had no family left, after her mum and dad died. And the notion that she was related to an aristo is nuts.

'She's posh. Very posh,' says Kim drily. 'Lives in a pile in Suffolk. You can look her up in Debrett's.'

I try to process. 'Could you give her my number, ask her to give me a call? So I can pay my condolences.'

'Sure.'

We're back at New Scotland Yard. 'Look after yourself, Gil,' says Kim. 'I know you don't believe it's suicide. But I can tell you that in more than twenty years in the force, I've learned that the simple explanation is usually the right one. Occam's razor.'

I don't reply. For a brief moment, I wonder if we should hug, then decide she'd be mortified. The assistant commissioner turns on her solid, sensible heels and walks towards the entrance. I can hear the 'Afternoon, ma'am's of her juniors.

Standing in the rain, as policemen and civil servants hurry past under their umbrellas, I'm alone. Again. I'm puzzled and shaken that there's a titled aunt. With a stately home. I thought I knew Marilyn. All those years with her are a dream. Were the delusions mine or hers?

I pull out the BlackBerry. The buttons are greasy in the damp.

Shall I come over now?

Sure. Let me feed Amy first. 7?

*

Jess's house is a mid-Victorian, semi-detached villa, light brown London-grime-brick, just off the Kilburn High Road. Estate agents would call it Queen's Park borders, and it is definitely on

67

the way up, just like Jess. Its relatively modest front is a deceit: the house is much deeper than it is wide, so on the inside it feels huge, a nineteenth-century Dr Who's Tardis. At least six bedrooms, three ground-floor reception rooms, shower rooms and loos everywhere. It's absurdly big for just a mum and a seven-year-old. Jess bought it when she was planning a vast family with wanker banker hubby, and she hasn't moved out because Amy's life has been disrupted enough.

I'm perched on a stool at the marble island in Jess's kitchen, which extends beyond the original back of the house into the hundred-foot garden. The sky has a ruby tinge, which glows through the sloping skylight. A fox stares at me accusingly through the French windows. I stare right back.

Jess has seen it too. 'They think they own the place,' she says. She puts a bottle of Sancerre in the huge, American-style fridge. For now it's strong brown tea in mugs. Mine has a decal of Les from the Bay City Rollers, hers David Cassidy in his prime.

'Where did you get these? There's no way you were a member of the Tartan Horde. You're way too young.'

'Hobby. Amy and I pick them up from junk shops. We have a thing for seventies kitsch.'

'The age that style forgot,' I say, though it's the seventies that made me. I slurp my tea. 'Whenever there's a huge stock-market movement, there are winners and losers. Who do we reckon made money out of the collapse of NewGate? And who was on the losing side?'

Jess leans back. She knows where I am going with this.

'Just to be clear, I know I can't prove the NewGate run is linked to Marilyn's death,' I add. 'But humour me. Please.'

She blows on the surface of the steaming brown liquid. 'All the talk is about Ravel,' she says.

I should have guessed. 'Chris Ravel? As in Lulworth Securities?'

'You know him?'

'We were at Oxford.'

Jess rolls her eyes. 'Of course you were.'

'He won a Gibbs Prize for maths. Brain like a supercomputer, classic on-the-spectrum genius. At university he was a tankie.'

'What's a tankie?'

'A Stalinist. Member of some *Life-of-Brian*-style Communist sect.'

'You're pulling my leg.'

'It's not so crazy. Stalinism is about focus, ruthlessness, discipline, and a refusal to be diverted by normal human instincts and emotions – all the qualities necessary to be an uber-capitalist hedge-fund manager.'

I think back to Chichele, queuing in the Junior Common Room at 2 a.m. for baked beans. 'He was a PLO supporter, too. There were rumours he was some sort of honorary member of Fatah. He spent most of his summers in Palestine, and wore a keffiyeh the whole time.'

Jess gets up to refill the kettle. 'This is so going into the *FC*'s next profile of him.'

'You'll need another source. It was a long time ago, before he became unbelievably wealthy. How much is he worth these days?'

'Hedgies never disclose. The rumour is at least a couple of billion. Maybe more.'

After Oxford, Ravel created one of the biggest hedge funds in the UK, Lulworth Securities. It has $20 billion of assets under management and an envied history of beating the market. Ravel has no small talk, doesn't suffer fools and is notoriously abrupt. In the City, he's cordially disliked but is tolerated because he makes so much money for investors and the banks that service his funds. He's also feared, because he's usually right.

'If he shorted NewGate, I can't imagine how much he's trousered,' I say. Short selling is when an investor borrows shares or bonds to sell, in the hope that the price falls and the shares or bonds can be bought back much cheaper, yielding a fat profit. The purpose of short sellers, like Ravel, is to identify and target vulnerable institutions. And there weren't many more vulnerable than NewGate.

If Ravel made a bundle on the NewGate rout, he'd have had no grudge against Marilyn, unless he illegally manipulated the shares in some way and she was planning to blow the whistle. That's plausible.

'As you pointed out, I should know this stuff,' I say. 'So don't be too cruel. Is Ravel bent?'

Jess sighs. 'There are two schools of thought about hedge funds, as I am sure you know. One is that they're all spivs and cowboys, that it's all disguised insider trading and market manipulation. The other is that they are genuine rocket scientists, who use algorithms and formulae to beat the market, fair and square.'

'Your view?'

'Somewhere in between. Yes, there are crooks. But there are others who are bona fide mathematical geniuses.'

'And Ravel?'

'We've agreed he's a brainbox. And, for what it's worth, his reputation is squeaky clean.'

'You can pay people to launder your reputation.'

'You're telling me?'

I remember the many times I've seen Jess humiliate PR executives. She thinks they're all liars and parasites.

'Can I ask another stupid question?'

'You don't normally ask my permission.'

'Ha ha.' I take a deep breath. 'If Ravel made a killing, does that mean someone else has lost their shirt?'

'Certainly lots of NewGate shareholders are much poorer than they were. But if you are asking if one investor in particular incurred a huge loss that corresponds precisely to whatever profit Ravel has made, that's unlikely – because Ravel may well have borrowed from multiple investors, who in turn may have hedged.'

I gulp the last of my tea. The kettle has boiled but Jess ignores it and goes to the fridge. She takes out the wine. 'I need a drink,' she says. She shows me the bottle by way of offering.

'Sure. But just to be clear, it's not impossible that someone's a big loser?'

'In theory? No. But, as I said, unlikely in that simple sense. Though if there is a mega loser, they'll be keeping very quiet about it. The humiliation would be worse than the monetary loss.'

'If you hear of a big loser, will you tell me?'

She gives me a long-suffering 'Yes' and adds: 'Just for the avoidance of doubt, I don't think Marilyn was bumped off by a disgruntled NewGate shareholder.'

'I didn't say she was.'

'It's what you think.'

She roots around in a drawer for a corkscrew, uncorks the bottle and pours each of us a large glass. Before I can make my disingenuous objections, the BlackBerry rings. I mouth 'Give me a minute' to Jess, who raises her eyebrows. But it's already out of my pocket and halfway to my ear.

'Is this Gilbert Peck?' The voice is lazily entitled, resonant of generations of private education.

'That's me.'

'My name is Cressida Dawler. The policewoman mentioned my niece, Marilyn Krol, was a friend of yours.'

It's the countess. Blimey. Thanks Kim. 'Yes. I'd known her for years. Please accept my sincere condolences.'

'Thank you, Mr Peck. As you probably know, she and I weren't close. But family is family.'

I have no idea how to respond, so say nothing. 'We're holding a small funeral, Friday week. In our chapel.'

Our chapel. Another thing I didn't know about Marilyn.

'It will be a small affair. I'd be grateful if you didn't mention it to anyone. But you would be most welcome.'

She gives me the name of a house in Suffolk, no street or anything common like that, and hangs up.

Without being conscious of it, I've been pacing the room. I face Jess.

'Marilyn's funeral,' I explain to Jess.

'Will you go?'

'Yes.'

She gives me a tight smile, the sort my big sister used to give me when I fell off the climbing frame and scraped my elbow. *Be brave. It won't sting for long.* 'You should.'

Looking for the Marilyn I never knew fills me with dread. But I have started a project that is more important than anything else, investigating why she died. *This is bigger than you think*, Marilyn said. Her last words to me. She wanted me to know. I glug the sharp, icy cold wine.

'I can't wait to meet the countess.'

Chapter 6

AMONG THE MANY THINGS I never noticed about Marilyn, while we were fucking and sharing confidential information about our respective employers, is that she wasn't boringly predictably middle class like me. She was posh. Thanks to Google, I have learned that she could trace her ancestors back to William the Conqueror and before. The Dawlers are toffs. In fact, as far as I am capable of understanding these nuances, they are the toffs' toff, Roman Catholic aristocracy who think they are better than everyone. They were recusants after Henry VIII's spat with the pope, yet clung on to their ownership of half of several ancient counties. Anyone ennobled after the dissolution of the monasteries is an arriviste to them. Which explains, presumably, Marilyn's supreme intellectual self-confidence.

I am pedalling languidly along country lanes in Dedham Vale, from Manningtree station. These are apparently the lanes of her hidden and privileged childhood. The public highways run through woods and farmland that have been in the Dawler family for generations. I drink in Constable's idyll. After three miles, it's impossible to miss my destination – because Dawler House rises up like a great Jacobean ship across a verdant ocean of parkland. 'One of the finest examples of its type,' says Wikipedia, of its red-brick, sharp-edged gables and mullioned windows. As I pedal between Corinthian pillars that announce the entrance to a vast estate, I see a simple Norman chapel on the left. Dismounting, I wheel the Brompton toward the iron railings that protect an ancient graveyard. At a wooden gate, a family retainer instructs me to leave the folded bike in the portico.

There are a pair of dark-suited men wearing earpieces loitering to my right. Security. It's obvious whose. I am disappointed Marilyn's aunt didn't choose to exclude a flashy former prime minister from her small family affair. I grind my teeth. I wonder whether the countess would evict him if I shared my conviction that he murdered her niece? Probably not. Too much of a scene.

The chapel is grey stone, lovingly and expensively restored. The ornate interior reeks of incense. On entry, I am ushered to the friends' side. In the fifth row, I am next to a sixty-something man whose full lips and exquisitely cut and swept-back grey hair – Trumper, I assume – are familiar, though he cultivates a certain kind of knowing aloofness, in the great tradition of Whitehall mandarins. We've never actually been introduced. Lord Ravel nods at me. 'Peck,' is all he says. 'Ravel,' I reply, to this former cabinet secretary. He was supposedly high-up in the Secret Intelligence Service, and is a man who by repute knows more dark secrets than God.

I can see the back of Todd's head, three rows in front. His hair is as dark as ever it was. 'Dyes it, you know, like a member of the Chinese politburo,' Ravel comments. 'Can't stand the idea he might be getting past it. How are you doing by the way? Must be very hard for you.'

I force a feeble smile. Of course Ravel knows about my fifteen-year affair with Marilyn, the affair we thought we brilliantly hid from the world.

'Is it well-known that she and I ... ?'

'I doubt it. It was my job to know these things.'

His utter confidence is familiar. Like father, like son. I shared tutorials with Chris, at Chichele. One time, discussing the

Philosophical Investigations, his demolition of a college fellow's Wittgenstein primer reduced the young tutor to tears. Ravel junior neither noticed nor cared.

'I have to say, and I hope this doesn't sound tactless, but I was surprised she took her own life,' Ravel says. 'She was the last person I would have expected, if you know what I mean.'

'I do. But the police insist.'

'I see they've put Kim Jansen on it. She's formidable. Or at least compared to the rest of them.'

The last of the mourners are sitting down. The Governor of the Bank of England is shown to a seat alongside Todd.

Ravel murmurs, 'The family agree with you and are refusing to acknowledge the suicide. Couldn't have a proper service and burial otherwise.'

'I thought the extreme Catholic prejudice about suicide was dropped by the pope twenty years ago.'

'Not for Catholics like the Dawlers. Hope your Latin isn't too rusty.' He turns to face the front. Through our conversation, Johnny Todd has rigidly faced the altar. He's still and contemplative.

The priest climbs the few steps up to the oak pulpit, and tells us we are gathered to celebrate the life of Marilyn Krol, taken from us cruelly and young. As the service progresses, I feel isolated and lonely. Almost everything is unfamiliar and alienating: the hymns, the Latin prayers, the depersonalised tributes from the priest and Aunt Cressida. Neither of them knew Marilyn. They measure her life in her first-class degrees and high-flying jobs. All this pomposity and ceremony is not my Marilyn. But I didn't know the real Marilyn.

The coup de grace. Todd walks to the lectern. He says a few sanctimonious words about how there would have been no Modern Labour without Marilyn's brilliance. And he reads Hopkins:

The world is charged with the grandeur of God.
It will flame out, like shining from shook foil;

It gathers to a greatness, like the ooze of oil
Crushed. Why do men then now not reck his rod?

I scan the chapel and marvel that no one is calling out Todd's apostasy. If *he* feared God's authority, if he *recked his rod* – if he hadn't stolen whatever he could get away with – my sister might still be alive.

The priest is winding up the service. He reads Psalm 22, in the traditional vulgate version:

> *Parasti in conspectu meo mensam adversus eos qui tribulant me;*
>   *impinguasti in oleo caput meum: et calix meus inebrians,*
>   *quam præclarus est!*
> *Et misericordia tua subsequetur me omnibus diebus vitæ meæ;*
>   *et ut inhabitem in domo Domini in longitudinem dierum.*

My Latin is limited and rusty, learned in a crash course in the lower sixth, just in case it might help secure me a place at Oxford. From somewhere I extract a well-worn phrase, about 'living in the house of the Lord'. Or something like that.

And then the priest asks us to sing the same psalm in the bowdlerised hymn version, which he has been led to understand was one of Marilyn's favourites. I manage to suppress a disbelieving snort. As it happens, I know the tune, and some of the words, thanks to my parents' insistence that I should attend the *goyische* assemblies at my North London primary school. A few Jewish kids sat and read for half an hour in the library, but Bernard and Ginger didn't want to mark us as different from the other children; they wanted Clare and me to assimilate Englishness.

I boom:

> *Goodness and mercy all my life*
> *Shall surely follow me;*

And in God's house forevermore
My dwelling place shall be.

It's done. Close family files out first. There are only about thirty mourners, forming a line in the aisle to pay our condolences. Lord Ravel is still next to me. I can't see Johnny Todd, until I look around. He's gone to the back corner of the chapel and is placing a lit candle on the iron stand. He contemplates it for a moment, hands folded, head bowed.

'I assume there's a photographer somewhere to capture that touching scene,' I say.

Ravel smiles. 'He read beautifully, don't you think? No one does faux sincerity like our former leader.'

He's invited me to risk saying what I think. 'It's funny how few people notice that our former prime minister is a charlatan.'

He answers elliptically: 'Towards the end, I think even our lovely Marilyn was beginning to see Johnny properly.'

Our lovely Marilyn. 'Did you speak to Marilyn often?'

'Not recently. We worked hand-in-glove ten years ago. Since she left, we tried to lunch a couple of times a year.'

'What about Christopher?'

'My son Christopher?'

'Was he close to Marilyn?'

'You'd know better than me. But I assume they knew each other.'

Only 'assume'? That's odd.

'I wondered if Christopher would be here today, actually,' Ravel continues. 'He's infatuated with Todd, you know.'

Why wouldn't he have telephoned his son to find out if he was coming? There is something off here.

'Why would Christopher have any interest in Todd?' I ask.

'Peas in a pod.'

I look quizzically at him. 'I'm sure you'll work it out,' he says. 'Now I've a question for you. Has Tudor asked you what to do about the banks?'

77

'The *banks*?' I reply. 'Plural?'

'Oh, don't play the innocent. Of course there'll be others in trouble. The question is what does the government do about them?'

'Well the official policy is caveat emptor. Banks go bust, depositors lose money, so everyone learns a lesson for next time.'

'The official policy is bunkum,' he says gravely. 'Do you think any government could survive depositors losing money?'

'Then there are two options: bail out depositors, or bail out the whole bank.'

'Quite. And protecting just the retail deposits is messy and complicated. Where would a chancellor draw the line? Would he say everyone with savings up to a hundred thousand pounds was protected and anyone with more than that would suffer losses? That would be bad politics and probably terrible economics. I assume foreign investors would head for the hills.'

'What then?'

'We'll end up nationalising of course. Back to state socialism.'

We shuffle forward. 'Do you think Tudor has come to that conclusion?' I ask.

'Not yet. He's such an old woman.'

*

We've reached the door of the church where – to my dismay – the priest is standing holding a collection plate. I've only got credit cards on me. Panicking, I fumble through the pockets of my black Lacroix jacket – the one with the intricately embroidered floral lining – and find three pound coins and a crumpled fiver. I put it all clumsily on the silver plate.

'Sorry, it's all I've got.' The cleric smirks contemptuously.

As we turn towards the porch, I see something – someone – so unexpected that I flinch as if shocked by touching a live wire. It's Marilyn. The angular cheekbones, slight sinewy frame, judgemental grey-green eyes. And then she becomes a shimmer of Marilyn, a mirage, an older Marilyn, with grey hair cut boyishly short, and wearing an exquisitely tailored, black wool-and-silk housecoat. The countess.

'I'm sad we've had to meet, in these circumstances,' she says, leaving me unclear whether her sadness is about the circumstances, or encountering me.

'It was a touching service,' I lie. 'Sincerest condolences, again.' The words stick in my craw. I have more right to mourn than she, not least because she seems made of the same unyielding steel as Marilyn, which the internet tells me was forged over the centuries of Dawler women keeping the show on the road against the mismanagement of feckless men.

She fixes me with black pupils as forbidding as a barred door. 'Can I ask you, Mr Peck, why the police insist on saying Marilyn took her own life? I don't believe it. That's not what we do.'

'The police insist the evidence points in that direction. But, like you, I am keeping an open mind.'

'I don't trust the police.'

Apparently no answer is required. The countess is already turning to greet Lord Ravel. I shuffle on towards Earl Woolard. His wavy, greying ginger hair is Brylcreemed back over his scalp, and the pink of his cheeks betrays someone who enjoys his wine cellar. He's wearing a camel coat, with a brown velvet collar, that's wearing thin and was probably made for him twenty years ago. It's too snug around fleshy upper arms and midriff.

'Ah, Gilbert Peck, no less. So sad about Marilyn.'

More regrets from another person who hardly knew her. I know *him*, though. Woolard, then known as Frank, worked for many years as senior partner of one of the City's older stockbrokers, the snobby kind that favoured the right school over brains. It kept itself afloat by illegally gaming stock exchange rules with a complicated scheme to charge clients twice for buying South African stocks, known as 'kaffirs'. I tried to expose both him and the scheme as a cub reporter on *Investors' Weekly*, my first employer, but the then chair of the stock exchange went shooting with the owner of the mag, and persuaded him to close me down. Woolard's firm continued to thrive, though it was swallowed up years ago by a Luxembourg bank with a reputation for facilitating insider trading. Plus ça change.

I murmur something banal about his loss, and shake his hand. 'Do have a sandwich before you head back to London,' he encourages me. 'See you in the drawing room.'

*

The house has thirty bedrooms, and staff to match – who polish, oil, stitch and mend the furniture and tapestries that have passed from Dawler to Dawler for generations. On the walls are sublime Canalettos, somehow kept out of the clutches of the tax man when death duties couldn't be ignored. I gawp at one of Whitehall, lost palaces on each side, familiar and foreign at the same time.

'Magnificent, isn't it?' Woolard pads up behind me.

'You are lucky to be able to look at this any time you want.'

'I suppose we are.' He shrugs, preferring not to acknowledge privilege. 'How are you finding the Beeb? I used to read you in the *Financial Chronicle*. Bit of a loss to the green 'un if you don't mind me saying.' The pages of the *FC* are a distinctive soft green.

'I was ready for a change. And I can't claim to be bored.'

'We have noticed. Are you planning to bring down another bank any time soon?'

I can't tell if he's joking. 'You never know. Are you still making a bob or two from the kaffir trade?'

He reddens. 'Ah yes. That. Ancient history. The City is a very different place, all Yank money now. Not necessarily a good thing.'

I suppress a smirk. Is he really too thick to know that in the absence of the torrent of cash into the UK from America, Russia,

China, Singapore, Japan and so on, the value of his estate would not have quintupled? Or is he just too entitled to care? When our paths first crossed in the 1980s, he was a down-at-heel, dodgy aristo. Now, thanks to soaring land values, he and Cressida are ultra-high net worth, in the jargon.

It's pointless challenging his insidious Anglo supremacism. More pertinently, I've spotted someone whose story I do want to hear. George 'Georgie' Edmunds, Governor of the Bank of England, is heaping a plate with cold cuts of beef and potato salad from willow pattern bowls.

'Will you forgive me?' I say to Woolard. Not waiting for a reply, I take the shortest route to the Queen Anne mahogany table where Edmunds is spooning horseradish onto the side of his plate. 'Governor?'

'Peck. I wondered if I'd see you here.'

OK, so literally everyone knows about Marilyn and me. Even the Governor. I take a plate and ladle salads onto it. I'm trying to cut down on red meat. I look at it and regret how much beetroot I've taken. I surreptitiously put some back.

'Do you have a minute for a chat?' Edmunds says.

'I do.'

'Let's sit over there?' He points to a long table in the adjoining grand reception room. 'I am not very good at eating while standing up.'

We sit facing the wall of French windows that open to lawns that slope gently to a manmade lake. 'If you look to the right, there's a beautiful Jekyll garden,' he says.

'How's your garden?' Famously, it's his pride and joy.

'At times like this it's about my only solace.'

'That bad?'

'Come off it, Peck, you know it's bad.'

I shovel a nasturtium and dandelion leaf, in honeyed dressing, into my mouth. I wonder if it's the earl or the countess who knows how to live: certainly one of them does.

I dab my mouth with my napkin. 'Forgive me for being blunt. I need to know whether anything happened to Marilyn at work that – you think – would have persuaded her to take her own life.'

'We're all asking the same question. The Bank is in shock. I know people always exaggerate the virtues of the deceased, but she was the brightest and the best. And so diligent.'

He prods at a piece of beef. 'In answer to your question, it was obviously a challenging time for her, for all of us. She was in charge of financial stability; and finance, markets, were not stable. Needless telling you, of course. But she was in her element, or so it seemed. She worked tirelessly to learn where the risks were, which institutions were vulnerable.'

I have another thought. 'Marilyn was very single-minded. Did you find her an easy colleague?'

'Funny you should say that. She saw things that some of us missed. That could be challenging. But she made the Bank stronger, even at the cost of upsetting her colleagues.'

I force a smile. 'That doesn't surprise me. What did she spot before others?'

'She was the first to work out that assets the banks thought were easy to sell and were as good as cash might turn out to be impossible to sell when most necessary.'

'Which is precisely what got NewGate into such trouble after bond markets shut down.'

'Quite.'

Shovelling garden leaves onto a fork, I love hearing my friend praised. But it's not a eulogy I need. 'What I really wanted to know is whether the two of *you* saw eye to eye. Marilyn was one of those people who was hard to shift once she had made up her mind.'

'What's the basis of this chat?'

'I've assumed we're talking off the record. To be honest, I can't promise not to use what you tell me, but I can guarantee I won't source it to you or the Bank in any way.'

'On that basis, then, Marilyn and I did have a significant disagreement, about whether and how to help NewGate, after we learned it was in trouble.'

Edmunds sips from his water glass, and stares to my left. I press.

'What did you disagree about?'

He pauses and reflects before replying.

'NewGate came to see us, to get our permission and support for a plan it had devised to sell itself to another financial institution, a rescue, an attempt to stave off collapse.'

NewGate was trying to sell itself. That's news. 'Who was the bidder?'

'It would be wrong for me to say, even off the record. Suffice to say it's a name you'd know.'

Shall I play the guessing game with him? Maybe in a minute. For now, it's better to let him continue.

'Right from the outset, Marilyn was in favour of the takeover. And I thought she was probably right, until we got right down to the wire, a few days ago. At the last moment, the bidder told us he would only do the deal if we guaranteed him access to billions of pounds of cheap credit, and underwrite losses over a specified level. He was asking for a giant subsidy, which was almost certainly a breach of European state aid rules, and therefore illegal.'

I'm intrigued by why Edmunds is describing the bidder as 'he'. An individual not a bank?

'You could have got a waiver from the government, surely?' I ask. 'Force majeure and all that.'

'Possibly. The involvement of the EU makes it complicated. There was another problem though. We would have been using taxpayers' money to protect bankers from the consequences of their own foolishness. I couldn't countenance that.'

'And Marilyn could?'

'That's the funny thing. To my amazement, yes, she continued to support the deal.'

I am nonplussed. I paraphrase Bagehot, the Victorian doyen of banking theorists. '"Any aid to a bad bank is the surest mode of preventing the establishment of a future good bank."'

'Indeed.'

'I had so many conversations with Marilyn about all this. She was adamant that the central bank should only act as lender of last resort to well-run banks, that to prop up incompetent or dishonest banks was the road to hell. Moral hazard really mattered to her.'

'You should work for us.'

I raise my eyebrows in comic disbelief. He presses on. 'As you say, in a general sense Marilyn was fastidious in adhering to central banking orthodoxy. So I was surprised, upset even, when she went on manoeuvres with other Bank executives, to try and persuade me to deploy our balance sheet to help NewGate. I felt let down and was shirty with her.'

He lets his head droop briefly, in sadness and maybe guilt. No one wants the last thing said to a friend or colleague to have been angry. I am tempted to reassure him that she would have shrugged off his displeasure. When we were in bed, she took the piss out of his intellectual sclerosis, as she called it. Even so, I am as intrigued as he is by why she would have wanted to use or abuse the Bank of England's financial muscle to help the mystery buyer of a failing bank.

'What's going to happen to NewGate now?'

'We'll keep it on a lifeline, for a while. But our support can only be temporary. It's not appropriate for NewGate to become a subsidiary of the Bank of England. Which means the prime minister faces a difficult decision: take it into public ownership with a view to selling it back to the private sector in a few years, or wind it up in an orderly fashion.'

'A dilemma for Neville Tudor.'

'It certainly is. As Marilyn doubtless told you, NewGate is not the only bank struggling in current market conditions. It is simply the most visible.'

I spear a new potato, and pretend it is completely normal for the Governor of the Bank of England to tell me that the entire financial system, the underpinning of our prosperity, is in trouble. I sort of knew already, but confirmation is a big deal. I've got to get it on air.

My conscience pricks. I shouldn't be thinking about my next big journalistic coup at my lover's funeral. And then I remember again what she said.

This is bigger than you think.

Marilyn was telling me that billions of dollars were at stake, considerably more than the price of a life, her life. When I find out why Marilyn was in favour of bailing out NewGate, I'll know more about why she died, and presumably too about the next dominoes to tumble.

I make one last attempt with Edmunds. 'Are you sure you can't tell me the name of NewGate's white knight?'

He gives me a resigned look. 'If you ask around, it won't take you long to work it out.'

*

Half an hour later I'm wheeling my bike out through the park's imposing gates. This time I notice that there are lions rampant on the top of the gate's pillars. How did I miss them when I arrived? It turns out that Marilyn, as a Dawler, was top of the food chain by dint of birth. Did she work selflessly for a Labour prime minister as a rebellion against her birthright, or to protect the privileges of her family?

I am so engrossed by my memory of her – I can hear her voice telling me that Todd explicitly rejected the politics of envy, that Modern Labour was all about rewarding success – that I barely register the low rumble of the navy blue Range Rover that pulls up beside me. The back-seat electric window purrs down, revealing a face known by everyone in the country. More

85

grey and more lines than the first time we met – more than nine years as prime minister will do that to you – but the same startling green eyes that wooed from a thousand billboards.

'That was all a bit odd, and sad, wasn't it?' Johnny Todd does a passable impression of someone who cares. He always did.

'There is no chance that Marilyn killed herself,' I find myself blurting. 'She was murdered.'

I've startled Todd, who flinches – just a millimetre or so. Then the front window opens. Alex Elliott, a PR man much more powerful than most newspaper owners, leans out and forces a grin.

'Peck. The evidence says suicide.'

'Evidence can be rigged.'

The bloom is definitely off Elliott's youth. He's a caricature of the public-school smoothie: hair still floppy, hairless cheeks sagging, another yard of poplin needed for the brilliant white Jermyn Street shirt that hides a tummy. His charm disguises unfettered malice.

'Calm down. We all loved Marilyn. That's why I wanted to have a word. I'm hosting a small gathering of her closest friends, Wednesday night, so that we can share memories of her, honour her. I'd love it if you would come. My place.'

Elliott is a snake, though an entertaining one. He is staggeringly well-connected, and I would be mad not to go, if only to work the room for stories.

'I'll try.'

Todd fixes me with a stare. 'Take care on your bike, Gil.'

Did he really just say that?

Before I can respond, the Range Rover accelerates with a spray of gravel. I'm dusting it off when I feel the number two BlackBerry vibrating with an incoming call. It's the Downing Street switchboard.

'Gil Peck? This is Switch. Are you in a position to take a call from the prime minister's press secretary?'

Click.

The next voice I hear is Jane Walters's. She's been minding Neville Tudor for fifteen years, and she's never softened around the edges. No small talk, no *How are you?* Straight in.

'There is a global crisis in the making, and Britain can take the lead in coordinating an international rescue. Are you up for interviewing the PM about his ambitious plans?'

I've been here before. In practice, Jane always promises much from an interview, and the cautious Tudor under-delivers. He doesn't have Johnny Todd's flair and sense of showbiz, though he's much more diligent in the day job.

'You know I'm never going to turn down an interview with the PM, Jane. When did you have in mind?'

'Next few days. Maybe Monday. I'll confirm over the weekend.'

Chapter 7

O N   T H E   T R A I N   B A C K   T O London from Manningtree
I write a blog on my BlackBerry. I want to take Walter
Bagehot's insight in *Lombard Street*, that the route to
good banks is to punish the bad bankers, and apply it to the
NewGate farce. Obviously I would discuss this with Marilyn.
Is it weird to address it to her? Probably.

Dear Marilyn,

*When you moved to the Bank of England, we talked about
moral hazard, that if someone is lending or investing, they'll do
so less prudently if they know someone other than themselves
will incur the losses when all goes wrong. We agreed that it is
an important idea, especially for someone in your job.*

*We agreed this goes wider than the banks. There is a systemic
abdication of responsibility by those in power. It is a cancer
in this supposed age of unbroken progress, the rot in the
foundations of almost everything. Today's leaders want lavish
rewards and praise for achievements that aren't theirs – low
inflation and economic growth imported from China would
be one example – but they always blame others when things
go wrong.*

*I've been thinking about how we restore the convention of
credit where credit is due, and punishment where punishment*

is due. I am not hopeful though, because testosterone-fuelled narcissistic sociopaths proliferate wherever there's money or power or both. They are everywhere.

If I was writing a mathematical forecasting model that built in the toxic consequences of moral hazard, the part that would challenge me is how to capture the subjective perception of risk. Or to put it another way, risk that would be water off a duck's back to one person – me, perhaps – may feel so extreme to others that it would terrify and incapacitate them. For the anxious, leaving the house to go to the shops is unbearable. For others, skydiving isn't thrill enough. It's all about subjective evaluations of the worst that can happen.

I am a case in point. Since the murder of Clare, my brilliant feted sister who kept me safe as a teenager, I've taken excessive risks for the sheer undiluted thrill of it, to dice with a kind of death, reputational death.

I've needed more than ever the adrenaline rush of humiliating the rich and powerful by revealing their secrets. It proves I'm alive. This pursuit of the sociopaths who run our lives, ruin our lives, doubtless feeds my own inner narcissist. I love all the attention after each scoop, the jealous bitchy asides of other broadcasters and hacks, the leak enquiries. And yes Marilyn, I know this is all a bit pathetic, that it's displacement activity for my failure to bring Todd to justice, a revenge binge on the whole boss class for my inability to execute the revenge that counts.

If one of my scoops goes horribly wrong, if I claim as truth something that isn't quite right? Fuck it, I deserve to be humiliated and punished. Because the worst that could happen has happened. Twice now. You and Clare. I didn't protect and save either of you.

It is a mental health issue, though my line managers couldn't give a toss. They are just thrilled that I am breaking business

90

scoop after business scoop, for the glory of the corporation. They love that the BBC has been telling the world about the evils of collateralised debt obligations when most of the competition is still confused about how financial markets have become radioactive and are poisoning us. It's two fingers to the Globe and the Daily Mail, which hate the BBC. My blarney to management is about how I scientifically calibrate the risks when I decide to publish a story that begins 'I can exclusively reveal.' The truth is much more gut feel, and the thrill of daring the gods to ruin me.

One day they will. Or at least I hope so.

I am the problem with Bagehot's theory of moral hazard. You could design a market, or even a society, to eliminate it, by making sure that banks and bankers, for example, are spanked properly when they take crazy risks. But some of us take stupid risks because we don't care about the consequences when it all goes wrong. What if the bankers – like me – aren't afraid of shame and humiliation? How many of them, how many of us, secretly crave disaster, perhaps to atone for past sins? If loss carries no fear, then there's nothing anyone could do to rein us in. Moral hazard is a useless concept when applied to sociopaths.

In a battle between sociopaths, there is no compromise, just a victor and a corpse. I will avenge you, darling.

G x

Tapping it out on the BlackBerry's dinky buttons takes most of the journey. I'm finishing when the train pulls into Liverpool Street. I read it through for sense and spelling, as a uniformed lady walks through the carriage picking up rubbish with a latex-gloved hand. She warns me if I don't get off soon I'll be going back the way I came. I thank her and start typing the address in the 'to' box. This will be a blog with fewer hits

91

than most. It's going to one reader: Marilyn.Krol@gmail.com. I press send.

*

Less than half an hour later, I'm back in Highbury Fields, turning the lock in the front door. A familiar bark greets me in the communal hall. Jackie, the dog walker from upstairs, has returned with Dog. He wags his tail and rubs himself against her legs, showing no interest at all in me.

'Why are you so disloyal?' I scold.

'Dogs are the best judges of character.'

I see her taking in my sombre clothes. 'I'm just back from a funeral.'

'Sorry Gil. Someone close to you?'

'Yes and no.'

I take the lead from her and tug a reluctant Dog towards my door. 'Pop in later so we can settle up.'

'Something came for you.' She fishes in the wide pocket of her anorak and pulls out a yellow jiffy envelope. 'Postman brought it just as I was going out.'

'Thanks.' I tuck it under my arm as I manoeuvre Dog and bike into the flat. It's only when I put the package down on the kitchen counter that I notice the familiar handwriting on the label. My throat constricts.

Kill me now, kill me now, kill me now.

I tear open the envelope. Inside is a battered and fraying copy of the Picador edition of Gabriel García Márquez's *One Hundred Years of Solitude*. I know this book. I open the cover and there's my name, in my handwriting, in the top right-hand corner of the first page. I must have put it there when I bought it, at university, along with pretty much everyone else at my college. I lent it to Marilyn shortly after we met: an exchange of the books that made a difference to us. On the cardboard of the inside of the front cover is new handwriting. My chest is squeezing all the air out of my lungs. Should I read it? The words swim before my eyes, empty of meaning. I take slow breaths and start again.

Darling Gil. I'm not going to see you again, so I am returning your book. I am sorry for everything. See you in the next life. Marilyn x

The dam fractures and the tears flood. I'm overwhelmed and don't immediately notice that Jackie is frozen in place in the doorway. I remember she was due to look in, to pick up her cash.

'What's happened?'

'It's fine, it's fine,' I splutter. I take deep, wheezing breaths. 'Jackie, could you come back a bit later?'

She retreats. I move to the kitchen counter, lean forward and lay my head on it. I am deflated, exhausted. Dog looks at me with concern.

How could I have been so stupid, so arrogantly sure of myself? Why couldn't I see what was in front of my eyes? I refused to believe Marilyn could have killed herself precisely because I refused to believe Clare had been murdered till it was too late. I wasn't going to make the same mistake again. Except I did. In reverse.

As usual I was blinded by vanity. I was so obsessed with being the first to prove the banks are bust that I could not see that someone I cared about for so long was in terrible trouble. What is wrong with me? Why are my priorities so fucked up?

The note in the book leaves nowhere for my delusions to hide. I am bleeding, knifed by the knowledge of how much I let her down.

Why did you do it, Marilyn? Why? We spoke only hours before she climbed on a chair and put the rope around her neck. Why didn't she ask for help, give me a hint of her desperation? She did though. She did. *This is bigger than you think.* If only I'd kept her on the phone longer, insisted we met there and then. But I was too intent on seeking my own glory, landing the scoop, humiliating the competition. Why am I unable to hear the people in my life when they're trying to tell me something important about themselves?

My tears splash on the book, staining the pages. I pick it up by the spine to shake it dry, and as I do a flimsy card falls face down on the marble. I turn it over and what I see has the force of a sledgehammer, almost knocking me unconscious. I'm dizzy, nauseous. I run to the sink and throw up. This is hell.

It's a colour photograph, the kind you get developed and printed in Snappy Snaps, except this one can't have been. It's Marilyn, younger, maybe about ten years ago. Around the time of the 1997 election, maybe just after. She's naked, lying on a sofa, smiling at the invisible photographer, eyes wide and dilated, lines of coke readied on the glass-topped coffee table in front of her, next to the other routine detritus of 1990s debauchery – open Krug, ashtray filled with roaches and filters, a half-empty bottle of Grey Goose.

Oh God. Oh God. Oh God. I remember this Marilyn. This is my Marilyn. Except I wasn't the photographer.

I retch again. Agony. There's nothing inside me to expel.

Where was this? When was this? Who was she with?

I don't recognise the furniture.

I go back to the book. There are two yellow Post-it notes. One is old and fading. The handwriting is unfamiliar: 'Don't forget your friends.'

The other is newer, in Marilyn's script: 'Find me, Gil.'

That's all. Nothing else.

I will, I will, I will.

The buzzing of the BlackBerry comes from far away. Maybe this is a nightmare and if I look at my phone I'll wake up and everything will be OK. I tug it out of my pocket. An incoming email. Auto-reply. *I am out of the office and not reading emails. Marilyn Krol.*

I crumple to the floor, wrap my arms around my legs, and rock back and forth, intoning over and over, *I'm sorry Marilyn, I'm sorry Marilyn, I'm sorry Marilyn.*

Chapter 8

I t's unnerving that the door to 10 Downing Street always opens before I can ring the white enamel bell. The duties of the normally jovial police officer inside is to monitor who's outside on the small array of CCTV screens.

'Good to see you, sir.'

'And you. Does it feel different with a new PM?'

'Every prime minister is different, sir. They have their ways, as you know.'

Johnny Todd was all charm, all the time – in public at least. Neville Tudor is not quite so adept at hiding his frustrations.

It's Monday morning, and I'm here to interview the PM. It's been a lost weekend. When I saw that photo, it was like being smashed to bits by an express train. For an indeterminate time, I was curled on the kitchen floor, sobbing and rocking. At some point, Jess rang to check in with me. I didn't take the call, but the buzzing of the phone reminded me there is another world. I should tell Jess that she was right, all along: *Marilyn killed herself, she killed herself, she killed herself.* But I can't talk to her, or anyone, about it. *Kill me now, kill me now, kill me now.*

I feel humiliated, diminished. All my bravado that we were so clever and superior in our open relationship was self-deluding hypocrisy. How could she have fucked someone else so soon and never have told me? How could I not have sensed the pain Marilyn was in?

After I moved from the foetal self-hug to sitting on my bum, Dog came over and started nudging me with his head. He was right. I needed a walk. We left my apartment and headed north, up the dreary Holloway Road, up the multi-lane Great North Road to Highgate, and on and on, through verdant, salubrious Muswell Hill and then round to Alexandra Palace. We walked and walked while just one thought resounded in my head. *Why Marilyn? Why Marilyn? Why Marilyn?*

We walked for hours, past traffic that thinned as night turned to early morning. Finally, as straggles of exhausted clubbers emerged blinking into the dawn, Dog and I returned home and I collapsed into my bed. Which I didn't leave for twenty-four hours. Then on Sunday I resorted to my new drug of choice: hours and hours at the gym, on StairMaster and treadmill. I avoided friends and colleagues with lies about chores and family obligations. Today, back in Westminster, I can function, detached from my feelings. I can still compartmentalise, thank goodness.

It's hard to linger long in the Downing Street hallway. The police officer suggests I sit, though I am too restless, and anyway the curved dark wood chairs look too much like ornaments for comfort. Important bewigged men painted in oils – presumably Walpole and the Pitts, though I've never asked – look down sternly. With its large black and white rectangular tiles, this is the entrepot, never a destination.

An official bustles in, introduces himself as Roger, and deposits me briefly in the small ante-room down a red-carpeted corridor to the left. The size of a walk-in cupboard, with the same deep red carpet, it can't be where they put visiting heads of state. I've been put in my place, though the King of Jordan and the Sultan of Brunei are missing out on great British eccentricity. The most conspicuous object in the room is an old safe, built into the middle of a small white marble fireplace. Above it, on the mantelpiece, is a large carriage clock made by Whitaker of Camberwell.

Again I pace rather than sit in the uninviting armchair with wooden arms. It's next to a Georgian glass-fronted cupboard filled with late-seventeenth-century silverware. I'm not an expert, but the ink stand, snuffer trays and candlesticks don't look refined. To my left, on the ledge of a single window that struggles to import any light, is a neo-classical bust of an indeterminate hero. Johnny Todd as seen by a latter-day Michelangelo?

I take out my notebook and read through my questions. As I scribble thoughts for follow-ups, Roger returns and says the PM is almost ready. I trail behind him up the wide staircase, with its perfect right-angle turns, watched disapprovingly all the way by the black and white portraits of past prime ministers. As we round towards the first-floor landing, there's a familiar greeting.

'Ah, Peck. We meet again, as they say.'

Lord Ravel. Why here? It's a couple of years since he was cabinet secretary.

'This is unexpected.'

'I do the odd special project for the PM.' As I step on the landing, he steers me away from the official minder. 'Roger, be a dear and give us a minute.'

Roger loiters a respectful distance away and checks his phone. Ravel pulls me into a doorway and lowers his voice. 'I've been reflecting on our chat about Marilyn. I am inclined to agree that suicide doesn't make sense.'

'But it was though,' I blurt, too loud. I risk making a fool of myself and try to calm down – though just the mention of her name summons her dead body on the slab, morphing into the drugged seductress of the photo. I raise my hand to my right lobe and squeeze hard.

Ravel sees the tic and looks at his shoes, wondering – I assume – if I am about to lose it. 'You seem sure. What have you learned?' He strokes the front of his silk Hermès tie, a subtle grey-blue pattern of tiny ovals, with the outside of his little finger.

What do I want to tell him? Nothing. 'I have reconsidered what assistant commissioner Jansen told me. She's right. Suicide is the explanation that best fits the available evidence.'

He lifts his eyebrows. 'Possibly. But there is more to this. You should follow your initial journalistic instincts and keep sniffing around.'

Why is he saying that, what he is holding back? He has that annoying Mycroft habit, cultivated by spooks, of implying hidden depths. It's often a confidence trick, a sleight of hand, so that interlocutors don't see the shallows they're galumphing through. Misdirection. Though maybe not this time.

'Can you be more precise?'

'You know what she was working on. Focus on that.'

I'm about to ask if he means NewGate, when Roger coughs loudly. He's respectful of Ravel, but knows Tudor will be unforgiving if we keep him waiting. 'Sorry, sir. I really do have to take Mr Peck to the PM,' he says.

'Quite so, Roger. Forgive me.' Ravel makes a 'shoo' gesture with his right hand and I nod goodbye. 'Keep in touch,' he says.

Roger steers me into the Pillared Room, the grandest room in Downing Street, full of gilded eighteenth-century furniture. Emma, Petra and a second cameraman have already arrived with two cameras, set up on the diagonal. Tudor's logistics advisors have decided they want the portrait of the first Queen Elizabeth to be looking down on the PM, presumably – they think – as some kind of regal endorsement. A union flag frames the shot on the other side. It is a terrible cliché, but I've learned from frustrated experience that no Downing Street spinner will ever be argued out of this kind of nonsense.

Petra sits me in my chair and hands me a lapel microphone. I attach the radio pack to my belt, and clip the mic to my right lapel. I then place my own mic, the one for my Olympus digital recorder, underneath it. Whenever I do an interview, I record it on this device too. It is how I keep a record of everything said off-camera. I rarely bother to seek the permission of interviewees for it – though I should – but it's my insurance against missing or forgetting anything.

Petra asks Roger to sit where the PM will be so she can frame the shot. 'You aren't as wide as the PM, but you'll do,' she says. Roger suppresses a smirk. He doesn't want to appear disloyal.

'Behave, Petsy!' Emma scolds. Her phone buzzes. 'Jane says Tudor will be with us in two minutes.'

I walk to the door. 'Can you do a set-up shot of the two of us walking in and sitting down?' I ask Petra. If it's framed well and the PM says anything pithy and appropriate while we are ambling, I will include this segment at the opening of my TV package. 'Emma, can you double-check it's OK with Jane?'

Petra swings the camera around and checks the focus. From the large double door that separates our room from the adjacent drawing room, I hear a Welsh baritone a few yards away. Emma rushes out to waylay Jane Walters, Tudor's press secretary, and sort the walking shot. Jane has total power over these things.

I walk to the door. Emma is schmoozing Jane. Tudor is to her right. He beckons me with a wave, and swallows my hand in his. I'm not sure if the painful squeeze is meant to be a warning, or is just insensitive.

Unlike his predecessor Johnny Todd, all gym-toned physique and lean perma-tan, Neville Tudor is a bear. In the fifteen years since we first met, there's been a battle fought on his body between his love of sugared carbohydrates and his obsessive hours on the treadmill. The doughnuts are winning. His mop of dark hair is greying at the tips, there are bags under his eyes and his skin is white and leathery – as if the generations of antecedents who spent daylight hours down the pits have been memorialised in his DNA. When he speaks, his voice is deep and melodic. Tudor is the last in Labour's long line of socialist orators, who've been stirring workers' emotions for a hundred and fifty years with the

101

poetry of the class struggle, replaced latterly by lawyers and management consultants.

'Causing trouble, as bloody usual,' he booms.

I try desperately not to look smug. Best to say nothing.

'The problem we've got though is the confidence of bank customers has been shattered,' he says, enunciating each syllable. 'Confidence is what it's about. We've got to restore confidence.'

He's provided me with my intro. Or at least, I hope he has. 'Prime minister,' I begin, 'would you mind repeating that point about the importance of customers' confidence as we walk to our seats? I'd like to film you saying it in a chatty informal way, if that's OK with you?'

He looks at Jane Walters. She nods.

Emma retrieves a radio mic and attaches it to his jacket. A minute later, we're walking into the room together, the PM leading, and Petra filming us. He repeats to me that what he wants to do is restore the confidence of savers – which is the 'upsot' or 'raised-up sound on tape' that I needed, a few of his words to be inserted in between my narration.

We take our seats. 'Shall I do a clap, Petra?' I ask.

'Yes. In three . . . two . . . one.'

I position my hands where both cameras can see them and clap. It's a technique to help the video editor synchronise the recordings on the separate cameras, when we get into the edit suite.

'In your own time,' says Emma.

I look directly at the prime minister. 'You've said that the confidence of bank customers, savers, has been blown up by the run at NewGate. What can you do to restore it?'

Tudor leans forward, hands raised like a preacher in the pulpit. 'What I want to set out today is our guarantee to protect everyone's savings.'

'*Everyone's*? That's quite an undertaking.'

'We are the people's government. So of course our promise is to everyone. As a temporary measure to ease the anxiety of the customers of British-based banks, the government will improve the generosity of the deposit protection scheme. We will provide a hundred per cent insurance to all savings.'

Bloody hell. He just wrote a blank cheque to every bank. 'That could be very expensive.'

'It's only temporary, mind you, but it's vital to end the risk of bank runs in these volatile times. If it works, it won't cost us a penny. It shows we have every confidence in the banks, which means everyone else can have that confidence.'

Bagehot starts bellowing in my head: this is the ultimate in moral hazard, by prime-ministerial fiat. Tudor is not only protecting depositors. He's also shielding bankers themselves from the consequences of their own recklessness and cupidity.

'But you are also bailing out the greedy bankers,' I say. 'You are removing from them any incentive to manage our money prudently, because you've said taxpayers will pick up the bill when it all goes wrong.'

Tudor gives an almost imperceptible glance towards Jane. 'As I've said, we don't anticipate any cost to taxpayers. But you are right in principle. Which is why, as I said, this can't be permanent. It's to get us all over the hump.'

He's given me a huge story, which will lead the news bulletins and splash tomorrow's papers. He has in effect nationalised all the risks taken by the banks, while securing none of the profits for taxpayers. It shows how frightened he is about how much cash is leaking from them – and he wants me to be his messenger to the country, because I'm seen to be the authority on the crisis, and savers may feel less anxious if I report on his plan to shore them up.

There are other questions. 'Prime minister, right now you are keeping NewGate alive through the loans being provided by the Bank of England, loans guaranteed by the government. In other words taxpayers are supporting NewGate to the tune of billions of pounds. Why not go the whole hog and take NewGate into public ownership?'

He squirms, and again looks for Jane. Together with Johnny Todd, Neville Tudor was part of the double-act that turned the beer-and-tripe Labour Party of 'up the working class' into the prosecco-and-prosciutto Modern Labour of Britpop, global trade, and tax incentives for the super-rich. Anything that hints of a renewed ambition for the state to own the commanding heights of the economy is anathema.

'With the Bank of England, we're trying to understand what went wrong at NewGate and what should happen now. In due course, we'll decide whether taking it into public ownership is in the interests of taxpayers.'

A classic non-answer. I twist the knife. 'So you are not ruling out nationalisation?'

I sense Jane Walters, out of my line of sight, directing curses at me. They're written in Emma's frown, who is standing to the right of the PM just out of shot. She's there to signal with her fingers how many minutes of our allotted time I've used. We were allocated a whole eight minutes, which may sound stingy, but is more than the five minutes Downing Street often allow.

'All options are on the table.'

I remember Ravel's cryptic remark at the funeral, about a potential buyer sniffing around NewGate before my story broke. 'What about selling it to another bank? Is that an option?'

'As I just said, all options are on the table.'

Emma purposefully holds up the index finger of her right hand. One minute left, and I am not going to waste it. My previous incarnation as political editor whispers a question to me.

'Prime minister, the British people didn't vote for you.' Tudor has only been PM for five months: he took over from Johnny Todd mid-term, after Todd had been in post for a decade. 'Shouldn't you legitimise your government by asking the electorate's permission to keep governing? Shouldn't you call a general election?'

Tudor's face darkens. It looks as if he wasn't expecting this.

'I don't need to remind you, Gil, that our political system is not presidential. It was the Labour Party as a whole that won the mandate. There is no reason, constitutional or based on convention, to have a general election. Callaghan didn't have one when he took over from Wilson, nor did Peter Ramsey after succeeding Thatcher.'

'But prime minister, look at the polls. Six months ago, the Tory lead over your party was in double digits. Since you took over, that deficit has been eliminated and you are ahead. Why not bank that, to coin a phrase?'

'Only the actions of a foolish prime minister are dictated by opinion polls. They swing all over the place. It's leadership that matters.'

Classic hedge.

'I note you are not ruling out an early election.'

'I am not ruling anything in or out. And you can't read anything into that.'

I can feel the heat coming off Jane, behind me. She is about to explode. Emma is frantically making a circle in the air with her right hand, the time-honoured gesture for *Wind up now or there'll be hell to pay*. I take the hint.

'The British people will draw their own conclusions. Thank you, prime minister.'

'Thank you, Gil.'

*

It's a wrap. Tudor looks like thunder as we unhook the mics. 'You bastard, Gil. Why did you ask me about the election? It's bloody obvious I have to consider it, but I can't talk about it.'

'You also know it would be a dereliction of my professional duty not to ask about it.'

Tudor harrumphs. 'You're the bloody business editor.' And then he grins. He knows the game: straight out of university, he was a hack, for the *Western Mail*.

105

'If you're going to call an election, you'll need NewGate's future sorted out first.' And there's something else that he and I both know, which I don't need to articulate. He is defining his time in office, for however long or short that turns out to be, by not being Johnny Todd, whom he supported as a steady-as-you-go chancellor for all those years. To be his own PM, he has to get past the financial crisis.

'That would be playing politics with the economy. You know my government won't do anything to undermine fiscal *rectitude*.' He catches himself just too late, raises his eyebrows and mouths 'Sorry.' 'Rectitude' is his catchphrase, the object of a thousand comedians' parodies. 'You're right we haven't got long. The Governor is worried the uncertainty is infecting other banks. The hedge funds are targeting any bank that looks vulnerable. It is a contagion. As you know, just the perception that a bank is in trouble can make the worst come true, if lenders withdraw cash.'

'But who on earth would take NewGate off your hands?' I ask. 'It's a dog.'

He pauses. He is reluctant to talk in front of my crew and his officials. He turns to Jane. 'Give us a moment love. I want to have a private word with Gil.'

He leads me to his office. At one end are the disproportionately large, dark blue double doors, their mouldings framed with gold paint. He sees me looking at them. 'They are bizarre, aren't they?' he says. 'They lead directly to the Cabinet Room. Johnny used to go through them to make a grand entrance. He loved to remind ministers of what it meant to be first among equals. Not my style. I walk round to the normal door that everyone else uses.'

'He really did think of himself as *il presidente*,' I mutter to myself. And then: 'I think you were about to tell me who's going to buy NewGate.'

'Don't get ahead of yourself.' He gestures me to sit on the white sofa, while he collapses into an overstuffed armchair to my right. 'We're not having this conversation, are we?' he says.

'I know the rules.'

'Right. So the thing is that when you blew the whistle on NewGate's funding crisis you also called time on a potential takeover. The Bank of England was in advanced talks with a prospective buyer about buying NewGate. But when the run started, all bets were off.'

'Who was the buyer?'

Tudor takes a moment to decide how much to tell me. And this time he can't ask Jane. I encourage him: 'If the City learns there's a buyer, that will flush out other potential bidders. It's all about confidence, as you say.'

Confidence.

He smiles. And looks almost relaxed. 'I've always loved your bullshit. You want a story. I get it. Though it seems to me you've done pretty well out of me today.' He stretches out his legs, gets up and walks towards the large window overlooking the well-tended garden.

Turning to face me, he says, 'Not in any way for attribution?' I shake my head. 'It was Harvey Jackson.'

'Wow.' Harvey Jackson is the most famous business leader in Britain, and arguably the most popular. All politicians crave his endorsement, in the way they craved Richard Branson's in the 1990s. Jackson set up and runs a private equity firm that donates a percentage of its profits to alleviate poverty in the developing world. The firm is called Make Hunger History, or MHH. Jackson's mantra is 'Profit for good', which cynics like me see as 'Profit for the good of Harvey Jackson'. But the bullshit has been swallowed by plenty of people who should know better, including members of the government. Jackson buying NewGate is a grade A story.

'Can the deal still happen?' I ask.

'Tricky. The run on the bank means the Bank of England has had to inject maybe twenty billion pounds into NewGate. And rising.'

Twenty billion. That's way more than the Bank has admitted. Wholesale funders, the other banks, must be withdrawing their lines of credit. The banks are panicking as much as – maybe more than – ordinary savers. *This is much bigger than you think.*

'If MHH was allowed to buy NewGate,' Tudor continues, 'we'd be accused of giving an unfair advantage to Jackson. It could look too cosy, unless we made it clear that every bank could have loans from the Bank on the same terms. And I don't think we could do that, because we'd be in breach of European Union state aid and competition rules.'

I choose not to tell him that the Governor of the Bank of England has already made the same point to me.

'There's something else. The Governor is wary of Harvey. Says no one knows how he funds MHH. He worries his business is too good to be true.'

No wonder the Governor was so upset when Marilyn backed the takeover. It's even more puzzling she wanted the deal to go ahead. I'm certain she thought Jackson was a spiv – she said as much.

Tudor arches his back and rotates his shoulders. He's making no effort to hide his stress. He mutters, 'Bloody Johnny says it's my public duty to force through the MHH rescue. According to him it will cement Modern Labour's reputation as the party of entrepreneurs.'

'Oh yes. I'd forgotten the Todd connection.'

Famously, notoriously, when Todd left Downing Street, he joined MHH's board. The *Daily Mail* went to town on Todd cashing in on the connections he made as PM.

Tudor turns to look out the window and drums his fingers on the sill. 'Jackson's paying him at least a million quid a year, probably more. He can fuck off.'

The door opens. The diary secretary apologetically tells the prime minister he's running late for his next meeting. Tudor grimaces. 'Stanley Blackwell,' he mutters. 'Another banker who wants to pick my pocket.'

'Why's Blackwell here?' I ask. Sir Stanley Blackwell is chief executive of Peking and Taiwan Banking Group, PTBG, the UK's biggest bank.

'Never you mind.' He clomps into the adjoining room, the so-called private office, where his official and political support staff all have desks, and he orders Jane to escort me to my team. 'All off the record,' he bellows at me by way of farewell, over his shoulder.

Upstairs, Petra and Emma have almost finished packing away the camera kit.

'Which line do you reckon we should lead on?' Emma asks. 'The promise that all savings in banks will be protected, or Tudor's refusal to rule out an early general election?'

'Probably the guarantee to savers. It's a big deal. I'm going to blog on both. And I've also just got another story.'

'Christ Gil. Justin's not going to like it.' Justin Blakely is the BBC's political editor, whose reports normally lead the bulletins.

'Diddums.'

The priority is to work out why Todd and Jackson were so keen to take possession of NewGate, and why Marilyn was supporting them.

Jackson is another contemporary of mine from Oxford. He was a Gucci-loafer-wearing, Mr-smoothy-chops even then. We weren't close, but I need to get to him. Not too much of a stretch, I reckon. He craves publicity, and as the BBC's business editor I am his gateway to millions of viewers and listeners. He won't refuse an interview request. No chance.

Chapter 9

'IT IS OBVIOUSLY IN HIS interest to do an interview with me.'

I hear myself and clock my tone is too urgent. I moderate it. I've been ringing Alex Elliott, Jackson's PR gatekeeper, for a couple of days and leaving messages, as if into a vacuum. I can't work out if he was instructed by Jackson to ignore me, or whether this is some kind of public relations mind game. Either way, now that I've got him on the phone I mustn't screw it up. Neither of us mentions the awkward conversation we had through the window of his Range Rover at Marilyn's funeral.

'Jackson tried negotiating behind the scenes,' I say. I'm in my tiny so-called office, in Television Centre. 'He was stitched up by the Bank of England. He should go public and put some pressure on.'

I am arguing a position I hope will massage the ego of my interlocutor. It is a technique I deploy as if by instinct. Sometimes my bollocks convinces me, almost, though privately I am sure the Bank was quite right to trip up these cowboys. Don't expect me to say that out loud, except possibly to Jess.

'I agree,' says Elliott. 'But the situation is delicate. And my client remains to be convinced. I can assure you, though, that if he does decide to go public, he'll do it with you. You have my word.'

The word of a man whose fortune was generated by an unrivalled ability to lie for his clients. Not worth the electrons that transmit his assurance via the loudspeaker in my BlackBerry. But better than a straight 'no'.

'You know what these private equity guys are like,' he continues. 'They hate the limelight.'

I just about suppress a contemptuous laugh. He is right with respect to most of the egregiously wealthy top managers in private equity. They worry – correctly – that their style would be cramped, that there'd be a national outcry, if everyone could understand precisely how they make their billions. Their techniques for making out like bandits are cloaked in phoney science but are simple in practice. They borrow cheaply to buy stable established businesses, sack loads of workers, sell off excess stock, remortgage the property and pocket what's left. It used to be called asset stripping. Now it's thoroughly modern financial capitalism, lauded and feted even by the Labour government – which increased the tax breaks available to the managers and their clients. It's the antithesis of socialism, reverse Robin Hood: appropriation and aggregation of cash freed up by depriving workers of their livelihoods, for distribution to a small circle of banks, privileged investors and the fund managers themselves. Take from the poor to give to the rich, the final triumph of Darwinian capitalism, summed up in the private equity managers' cherished remuneration precept, the notorious 'two and twenty'. They trouser two per cent of all money they manage and twenty per cent of all profits made, which – in an era of economic stability and falling interest rates – is generating personal fortunes faster and bigger than in the robber barons' heyday. The Dawlers, Marilyn's forebears, constructed their pile and acquired their Canalettos through centuries of feudalism. Jackson and the new financial aristocracy are buying England by the ton – acres of parks and farms, mansions and palaces – on the proceeds of flipping high street retail chains and world-famous manufacturers. If the 1980s were about the soaring salaries of Thatcher's liberated business executives, who ran the companies that were listed on the stock exchange and were owned by all of us via our pension funds, the first years of the new century are the hegemony of a new breed of owner, those who become billionaires by buying and taking private those very same stock exchange companies.

Jackson, though, is different from most of his private equity competitors for two reasons. First he has sanitised his asset stripping by pledging to share a proportion of his business profits with the poorest people in the poorest parts of the world. And secondly, he has a panic attack if people are not talking or writing about him.

'Alex, we are talking about Harvey Jackson here, not your normal private equity recluse.' I don't want to sound too exasperated, but really. 'He loves being on telly. Plus, there's talk he wants to turn MHH into a retail brand, the people's private equity. True?'

'No comment.'

'On the basis of your non-denial denial, it's clear he needs as much publicity as possible. Brilliant for you, of course. Much easier to get him in the *Daily Mail* than to keep him out.'

I don't know how many times I've had this kind of conversation with Elliott. His clients hire him to manage their reputations, groom their images, airbrush the warts. They trust his judgement about when it's in their interest to be out in the world, and when the better part of valour is to hide. His greatest triumph is the legend he has created about himself, that he has unrivalled access to and sway over media bosses and owners. His clients pay him a fortune to control when they are and when they are not a double-page spread in the tabloids. His prowess is in calibrating the bribe to an editor – perhaps with a salacious story about a celeb foolish enough not to pay his exorbitant fees, or by offering first dibs on an interview with another client. As one of the many sociopaths hiding in plain sight at the heart of the establishment, Elliott also collects dirt on journalists and editors, just in case the bribe has to be reinforced with a threat.

113

He lives by the idea that if his client has to resort to suing a paper or TV station, if libel lawyers have to be instructed, then he's failed. Far more effective to float the possibility that an exclusive interview with the heart-throb, drug addict lead singer of mega group Synapse Short Circuit is yours, so long as you don't print that the chairman of Tyranno Bank is boffing his PA. He collects and puts in the deep-freeze the dark secrets of foes and friends, just in case. He'll thaw them and trade them to promote the interests of whichever client is currently raining sterling, dollars and euros on him.

If I want to get to Jackson, Elliott will have to open the door. And I am waiting for him to name the price.

'I'll do what I can. And by the way, I hope you're coming to my soirée for dear Marilyn.'

Dear Marilyn. He is goading me, but I won't rise to it. If all he wants for the access to Jackson is my presence at his party – so he can swagger to clients that the BBC's business editor is one of his 'friends' – that's an offer I'll take. Cheap at the price.

'Sure. It's in the diary. Anything else you need?'

'We can talk about rules of engagement. But I'll need your word you'll only ask about Harvey's future plans, not about who he may or may not have already spoken to about buying NewGate.'

'His plans are far more interesting than what's just happened,' I evade. 'I'm a journalist, not a historian. You can relax.'

'It's a moron who relaxes with you, Gil.'

*

A couple of hours later, I arrive at the Adelphi, an art deco jewel on the Thames just off the Strand. Many of Jackson's competitors prefer more discreet addresses, but he's a show-off. The river side of his office has perhaps the most essence-of-London view of anywhere in the capital. It is the Thames snaking between

Parliament and St Paul's. The river is the life-giving cord between the Commons and the City, though it is unclear which end of town, SW1 or EC2, is the feeder and which is the fed. There is a mutual dependence between politicians and bankers, they need each other – even when they resent and despise each other. The bankers can't operate without the licence granted by the lawmakers. The government can't function without the tax revenues generated by the bankers. That interdependence doesn't change when Labour and Tory take turns to govern us. A Labour government is just as wary of alienating the bankers as a Tory one is mindful of cultivating them. And although most bankers vote Tory, they need an accommodation with ministers of any and every political persuasion. Jackson has ostentatiously made his working home at the fulcrum of politics and finance. To be here is to play each off against the other, to amass power and money.

I am collected from an airy hall of veined white marble by a gawky young man – Crispin – who describes himself as Jackson's assistant, though he reeks to me of unpaid intern. I guess he's on a gap year between one of the better public schools and Oxford. He's presumably here to reassure his ambitious parents that he understands the necessity to turn his expensive education into something lucrative in finance.

'Yah. I've seen your work on the BBC,' he says, as we ride the lift up. 'I think what you do is great, though you probably don't want to hear what my pa says about you.'

On exiting the lift, every wall is a frieze of almost life-size colour photos, mostly of beaming African farmers and their energetic children. In more than a few, Jackson is being hugged or is shaking hands with a local leader, white saviour stuff. I make a mental note to investigate whether Make Hunger History, his firm, actually honours its promise to donate twenty per cent of profits to research into improving crop yields in places where food poverty is rife. Who actually audits and assures this? How would any of us know for sure that MHH's cash is modernising farms in hostile climates rather than financing superyachts for Jackson and his cronies?

Crispin guides me to the boardroom, where the team are setting up. Petra – in a black T-shirt that shows off more impressive biceps than mine – is not happy. She can't get the shot she wants because the boardroom is dominated by a long walnut table.

'The interview will look shit if we do it here,' she says. Crispin looks anxious.

'Gosh. What can I do?'

'Can we look at other rooms?' Emma suggests.

'They're being used for meetings, I think.'

'What about Mr Jackson's office?'

'I don't know. I can ask his PA.'

Emma and Crispin go out to investigate. Emma returns beaming. 'Jackson's office is amazing. Filled with modern art. I think there's Jackson Giacometti, one of those stringy, lumpy people sculptures. And maybe a Matisse on the wall. Honestly, it's unbelievable.'

'But can we film there?' snaps Petra, out of patience.

'Yes, but we've got to be all done in an hour. Tops.'

Petra nods. 'Tight. We'll make it work.'

Emma winks at me. A television producer's hour is – let's say – elastic.

Emma and Petra disappear into Jackson's office to set up. I stay in the boardroom to go through Jackson on my BlackBerry. The door is open. After a few minutes, there's the sound of some kind of argument just yards away.

'Harvey, it is a privilege to be working with you, but you are aware, I presume, that the loss on my investment is now very significant?' The voice sounds East European: deep, firm, menacing.

'Don't worry, Petr.' It's placatory, honey-sweet Dublin. Harvey Jackson. 'Your loss hasn't crystallised. It's not a real loss. The shares will recover. You'll end up making a fortune.'

'Maybe. I assume you understand the consequences if I lose one.'

'There's nothing for you to worry about, Petr. Relax.'

I move to the door. A man who looks as relaxed as a steel girder walks slowly and deliberately past me towards the lifts. He has the tan of a tax exile hiding in Monaco, prominent Slavic cheekbones, a nap of almost white, ultra-short hair framing a perfectly circular skull. His immaculate suit, that drapes in perfect lines with no creases or lumps, probably cost the same as most people would spend on a new bathroom. Zegna, maybe. He is presumably Russian, maybe Ukrainian, an investor, an oligarch.

Petr. Petr who?

The lift's steel doors close behind him, just as Crispin comes back to escort me along the corridor to Jackson's office.

'You look too young to be on staff here,' I say.

He gives a self-deprecating laugh. 'I'm not really on staff. Just helping out before going to uni.'

As I thought. 'Interesting work?'

'No, not really. I'm mostly a messenger boy.' He looks glum. 'Though I get to meet amazing people.'

'Like who?'

'Well that guy who used to be prime minister ...'

'Johnny Todd?'

'Yeah, him. He's here all the time.'

We're walking past more life-size photos of African farmers, often standing next to heaps of cassava, or plantain or wheat. Jackson is in a striking number of the pictures, and an MHH-branded Land Cruiser is in almost all of them. There's no possibility of ignoring Jackson's philanthropic intentions. It's so Modern Labour: a hand up, not a hand out, never mind that the price is paid by the British working classes, made redundant when MHH buys their respective employers. 'Todd was always big on development,' I say, trying to draw out Crispin.

'I suppose.' Crispin is too young to have experienced the Todd of the opposition years in the 1990s as the UK's JFK, the young optimist who seemed to understand the modern world and promised to unite the country after years of Thatcherite division. Crispin grew up with Todd as a disappointed realist, aged and wearied by the compromises of governing.

'Before I worked here,' Crispin says, 'I always thought nothing could bother Mr Todd. On TV, he's so calm, in control. I shouldn't tell you but this morning he lost it. Everyone could hear. He was shouting and swearing.'

'That does surprise me.' I am not being disingenuous. 'What wound him up?'

Crispin blushes. 'Harvey would kill me if I told you. About the only thing he said when I started here was that I wasn't to talk to outsiders about what I see and hear. Not even to pa.'

'Course.'

He looks relieved. 'By the way, I think you know him – Dad, that is.'

'OK.'

'Alex. Alex Elliott. I've heard him mention you.'

I should have guessed. 'Oh yes. I definitely know Alex. In fact, I'm going to a party at your house.'

'You won't see me. I live with Mum most of the time.'

He hands me over to Jackson's secretary, who directs me into Jackson's office. As Emma said, it's filled with what looks like priceless twentieth-century art. And a Bauhaus bookshelf displays framed photos of Jackson with world leaders. Todd features in a disproportionate number.

I'm drawn to a dark marble sculpture of a reclining headless nude to the right of a river-facing window.

'Moore, or Hepworth?' I muse out loud.

'Hepworth, of course. By far the more important of the two. Underrated.' Jackson has padded in behind me. His black polo neck covers the hint of a middle-aged prosperous paunch, minimised by a personal trainer. He's wearing velvet smoking slippers, symbol that here he is *le patron*. The most striking thing about him is the same as ever it was, hair that is albino white, Andy Warhol white.

'Good to see you, Gil.' His Dublin accent is warm and welcoming, such an asset. It makes him classless in class-riven Britain.

'And you. I can't remember the last time we met.'

'An age ago. I've been watching and admiring your relentless progress, though. Congratulations on moving to the Beeb. Perfect for you.'

I smile a thank you. I know his patter, and I need to be immune to his flattery, the implied friendship.

'It's a good idea if we kick off.' I direct him to the chair that has the desk and bookshelf behind him. While he's sitting down, I turn my back and switch on my private tape recorder. Petra asks Jackson if he would allow her to insert the mic cord up the back of his jumper, and then if he could clip the mic itself to the front of the neck.

'Blimey, this is soft,' she says, as she slips her hand under the black sweater. He laughs. She's embarrassed him. I love Petra.

I attach my own mic to my lapel, clap for the synchronisation and we're off.

'Let's start with why you want to buy NewGate. What's the attraction?'

Jackson is a natural on camera. He knows how to perform, no hint of nervousness. He looks earnestly at me. 'What I see is a great institution that's hit a patch of bad luck, and just needs a bit of support to get back on its feet. NewGate is such an important institution in the north-east. The repercussions of its problems go far wider than anxiety for its savers and shareholders. Here at MHH, we believe business has a responsibility to support the wider community. And we think we have a great opportunity to do that with NewGate.'

'So buying NewGate is altruism? You're surely not telling me profit doesn't matter?' I'm trying to sound sceptical but not hostile. It's hard.

Jackson leans back in his chair. 'Don't misunderstand me,' he says. 'This is not an act of charity. We wouldn't be doing this if we didn't think Newgate can return to profit and be a strong and sustainable business once again. But you are being too cynical about businesses like ours. We can be a force for good. And by the way, profit isn't a dirty word. If there's no profit, there's no investment and ultimately no jobs.'

In my lap, I'm holding an A4 sheet of paper. It contains a dozen questions. I probably won't need to ask all of them, because he may well supply the answers without prompting. I've left the ones that are most likely to infuriate him till nearer the end: I don't want to risk him terminating the interview in a huff before I've got anything broadcastable.

'How far advanced are you in your preparations?'

'We've done a lot of work. And it's not just about the finances. It's also vital that we're seen to be going with the grain of what local people want. You know that Meathead has thrown his weight behind us?'

Meathead is a Geordie rock legend, and international campaigner for peace in the Middle East. His recent Concert for Palestine raised millions of pounds to improve the supply of potable water in Gaza. Having him as the figurehead of the takeover will increase the popular pressure on the authorities to allow it.

'And of course, you have our former prime minister Johnny Todd on the board. Is he very involved here?' I nod at the photos of Todd, to Jackson's left. I am praying they are in shot, and cursing myself for not checking before I sat down.

'He's a great source of advice,' Jackson enthuses. 'We're lucky to have him.'

'And does he share your view that it would be better for NewGate customers and the wider economy for MHH to take over the bank, rather than see it nationalised?'

'Johnny agrees with me that nationalisation would be a huge mistake.'

I look at my notes and see a scribble: *ask about the Russian complaining of losses.*

'Is that because you are sitting on huge losses on NewGate shares, and buying the whole bank is the only way of getting the money back?'

At this point, his habitual smiling pose vanishes. His lips scrunch up, as though slapped. 'I can't imagine why you would ask that. We have no shares in NewGate.'

'But you were negotiating to buy NewGate before the run on the bank, before its financial difficulties became acute. You were the potential white knight.'

He shuffles his left leg. This is not what he wanted to be asked. This is not what Elliott told him he would be asked. I am prepared for Elliott's bollocking.

The lilting easy charm has vanished. He says coldly, 'NewGate needed a stable owner. We were happy to be that owner. We still are.'

'It's a bit of a pain for you that you couldn't do the deal back then. Since the run, the Bank of England has injected more than twenty billion into NewGate. Who is going to lend you that kind of money to replace all the Bank of England's support?'

He shakes his head. 'Obviously we're going to need Bank of England funds until markets recover. But the government's best chance of getting all its money back is to sell to us.'

I can see Jackson looking hard at Emma, hoping somehow he can signal he is desperate for the interview to end. He'd probably tear off his mic and walk away, if he didn't know how bad that would make him look, how much we'd love that. I assume he regrets that Alex is not here to protect him. It's time I asked the one question that matters to me.

'The Bank of England's director of financial stability, who tragically died recently, she was backing your takeover, wasn't she? How did you persuade her it was a good idea?'

Jackson realises petulance would be the wrong look. He becomes grave. 'I was shocked and saddened to hear of Marilyn Krol's death,' he says. 'As it happens, I wasn't aware she was in favour of our offer. But if she was, that would be because she grasped the national interest.'

Do I imagine it, or is there the faintest trace of a smirk on his face? I'm going to study that back in the edit suite later. I glance at my notes, to check there's nothing else vital. There isn't.

'We'll see what the government thinks about that,' I say. 'Thank you for talking to us, Mr Jackson.'

And that's it. I unclip my mic, stand up and walk towards Jackson. Petra is gently pulling his mic out, careful not to snag the cashmere. Jackson fixes me with his blue eyes.

'God, you're a pain, Gil,' he says. 'I thought you agreed we'd talk about our future plans, not our earlier offer.'

'But the two are the same, aren't they?' I bullshit. 'And surely it's important for people to know just how serious and committed you are.'

'Don't kid a kidder, my friend.'

I smile.

He relaxes. 'Just awful about Marilyn. Really shocking.'

'Did you know her?' I wasn't aware he did, other than in a distant professional sense.

'We met a few times, over the years.'

He's not telling me something. But he doesn't leave me time or space to probe. As he guides me into an adjacent meeting room, the charm is replaced by focused interrogation: 'You blew up our deal. Who set you up? Who leaked to you?'

'Oh come on, Harvey. You know I can't talk to you about any of that.'

'Did you know you were blowing us up? Were you in on it?'

'Good grief. Of course not.' My ego has got the better of me. I shouldn't respond at all, but my entire professional identity is as an impartial journalist. 'It was a story. A bloody good story. That's all.'

'Then you were used, my friend. And that should bother you.' The seduction has gone. There's an uncomfortable edge to his voice, perhaps an implied threat.

'What do you mean?'

'Someone wanted NewGate's share price forced lower. To make a killing. And when you told the world it needed a bailout, that's what you achieved. You've been manipulated.' His hands have become balled fists. 'You went on TV to tell the world NewGate had run out of money. Its customers then went to their computers to check their accounts. But they couldn't. The website had been sabotaged. No one could log on. They panicked and headed straight to the branches. Hey presto, you triggered the first bank run of modern times, and in the process you fucked me up.'

I process. 'You are saying there was a conspiracy to break the bank?'

'That's exactly what I am saying. It was genius. Whoever shorted the shares has made a fortune.'

He doesn't attempt to disguise his admiration for the short seller who frustrated him. His contempt is for me. 'It's not brilliant for your brand to be turned over like that. You were done up like a kipper, my friend. And I reckon you already know who played you.'

I want to protest, but I know he's on the money. The customers in the queue told me they became anxious after the website crashed. I sowed the initial uneasiness with my scoop. I'd been assuming it was a terrible coincidence that the website couldn't cope when NewGate customers tried to log in. But what if the servers were hacked, taken down?

Marilyn's warning that this is all much bigger than I thought is in my head again. Did she know who was pulling the strings?

'So who wanted to blow up NewGate?' I ask.

He looks at the ceiling. 'You know the answer.'

Maybe. Journalists like me obsessed with getting scoops are susceptible to manipulation but I pride myself it never happens to me. I need to get out of here, and I have to go back to my source, Robin Muller. What was his game? Who was he acting for?

I have a suspicion my former partner in small-time dope dealing at Oxford has flogged me dodgy gear.

Chapter 10

I F YOU WANT TO KNOW which boss is trying to get his millions of share options into the money by flogging his lacklustre company to private equity, have a meal in the Wolseley, on Piccadilly. It's the works canteen of *Le Tout Money*: hedge funders being schmoozed by bankers being schmoozed by MPs being schmoozed by newspaper editors being schmoozed by PRs. No one goes there for a discreet rendezvous. It's a place to see and be seen.

It's London's take on a Parisian brasserie, art deco and cavernous, built in the 1920s to show off sleek Wolseley sedan cars. I've got my normal table, middle left as you look from the entrance, in the central area reserved for what Bruno the restaurant manager marks in his book as PWK, or People We Know. It's the best place to spy PWM, or People Who Matter. Lucian Freud is at his regular table, a pewter mug of cold Atlantic prawns in front of him. While I'm waiting for Jess to arrive, Kate Moss is escorted by Bruno to her seat next to him. The Wolseley is the best show in town. I can't help but gawp at the tableau of the artist and the model. The owners Chris and Jeremy walk the floor, assiduously checking we're all being properly looked after. Everywhere I scan, deals are being finessed, secrets traded.

Unusually, I'm on time. Jess isn't. While I wait, I look at the BlackBerry, and note that I missed a call from Mum. I must ring her later. See how she's getting on. I text Lord Ravel. *Do you have two mins for a quick chat?*

He rings instantly. 'How can I help?'

'It's been suggested to me the collapse of NewGate's servers, the night before the run, was more than just the sheer weight of too many of its customers trying to get online at the same time. I've been told they were sabotaged. Do you have a sense of whether that's true?'

A pregnant pause. Theatre? I still don't know whether Ravel knows as much as he implies. 'Who is your source?'

'Someone close to NewGate. I can't say more.'

'But not someone at NewGate?'

'Does that mean you think it's not true?'

He goes silent again. I think I can hear him scratching his face. 'I can't give you a definitive answer,' he says. 'There may be something in it. Leave it with me.'

'Thank you.'

'We should find a date to meet and talk properly.'

'I'd be delighted. When would suit?'

'I am not sure you are going to approve, but I am on the board of a North London football club, not the one you hold in highest affection.'

On Radio 4's *Saturday Live*, I've talked about my tribal and familial obsession with Tottenham Hotspur: Spurs till I die. He's talking about the other club, the hated Gunners.

'Why don't you come to the Emirates for the North London derby? Directors' box. Surprisingly decent food these days. But I'm afraid you'll have to wear a jacket and tie: we're old-fashioned like that. Her Majesty's football club, as you know. I'll get the details to you.'

Oh no. How will I explain to Dad that I'm going into the enemy's bunker? I'll say it's for work, but he'll see it as a compromise too far.

I try to keep the anxiety out of my voice. 'That's a date.'

126

I hang up, and see Jess manoeuvring around black-uniformed waiters. She looks flustered, a bit red in the face, hair in need of a brush. Very unlike her.

'Sorry I'm late. I had to go to Amy's school. There's been a bit of a thing with her. The head called me in.'

'Oh no. What happened?'

She keeps talking as she bends down to kiss me on the cheek in a maternal way and sits down. 'It was during assembly. Some of the children were asked to go to the front and tell an interesting fact about their parents. When it was Amy's turn, she told the whole school that her dad is – and apparently these were her precise words – "a world-class cunt who never rings and never helps Mummy".'

I burst out laughing. 'Oh my God.'

Jess looks around for a waiter. 'I'm desperate for a drink but I'm going to have a coffee.'

'How did the school react?'

'The head has experience of the world, thank God. She was understanding. I told her it was all my fault, that Amy was repeating what she'd heard from me. Obviously I've promised to be more careful about what I say in front of her.'

I see a mother's anxiety in her eyes. 'I get this is difficult. For what it's worth, you are obviously a brilliant mum. I have no idea how you keep the show on the road.'

'I'm not. There's a pattern developing with Amy. A worrying one. There was another incident, last week. One of her friends was being bullied by a boy. Amy doled out what she insists is justice. She pushed him up against a wall in the playground and told him if he did it again he would know the meaning of the word "pain".'

'OK. I think we can see what's happening. She's taking after her mother.'

'It's not doing her any favours. The boy ran away in floods of tears and his parents have made a formal complaint.'

'Bloody hell. Will she be OK? Is she being punished?'

'The head is on Amy's side. But they can't condone or turn a blind eye to threats of physical violence. If she does anything like that again she'll be suspended for a couple of days.'

'I'm so sorry. Please give Amy my love.'

'She'll like that. When are you coming over to hang out?'

'As soon as I'm invited.'

Robert, a waiter I've known for fifteen years at assorted fashionable London restaurants, arrives to take our order. I'm having the marinated herring, with horseradish, the Wolseley's version of Jewish schmaltz herring; and then a Niçoise salad with fresh tuna. Jess is less fastidious than me about what and how much she eats. I don't know whether it's her metabolism or her relentless nerve-fuelled activity, but she seems to be able to consume anything and everything. She has a prawn cocktail – which is a Wolseley retro classic – and the Wiener Holstein, a huge piece of breaded and sautéed veal, topped with a fried egg and anchovies.

'Still or sparkling?' asks Robert, though he knows it's always sparkling.

'And can I have a black Americano, now if possible?' says Jess.

As soon as he's gone, Jess runs her hands through her hair and asks me if she looks a frightful mess. 'Not at all,' I fib.

'You're a rubbish liar, always were,' she says. 'How are you doing?'

My hands are on the table and she reaches out with her right and squeezes my left. Just for a few seconds. I look down, then back up at her and blurt: 'A package arrived. From Marilyn. She sent it before she died. You were right all along. I was wrong. She killed herself.'

My black rucksack is under my chair. I pull it out, unzip it and hand the Márquez paperback to Jess. She reads the inscription at the front.

'I'm so sorry. I can only imagine how you feel.'

Oh God, I'm about to cry.

I gulp and keep talking. 'There's something else.' I remove the photograph and Post-it notes from the back of the book. I am careful to make sure no one but Jess can see the photo as I pass it to her.

'Heavens,' is all she can manage. She's too embarrassed to talk for what feels like an age, and I don't know what to say.

'Did you take this picture?' she eventually asks.

'No. That's part of why it's upsetting. She was with somebody else. I've no idea who.'

'So why did she send it to you? It feels cruel, needlessly cruel.'

I shut my eyes and try to think. This is hard.

'There were two Post-it notes with the photo,' I say. 'One was old, written in block capitals. All it said was "DON'T FORGET YOUR FRIENDS". The other was from her to me.' I show it to Jess.

'"Find me, Gil",' she reads. 'Marilyn wants you to find her?'

'So it would appear.'

She looks carefully at the photo, and squeezes her lips together. 'She looks totally off her head, almost unconscious. Any idea at all who took this?'

I shake my head.

Jess reaches across and squeezes my hand for the second time. 'You should have rung me, you idiot.'

I nod meekly.

'Even though I never liked her,' she says, 'I am sure she cared about you. She wasn't trying to hurt you. My hunch is she's asking you to be her knight in shining armour.'

'Really?' I am definitely going to burst into tears. I fight it.

'Somebody did something really bad to her, and she wants you to stand up for her.'

I wince. It sort of makes sense. But not completely.

'Why not give me a name? Why involve me in a guessing game?'

129

'I am not sure. But she was distraught enough to kill herself. Which means, in my book, she wasn't thinking straight. Or maybe she thought you'd be able to work out who was behind the camera from what's in the picture.'

'Well I can't.'

Up to now, Jess has resisted handling the photo, as though it's toxic. Now she picks it up and studies it, holding it gingerly at the very edge, between finger and thumb.

'She was with someone ostentatiously wealthy,' she remarks. And then I see in her face that eureka moment I've seen so many times, when she's made a breakthrough in a story. 'Marilyn has told you who it is. See behind the sofa. The red and brown. That's a Rothko. Won't be hard to find a dealer or expert who knows the owner. Within the art world someone will know who it belongs to.'

I hadn't properly grasped the significance of the fuzzy rect-angles of intense colour behind the sofa. I was too mesmerised by Marilyn. 'It could be a repro.'

'Possible, but nah. Your ex-girlfriend didn't write down the name, because she thought you would know him the moment you saw this.'

I am sceptical, but say nothing.

'And another thing,' Jess continues. 'That note, "Don't forget your friends". Surely you've thought about that?'

Now I feel embarrassed. I've been so focused on my own misery that I dismissed it as a random piece of paper, maybe a bookmark.

'The photographer wrote that,' Jess says. 'I'm almost certain of that. It's really nasty. Reads like a threat.'

'Blackmail?'

'Don't you think?'

'But it's sloppy. If he can be identified by the painting . . .'

'Except that he assumed she would never show it to anyone. He wouldn't expect his victim to commit suicide and send the evidence to her lover.'

Jess hands the photo back to me just as the waiter arrives with the starters and Jess's coffee. I eschew the rye bread and concentrate on the clove-infused herrings. Jess ignores hers completely.

'I didn't know Marilyn well,' she says. 'Actually, I think she had a problem with women, she definitely preferred men.'

I don't argue.

'She was complicated,' Jess says.

'You could say that.'

'The photograph is so ... violating. She's exposed, helpless. It may have been taken without her really knowing, if she was totally off her head. She would not have sent it to the most important person in her life – that's you, in case you didn't know – unless you needed to learn something really really important.'

'What do you mean?'

'I think she's protecting you in some way. It's not just about who harmed her, it's about who may want to harm you.'

I put my fork down. There is too much for me to take in. I am feeling overwhelmed, and I've lost my appetite. I need space to work this out. I gingerly put the book, with photo and notes carefully reinserted, back in my bag. At the moment it feels like the most precious and important object I will ever own. I need to change the subject.

'Where are you and the *FC* on subprime? Do we have more of an idea of how bad it will be for the banks?'

Jess doesn't even hint an objection that I've reverted to type and chosen to displace the upsetting stuff with a comforting conversation about numbers and money. 'That's pretty much all we're working on, at the moment. This is financial global-isation being stress-tested to breaking point. The remarkable thing, as your bloody story captured, is that so much of the pain has been shunted to Europe rather than being kept in the US.

'Pretty much every European bank has a problem. Schon and the other bulge bracket Wall Street firms did an amazing job of packaging up the toxic waste and persuading naive European investors to buy it. With the help of the rating agencies of course.'

I shovel in the last of the herring and crème fraîche. 'I am sure Harvey Jackson was burned, though he insists he wasn't.'

'I meant to congratulate you on the interview.' Is there just a touch of envy in her tone? There should be, given her paper is supposed to be the house publication for the Jacksons of the world. 'You got a decent line.'

'He said something much more interesting when the cameras were off. He alleged that NewGate's website was blown up on purpose by a cyber-attack. He thinks the whole bank run – including my scoop – was designed to bring down NewGate.'

She uses her hand to push her hair off her eyes. 'That's quite a claim, dynamite if true. Did he offer proof?'

I shake my head. She breaks off the end of a piece of the Wolseley's trademark mini baguette – the size of a fat finger – and wipes up pink Marie Rose sauce, which she devours with the relish of a child. 'Amazing story,' she says.

'Good of you though not to articulate the problematic implic- ation. So before you ask, no, I had no clue I was part of a scam when I revealed NewGate was asking the Bank of England for cash.'

'Hang on,' she says. 'You may not have been. But . . .'

'Yes, I know. I need to go back to my source, find out what he knew, what his motives were in talking to me. Believe me, I've been trying.'

Since the interview with Jackson, I've been ringing Robin Muller almost hourly. The mobile goes straight to voicemail, my texts are ignored and the landline is picked up by a PA who has plainly been instructed to humour me and block me. I'm not surprised. Pretty much my entire adult life, Robin Muller has been invisible until he needs something.

'Why would someone orchestrate a bank run like that?' Jess asks, rhetorically. We know the answer.

'The question is not *why*, it's *who*. Whoever bet on NewGate's share price falling before I put out my story would have made a fortune.'

'Who would be quite so ruthless?'

I think back to my train blog, my final letter to Marilyn. *Wherever there's money or power, there are testosterone-fuelled narcissistic sociopaths.* 'I fear it may be quite a wide field. Who do we know had short positions in NewGate?'

'Chris Ravel of course. We talked about it.'

I slap my forehead. *Moron.* 'I forgot Chris Ravel bet against NewGate.' I've been too sidetracked by pursuing what happens next to NewGate. I wonder how much to share with Jess. I might as well give her everything.

'Believe it or not, before you arrived I asked Ravel's dad if he had any intelligence on whether NewGate's website was targeted by cyber terrorists. I thought he might be able to find out through his GCHQ connections.'

Jess looks at me with incredulity. 'You in effect asked Ravel's dad whether his son had engaged in criminal market manipulation. It's almost funny.'

Shit, shit, shit.

'OK, yes, maybe not the brightest move I've made. Although when I met him at Marilyn's funeral, I got the distinct feeling they're not close. But yes, I am an idiot.'

My life has become a study of assorted bungles. I feel dazed and look past Jess. A couple of tables away, Kate Moss is playing with her salad, stony-faced, as Freud consumes in silence. I see and I don't. I'm in my own head trying to understand why Marilyn ended her life so violently, who or what drove her to that bleak despair. It was connected to NewGate, of that I am

133

sure. But precisely how? I am in quicksand. Each time I struggle to reach land, I sink further.

There's a voice calling my name. 'Gil, where've you gone?

'I was miles away.'

'You're telling me.'

I need to find out more about the relationship between the two Ravels. I reach into my jacket pocket for a small notebook to write a reminder and feel a heavy piece of rectangular card. Oh yes. The invitation from Alex Elliott to his party. It is headed *Remembering Marilyn*, in heavy waxen lettering. Underneath is today's date. I pass it to Jess. She grimaces.

'Poor you,' she says.

'I've got to go,' I say. 'Do you think ... ?'

She snorts. 'Fuck off, Gil. That's too much to ask. You know how much I hate Elliott.'

'Think of it as work. Everyone will be there. It'll be story city.'

'Honestly, I can't face it.'

'We can go for an hour. Quick schmooze. In and out.'

'You know that's never going to happen. You'll schmooze some great-and-the-good monster and we'll never leave.'

'Please, Jess. I don't ask much of you.'

'Are you joking? You're the neediest fucker I know.'

'Please, Jess.' I do my winsome puppy face. 'Please.'

'Jesus. Why did I ever agree to be your friend? OK. If I can get a babysitter.'

Chapter 11

A T JUST AFTER TEN THAT evening, Jess and I pitch up at Alex Elliott's Notting Hill mansion in a grubby minicab, a Vauxhall Vectra that smells of stale Silk Cut. Super Cars of Holloway. He's struggling to pull over because black limos are double-parked all the way up the street.

'My God. Literally everyone who's ruining Britain is here,' Jess says grimly. 'I'd forgotten that apart from you, Marilyn only fucked upwards.'

I don't respond. I am morose: this is not in any meaningful sense an event to celebrate my friend. The billing on the invitation – 'Remembering Marilyn' – is just an excuse for another of Elliott's networking events, given cachet by the tragic suicide of a rising Bank of England star. Maybe he doesn't even recognise his own cynical exploitation anymore. If he still has friends, what he expects of them is to entertain his more important, remunerative clients.

The entrance is brightly illuminated by lanterns. The guests' personal security, with their regulation earpieces on curly-wurly flex, are in a huddle on the right. The doorkeepers, with clipboard lists of the invitees for ticking off, are long-legged, short-skirted Sloanes.

'Gil, so pleased to see you,' says a blonde I've never met before. 'And who are you?' she asks Jess archly.

I see Jess bristle, and hope she won't react too brutally. Jess gives a freezing scowl. 'Jess Neeskens. *Financial Chronicle.*'

The blonde smiles, unperturbed. 'Of course.'

The moment we step through the door, glasses of vintage Deutz are thrust at us. There's no non-alcoholic option. This wake seems like every other one of Elliott's parties, or what he calls his little gatherings. It's already mobbed with those whose wealth passes the ultra-high net worth threshold, the famous, the powerful and a few hangers-on. Their connection to Marilyn is tenuous.

'I know you loved her, in your own fucked-up way,' she says.

Did I? Maybe. It turns out I hardly knew her. Imagine spending so much time with someone over so many years and learning literally nothing about their family and background. 'I miss her,' is all I manage, staring at my faux-alligator-skin Chelsea boots.

An image suddenly comes to me of Marilyn standing over the gas hob in a bright red kimono, gingerly lifting the hissing aluminium espresso pot. Why is that in my head? Time to put up the shutters. Time to have a drink. Jess slips her arm around my waist and squeezes. 'Shall we get a glass of wine?'

As a habitué of too many Elliott dos, I know where the good stuff is to be found: his specially built claret room, where magnums and jeroboams of vintage red are being dispensed. The sommelier loiters outside, looking grave and unwelcoming – a deliberate ploy to deter the unfavoured majority of Elliott's guests.

'Hello, Mr Peck, and Miss ... ?'

'Jess.'

'Of course, Miss Jess. Can I offer you a proper drink?'

'That would be amazing,' I say.

We go inside the Aladdin's cave, with its floor-to-ceiling shelves of magnificent wine. It's a microclimate, where tempera- ture, humidity and light are all regulated to maximise the longevity of the contents of the hundreds of bottles, each of which is worth more than Elliott pays his driver or his cleaners for a week's work. On the counter is first-growth claret that is way out of my league. But I know Elliott well enough to be confident there will be something more recherché hidden under the counter.

'Michael, where've you put the good stuff?'

He winks and brings out a jeroboam of 1982 Château Latour. I can't believe my eyes. That's about six thousand pounds in a bottle.

'Our little secret, sir,' he says. 'Probably best you don't tell Mr Elliott.'

He hands a glass of the deep purple nectar to each of us.

'Thanks so much, Michael.'

We exit to the hubbub, and walk up a grand flight of stairs to a gallery where a liveried custodian is serving Russian caviar on blinis. Another, the former head barman of the Savoy, is mixing dry martinis. I spy a louche, unshaven man with wispy long greying hair. Raoul, the cocaine supplier to fashionable London. I assume there's a recreational drug dispensary set up in the house somewhere. I've been clean for years, but for the first time in a very long time, I am tempted.

'Keep an eye on me please, Jess. I don't *want* to get off my head, but I'm slightly in the mood. You know what it's like.'

Jess raises her eyes to the ceiling.

'One other thing,' I say. 'Todd will be here. It's impossible for me to talk to him. If you bump into him, can you ask what he thinks about Marilyn's death?'

'I doubt he'd confide in me, but—'

'I thought I'd run into you.' The shadow chancellor Patrick Munis has interposed himself between us. 'Sorry, am I interrupting?'

Jess makes an excuse about having seen a friend, and detaches herself. She is not a Munis fan.

'Tragic what happened to Marilyn,' he says.

Despite myself, I am fractious. 'What do you mean, "what happened to Marilyn"?' I can't hide my annoyance. 'Nothing happened *to* Marilyn. She killed herself.'

Patrick is subdued. 'Yeah. You'd known her for years, hadn't you?'

I had and I hadn't. At the back of my brain is that gnawing anxiety that will incapacitate me if I don't grip my ear with thumb and forefinger and say the spell. *Kill me now, kill me now, kill me now.* Has Munis noticed my OCD ritual? I've never known if people are aware of my weirdness and are too polite to mention it.

'She was a genius,' he adds. 'Todd relied on her more than he'd ever admit. If she hadn't left Downing Street, he would probably still be there and I wouldn't be on Elliott's guest list.'

'What do you mean? I thought you and Alex had been friends since university.'

Munis shrugs. 'Actually this is the first time he's invited me to one of his dos for years. After Todd's landslide, I wasn't of any use to him. He couldn't be bothered to waste time on us. I don't blame him. I had nothing to offer.'

Munis's realism is impressive. 'Weren't you offended?'

He laughs. 'You are a romantic. Business first, always, for Alex. When the invitation turned up, for me and Mrs B, it was the clearest sign our party is back, that we matter again.'

Mrs B is Citronella 'Stella' Barnsbury, the Conservative Party's newly elected, young, reforming leader. Not far away, in the gallery on the floor immediately above us, I can hear her jovial Cheltenham Ladies' College chortle reverberating down the stairs.

'You're being serious?' I ask.

'Deadly. The guest lists at Elliott's parties for the past decade have been the best measure of who has power. We haven't been anywhere near it for years.'

While he's been speaking, I've drained my glass of the Latour. That's a couple of hundred quid Elliott will never get back. I am annoyed with myself for not concentrating enough on its magnificence. 'I'm not sure Labour is as certain to lose office as you imply. You've lost your lead in the polls, and the election is years away.'

'Until you blew up NewGate I would have agreed,' he says. 'But ... events, dear boy.'

I make a theatrical grimace. It grates to be cited as the trigger for Labour's potential undoing. And he's wrong about my role. I look to Jess to back me up, but she's lost in the melee.

'I've been chatting to Ravel,' Munis goes on. 'He's convinced the NewGate debacle is just the start. He says you've blown the whistle on the biggest scam in financial history. All the banks are in trouble. And it's happened with Labour asleep at the wheel. If we can't win an election against that backdrop ...' He tails off as he sees the look I'm giving him. 'What?'

'Lord Ravel? Here?' I shouldn't be surprised, because he's certainly important enough to be courted by Elliott. But I didn't think coke and hookers were his scene.

Munis laughs. 'Wrong Ravel. *Le fils.*'

'Of course.' The billionaire who bet heavily against NewGate, according to Jess, and won huge. 'Where is he?'

'Upstairs, with a couple of members of the Saudi royal family.'

'Presumably Elliott's clients?'

'I would have thought so.'

At that an older woman I don't recognise, plummy voice, tweed skirt, forcefully inserts herself between us. Ignoring Munis, she says to me: 'I just wanted to say how much I love you on the *Today Programme.*'

Munis winks mischievously at me, mouths 'Lunch, soon,' and sidles off.

'That's very kind,' I say to the woman.

'Not at all. I'm afraid my son is not a fan. He and I disagree about you.'

'Forgive me for not knowing – who is your son?'

'I'm Nan Elliott. Alex's mother.' She lowers her voice into a stage whisper. 'He is a bit of a wanker, isn't he?' *Fucking priceless.* 'His father and I always hoped he'd do something serious. Instead he went into PR.'

She looks around the lavish reception room, covered in expensive art by assorted Saatchi-promoted artists. 'Well, at least he's made some money. That's something, I suppose.'

I need to find Chris Ravel. 'A genuine pleasure to meet you,' I tell her truthfully, before lying that I've got to leave soon and need to find the friend I came with.

The party is sprawling upstairs and downstairs in what used to be three multi-million-pound houses that have been knocked together, excavated, broadened and heightened. In the basement is Elliott's favourite toy: a heated swimming pool with a retractable cover, made of tiles pillaged from a sixteenth-century Ottoman palace. I climb the four storeys to the top of the house, scanning each reception room for Ravel and Elliott. At the apex, I am about to give up when I hear a noise coming from behind a bookshelf at the end of a corridor. It is a sort of moaning. And maybe laughing, too. Then I notice the bookshelf is an illusion: it's actually a sliding door. Should I move it?

I cough, and say a quiet, 'Hello?' No response. There's nothing really to knock on before entering, because the books are real and would dampen any banging. Oh well, there's no sign saying keep out, so I gingerly nudge the bookshelf to the left. It slides effortlessly.

I've got it half open when I am assaulted by a Dantesque sight. On a vast bed in a huge bedroom decorated in the debauched gaudiness of Louis XIV are two naked women. One is on all fours, and is being penetrated by the other with a black leather strap-on, while a group of men – including Elliott – spectate.

140

For the first time, I understand what people mean when they say, 'I didn't know where to look.' I mutter 'Sorry, sorry' and back away. But Elliott has spotted me.

'Come in, dear boy. Don't be shy. You know Lydia, don't you?' Lydia is Elliott's Russian model wife. She's wearing the strap-on.

'Gosh, er, sorry to interrupt.' I notice that Chris Ravel and two Saudis are to the left of Elliott. 'As it happens, I was actually trying to find you and Chris. But I should never have interrupted your ...'

'Well you've found us now. Come in, come in.' He won't be dissuaded. 'Chris, our friend Peck is here. Says he wants to talk to you.' He talks as though I've just bumped into them at the bar of Soho House, as though there's nothing unusual about any of this. I assume he's coked to the gills.

It's a long time since I've seen Chris Ravel. He never seems to age. He is as stringy and sinewy as when we exchanged half nods of recognition in the Chichele quad. Any possibility of fat or flesh is presumably consumed by the sheer number of neuron sparks in his brain. He's wearing Savile Row, Huntsman I guess: dark blue jacket, almost black, over a grey T-shirt. His blond hair is razor-cut to skinhead, and he's got gold John Lennon glasses. You could draw him with compass, ruler and protractor, all angles and perfect geometry.

He's staring at something on his BlackBerry and ignores me. *Where am I supposed to look?*

'Hi, Chris. Do you have a minute?'

Ravel stops typing and turns to me. 'What do you want to know?'

How Lydia's breasts defy the rules of gravity? Not that. 'I'm trying to understand quite how systemic this crisis is, and which banks will be next to fall over.'

I actually said that. In Elliott's madhouse. I am the living embodiment of cognitive dissonance.

141

He nods. 'Happy to chat. Probably best if we have a bit of privacy.' He turns to Elliott. 'You don't mind if we use your office, Alex?'

'You know where it is.' Elliott is more interested in the performance, which has seemingly been arranged for the benefit of the Saudis. Ravel turns to them.

'You have my number. Give me a ring and we'll meet next week.'

'Do you think Sir Stanley will agree?' one of them asks.

'Ask him yourself,' says Elliott. 'He's downstairs. I'll introduce you.'

Blackwell? The PTBG bank boss is here too? What do the Saudis want from him?

'Give me a few minutes. I just need to have a quick chat with our friend here.' Ravel puts his hand to his heart. '*Shukran. Ma'a salama.*'

He nods at Elliott and we escape to the corridor. 'Thanks for rescuing me,' I say. Ravel shrugs. I follow him to a room on the right, which is a temple to pre-Nazi German expressionism. There is a brutalist desk at one end, and the walls are covered in paintings by Dix, Grosz and Klee. The one post-war work is a floor-to-ceiling photograph of The Who peeing on the stranded monolith, the cover of *Who's Next*.

'I love that image,' says Ravel. 'Sums up everything, don't you think?'

'Possibly the City right now.' I would elaborate, but I am suddenly feeling woozy, a bit sick. I must have done precisely what I feared, which is to let my glass be replenished till I can barely stand. Except I don't remember any top-ups after that first near-priceless glass.

'You know the whole system is fucked, don't you?' says Ravel.

'The system?'

'Every bank. Fucked.'

Christ. My anaesthetised brain can't think of anything intelligent to say so I keep schtum. I must be drunk because I can hear my dad telling me intelligent people know when not to say a word. At the time I thought he was trying to shame me about my hyperactivity, my compulsion to talk and talk and talk.

'Greed,' Ravel sighs. 'They've been killed by their own idiotic greed. Still, I'm not complaining. Their stupidity is adding considerably to my wealth.'

That is an invitation. 'Did you short NewGate?'

'Of course. It's the job. Find a company's weak point, progressively apply pressure, ignore the squeals, put it out of its misery.'

'Lucky for you, then, that NewGate's website was sabotaged the night I told the world it was in trouble. That turned what would have been a fall in the share price into a rout.'

Ravel fixes me with magnified eyes behind the circular glasses, and smirks. 'If that's what happened, then yes, I was lucky. But I was going to win anyway. Just maybe not quite so fast.'

If he's lying that he had no knowledge of the attack on NewGate servers, he's adept at it. He continues his sermon. 'People who removed their savings from NewGate weren't panicking: they were being rational. There's nothing left in the kitty. The bank believed its own bullshit that it had special technology allowing it to lend more than the value of a house and never incur losses. Well done you for calling it out.'

He wants me as an accomplice in his profiteering. I won't have it. 'Was it you who arranged for the story to be leaked to me?'

He becomes petulant. 'I told you, NewGate brought itself down. And they're only the canary in the coal mine.'

This is bigger than you think. 'Marilyn Krol agreed with you.'

He shrugs. 'Didn't really know her. I'm a bit of a fraud being here tonight.'

At last someone's admitted to the hypocrisy of this event. 'I suppose you knew she supported Jackson's bid for NewGate.'

'I didn't, but it's irrelevant. That takeover was never going to happen. Even if the Bank of England had allowed it, the deal could never have been completed. Not once the buyer's accountants saw the balance sheet was a lie.'

I am not sure I believe him. 'If Jackson had been successful, your short positions would have been worthless.'

He shakes his head. 'The numbers never lie, Gil. NewGate was always going down the pan. There was nothing Marilyn or Jackson could have done to stop it.'

His voice has a contemptuous edge. He's saying we're all going to hell. 'Was there anything else you wanted?'

There must be a hundred things, but my brain is continuing to fog up. I wish I wasn't so tired. I force myself to keep going. 'Who are you targeting next?'

He laughs. 'Good one Gil. You know I'm never going to tell you that. If I did, no one would lend me the stock. And I wouldn't be able to make even more money that I don't need.'

He walks over to a bronze sculpture that looks like moulded plastic. Hans Arp, I think. Probably worth a million. He starts rocking it compulsively.

'The weird thing, though, is that even when a bank is as shit and bust as NewGate, there's always some idiot who *thinks* they want to buy it.'

He walks away from the Arp sculpture, thank God. He grins. 'You and me aren't so different. We tell the entitled and smug what they don't want to hear, that they're arseholes or crooks or both. And we feast off their carcasses.'

I utter a limp, 'Maybe. I'm not sure.'

'I've got one piece of advice for you. Keep doing what you're doing.' He walks to the door. The audience is over. 'I'd better check Elliott's not leading my Arab friends astray. You coming?'

I've had enough. 'I think I'll head home.'

I want to find Jess and get out of here. Down one floor, having done a recce of a reception room with floor-to-ceiling French windows that give on to a huge balcony – where Elliott has placed gas heaters for the smokers – I am almost knocked over by a furious Geordie voice.

'Peck, you southern piece of shit. Why did you wreck NewGate? You hate the north.'

Shaved head, wrap-around shades, black T-shirt over middle-aged spread, Nashville-stitched cowboy boots. *Essence of wanker.* It's Meathead, lead singer of stadium rock band I-Test, Newcastle's very finest.

'You vandalised the best business on Tyneside,' he booms, jabbing his finger at me.

'Calm down, Meat.' A calming and placatory Dublin accent. Jackson. This time in a tailored blue suit, though the cashmere polo neck is under the jacket. 'We've got a plan, remember? And Gil was only doing his job.'

Meathead snorts. Behind him, next to Jackson, is the Russian from Jackson's office. Petr. Petr … *who*? I want to introduce myself, but my head is throbbing and I think I might throw up. I nod to Jackson and say goodnight.

Where is Jess? The stairs are like one of those Escher paradoxes, round and round with landings on each floor. Halfway down, no sign of her. I go all the way to the basement. There's another sitting room there, quiet, soft lighting, deep sofa, a wall of linked TV screens. No one in it. I'm so tempted to sink into the sofa and sleep. I walk towards it, when I'm electrocuted awake by the painting behind the wall above the sofa.

Three fuzzy red and brown rectangles. Rothko.

That Rothko.

Chapter 12

I'M WOKEN BY SANDPAPER RUBBING on my face. It's not unpleasant, just unexpected. I open my eyes. Mistake. My head throbs. I need water, painkillers. I orientate myself. This is not my bedroom. Where on earth am I?

'And who are you?'

My question is directed at a giant tortoiseshell cat, which has been licking my cheek and is now padding on the duvet and purring.

A small girl calls out, 'Mr Volcker. What are you doing? You shouldn't be bothering Gil. Naughty cat.'

Amy. Jess's daughter. In bright blue blazer and grey skirt. I'm in Jess's spare bedroom. How did I get here? What happened last night? The pounding in my skull is agony. Nurofen. I need Nurofen.

'Amy. How lovely to see you,' I say.

'I've brought you tea. I made it myself. I put it in my favourite mug.'

This time the picture on it isn't a seventies teen idol. It's Bagpuss. 'Mum and me found it in the Oxfam shop. It cost a pound. That's a bargain.'

She deposits it on the bedside table and stands there expecting me to drink. It's far too milky but I know my duty and slurp.

'Delicious. Thank you so much.'

'I would have made you breakfast, but Mum says you never eat it.'

'Mum's right.'

'Anyway, I didn't have time. I had to wash my hair and then Mum had to braid it.'

'Your hair looks great. Any idea what the time is?'

'It's about quarter to eight. I need to leave for school in a minute.'

She walks to the door and shouts, 'Mum. Gil's awake.'

'Tell him we'll talk after I've dropped you at school,' Jess shouts back. 'And that there are fresh towels in his bathroom.'

Amy turns back to me. 'Did you get all that?'

'Yes I did. Have a great day at school.'

'Thank you. It's nice to have you stay over. Will you be here when I get home?'

'Probably not. I have to go to work. But I'll see you soon.'

'You'd better.'

*

After she's gone, the inevitable happens, an attack of the screaming 'oh-no's. Fragments of what happened after I saw the Rothko come back to me. Returning to the claret room, taking a glass of Latour and downing it in three gulps. I apologised to the sommelier. Charging around the house looking for Elliott, thankfully not finding him, because I would have struggled to explain to the DG and the director of news why I assaulted the most powerful PR in London in his own home. I ran into Meat again. The Russian, Petr, inserted himself between us, before Jess swooped in and bustled me out, just in time to throw up in the street outside Elliott's mansion. Wondering which guests might have seen me, I am mortified. *Kill me now, kill me now, kill me now.*

None of that is the real humiliation. It's the idea that Marilyn had a fling with Elliott, that he fucked her. I want to punch myself in the face, to stab myself in the thigh. *You picked the single person I despise most. Why, Marilyn? And why didn't you tell me?*

I hear the front door close. It is my cue to creak out of bed, careful not to move my sore head too fast or too suddenly. For the first time, I notice I am wearing only my boxers, and I cringe again. How did I undress? Did Jess undress me? I have almost no memory of the taxi ride back, or getting into bed.

I walk to the adjacent bathroom and stand as still as I can under the powerful shower, hoping the jet and the heat will wash away the poison. After ten minutes, I slather myself in Jess's Jo Malone cypress and grapevine shower gel. The astringency begins to cleanse me of the horror of last night. *I want to die, I want to die, I want to die.*

I stagger out of the shower, towel around my waist. Where are my clothes? Not flung on the chair. Someone hung my suit and shirt in the cupboard. Jess must have put me to bed like an invalid. I can't bear it. I dress, except for shoes and socks, pad to the kitchen and fill the kettle. I grind enough coffee for several mugs, add the lot to the cafetiere. When I press the filter down with unthinking force, coffee spurts like a geyser.

There's coffee everywhere but I can hear the buzzing of my phone. I run to the bedroom. My parents' number. Fuck, I forgot to ring them.

'Gil.'

'Hi Mum.'

'Didn't you get the message?'

'I saw you rang. I meant to call. But no, I didn't get a message.'

'That's odd. It wasn't urgent. Dad and I just wondered how you are. We remembered Marilyn was a friend. Are you OK?'

'I'm fine, Mum. Have you heard from the doctors? How are you?'

'They are pleased with me. And I'm feeling good. Your dad's a bit tired though. Will you come and see us?'

'Yes of course. Maybe this weekend?'

'That would be lovely.'

We say goodbye. I sit on the bed. Why didn't I get a voice-mail notification? I press the button to retrieve messages. I have no new ones, but thirty-five saved ones. That seems a lot. The first one is from my mum, asking me to ring her. Then there are several I did retrieve: from the office, from Elliott telling me to ring about the Jackson interview, another from the Downing Street switchboard saying Jane Walters wants me. For some reason I decide to keep listening. I have a hunch. I'm praying I'm wrong, but I'm not. It's the voice I both wanted to hear and dreaded.

'Gil. Where are you? I need to tell you something. It's urgent. Call me.' Marilyn. Recorded shortly after we spoke on the day she died. Was she helping me or was I supposed to help her? My head is spinning.

I hear a key turning in the front door. 'Gil! Have you made coffee? I'm gagging for one.' Oh fuck. The coffee is all over the kitchen floor. I run back, scrabble under the sink, find a dish-cloth, soak it and start mopping the quarry tile floor. I'm on my knees when Jess walks in. She bursts out laughing.

'Look at you, in your Versace suit scrubbing the kitchen floor.'

I look up and whisper, 'Not feeling well.'

'You've got most of it up. Come and sit down. You look terrible.'

'I feel awful. You wouldn't have a Nurofen, would you?'

*

After two ibuprofen and two paracetamol, and a couple of mugs of strong black coffee, I am almost functioning again.

We've moved to Jess's book-lined sitting room where I have sunk into a deep sofa. Jess sits in the hard-backed mahogany Regency chair to my left, looking like an indulgent but disappointed parent.

'Is everything all right?'

'Not really.'

'What happened?'

'I just heard from Marilyn.'

She looks at me as though I've lost my mind.

'She left a voicemail for me on the day she died. I've only just heard it. She warned me we were both in trouble.'

'Fuck.'

'I'll play it to you.'

Her face darkens as she hears: *It's urgent. Call me.*

'We know she killed herself, right?' she asks.

'Obviously. But someone was trying to harm her, to shut her up.'

'Maybe. But what's the connection with you? Why are you at risk?'

The question is otiose. She knows as much or as little as I do, which is to say it's all to do with NewGate, but we can't see the whole picture. She changes the subject. 'What on earth did you drink last night?'

'I saw the Rothko. The one in the photo. It belongs to Elliott.'

We look at each other, for what seems an age.

'That's awful. Do you think . . . ?'

'Yes. Possibly. Probably. After the '97 general election, when we had that terrible row about Clare, we didn't see each other for a year. That picture could have been taken then. She looks the right age. She obviously had a fling with him. She never said. But there's so much she never said.'

An image from Elliott's bedroom last night comes into my head, his wife Lydia degrading and degraded for his and his clients' entertainment. In halting sentences, I recount the choreo-graphed debauchery, trying to make a joke of it. 'I'm not sure I've ever been so embarrassed. Honestly, I just didn't know what to do.' I make a feeble smile.

Jess stands up, walks towards me and wraps her arms around me. The tears come. Not in a torrent. Gently. 'Don't worry, Gil. It'll be OK. We'll make this right.'

'I'll pull myself together. I just had too much to drink, that's all.'

I wipe my eyes with the back of my hand. Jess goes to the kitchen and returns with two sheets of kitchen paper, which she hands to me. I blow my nose.

'Something's bothering me,' she says. 'Why didn't you get Marilyn's voicemail till today?'

'That's easy. My phone has been hacked.'

'What?'

'Someone dialled into my mailbox, pretending to be me, and accessed my messages. Once they heard the message, they would no longer register as new messages for me. So I would never have known to listen to them.'

'So why did you listen today?'

'Because my mum said she left a message but I never got it. So I worked out what was happening.'

'How?'

'You honestly say you don't know about phone hacking?'

She shakes her head. I'm amazed.

'Every paper is at it,' I say. Except perhaps the *FC*. 'It's how they steal the secrets of the rich and famous. They blag officials working for phone companies to reset the PINs for accessing messages of people they want to target. Celebrities, footballers, politicians, you name it. Once they have the PIN, they can listen to messages and steal secrets.'

'You've never done it, have you?'

I pause for too long.

'Fucking hell, you have! Gil!'

'Years ago, when people were too thick to reset their PINs from the factory setting, 3333, I tried it a couple of times. But it felt dirty. I haven't even thought about doing it for years.'

The disappointed parent becomes the angry parent. But then there's a change. 'Someone's targeting you. It could be a journalist trying to nick your sources and your stories. Or if Marilyn's right, it's someone who wants to harm you.'

For a minute, we sit in silence. If I am in danger, do I go home, lock the door and climb under the duvet? It's tempting.

'What do I do?'

'What we always do. We need to do some digging. And you need to go to work.'

'Maybe.'

'Not maybe. Definitely. You're only a fraction of the way through the biggest story of your life. And if someone's trying to stop you, your best defence is to expose them first. Stop feeling anxious and sorry for yourself, and get out there.'

'OK, Mum.'

I stand up and assess myself. I think I can move without throwing up. I walk toward the front door.

'Attaboy,' Jess encourages me. 'But Gil, you can't leave yet.'

'Why not?'

'You need to put your shoes and socks on.'

*

At lunchtime, I am pedalling down Scrubs Lane to Television Centre. The analgesics have worked their magic, I am fragile, but I am back on the mission. The A40 flyover looms. As I swing right into the straight-ahead lane that takes me under the bridge, a black cab driver beeps, gesticulates and shouts something that might have been 'Love your work, Gil,' but I suspect was less flattering. I mouth 'Sorry' and zip through the lights. The doughnut looms ahead.

As soon as I enter the bustling business and economics unit, I head to the long table where the assorted national producers and correspondents sit at their PCs scrolling through wires, arranging shoots and filling in tedious risk assessment forms. Emma has her hand over the mouthpiece of a landline handset, and is trying to have a discreet conversation. As I hover next to her, I hear the time-honoured ritual of a producer trying to placate an interviewee, who gave up several hours of his precious time yesterday to be filmed by one of my colleagues but who never made it into the final edit. Emma is using the tried and trusted 'a big story broke late last night and we were ordered to make emergency cuts' line, rather than the truer 'you were incoherent and unusable'. She hangs up.

'I literally hate this job,' she says.

'Don't talk bollocks. You love it.'

'Sometimes. Though if you've come to see me, I assume my day is about to get a lot more complicated.'

I stick out my bottom lip and put on a hurt face.

'For fuck's sake Gil, what do you want?'

'I'm really keen to do some filming on Schon's trading floor. Can you sort it?'

'I can try the PR, but what do I tell him? You know how much they hate publicity. It's incredibly hard to persuade them to do TV.'

'Can you tell him we're doing a piece for bulletins on credit derivatives, credit default swaps, all those insurance policies that underpin the triple-A ratings of collateralised debt obligations. We want to help our viewers understand the innovations that have made it cheaper for people to borrow, especially for mortgages.'

She gives me a disbelieving look.

'Are we really doing that piece? Have bulletins told you they want it?'

'Not yet. But obviously don't tell him that.'

She puffs out her cheeks. 'I hope you're not trying to get me into trouble.'

'Would I, Em? If we get inside, and we extract decent footage and interviews, we'll definitely use them. The financial crisis is the only game in town, and the explosive growth in the use of these derivatives is associated with the extreme risks the banks have been taking. It's part of the story of banks going bust. Even if we don't use the footage immediately, it'll get used. You'd be telling Schon the truth. Sort of. Trust me.'

'A little voice tells me I am making a stupid mistake.'

'If the PR is iffy about it, I'll reassure him.'

An hour later, Schon's PR, Dougie Pescod, rings me to double-check that I'm not planning to turn over Schon. 'This is a film about the market, not about us?' he asks in his Texan drawl. 'Right?'

'One hundred per cent. It's about why credit derivatives have cut the cost of borrowing. It's about financial innovation that has improved lives, especially for those on lower incomes.' *Please let him swallow my bullshit.*

'OK. Swing by tomorrow at eleven; I'll warn the guys on the desk. And I'll be with you every minute,' he adds.

'Magnificent. See you tomorrow.'

*

The following morning, I walk onto Schon's vast trading floor, to be greeted with a whooping noise, and shouts of 'It's the Peckmeister!' I squirm. This is embarrassing.

'You're a legend among the traders,' says Pescod. 'They love Peckonomics. I assume you know you've been moving markets with it.'

'Shut up Dougie, his head's big enough as it is,' says Emma. She takes the tripod off her shoulder, which she has been carrying for Petra while also dragging the rigid case filled with lighting equipment, and hands it to me. 'You can lug this, Peckmeister.'

We walk to the middle of the floor, so that Petra can film a three-hundred-and-sixty-degree panorama of the twinkling, blinking lights of hundreds of trading screens, and the giant ticker that flashes share prices, bond prices, and breaking news in a frieze running all the way around. The rows and rows of desks are like ploughed furrows in a dystopian digital landscape, peopled mostly by white men, navy blue jackets off, tieless, white shirts, top buttons undone.

'Do you have another floor where all the women traders work?' Emma asks.

Pescod colours. 'We know. It's not a great look. We're actively trying to recruit more women.'

Emma rolls her eyes. 'I'm just messing with you. Can we interview a couple of the guys? Nothing terribly detailed or lengthy.'

'I assumed you'd ask. Most of them prefer to stay anonymous, but I've found two or three who are up for it.' Pescod introduces us to Didier, who is thirty-something, floppy brown hair, spectacles with rectangular black rims – perhaps an homage to the young Yves Saint Laurent. His English is fastidiously perfect, his faint French accent is a chic luxury.

Petra gives me the handheld mic that's wired to her cumbersome on-the-shoulder camera. I switch into focused, broadcast interview mode. 'Good to meet you, Didier. I understand you trade credit. Tell me about the state of the market.'

'It's crazy. So much volatility.' He gives a lengthy explanation that involves phrases like 'the widening spread between three-month LIBOR and Sonia'. I let him talk and talk, while Emma gives me her 'this is unusable' stare.

When he's finished his discourse on the semiotics of the trading floor, I have another go.

'That was really interesting, but perhaps a bit too complicated for some of our viewers. So can I put it another way. If you were telling your grandmother what's going on, how would you put it?'

He tries his best. 'Banks are increasingly charging considerably more to lend to other banks than the risk-free rate of borrowing.'

OK. If my grandma had been a hedge-fund manager she'd have understood every word. She wasn't. She sold ladies' suits in a shop in Jewish Stoke Newington. But I am able to translate Didier. He just told me banks are significantly increasing what they charge other banks who want to borrow from them. The reason this matters is that it implies there's an open secret in the financial industry that many banks are in deep trouble, and that therefore interbank lending, as it's called, has become a very risky business.

We do a couple more of these chats, so-called voxes, while I scan the room and work out how I can escape Pescod and seek out Muller. Pescod is all Texan homespun 'y'all' charm, but he's keeping me on a short leash. It won't be long before I'll have used up all the traders brave enough to appear on television news. I need to escape now.

I turn to Pescod and, with faux embarrassment, say I'd like to use the men's room – which I noticed was beyond the trading floor by the lifts.

Emma lifts her eyes to the ceiling. Petra is busy walking down the rows gathering shots for coverage, and I can see Pescod has been looking anxiously in her direction, in case there's sensitive information on the monitors she's filming, or something wholly inappropriate on a trader's desk. As I hoped, he judges it's more dangerous to leave her alone with a camera than let me go to the loos without him.

'How do I get back in?' I ask.

Pescod unclips his door pass from his belt and hands it to me. I walk briskly off the trading floor, craning back to check he isn't observing me. He's looking at the tiny review screen on Petra's camera, reassuring himself she hasn't filmed anything that could get him into trouble. *Perfect.*

I head for the stairs. I've been here before when I was at the *FC*, and I know Muller is on the floor above. What I can't remember is whether Corporate Advisory, where he's a senior managing director, has its own reception desk. *Shit, it does.* Behind a block-like, dark wood table sits an immaculately turned-out young woman – brunette hair in severe bun, crisp white silk blouse, manicured nails.

'Can I help you?' she says.

'I wanted to have a quick word with Robin Muller.'

'You're Mr Peck, aren't you?'

I give her what I hope is a winning smile. 'That's right.'

'My mum loves you. When you're on the news she always shouts for me to come and watch. We love the way you explain things.'

'So lovely of you to say that. Thank you.'

She looks left and right, as if checking we're not being observed. 'I'm not supposed to do this,' she murmurs, 'but could you scribble her an autograph? Things haven't been great for her recently. She'd be so pleased.'

'I'd be delighted.' She hands me a Schon compliments slip. 'What's her name?'

'Doreen. "To Doreen", please.'

I write: *To Doreen. Thanks for being generous about my eccentric broadcasts. Best wishes, Gil.*

'She'll be made up. Thanks so much.'

Doreen's daughter then reverts to her role as gatekeeper for Schon's masters of the universe, and scrolls down her screen.

158

'The thing is, Mr Peck, there's nothing here to say Mr Muller is expecting you. Should I call his PA?'

Shit. What do I say?

I begin to mutter something about how he's an old friend, and could she ring him rather than the PA, when I hear the voice I encountered in the Chichele Junior Common Room more than twenty years earlier. At the time he was passionately arguing we should go on strike to force the college's endowment fund to stop investing in apartheid South Africa. I've often wondered what happened to Muller's conscience when he joined the world's most opportunistic and ruthless investment bank, Schon. Maybe I will ask him at last.

He steps out of his office and pauses, holding the door open. As he glances around the reception area our eyes meet, but he wilfully refuses to acknowledge me. Instead, he turns away and focuses on the man walking into the corridor.

Chris Ravel.

'Hi, Chris,' I say, so loudly that Muller can't possibly pretend I'm not there. 'Did you enjoy the party?'

Muller's gaze flits between us. 'Of course, you two know each other.'

Ravel ignores him. 'Classic Elliott party,' he says. 'If you wrote an algorithm to identify the most important people in the country, most of them would be on his guest list.'

I brace myself for him to comment on my inglorious drunken exit, but either he didn't see it or he's not interested. I think of the Rothko and the photograph, and Elliott's wife in the upstairs bedroom. 'Definitely classic Elliott.'

Ravel tries to detach himself from Muller and head for the lifts. But Muller reaches out and grabs his arm. Ravel freezes. He does not like being touched.

'What are you doing, Robin?'

'I have a family, young children.' That is odd. If I didn't know better I'd say Robin Muller is scared. In all the years I've

159

known him, I've never known him show vulnerability. What's eating him?

Ravel shakes him off. 'Relax, Robin. There's nothing they can do. They're up to their necks.'

He winks at me, as if to a co-conspirator. But he's given me the clue I need. I don't know for sure whether Muller leaked NewGate's desperate state to me on Ravel's instructions, but I'm fairly certain neither of them will want me talking about it here, in front of the receptionist.

'Robin,' I say. 'We need to chat. About that conversation we had, when you telephoned me, just the other day.' I turn to Chris and speak slowly and clearly. 'Chris, would you be able to join us for a few minutes? What I want to discuss is relevant to you too.'

Muller's control freakery is to Olympic standards, and this is not how his morning was supposed to pan out. He is flustered, and there is an involuntary twitch in the corner of his mouth. The last thing he wants is to be interrogated by me in front of Ravel.

'Don't worry, Chris, Gil's an old friend. You're in a rush. I'll brief you later,' he says, jerkily. The practised charm and composure, that he had even at college, has evaporated. 'Let's go to my office, Gil. I have precisely five minutes.'

I transmit a victory smile to the receptionist as I follow Muller to a corner room, which is the size of a well-appointed London apartment. It looks directly on to the dome of St Paul's. The view says everything about Schon: it has privileged access – the best view imaginable – even to a national treasure like Wren's masterpiece.

No time to admire it: my five minutes have begun. 'Why did you tell me about NewGate being in such trouble? Actually that's a stupid question. You knew telling me would blow up Jackson's takeover of NewGate. Why did you want to kill that deal? Surely Jackson's a Schon client?'

Muller collapses into the chair behind the desk and snaps shut the screen on his laptop. 'You are trespassing. I should get you thrown out.'

'Jesus, Robin. Don't be an arse. If you did get me thrown out, do you think I would keep quiet about it? Don't you think your partners in New York would want to know why the BBC's business editor risked his career to talk to you, what you might be hiding?'

He goes quiet. There's an antique grandfather clock in the corner and its tick is an ultimatum.

'Why did you blow up the MHH deal?' I try again.

'Bigger fish to fry.'

That again. Marilyn's *this is massive*.

'What fish?'

'Don't be so disingenuous. You know what I'm talking about. You mentioned in one of your blogs how the crash of NewGate's website contributed to the run. You have the pieces. Join them up.'

Chris Ravel's cold-eyed certainty at Elliott's party comes back to me. *Numbers can't lie, Gil. NewGate was always going bust. There was nothing Marilyn or Jackson could do to stop it.*

Did Ravel also confirm that he'd ordered Muller to leak the story to me? I can't remember. Why did I drink so much?

'You screwed Jackson so that Ravel could make a killing. But why?'

This is sort of a rhetorical question. Ravel's trading flows and information are priceless for a bank like Schon. The occasional deal fee from Jackson isn't in the same league.

'As I said, you are capable of working all this out for yourself. But I wouldn't lose sleep over it. You fucked up a very bad person.'

'Jackson?'

Muller just looks at me, hands in trouser pockets, fiddling with what I assume is a set of keys. I've never known him nervous and wired like this. I bulldoze on. 'Ravel went massively short on NewGate. You used me to force the price down. That's market manipulation. I should report the two of you to the Financial Services Authority.'

'I'm not sure that would be career enhancing for you. How would you explain your role in all this?'

'I'm not implicated.'

'Really?' He's stopped jangling his keys and is resting his hands on the desk. 'If the regulators did contact me, I'd be obliged to say that you told me you'd been informed by hedge-fund contacts of yours that NewGate was in trouble, and you asked me about it. I refused to comment. Schon's rules, everyone knows that. So the question would then be why you didn't mention that your contacts – perhaps your friends – were shorting the stock when you put out your story?'

'But none of that is true. You rang me. I had no idea about short sellers.'

'Good luck with proving that. In the meantime, what do you think your BBC bosses would do? And now that you are so famous, or perhaps notorious, who else would give you a job?'

This is getting wild. Which never happens when Muller is involved. I'm missing something. Muller is not frightened of what I may do: I'm just an annoyance, a bit of a sideshow. There's something else. Why did he tell Ravel about being worried for his family? Someone's threatening him.

'Has Jackson worked out what happened? Is he going to report you to the authorities? Or has he already? Did he shop you to Marilyn on the day of the run?'

The day Marilyn died.

'Gil. You're out of your depth. Walk away, while you can.' Which was pretty much what Marilyn was telling me to do in her voicemail.

The BlackBerry hums against my thigh, the buzz so loud in the quiet of the office that Muller can't miss it. He glares. 'Answer it.'

It's Emma. 'Where are you, Gil? The PR is going mental.'

'On my way down.'

I hang up and turn to Muller. 'You are a cunt.'

Chapter 13

DAYS PASS IN A FRENZY of blogs and broadcasts. The great Jenga tower that is the banking system seems about to topple over, wreaking heaven knows what harm to the rest of us. No one can be sure which block will next be removed from the tottering tower, which bank will be next to collapse. I have somehow become the commentator for the nation of this monstrous game, and I am struggling to be neutral, impartial – because the more I see, the more I know that the greed of bankers has imperilled us all, while regulators slept. Inevitably, because I am excited and under pressure, my OCD has kicked in with a vengeance. It's been the same since I was twelve years old: I doubt the evidence of my senses, and indeed my memory, and engage in repetitive rituals of checking and double-checking that I've done something, such as switch off the oven or the hob.

This morning, OCD is delaying my cycle to the BBC. Having said goodbye to Dog and left the flat, I go back to the front door to check it's properly shut. I press it, walk a few yards, and then feel anxious that I haven't double-locked it. I return. The key won't move any further in an anti-clockwise direction. So yes, it must be double-locked. I try to get on my way again. But what if the lock is just stiff? I go back, unlock and then lock. Again. And again. Till eventually I get to the final test of whether all is secure. I press with my knuckle so hard on the door that it hurts the bone. My knuckle will continue to hurt for a few minutes, long enough for me to reach the street. The pain is the proof I need that I really did lock it. No turning back now. Yes, the back of my hand hurts. I can unfold the bike and mount it.

As I cycle round the fields, I tell myself that I am being mad and irrational. I don't understand how I can observe my rituals, know that they're crazy, and yet not master them and abandon them. I take a few calming breaths while I pedal. In through the nose, out to the count of five between pursed lips. I am assaulted by all the duties I've neglected, like checking in on Mum and Dad. I'll ring them later. Now I've got to get my head in the right space for lunch with Peter Law, the BBC's director of communications.

I've known him for years: we first met when he was Johnny Todd's deputy spin doctor, before Pete left for the more lucrative world of public relations. He rang me for mutual condolences after Marilyn died, and we said we'd get together, for our own private wake. His idea. But there's something I need from him.

We're meeting in the BBC Club, where the food is marginally better than the canteen, and where legendary television executives and actors were for decades able to get rat-arsed drunk any time of the day or night. Not many of the cravat-wearing, lecherous, alcoholic producers are still alive. National treasures all of them, though they wouldn't be if the young female producers coerced into having sex with them ever told their stories. When I arrive, Law is already at the table, grazing on a bowl of crisps. I can see from the open bottle of Chablis that he's at least two glasses in. I hate drinking at lunch, but I want Law to be relaxed enough to give me what I want. So I need to encourage him.

'Glass of Shabbliss, old cock?' he says.

Pete's Yorkshire, from Halifax, he's carrying two stone that are surplus to any kind of requirement, and he has a brain that processes information at the speed of light. Obviously I hate anyone and everyone who works in PR. They are the enemy. But he's never dull, and is both off-the-charts outrageous and a trove of gossip. I've been meaning to follow up what he told me about the relationship between a member of the royal family and an American billionaire for ages. He's also got an unexpectedly strong moral core. When he quit Downing Street, most – including me – thought it was greed, a desire to monetise his relationship with the new regime. Years later, off his bonce in the Groucho, he told me it was because he had come to the conclusion that Todd was driven solely by his insatiable narcissistic appetite, and that – in his words – 'his commitment to the Labour cause is a tissue of self-deluding fiction'. He is one of the few people I ever told about Todd's affair with my late sister. It turns out he already knew. 'Probably no comfort,' he said, 'but now he's fooking everyone up the arse.'

I haven't pre-warned Pete that I am going to ask him about his life after Todd, and more precisely about the months after Modern Labour's landslide victory in 1997. He'd left Downing Street to work with Alex Elliott, who had quit Media Corp to set up his own PR firm. Tory-supporting Elliott, whose first job out of Oxford was in the Conservative Research Department, desperately needed privileged access to the new Labour prime minister. Pete's inside track was so valuable that the firm was renamed Elliott and Law. They were joint owners, and accumulated considerable income and wealth, until in 2004 they had a spectacular row. Without consulting Pete, Elliott had signed a contract to launder the reputation of a repressive Gulf state. Pete's capacity for ethical compromise was tested beyond endurance. His unexpected moral core became a bother to him again. As he explained it to me, 'I told Alex he was corrupt, and I wasn't going to work for tyrants who torture and execute their opponents.' He walked out, and a few months later he joined the Beeb.

He splashes Chablis into my glass, and tops up his own. 'I'm only drinking because I can't get over Marilyn topping herself,' he explains. 'It's a disgrace. I loved Marilyn.'

'I know you did, Pete.'

'I wish she'd let me fuck her. I tried often enough.'

'Pete!'

'Sorry, old cock. I was always jealous of the two of you.'

I should have remembered there's never any need for foreplay with Law. I might as well just ask. 'You know when Marilyn and I broke up for a while, after the election, did she take up with anyone?'

Law grunts and fills up his glass. 'Bottle's empty already. I'll get another one. What were you asking?'

'Whether Marilyn was dating anyone, or was with anyone, after we stopped seeing each other for a bit in '97.'

Law looks around for a waiter. They've all vanished.

'Why are you asking?'

'Because it turns out there's lots about Marilyn I didn't know, and I want to fill in the gaps.'

Law has finally managed to catch a waiter's eye. He shakes the empty bottle at him. 'I meant why are you asking *me*?'

'Because you used to be close to Elliott.'

'Well then you have your answer.'

'Not really.'

'Are you sure you want to know? It was a pretty dark time for Marilyn.' I nod, though my chest tightens. 'After the two of you broke up, Marilyn was in a terrible state. I'd never known her messed up. She was drinking too much, doing way too much coke. Quite how she managed to hold it together at work I'll never know.'

'You and I were supposed to be friends. Why didn't you tell me?'

'She swore me to secrecy. Anyway, long story short, Elliott saw an opportunity and moved in.'

Now that he's confirming my worst fears, I'm not sure I do want to hear.

'How long did it last?'

'A few months, maybe. Towards the end, she even moved into his place.'

His words hang in the air, taunting me. *Why, Marilyn, why?* I'm afraid to ask, but I need to put my finger in the wound, to clean it out. 'Did she ever tell you what she saw in him?'

'Sort of. Years later, after I fell out with Alex, I asked why she did it. She didn't really answer, just said it was a time in her life when she'd done a load of terrible things. I guess fucking Elliott was a test of how much humiliation she could endure.'

Pete scoops up a handful of crisps and starts to speak and munch at the same time. 'If it's any consolation, she said she felt really bad about how she'd let you down. She wouldn't explain what she meant, but she started crying.'

I look at him in disbelief. Marilyn never cried. My mind is racing. I remember Jess's verdict when she saw Marilyn's photograph. *The photograph is so . . . violating. She's exposed, helpless.* Marilyn sent me the photo to tell me she'd fallen back into darkness, and this time she could not tolerate the loneliness and the pain.

A decade ago she pulled herself out of the swamp. How was she dragged back in? *Find me Gil.*

Law raises his glass and clinks it against mine. The sound is clinical, icy.

'To you Marilyn. I miss you.'

*

An hour later, I'm in my Ikea cupboard of an office. I did once complain about its size to Janice, and she made clear I was being a self-important, pampered tosser. I've logged on to my

PC and am browsing the website of Elliott and Partners, which is what Elliott and Law became after Pete walked out. It doesn't display a formal list of clients, but in a section about recent assignments there are photos of various reputation-enhancing projects that the firm has created for assorted businesses.

I am struck by Elliott's commercial promiscuity. One article on the site is about how Elliott helped MHH and the Johnny Todd Peace Institute launch and run the 'Jackson Development Economics Prize'. It's illustrated with a picture of Johnny Todd awarding the prize to a young black doctoral student from the London School of Economics. Another 'story' talks of a press trip Elliott organised to show off a massive Gulf property development. It lists Chris Ravel's Lulworth Securities as an anchor investor, and includes a quote from him about the rapid modernisation of the region. A third page shows a photo of Elliott grinning in a hard hat and high-vis jacket, standing next to a lean man with close-shaved hair, wide Slavic cheekbones and a broad nose. He's leaning on a pick-axe, and somehow his smile conveys menace. The caption reads: *The Russian investor and philanthropist Petr Primakov breaks ground on oil refinery upgrade, Odessa, Ukraine.*

'I've found you,' I mutter. Petr Primakov. The Russian from Jackson's office, who interceded when I embarrassed myself with Meathead at Elliott's party. There are so many routes to learning more about him. I choose the laziest, and dial on the landline.

'What do you know about Petr Primakov?' I ask Jess, the instant she picks up.

There's a nanosecond pause, as she accesses the database in her head.

'Worth billions. Proper oligarch. Picked up oil, gas, metals in the fire sale of state assets after the collapse of the Soviet Union. He's kept a lower profile than many. Close to Putin,

170

of course, the normal insurance policy. We think he's moved to the UK. Can't be sure.'

'How dodgy is he?'

She laughs. 'He's an oligarch.'

I remember the fragment of conversation I heard outside the lift in Jackson's office. 'Would he be interested in buying NewGate, do you think?'

'It could make sense. NewGate massively promotes its work in the north-east, as a community bank. Buying it would be a way to put down new roots, acquire new friends. A bit like Abramovich buying Chelsea.'

'Reputation laundering.'

'You said it.'

'Thanks, Jess.'

'Why are you so interested in him?'

I'm about to tell her when the bat-phone BlackBerry buzzes. It's Kim Jansen. 'Sorry, Jess. Must take this.' I don't need to hear Jess's sigh to feel it as I hang up.

'Hello assistant commissioner.'

There are no formalities from Jansen. 'I went back to the pathologist to raise the point you made, to double-check whether or not someone with so much ket in their system would have been capable of hanging themselves. He confirmed it depends on the scale of her habitual use, her tolerance of the drug. His assumption is that Marilyn's system had adapted to regular, heavy intake.'

For a few seconds I say nothing. I am taking this in. I don't understand how she could disguise such recreational drug excesses from her work colleagues, from me.

'Are you still there, Gil?'

'Yeah. I was processing. And I need to apologise. I shouldn't have put you to that trouble. I've been reflecting on what you've been saying and I no longer doubt she committed suicide.'

I don't explain about the note in the book. It's my most important physical connection to Marilyn, and the idea of passing it to Kim, of it vanishing forever into some warehouse of forgotten evidence, is too troubling.

'It's my job to cover all angles.' I think I hear relief in her voice at my capitulation. 'Can I just follow up on one thing, though?' she asks. 'Last time we spoke, you said you were unaware she still had such a serious drug habit.'

I wince. 'Yes. That's true.' It's painful being reminded of what Marilyn hid from me.

'Even so, I don't suppose you have any clue where she sourced her Class A substances?'

'Why would that matter?'

'In case you hadn't noticed, drug dealing is still a serious criminal offence. I can't ignore it.'

I do have an idea, actually: Elliott, via Raoul. But I'm not going to mention them. Elliott would deny it, and there'd be no proof, just a world of recriminations and pain for me.

'I accept she killed herself. But I don't understand why. You haven't found anything that helps explain it, have you?'

'The drug abuse could be part of it. But we'll keep looking. It would probably help if you and I could meet. I'd love to understand more about her.'

So would I.

'Sure.'

'Have you got your diary there?'

A diary. I suddenly recall Marilyn's routine, a nightly ritual. Before going to sleep, even after sex, she'd scribble down what was in her head, the events of the day. It would take five minutes, maximum. She'd never discuss what she wrote, never show me. It was just a thing, like brushing her teeth.

'Just out of curiosity,' I say casually, 'did you find anything like a diary?'

'I'll ask.'

We make a date to meet and Kim rings off, leaving me agitated. I can't believe I forgot about the diaries. I don't trust the police and Kim not to bury them. If they haven't found them, I need to. I telephone Jess.

'You're kidding me, Gil. We're not breaking into Marilyn's flat.'

'I have a key.'

'The police have explicitly told us to keep out. We'd be committing an offence.'

'I'm not asking you to come with me. I'll do it after the news tonight. I'll be in and out in ten minutes, and I'll report back in the morning.'

*

Once I've done the *Ten*, I walk up Wood Lane towards Shepherd's Bush Green, till I flag down a black cab. I tell myself I am well within my rights to enter Marilyn's home. She gave me a key. She would have expected me to find out what happened. Even so, I'd rather no one saw me go in, and I ask to be dropped thirty yards from the house.

My wariness is justified. As I walk up the opposite side of the street, I spot someone loitering to the right of the entrance. That's unsettling. Why would Jansen leave an officer on duty here, so long after Marilyn's death, and when she's already decided it's suicide? The best course may be to cut my losses and go home.

Before I can make up my mind, the figure spies me and hurries across the road. Jess.

'I wasn't expecting you,' I whisper, trying to get my heart rate under control.

'That's because you are spectacularly thick. What in our history led you to think I would let you do something so idiotic on your own?'

173

I take out the keys, we go in the front door and climb three flights to the top floor. There's still police tape across Marilyn's door, but it's starting to droop and peel away.

'We shouldn't be here,' Jess says, for form's sake. She knows I'm going to ignore her.

'You're right.' I put the key in the lock, break the tape and we enter.

The moment I step inside, a digital beeping sounds from a box on the wall, broadcasting our transgression. *Shit.* I forgot about the alarm. The police must have found an electronic fob and turned it on. I run to the keypad on the left of the corridor and frantically try to remember the back-up code, before the beeps become a wailing siren.

'This could be over quickly,' says Jess.

Numbers suggest themselves. Marilyn's birthday? *No.* My birthday? The beeps seem to get more urgent, mocking me for my egotism. What's Johnny Todd's birthday, for fuck's sake? *How many attempts do I get before it locks me out?*

I need to think. What would be a significant number sequence for Marilyn? Something clicks in my head, as the beeping increases in volume, a warning of the deafening blast to come. If this fails, we're toast. *Zero one zero five nine seven.*

The beeping stops. I can breathe. *I did know you, Marilyn. A bit.*

'You remembered,' says Jess.

'More deduction. The date of the 1997 general election.'

'Todd's apotheosis.'

'Marilyn's.'

We move into the flat. 'Don't turn on any lights till I've drawn the curtains,' Jess says, whispering even though there's no one to hear. 'And I don't think we should put the lights on.' She takes two small torches with powerful beams from her coat pocket. 'Here.'

I give her an admiring look. 'You've done this before.'

I walk to the floor-to-ceiling windows in the main reception room that give on to a small balcony, with its black wrought-iron balustrade. As I cross the room, I try to keep my eyes on the wooden parquet floor, away from the steel beam that spans the mansard. They've removed the rope. I press hard on my right earlobe, to exorcise the image. *Kill me now, kill me now, kill me now.*

I fumble for the drawstring, pull and close the heavy damask curtains. The beam hides in the shadows.

'Let's start in the bedroom,' I say.

It is a mess, more or less as Marilyn left it. Our torchbeams move over unwashed coffee mugs, wine glasses stained red at the bottom by dregs, knickers and bras all over the floor. Her habitual chaos. This is even more upsetting than I expected. The growl of anxiety in my head is becoming louder. On the desk, there is a picture of Marilyn. She's about five years old, standing proudly in front of a sandcastle, bolt upright with a spade sloped across her shoulder, like a soldier, beaming. Mum and Dad are crouched next to her. Untroubled happiness. No clue to the darkness that awaits.

I open the desk drawer. Random bank statements. Nothing much else. I shove them in my rucksack, just in case. I check that Jess isn't looking in my direction and surreptitiously add the framed photo.

'Have you found anything?' I ask.

Jess is on her hands and knees, at the bottom of a cupboard, torch held in her mouth. She's gingerly removing cuddly toys and teddy bears, old, patched and loved too much. 'Your girl-friend was more sentimental than she let on,' says Jess.

'I'm as surprised as you.'

Jess pulls out a heavy-duty plastic shopping bag from the back of the cupboard. Harvey Nichols.

'This looks promising.'

It contains maybe half a dozen cloth-bound, greeny-brown Letts diaries. Two pages per week. The kind many of us were given by optimistic parents when we were eleven or twelve, and maybe wrote in for a couple of weeks or months before getting bored and losing them. There are also Filofax diary pages, in brown paper envelopes with a year written on the front. Jess spreads them on the bed. They go all the way back to Marilyn's early teens, and she's written on every page.

There is a problem, however.

'They're in code,' Jess says. 'Some kind of runics.'

'What?'

'It's what swotty kids used to do. Didn't you?'

'I wasn't the *Swallows and Amazons* type.'

We rummage through the papers, looking for the most recent set of Filofax diary pages. They are missing.

'Where do you think 2007 might be?' Jess asks. 'You checked the desk, didn't you?'

A memory is triggered. I feel under the mattress on Marilyn's side, and sure enough a brown leather Filofax is there. I stuff it in my rucksack.

As I do, Jess freezes and puts two fingers to her lips.

'There's someone outside the flat,' she whispers.

'I didn't hear anything.'

Jess clenches her fists as someone turns a key in the latch. *Fuck.* Who else would have a key? No one we should meet.

The front door opens. The alarm is off. Will that tell the visitors we're here? What if they noticed the tape was torn?

I hear heavy footsteps in the hallway. Maybe there are two people. There's no way out. I scoop up the diaries and papers from the bed and stuff them in the Harvey Nicks bag. I gesture at Jess to follow. Stepping as quietly as possible, we return to the living room. The light has been switched on in the hall. Muffled men's voices are conferring by the front door. I lead Jess

176

to the window. We step behind the curtains. I delicately turn the key and open the glass door. We step onto the balcony. The curtains fall shut behind us, just as the living room door opens. Did they see the curtains twitch?

'This is mad,' Jess hisses. It's a bitingly cold early October night, and her breath comes out in puffs of mist. 'I can't believe I've let you do this to me again.'

Through the glass, there's the muffled sound of furniture being lifted and drawers emptied. They are ransacking. This is not the careful systematic work of the Met.

What if they look behind the curtains? The balcony is tiny, only about two feet deep. Looking down, I feel queasy. A fall from here, onto the pointed tops of the railings below, would be messy.

Out here, on this ledge, hiding from intruders in her flat, I suddenly wonder what kind of physical threats had been made to Marilyn, whether she feared she would be killed. I'm not going to articulate that. Jess won't want to hear it. But there is something I can say. 'What is the big secret they want to find?' I whisper. Jess shrugs and puts her finger to her lips.

The cold has gone deep into my bones. Suddenly it's quiet. We wait ten minutes. Still no sound. A few moments later, I hear the building's front door open. Peering over the balcony, I see a man walk down the steps. A second follows. They're wearing puffer jackets, and baseball caps shield their faces.

I recoil, flattening myself against the window in case they look up. They don't. We wait until they've sauntered down to the end of the road, then I open the glass door and peer through the curtains into the sitting room. No one.

'They've gone,' I whisper to Jess.

We creep out through the flat as quietly as we can and walk down the stairs. I'm clutching the Harvey Nicks bag to my chest, terrified that it'll split. After everything I've gone through, I'm not going to lose her testimony.

As soon as we get to the downstairs hallway, we realise our error. There weren't two of them: there were three. A man with long blond hair in a ponytail, hazel eyes, wearing a blue Adidas tracksuit, is waiting by the front door; and the look he gives implies he's been expecting us.

'Hello, you two. Do you mind if I look in your bag?'

He walks towards us. Jess looks at me. 'You should probably give it to him,' she says.

His guard is down. He turns towards me, so fixed on the bag that he doesn't notice Jess reaching into her pocket. Her hand comes out holding a can of Mace. An acrid mist spews into his face, and when he's screaming about his eyes she walks straight up to him and knees him in his testicles.

He doubles over. There are lots of things I need to ask Jess, but now is not the time. Before he can recover, we bolt.

I glance back. The two men in puffers have seen us and are running back up the street. We'll never outpace them. I hear a familiar and comforting rumble. It's a black cab coming towards us with the yellow light on. I run into the middle of the road, to eliminate any risk he won't see us. He stops.

'All right, all right,' the cabbie says. 'Where's the fire?'

I give Jess's address, and he unlocks the back door.

When we're settled on the bench, I look back. I see a huddle of three men outside the house, but they're making no effort to follow. The blond man still looks in some discomfort.

The cab turns the corner and they're lost from view.

'Where did that come from?' I ask Jess, pointing to the Mace can she's still clutching.

'Kilburn Community Centre self-defence classes. I knew it would come in handy one day. We learned all sorts of throws but the teacher had a simple golden rule. "If in doubt, kick him in the nuts."'

For five minutes, we sit without talking as the taxi drives along the edge of Hyde Park to Marble Arch.

178

'You OK?' I ask eventually.

'Yup. You?'

'Not sure.'

She puts the Mace back in her coat pocket. 'Who were they?'

I've been wondering the same thing. 'They weren't random burglars. Maybe private contractors?' What is euphemistically termed corporate security has become a growth industry in the last five years, thanks to Johnny Todd's policy of turning London into the billionaire's tax haven of choice, the hot-money capital of the world. Former special forces operatives and spooks are making serious cash by offering bespoke protection and investigation, with the limiting factor on the offered services being the amount of money the client can offer, rather than the criminal law.

'Who would have employed them?' I ask.

'Presumably whoever you've pissed off most.'

But who would that be? Jackson? Muller? Elliott? Absurd suggestions surely. They're pillars of the City. 'I've no idea.'

'But they seemed to know about the diaries.'

'Maybe. I agree they expected us. So they would want to take anything we'd removed from the flat.'

For a second I allow myself to feel the danger we've just outrun. Jess reaches for my hand and covers it with hers. I turn and mouth 'Thank you,' and we revert again to our own thoughts.

'Shall we have a look at the Filofax?' she asks.

I take it out of the rucksack. A quick flick through shows every page is in the same bloody code.

'It's daunting, the sheer number of pages we have to translate,' I say, as the Edgware Road's Middle Eastern supermarkets and cafes morph into the Kilburn Road's grittier pubs and Turkish kebab takeaways. 'Even if we knew how to crack it.'

'I've got an idea about that.' Jess takes out her phone. It's the new Nokia that has a built-in camera. 'Give me the Filofax.'

She positions it on her knee and takes a picture. She then sends it to someone as an MMS.

'That's the first time I've ever seen the point of a camera on a phone,' I say. 'Who are you texting it to?'

'Bloke called Tim. Works in IT at the *FC*. Geek. Plays Dungeons and Dragons every weekend. Loves codes and codebreaking.'

'Will he be awake now?'

Her phone buzzes. 'There's your answer.' She presses the button and puts Tim on loudspeaker.

'It's a very basic cipher,' he says. 'An old one. Pigpen. Incomprehensible, without the simple rules.'

'It doesn't look simple,' I say, trying to make sense of'

⊐⌐⌐⌐⌐⌐⌐

'The letters are placed in a noughts and crosses grid, with dots next to letters. Each letter is represented by its frame. What you sent me says "Marylin's Diary".'

I just about get it. Marilyn had a computer brain that allowed her to write it fluently.

'Thanks, Tim,' Jess says. 'I owe you.' She disconnects. 'So now all we have to do is take a week off work to translate them.'

'A week?'

'Maybe not that much. But it's a chore.'

'OK.' I've got an idea. 'Do you think it's too late to ring a seventeen-year-old boy?'

She gives me a disbelieving look. 'Have you really forgotten what it's like to be a teenager?'

I dial Luke, Clare's son, my nephew, and explain what I want him to do.

'I'm revising for mocks, but yeah, sounds good.'

'I'll give you a tenner a diary.'

'Thanks, Uncs!'

'Don't thank me till you see the code. It's not easy.'

'It'll be a doddle.'

We pull up outside Jess's house. 'You'd better come in,' she says. 'Lots to discuss.'

Until she invited me, I hadn't realised how desperate I was not to be alone. 'You sure? Won't you need to be up early to get Amy to school?'

'I'm way too wired to sleep.'

We go into the kitchen where Jess's mum, Joyce, is waiting up with a crossword. She's been babysitting while her daughter was out burgling. I feel a stab of guilt at dragging Jess into my mayhem. Again.

'You know Gil, don't you Mum?' says Jess.

Joyce gives me a broad, genuine smile. 'Lovely to see you. Though of course, I see you all the time on the news. Have you two been to some boring business dinner tonight?'

'It wasn't that boring,' I say.

Joyce turns to Jess. 'I'm afraid Amy's only recently got off to sleep. Sorry, darling, but she insisted on teaching me stud poker.'

Jess calls a cab for her mum and shoos me into the sitting room. 'I'll bring you a glass of wine.'

I collapse into the sofa. There's no point looking at the pigpen diaries, so I spread out the bank statements from Marilyn's desk. Lots of payments to Tesco, salary received from the Bank of England, cash withdrawals of £120 every time. After a few minutes, I hear the beep of the cab outside, the sound of the front door, and then Jess comes in with two glasses of red.

'Chianti. Gallo Nero. Is that OK?'

I take a sip. 'Delicious, thanks.'

Jess sits at the other end of the sofa, feet tucked under her and the papers between us.

'Do you think Marilyn was as OCD as me?' I ask.

'Not by the look of her bedroom.'

'It's just the weirdness of only ever taking out a hundred and twenty pounds in cash. Every single time. It's the sort of superstitious thing I do.'

I continue messed running one eye down the columns of figures, till I hit one that stands out.

I hand the paper to Jess. In late August there was a deposit of $5.2 million from a Cayman Island account.

'Blimey. You said her family is wealthy. Could it be an inheritance?'

'From the Caymans? Where pretty much every hedge fund and private equity fund is registered.'

Jess says what we're both thinking. 'Did Jackson bribe her to support his bid for NewGate?'

I down a large mouthful of the wine. It tastes of smoke and earth: simple, basic pleasures. 'We should talk to the police about this, shouldn't we?' I say.

Jess gives me a pitying look. 'I can see the headline in the *Globe* after you're charged with breaking-and-entering. "Beeb burgles Bank of England babe".'

I laugh. 'You're at the wrong paper.' For the first time in I don't know how long, I start to relax. Jess pours me another glass of wine, and the stresses of the night dissolve. Soon my eyelids are getting heavy.

'Let's get some sleep,' Jess says. 'The towels you used should still be in the bathroom.'

I ought to protest, call a cab and go back to my place. I don't.

I check my diary just to make sure I've got time in the morning to go home and put on a clean suit. Looking at my schedule, I burst out laughing, maniacally.

'You OK?' says Jess.

'Yeah. It's just that most of tomorrow I'm with a crowd who think of me as the embodiment of evil.'

'Bankers?'

'Bankers.'

'Ah. Hug?'

She wraps herself around me. Not everything is shit.

Chapter 14

Honestly I'm not too bothered whether people warm to me. If people dislike me for things that I consciously meant, then that's their problem. I can usually detect when people are wary of me, and sometimes I try to work out what's going on. Often I've got better things to do. Today I know I'm going to be surrounded by men who wish I didn't exist. But a contract's a contract, and the show must go on.

I was booked to chair the annual conference of UK Finance, the trade organisation for banks, insurers, fund managers and other City firms, *before* I became notorious for blowing the whistle on NewGate. Poor Moira Squires, the director general, regrets offering me the gig. She said as much in the briefing call a few days ago. But it would have been embarrassing for both of us to replace me, in these fraught circumstances. So here I am on a raised platform at the front of the hall in Chiswell Street's Old Brewery, facing a couple of hundred hostile bankers, jaws tight, wide-eyed gazes on me. Am I intimidated? Do I give a fuck? Not really.

The Old Brewery is what its name suggests, a Victorian ale factory repurposed as a conference centre on the Barbican's east side in the City of London. I am here to moderate a discussion with Sir Stan Blackwell, boss of Peking and Taiwan Banking Group. PTBG is one of the world's biggest banks, created in the mid-nineteenth century by intrepid Scots who were the backbone of the East India Company and the Indian Civil Service. Its headquarters are in Edinburgh, and it is fiercely proud of not being part of the City of London. Sir Stan, its lantern-jawed chief executive, is a working-class Glaswegian who started at sixteen as a bank messenger, and has been sucking up and punching down ever since.

He's just wrapping up his speech about how the problems at NewGate are a blip, an exception to the generally sound state of the banking industry, and why technological change means banks have never been stronger and sounder. While I listen, I'm calibrating what to say when he's finished. Should I go in guns blazing, stating for the record that he's a wanker, and a dangerous one at that, in denial about the crisis engulfing his industry? Or do I humour him, because we're both British after all and also because presumably no one in this room cares what I think?

Blackwell is waxing lyrical about how collateralised debt obligations and credit default swaps have allowed credit risk to be dispersed safely to investors all over the world, thus making the banks themselves much less vulnerable to losses when borrowers struggle to repay. *It's the big lie.* Should I say that out loud?

'When credit risks are shared with other investors – fund managers, insurers, hedge funds – the banking system is strengthened. What we are seeing in markets right now is the kind of temporary disruption and malfunctioning you often witness during important industrial revolutions. It will settle down, just as soon as these financial innovations are more widely understood.'

I am incredulous. Scanning the room, I see Chris Ravel sitting three rows back. He's the top of the food chain, the predator, surveying the complacent lambs ripe for the slaughter. Ravel latches on to my gaze, and feigns a theatrical yawn. I don't want to conspire with him, but the urge to wink is almost irresistible.

Blackwell is wrapping up. 'These are challenging times for our industry. But I am confident we will emerge stronger, and will continue to be the strong and stable foundation of our economies.'

Polite applause. I stand up, shake Blackwell's hand and guide him to a white chrome and leather armchair next to mine on the stage.

'Thank you for that enlightening and fascinating talk, Sir Stanley.' My sarcasm is lost on this crowd. I turn to the audience. 'Who wants to be first with a question?'

Hands go up. I point to a dark-haired man in the middle of the room. An usher brings a wireless microphone, and he stands. This won't be dull. It's Maurice 'Mo' Levine. He's a brash billionaire, who made his fortune by buying businesses that were temporarily undervalued on the stock market when they fell out of favour. Which no doubt is why he is now eyeing the banking sector.

'Sir Stanley. Very interesting presentation. But if you'll indulge me, you have a trillion-dollar balance sheet, is that right, sir?'

Blackwell nods.

'Well, I have your latest report and accounts here with me, and it shows balance sheet footings of one point six seven trillion. In other words, sir, your bank is roughly the same size as the British economy.'

'Some would say it's a mistake to compare a stock, the debt we hold, with a flow, like GDP,' Blackwell replies. He gives a condescending smile. 'But, yes, we *are* a big bank.'

Oh my God. Blackwell has just made the schoolboy mistake of patronising Levine. This will be interesting.

'Thank you, Sir Stanley, for that tutorial.' I look at Sir Stan, who seems in that instant to have become older and greyer. 'Now, there are three hundred and twenty-five pages in your report and accounts. That's a lot of pages, and a lot of numbers, and I've been through every one of them. Nowhere can I find your exposure to US subprime. In view of what we know about

187

losses in that basket case of a market, it is the only number of relevance to your owners. Would you care to enlighten us now and share with us how much subprime is on your books?'

There's a pregnant pause. A hush in the room. Blackwell grinds his teeth.

'Mr Levine,' he begins, 'we are fastidious in following stock exchange and SEC disclosure rules. If we had a material problem with subprime, you can be assured we would have disclosed it.'

Levine blows a raspberry that everyone can hear. Should I follow up? Of course I can't resist. I look hard into Blackwell's grey eyes.

'If I am correct in understanding your answer to Mr Levine, you are not saying you have no exposure to subprime. I think you are saying that you have eliminated all or most of the risks by holding it either in the form of collateralised debt obligations, or getting it insured?'

Blackwell smiles, mistaking my intervention for support. 'Exactly so.'

'But what if the losses on subprime turn out to be so great that they overwhelm all your protection strategies? What if none of the subprime loans are serviced by borrowers, and insurers go bust – and even the CDOs with first dibs on interest payments get nothing? What would be your exposure in those circumstances?'

Even though Levine no longer has the mic, I hear him say, 'That is the question.' Blackwell twitches the left side of his mouth.

'We could all have fun playing "what if?" games,' he barks. 'But that is not the world I see. It's no secret that we hold assets fashioned out of subprime. But we and our auditors have meticulously examined those assets and see no reason to make provisions for current or future losses. Those assets are worth a hundred cents on the dollar.'

Levine snorts disbelievingly. I say nothing. Another hand goes up. This time it's a bespectacled man I don't recognise.

'Could you say your name and organisation, just for the record?' I say.

'Peter Brown. Independent financial advisor. This is actually a question for you, Mr Peck. I'd like to know why you hate your country and how you have the impertinence to show your face here today. Your story about NewGate was scaremongering, pure and simple. There is nothing wrong with that bank except a temporary liquidity hiccup, which has happened to all banks throughout history. Your sensationalist reporting is undermining Britain's most successful industry and threatening to drive Britain into a recession. You and your lefty friends at the BBC should be ashamed of yourselves.'

There is silence in the room for half a second, and then malicious applause from perhaps half the audience. The rest – including Sir Stan – shoe-gaze.

I shoot a glance at Moira Squires, UK Finance's boss, at the side of the stage. Her eyes implore me not to throw petrol.

'This is Sir Stan's presentation, not mine. But Sir Stan, if you will permit me, I would like to say just one simple thing. NewGate, seemingly with the permission of regulators, thought it was prudent to increase its borrowing and lending by twenty per cent every year, while reducing the amount of cash and capital it held for a rainy day. NewGate wasn't alone. Many of you in this audience have done pretty much the same. I under-stand why. As a pure matter of mathematical logic, the less low-yielding cash and capital you hold, the more profitable you look, in the short term – which does wonders for your share price and the value of your share options.

'You were convinced you would never lose proper money on your lending, thanks to all that financial innovation Sir Stan has been waxing lyrical about, so it would have been insane to hold surplus capital. And as for cash, depositors were never going to fear it was safer under the mattress than with you; they were never going to ask for it back. So why would you want to hold

189

more cash and capital than the bare minimum? Only a moron would. Or a perfect bleeding-heart lefty.

'It's as though you think capitalism has only been around for fifteen years, that the booms and busts of the past five hundred years are fairy stories. Either that, or you were seduced by the most dangerous axiom ever formulated: "This time it will be different."

'I have news for you. It's never different. There have always been rainy days. And the banks that survive the storms are those with sandbags and pumps, those with cash and capital. There is a storm coming. An almighty one. The worst we've ever lived through. I look around this room and I don't even see an umbrella.'

I think about leaving it there, but what the hell. 'Mr Brown, why do you believe NewGate hadn't failed as a business when it asked for emergency help from taxpayers, from the Bank of England? What would you think if Marks and Spencer asked taxpayers for a bailout? Would you think that was OK? And, by the way, NewGate's chief executive just trousered four point eight million in pay and bonuses, for driving his bank to the cliff edge. That's OK, is it? Really?'

The silence in the room reminds me of when my primary school teacher, Mrs Needham, asked us to be quiet so we could hear a pin drop. Mr Brown won't make eye contact. Moira has gone bright red. I don't think there is a clause in my contract specifying I mustn't tell the truth, so presumably I'll still be paid.

A single slow handclap begins. Levine is back on his feet. And a naive or perhaps anarchist usher hands him the mic back.

'You may not like what Mr Peck just said, but do any of us seriously believe he is wrong?' There are shouts of 'Shame' and 'Sit down.' 'I will sit down in a moment. But you ought to know that the markets have already reacted to Sir Stan's reckless subprime denialism. His refusal to quantify the exposure has seen PTBG's share price fall ten per cent in the last fifteen minutes. His shareholders are close to ten billion pounds poorer as a result of a smug, self-satisfied speech. Draw your own conclusions.'

I am trying to work out what on earth the protocol is now. Blackwell, still on stage, has pulled out his own BlackBerry and is gawping at it, presumably to assess the seriousness of the rout in his shares. Then at the back of the auditorium, though for a moment I can't see her, a woman starts speaking. Her clipped, staccato voice reminds me of the posh mums of friends who, when I went to their houses as a child, made me feel like an interloper. Their 'Where exactly does *your* family come from?' implied 'You're not one of us.'

'Mr Peck. What we are living through in the City is the equivalent of war.' I can see she is wearing a black fine-knit Chanel suit with brass buttons, and her hair is in a severe bun. 'Usually in wartime journalists like yourself show responsibility, so as not to create unnecessary panic. In my view, the government needs to issue a D-notice to you and the BBC, to shut you down.'

D-notices again. *Flip.* At this there is enthusiastic applause. I mutter something about the importance of free speech, while Moira is waving at me, pointing at her watch, and mouthing 'Wind up.' I face the room.

'My job is to give British people and British businesses the information they need to make important decisions about their lives. Inevitably, given the stresses and challenges you face, you won't like some of what I have to say. That's how it is. Thank you all for coming this morning. The presentations have been thought-provoking. I understand a buffet lunch is being served in the room next door.'

I hastily leave the stage. I want to apologise to Moira, not because I actually feel sorry but because I've known her for years. She pre-empts me. 'Bloody hell. Did you have to make it all about you?'

'Oh Christ. Did I?'

191

'You did. For goodness …' She stops in her tracks, because she can see the journalists in the audience have made a circle around Sir Stan. He's trapped.

'Look at what you've done.' She points at the melee. Before I can insist it's not my fault, she rushes over to rescue him.

'Into the valley of death rode the six hundred,' I whisper.

'What was that?' shouts Moira.

'Nothing.'

I walk slowly towards the exit and take out the BlackBerry, which I had on silent while on stage. There are stacks of unread messages, the most recent from Jess.

You wanted to know which bank Chris Ravel would target next? PTBG

Ravel? I remember the smirk on his face when I saw him in the audience. I thought he was just laughing at Blackwell's naivete: in fact, it must have been the smile of a man who was about to make tens of millions of pounds from Blackwell's self-harm.

I survey the room. Everyone's filing slowly out, chatting in small groups or scrolling their BlackBerries. No Ravel.

Moira has retrieved Blackwell. I hurry to him. He cannot hide his discomfort. 'Back for more?' He tries in vain to make a joke.

'You did well, in difficult circumstances,' I lie.

I'm sure he doesn't believe me, but he'll clutch at any lifeline. 'Thanks. Your colleagues in the press were less understanding.'

'Everyone's on edge,' I say. 'Just so you know, the word is that Chris Ravel has gone massively short of PTBG, that he's betting your price will crash.'

No more jocularity. He looks shocked. 'Chris is an old client, a friend of the bank. He wouldn't be doing anything to undermine confidence in us.'

'That's not what I'm hearing.' Admittedly, only one message from Jess, but she never takes flyers.

'Ravel knows not to shit where he eats.'

'What do you mean?'

Blackwell lowers his voice. 'Off the record?'

'Of course.'

He gathers his thoughts. 'We've been prime broker to Lulworth since the beginning. Ravel needs our services, and our credit. As his prime broker, I know his positions. Yes, he's betting large that the banking sector is in trouble. He is not betting against us.'

What the fucking fuck? If Blackwell does know Lulworth's stock positions, he's driven a bulldozer through the so-called Chinese wall, the rule to protect client confidentiality and minimise conflicts of interest. I'm pretty sure that's against the law. I file the transgression for future reference and let it pass, for now. But I struggle to believe that since PTBG's shares are so obviously a one-way bet down, Ravel would give up the opportunity to make a bundle by shorting them. Ravel believes in historic determinism, money and the tragedy of the Palestinians, but loyalty to friends has always been an alien concept.

Before I can probe more, PTBG's director of comms catches his boss's eye and waves at him that they have to leave. 'Got to skedaddle,' Blackwell says.

Moira is having a heated discussion about what's reportable from the conference with the City editor of the *Telegraph*. I wave at her and head for the exit. In the large entrance hall, there's a huddle of investment bankers looking grave. A woman I know who specialises in EU banks for Schon is crying. I dismiss the idea that they've taken to heart anything I've said. A man next to her says something about having seen Robin only last night. Or at least that's what it sounds like.

I am about to inveigle my way in when I notice the large art deco wooden clock on the wall above them.

Shit. I'm meeting Munis for lunch in Mayfair – fifteen minutes ago. I run across the courtyard to the wide-arched exit. Thank God there's a cab on the other side of Chiswell Street: the driver sees me wave and pulls over. I step off the kerb to reach him.

From the corner of my eye, I catch a blur of motion hurtling towards me. A racing bike streaks out of nowhere the wrong way down the street. I lurch backwards, a panicked attempt to get out of the way. Catching my heel on the kerb, I land flat on my bottom as he skids to avoid me and stops.

'Watch where you're going, you moron,' says the rider, a messenger, in a balaclava and skin-tight Lycra. He hauls me to my feet. I want to shout at him that he's the moron, but the fall knocked the breath out of me.

There's something about him that rings a bell, but he isn't hanging around for me to find out what. 'See ya, sucker!' he spits, then jumps back on his bike and speeds off.

I'm embarrassed, a bit bruised on my bottom, but in one piece.

The cab waited. The driver rolls down the window and shouts, 'You still want me?' I give a thumbs up and gingerly walk towards him, checking the traffic three times. Once I'm safely on the leather bench in the back of the cab, I reach for the bat phone.

It's not there. Neither of the BlackBerries is where they should be. I frantically pat all my pockets. Nothing.

'Just give me a minute,' I tell the driver. I jump out and run back to the kerbside where I fell over. No trace, and no drain or grate that the phones could have fallen through.

I am a sucker. He mugged me.

Chapter 15

LOSING THE PHONES IS ALMOST my worst nightmare. I am powerless without them. The weirdness of the mugging is sinking in. The cyclist didn't take my wallet. Is the resale value of a brace of reprogrammed BlackBerries worth the hit and run?

Everything happened so fast. It felt like an accident. When I noticed my phones had gone, I assumed it was a random mugging. But was it? I screw up my eyes and try to recall any tell-tale detail about the rider. Did I see the end of a blond ponytail poking from his balaclava? The same as the thug's in Marilyn's hallway? Is it my imagination? I have to talk it through with Jess. I fumble for my phone, before I think *Oh yes.*

'You all right, mate?' The cabbie has been studying me in his rear-view mirror.

'Bit bruised.'

'You took a nasty knock.'

I become aware my right elbow is achy, where it hit the kerb. And the palm of my hand is grazed.

'The arsehole took my phones,' I say.

'You should call the police. Not that they'll do anything.'

He drives me to Scott's in Mount Street, where I'm due to meet the shadow chancellor Patrick Munis for lunch. Trevor, the front of house manager, is at the desk, greeting customers with his reassuring, silken understatement. I've known him for almost twenty years. We've risen through the ranks in lockstep. I pour out my heart about the cycle-by robbing.

'Is there anything we can do to help?'

'Could I use your phone?'

He leads me to a private office, where I explain my disaster to BBC tech support. The technician says they will block the numbers, and if I go to their office this afternoon, they'll lend me a bog-standard Nokia for a few days till the new phones arrive.

'How long will it take?'

'Depends if our suppliers have them in stock. Could be a week.'

A week? How will I cope? The idea of all those messages from contacts being sent into a black hole is terrifying. I am Major Tom, drifting aimlessly in space, trying hopelessly to connect to Ground Control.

'Is there nothing you can do to speed up the procurement?' I hear the pleading in my voice. I'm humiliating myself. 'They're the most important tools of my trade.'

I hear a sigh of pity, or maybe exasperation. 'We'll do what we can, Gil.'

By the time I'm finished, Munis has been at the table for fifteen minutes. I launch into frantic apologies and explanations even before I sit down.

'Think nothing of it,' he says. Munis – whose fleshy face and full lips betoken a voracious appetite for booze, food and power – sees that I've clocked the bottle of Puligny-Montrachet beading condensation on the table. 'I hope you don't mind, but I took the liberty.'

I do mind. He's ordered a bottle that on its own will bust the Beeb's expenses limit. Goodness knows how I'll explain it to Janice, after I submit the bill and she rejects it. But I try not to let my consternation show. 'I hope it's good. And since the corporation is entertaining you, perhaps you'll think twice next time before giving a cheap quote to the *Daily Mail* about our supposedly extravagant use of licence-payers' cash.'

Munis grins, and pushes the bridge of his rectangular tortoise-shell spectacles up the bridge of his nose. 'Excellent point well made, if I may say so. And can I also say how appreciative I am to you and the corporation for the privilege of dining in Scott's. Best Dover sole in London, by a country mile.'

It's certainly the most expensive. The owner, Richard Caring, made a fortune supplying cheap-and-cheerful schmutter to the billionaire owner of BHS and Topshop, Philip Green. Caring spotted the potential of outsourcing manufacturing to the low-wage Far East, long before management consultants put the 'global supply chain' label on the decimation of manufacturing from Bradford to Detroit. And then he bought and created some of the most expensive restaurants in London with the proceeds. Scott's is a microcosm of globalised Britain: the prices of the Cornish line-caught turbot and Breton langoustine are a force field that keeps out the jobless ex-factory workers.

The waiter hovers. I'm struggling to play the cheerful host. I can't stifle my anxiety about the stolen BlackBerries, and I've become aware that my coccyx is sore. Happily, Munis is too self-obsessed to notice.

'What are you having, Patrick?'

'So many treats, but I'll stick to the old favourites. Dressed crab, and a grilled Dover sole, on the bone, with a side order of wilted spinach. Yum yum.'

I'm already busting the expenses budget, so no point in holding back. I order the heritage beetroots, followed by grilled turbot and green beans in olive oil and garlic. The waiter tries to fill my glass with what I am sure is exquisite white Burgundy. I cover the top of the glass with my hand and decline.

'You're not drinking?'

'Not today.'

'If I'd known I'd be drinking alone, I wouldn't have ordered a bottle,' Munis insists.

'You'll manage.'

Munis's tolerance of alcohol is legendary. When the Tory leader Mrs Barnsbury was abroad, he notoriously chaired a three-hour shadow cabinet committee having consumed two and a half bottles of claret. No one would have known, except the shadow home secretary was at the same lunch. I was at a dinner with him once during which he delivered a seamless thirty-minute exposition of the neo-conservative mission to roll back the frontiers of Islamism, punctuating each paragraph with a gulp of red, and then collapsed unconscious only after he left the building. In all the years I've known him, Munis when drinking is like the frog in water that's gently being heated: everything is fine, until it isn't.

He takes a huge swig and sighs contentedly. 'Does it never frustrate you that your reports move markets and make other people wealthy, not you?'

It's a question I have asked myself. 'Not really. I chose long ago to be the messenger, the reporter. If people thought that I was profiting from what I was telling them, they wouldn't trust me, would they?'

'Maybe not. So what's it about for you, if not the money?'

That's not an easy question. Munis has always liked discomfiting me.

'That's hard to answer without seeming like a prat.'

'We're friends. We've known each other for years.'

Are we friends? Yes, I've known Munis since university. But you're supposed to trust your friends, aren't you, and I've never trusted him. Happily, he's riffing and doesn't wait for me to respond.

'There's no need for you to say,' he says. 'I know the answer. You're addicted to power. You and I are the same. In fact you probably have more power than most members of the government.

The difference is no one holds you to account. You can do what you like, with impunity.'

My hand moves to take a wedge of warm baguette, and then I think better of it.

'That's bollocks, Patrick. Journalists like me have influence. Of course we do. But that's not the same thing as the power to raise taxes, or criminalise anti-social behaviour or go to war. My job is to give people the information they need to live their lives and also to decide whether to elect you lot or the other lot. We might have an impact on who has the power and what they do with it. But in the end the buck doesn't stop with us.'

'As I said, you have power without responsibility. It's a drug. You are high on the noise you make. That's why you don't care about making proper money.'

He beams and swallows another twenty pounds' worth of Burgundy. I hope to God this isn't a two-bottle lunch.

'Do you?' I ask.

'Do I what?'

'Care about making proper money?'

He stuffs a wodge of bread in his gob and chews. 'I didn't used to. But so many of our friends, who went into the City, they're now so wealthy. They live in a different world.'

'So do you regret becoming an MP?'

'I wouldn't put it as strongly as that. But when I look at Chris Ravel, who has so much money, and at the incredible power that goes with being so rich, I do wonder whether I made a mistake.'

Ravel. Again.

'Surely the power you care about is meaningless to Chris. He can live anywhere in the world he chooses, so what happens in any particular country, such as the UK, is irrelevant to him. Surely all he cares about is making sure his assets are registered in a tax haven.'

'I think that's to misunderstand Chris. He's always had a purpose. The money is the means to an end.'

The starters have arrived; Munis takes a large mouthful of crab meat but keeps talking. 'Billionaires like him think they know everything. They like to tell us what to do – and we indulge them, because we're seduced by the proximity to all that wealth. We go to Chris's dinners, to his parties, we give him the opportunity to bend the ear of prime ministers and chancellors. People equate his unconscionable amount of money with wisdom. A billion pounds shouldn't give added weight to someone's views, but it does.'

That is true. Both parties, Tory and Labour, pursue the billionaires for funding. And in return the billionaires assume they've bought the MPs.

'Aren't you overglamorising Chris?'

'I've known him forever. He is terrifyingly clever, usually several steps ahead of the rest of us. Did you know I was his best man?'

I shake my head. 'Obviously I came across him a bit at university, but we were never in the same circle. I didn't even know he was married. No sign of his wife at parties and whatnot.'

'Divorced years ago. Poor Mags lives in a mansion in Hampstead with two young children. Tennis courts, indoor swimming pool, private cinema. Round-the-clock nannies.'

It's my turn to embarrass Patrick. 'I'd forgotten you and he were so close. So were you also a Stalinist tankie at Oxford?'

Munis reddens. 'Erm. It was a long time ago. Maybe for a term. Chris was seductive. You remember how confusing and exciting it all was in that first year. A rite of passage, you might say. I quickly learned the error of my ways and joined OUCA.'

OUCA is the Oxford University Conservative Association, the training ground for members of the Tory front bench. As for Munis's flirtation with the Communist Party of Great Britain, that's a wonderful scrap to throw to Justin, the BBC's political editor, a peace offering.

'Isn't it wonderful how Chris is still trying to overturn capitalism,' I say. 'Rumour has it he's behind the collapse in PTBG's share price.'

Munis shakes his head emphatically. 'It's never that simple with Chris.'

'What do you mean?'

'Sure he's making a fortune betting against the banks. But my hunch is that any minute, when the price is low enough, he'll do a reverse ferret and buy one.'

This feels important. I'm glad I dodged the Montrachet and kept a clear head. 'Which one?' Munis pulls a 'search me' grimace.

'Maybe the City rumour is upside down?' I hazard. 'Could he be after PTBG?'

'It's possible,' Munis replies. 'He thinks that idiot Blackwell has overextended the bank. But its retail operation in the UK is a licence to print money. Come to think of it, I reckon when the shares are cheap enough, he'll buy them all. He's going to end up owning it.'

'That's quite a prediction.'

Munis gives me a look that says he knows more than he's admitting.

'If I wasn't an MP, I would track PTBG's shares and buy them on the turn. I'd literally fill my boots.'

'I don't think your constituents would understand.'

The waiter arrives with the main courses. Munis asks for another glass of white – not another bottle, thank God. For a few moments, we eat in silence, savouring. My turbot has the elasticity of fish that was in the ocean only hours earlier. I experience almost sexual pleasure.

'I loved your interview with Tudor,' Munis says. 'Especially the moment when you asked him if he would nationalise NewGate. I was staggered he hadn't prepared something less revealing to say. Such an obvious question.'

'It was odd. They ought to nationalise NewGate, don't you think? It's the way to reassure savers and the markets, but Tudor's terrified of being accused of reverting to pre-Todd socialism.'

Munis laughs. 'Well that's exactly what we'd accuse him of, if he did it. Reverting to Labour's wealth-destroying, public-ownership habits.'

'And if you were in government?'

'We'd nationalise.' No hesitation. 'Our internal polling shows it would be a vote-winner, though you'll never hear me admit it.'

'You are such hypocrites.'

'Thank you kindly.'

'Don't you think that kind of game-playing is destroying voters' respect for all politicians?' I stress 'all'.

'That horse has bolted, I'm afraid. Principle died when Margaret Thatcher was kicked out. Now it's all about what the focus groups tell us they love and hate. As you know. So back to your marvellous interview: do you think Tudor will call the election soon?'

'He should. According to the focus groups you worship, he's enjoying quite a honeymoon. Labour is ahead in the polls.'

'You don't think he'll wait until he's had more time in Downing Street?'

I've asked myself the same question. 'This turmoil in the markets is going to get worse. We're heading for a recession, and he can't go to the country during a recession. So he needs to have an election soon.'

'A recession? Really?' Munis looks sceptical. 'None of the reputable forecasters are calling it. Why are you so gloomy?'

'Pretty much every mainstream forecasting model has a structural flaw. They are built on an assumption that banks always finance economic activity in a steady and predictable way. They've got no way of incorporating the impact of a credit crunch, of the sort of financial crisis that we're living through. Banks' access to wholesale markets is impaired. And when banks can't borrow, they can't lend. And when banks can't lend, the economy grinds to a juddering halt. If you've been around financial markets as long as I have, it's blindingly obvious. Most professional economists are making the error of ignoring the evidence of their eyes. Tudor, as the longest-serving chancellor in more than a hundred years, also understands how serious it all is.'

Munis puts down his knife and fork. 'If you're right, and you usually are, then we've got to stop Tudor. We need the election to come after the economic shit hits the fan. Voters must feel poorer and angry so that we can blame it all on Labour and Tudor. It's vital for us that there is maximum mayhem in markets and the economy before we go to the polls.'

Even by his standards, this cynical calculation is quite something.

'Please stop saying "we",' I say.

'Whether you like it or not, you and Chris Ravel are doing us a big favour.'

I stare at the detritus of beans and white fish on my plate. I hate the turn this conversation is taking.

'You and Chris are the Horsemen of the Apocalypse,' he chuckles. 'With his short selling and your reporting, you are destroying confidence in banks and the banking system. The more chaos you cause, the weaker the banks become and the less money they'll pump into the economy. Which means everyone is getting poorer, as you've been pointing out so astutely. And we're going to make sure voters know the real villain is Neville Tudor. You and Chris are ushering in the first Tory government for more than a decade.'

Just fuck off.

I have to pop his bubble. 'The election will happen when Tudor wants it. He has the power, not you.'

I excuse myself and go for a wee. When I am stressed, I drink even more coffee and water than normal. One price of ADHD is too many trips to the loo. When I get back, Munis is on the phone, concentrating too hard to notice me.

'Obviously we can't let the election happen now,' he snaps. 'For God's sake, Jimmy, it's time to bring out the dogs.'

He glances up, catches sight of me and hurriedly says, 'Thanks, my friend. See you soon.'

I sit down, and take a guess at who he was speaking to. 'I'd forgotten how close you are to Breitner.' Jimmy Breitner is the owner of Media Corp, one of the world's most powerful media empires that includes a clutch of influential UK newspapers.

Munis is hunting in the sole's elegant skeleton for just a touch more of the delicate flesh. 'Different Jimmy.'

I snort. I don't believe him. Banks are failing, the economy's on a precipice, and for people like Munis and Ravel, the only question is how they can exploit other people's misery.

*

As I speed-walk from Scott's to Bond Street underground station, I rehearse in my head how I'll explain a lunch bill just shy of three hundred pounds. I can't pass it off as a goodwill gesture to woo the Tories, since I have a dispensation from the BBC that means I don't have to disclose the identity of those I enter-tain, to protect my sources. The only thing she'll see is the bald number. I brace myself for Janice's censorious email.

When I get to TVC, I run to tech support, to pick up the Nokia. It's shit, but better than nothing. I suppose. My next priority is to log on to my PC and email the temporary number to contacts. Almost immediately after sending, the Nokia plays its annoying signature tune. It's Dad.

'Everything all right?' is my neurotic question. The lesson of history is Dad rings when there's a crisis.

'Yes. In fact, that's what I was ringing to say. The doctors believe Mum's illness may be in remission.' He still can't bring himself to say *cancer*.

'I'm so relieved. I bet you are too.'

He brushes off the question. Dad would never talk about his feelings. 'What's your news, son?'

'Keeping busy.'

He chuckles. 'I've seen all the criticism you've faced for your story about that bank. Ignore it. Mum and I think you are doing an important job. A great job.'

I smile. This is unusual. Dad almost never remarks upon my work in any way. And praise is almost unheard of. Mum insists he's proud of me, but I've never heard him say it. Till now.

'I hope the government isn't making things difficult for you. They should be grateful you are finding out what's going on.'

'I am not sure they are, to be honest. But that's OK.'

Despite the good news about Mum, I hear weariness in his voice. I should ask if he's all right, but he wouldn't tell me the truth, so I broach another difficult subject.

'Guess what? On Saturday I'll be in the directors' box at the Arsenal. For the North London derby.'

'That's going to be tricky. What will you do when we score?' By *we*, he means Spurs, the erratic North London team he bequeathed me as the nearest thing we have to practising religion.

'I don't think I'm allowed to shout or cheer in the directors' box. It's an etiquette thing. But Dad, quite honestly, Spurs' chances of winning are slim.'

'Never lose hope, son.' He goes quiet, and I guess he's scratching his right temple, which he always does when stressed. 'Gilbert, you're not going over to the enemy, are you?'

Gilbert? He only uses my full name when worried.

'No, Dad. It's business.'

'Glad to hear it. No Peck has ever been a Gooner. Will you come and see us soon? It's been a while.'

'I promise. We can celebrate Mum's good news.'

I hang up and hunt for Janice. I need to brief her on the furore at the bankers' convention, in case it's written up in a

205

newspaper. She's not in her office, but her PA tells me she's downstairs talking to the *Ten O'Clock News* team.

When I get there, Janice is deep in conversation with the programme editor and Emma. Janice waves me over.

'I've been trying to get hold of you.' She is tense. Has she got wind of the cost of lunch? How?

'Lost my phones. I was mugged at lunchtime.'

'What a pain. Are you OK?'

'A bit bruised.'

She steers me and Emma to the *Ten*'s small meeting room. Is she going to bollock me for losing BBC property?

'Emma tells me Robin Muller was an old friend of yours.'

'Er ... yes.' What does she mean, 'he was a friend'? Do they know he leaked the NewGate story to me?

Janice looks at Emma. Emma's mouth tightens; she takes a step towards me and puts her hand on my arm. 'When was the last time you looked at your phone?'

'About eleven o'clock.' Just before I went on stage with Stan Blackwell.

'You haven't heard, then?'

She's still clutching my arm. 'What's happened? What have I missed?'

Janice looks at Emma, and then at me. 'Robin Muller is dead.'

Chapter 16

HIGHGATE MEN'S BATHING POND IS a rectangular, artificial pond, on the eastern edge of Hampstead Heath, below the summit of Parliament Hill. It was dug in the eighteenth century as a reservoir for London's water supply. The water came from a tributary of the River Fleet, the same river which gave its name to Fleet Street – which is now populated by overpaid bankers, replacements for alcohol-abusing journalists. The subterranean river has become a sewer. What goes around, comes around.

The pond is in a hollow surrounded by sloping grass banks, trees and reeds. In summer, the lawns are filled with dog walkers and picnickers, while pink-fleshed men queue along the pontoon dock for the diving board. On a cold October afternoon, twilight, the pond is closed. There is police tape by the entrance.

I am on the edge of the water with Kim Jansen. 'We got a call at just after seven this morning, from one of the other bathers,' she says. 'Muller was struggling to breathe. Two swimmers dragged him to the bank, and rang for an ambulance. He was dead before the paramedics arrived.'

I stare at the still water, which is a gunmetal grey as dusk gathers. I'd known Muller more than half my life. Although it was always a relationship based on trade – first dope, then information – I might have called him a friend. If I called anyone a friend.

'What happened?'

She shrugs. 'I'm waiting for the coroner's report, but it looks like a heart attack. His wife Meghan says he'd been swimming here for years, but maybe there was something wrong that never got picked up.'

'That would be odd,' I say. 'Bankers like him have medical check-ups all the time. If he was prone to a cardiac arrest, he would have been told.'

'Well, let's wait for the report.'

'I saw him recently. He was behaving oddly.'

'How do you mean?'

'He was anxious, almost as if in danger.'

Kim starts to laugh and then thinks better of it. 'He was a banker. They're all worried these days, aren't they?'

'Not like that. Something, someone, was scaring him.'

She sighs, perhaps anticipating another of my conspiracy theories. 'Seriously, Gil, this doesn't look suspicious,' she says. 'I came here as a favour, and because he was my friend at Oxford too. But it's open-and-shut.'

Kim is right about one thing. I do miss him. Even if he was the most self-serving person I'd ever known.

'It's hard for you,' she says. 'First Marilyn, now Robin.'

I wilfully misunderstand. 'As you say, it must be more than coincidence they've died, so close together.'

'That's not what I'm saying. How can a heart attack be connected to a suicide?'

A Canada goose honks and lands in the middle of the pond. *Yeah, she's talking shit, I agree.*

'As for Marilyn, I followed up your question, Gil. No joy.' I've no idea what she's talking about. 'The diaries. The team didn't find them. Are you sure she kept them?'

208

'Maybe I misremembered.' This is not the moment to admit I've removed evidence from a crime scene. 'Thanks for coming here, Kim. Much appreciated.'

*

Muller's death is a short item on the local news, but isn't big enough for national bulletins. I am speaking to Jess from my office. She says it will be a nib on the front page of the *Financial Chronicle*. He was a big fish in the City.

With Jess I am less restrained than with Kim, even though I don't expect a more sympathetic hearing. 'Heart attacks can be induced,' I say. 'Jess, he was terrified when I saw him. I'd known him for years; he wasn't normal. Something was up.'

There's a long silence. I assume she's calculating whether I am strong enough to be told that I'm a hysterical idiot. But she surprises me.

'So much has happened since we were chased out of Marilyn's flat. You've been mugged for your phones, Muller is dead. So yes, I agree some of this is linked to Marilyn's death. Perhaps it all is. We need to work out what to do next.'

Time to fess up. Time to break the golden rule and reveal a source, now that no harm can come of it. 'It *was* Muller who gave me the NewGate story,' I say. 'NewGate is what links everything.'

I think of the woman with the cut-glass accent in the Chanel suit at the UK Finance conference. *What we are living through is the equivalent of war.* I assumed it was hyperbole induced by losing money, but it is war.

'Has your nephew made any progress decoding the diaries?' Jess asks.

Hell. I haven't handed them over. 'I'll cycle them to him now.'

*

Before climbing on my bike, I ring Dougie Pescod, Schon's PR. 'I wanted to say how shocked I was about Robin. I'd known him for more than twenty years.'

'We're all in shock. He was a huge part of the Schon family.'

'When's the funeral?'

'They want privacy. No press.'

'I was a friend. We knew each other at university.'

'I'll pass on your interest.'

He rings off.

*

Half an hour later, I carry my bike up the stairs of the amply proportioned grey-brick Victorian family house in Chalk Farm. Luke, in grey Nike sweats and mid-top Air Jordans, answers the door.

'Hi, Uncs.'

We hug. 'Is your dad here?'

'Not back from work.'

We walk through the hall, a geometrically white cuboid, with no clutter and a couple of bold Expressionist paintings, dazzling blue. My brother-in-law remade the house with straight lines and the obliteration of memories five years after Clare's death. I understood, though I was sad at the disappearance of the Toby jugs and thirties cigarette cards that had been collected by my sister and distributed randomly on mantelpieces and bookshelves.

Luke and I sit at the oak table under a glass roof at the garden end of the kitchen. I take the diaries out of my rucksack and spread them out.

'Bloody hell. There's a lot of them.'

'Yeah. Sorry. I'll try to explain what you need to do.'

I take out the brown leather Filofax containing the latest diary entries.

210

'It's like hieroglyphics!' says Luke. 'Or maybe mediaeval runes.'

'I thought the same thing. It's actually a pretty basic code called pigpen, where letters are placed in a nought-and-crosses grid. I've printed off a cipher from the internet, which should speed things up.'

I rummage around in my bag and retrieve the cipher, which I've put in a plastic cover.

'It all looks pretty straightforward. I'll get on to it. You said twenty pounds a diary?'

'I said ten.' I look at all the pages on the table and realise it's a mountain of work. 'Twenty quid's fine.'

Luke beams. He can see at least three hundred pounds on the table. Should I be giving a teenager so much cash? I remember the money I spent on illegal substances at his age. Also, should I be distracting him from exam revision?

'Have you mentioned this to your dad? You sure he'd be OK with it?'

'Dad'll be fine.'

'Do me a favour, don't let it get in the way of your revision.'

'Honestly, don't worry.'

I'm about to leave him to it, when I notice the document pocket in the Filofax's leather binder is bulging. Funny I missed that before. It contains a neatly folded envelope, which I extract. I look inside, without removing the contents. Photographs, maybe half a dozen. Colour. Pictures of a ghost.

I hastily put the envelope in my pocket. I feel assaulted again, but I have to pretend everything's OK. The best thing is to engage in mindless tidying.

'Let's put these diaries in a neat pile, in date order.'

When we've sorted them, I turn down Luke's offer of tea, give him a hug and head for the front door. On the street, before unfolding my bike, I take out the photographs. There are five: Marilyn is naked and seemingly off her head in all of them. There's also a short note on cream notepaper, written in meticulous italicised script. *I was thinking of sending these to Jimmy. What do you think the* Governor *would make of them? Love Q xxx*

I look at the envelope. The postmark is 28 August.

*

I cycle straight to Jess. As soon as she lets me in, before removing my helmet, I breathlessly pull out the photos and the card. 'We've now got proof Marilyn was being blackmailed.'

She scans the note. 'It looks that way.'

I leave the folded bike in her hall and follow her to the living room. The new information has triggered my hyperactivity. I have to spew out everything that's on my mind.

'The blackmailer is somebody who signs himself "Q". He warned Marilyn he would send the devastating photos to Jimmy. That must be Jimmy Breitner. It's a threat that her sex-and-drugs past would be plastered all over the *Globe* – curtains for her career.'

I am snapping the fingers of both hands with the tension of it all. 'Try to calm down,' Jess says. 'You're overwrought.'

I collapse into her sofa.

'Careful.'

'Sorry.'

'Would it have been so bad for Marilyn?' she asks.

'God yes. Don't you remember the humiliation the Bank went through when its Deputy Governor had sex with a journalist in the Governor's dressing room? This would have been far worse.'

'Can I see the envelope?'

I hand it to Jess. 'Look at the date stamp. It's a few days before NewGate went cap in hand to the Bank of England for the bailout. It's when Jackson was trying to get Bank of England approval to buy NewGate.'

'So do you reckon Jackson was blackmailing her?' she asks.

'Probably not Jackson directly. Someone on his behalf. And it's pretty obvious who. Marilyn sent me the picture of the Rothko to point me to Elliott.'

'But the note's signed "Q". Not "A" for Alex.'

'Oh yes. Annoying.'

Jess bangs the arm of her chair, startling me.

'What?'

'I've worked something out. Those millions of dollars transferred to Marilyn's account from the Caymans. It wasn't a bribe: it was part of the blackmail. They were trying to make her look corrupt. They were messing with her.'

I lock my fingers together and squeeze hard.

'That would mean Elliott wasn't freelancing. Jackson was in the thick of it,' I say. 'Elliott can't afford to lose that kind of money.'

Jess pinches her chin, her thinking tic.

'I'm not sure even Jackson can write off five million dollars without feeling it.'

'So who do we know who would regard a few million dollars as loose change?'

'Primakov,' we say, in unison.

Jess leans forward. 'I had our investigations team do some digging. He's dangerous. According to an ex-spook who infilt-rated the FSB, a Russian journalist ended up at the bottom of a lake in his car after writing about alleged bribes paid by Primakov to government officials. Blackmail wouldn't trouble him.'

The bottom of a lake. Or maybe the freezing waters of Highgate Pond, shrouded by willows. I tell Jess what I heard Primakov say in the corridor of Jackson's office: *the loss on my investment is now very significant.*

'It's obvious who employed the heavies we met at Marilyn's flat, and who arranged to mug me for my phones,' I say. 'Isn't it?'

Jess stares into space. 'Do you think we should be frightened?'

The buzz of Jess's phone interrupts us. 'It's the newsdesk,' she says. After listening, she responds, 'That's a story. Thanks for letting me know. Can you scan it and send it over?'

As soon as she hangs up, she switches on her laptop. 'What was that about?' I ask.

She brings the laptop and sits next to me on the sofa, so we can both see the screen. It's the front page of the *Globe*, Jimmy Breitner's mass-market tabloid.

'Wow,' I say.

The splash is quite a thing. There's a picture of the prime minister, Tudor, with the downward red line of a markets graph superimposed on his face. The conceit is Bowie's *Aladdin Sane*, but not in a flattering way. In the photo, Tudor looks petulant. The headline is 'A Lad Insane'. The two-paragraph write-off next to it says, 'The value of our businesses and savings is being sunk by an arrogant, know-it-all prime minister. He's bailing out the fat-cat bankers for mistakes he made in failing to regulate them properly. Although the *Globe* was an early supporter of Modern Labour, Tudor is no Johnny Todd. He's tired. He's run out of ideas. Enough is enough. Stella Barnsbury is the new broom this country needs. The *Globe* is today saying that the new Conservative Party of Mrs B is best for Britain.'

This is significant. Breitner's conceit as a media baron is that he can make or break governments. It's not a myth. If he's switching to the Tories after ten years of supporting Modern Labour, it's an earthquake.

And it started at lunch today. My lunch with Patrick Munis. *Time to call out the dogs.* I was sure he was talking to Breitner, negotiating his sordid deal to stitch up Tudor and scare him off calling an immediate election.

Breitner's endorsement won't have come cheap. What did Munis and Barnsbury promise him? I pull out my phone, and then remember it's the temporary Nokia, so none of the numbers of my contacts are stored on it. I ask Jess for Munis's and text him.

I tap, trying to remember how to use a number pad to retrieve the appropriate letters. It's clumsy and slow. But eventually it's written.

What did you promise Breitner in return? I press 'send'.

Munis replies instantaneously. *The pendulum swings.*

I read it to Jess and toss the phone on the sofa. 'It's just a game for him. He doesn't give a stuff about how the banking crisis is going to crash the economy, that people will lose their jobs, their homes. All he cares about is that Tudor gets the blame and he becomes chancellor.'

She shrugs. 'Plus ça change. Where do *we* go from here?'

'I have a meeting tomorrow that may shed light.'

'On a Saturday?'

'I'm going to the football, with Lord Ravel.' Jess looks at me disbelievingly. 'He's a director of the Arsenal. He invited me to join him in the directors' box.'

'He knows you're Spurs, I suppose?'

I nod, grimly.

Jess laughs. 'The former cabinet secretary has a sense of humour. Who would have guessed?'

Chapter 17

ARSENAL'S TWO-YEAR-OLD EMIRATES STADIUM IS the new Britain of tax-avoiding, non-dom billionaires. On match day, the roads from leafy Hampstead – home of a few of Arsenal's plutocrat supporters – to urban Drayton Park are rammed with Bentleys, Porsches and Mercs. The private conversations on either side of the directors' box are as likely to be about how to structure the acquisition of an asset to avoid tax as about how much the team misses Thierry Henry, Arsenal's greatest modern player.

When I arrive, escorted from the reception area on the Hornsey side by red-suited hostesses, Lord Ravel is in the directors' restaurant. It's a Saturday twelve thirty kick-off and we're having an early lunch. I've chosen a navy blue Paul Smith suit, blue knitted-silk tie and crisp white Charvet shirt. My subtle homage to my team. I've been warned that football scarves are not permitted.

I find Ravel in conversation with Bob Wilson, an Arsenal legend and former TV pundit. Wilson is famously a gent, so I park my loyalties and say what a pleasure it is to meet him. Ravel has forewarned him I'm with the other team.

'I'm expecting it to be a painful afternoon for you, but you never know,' says Bob.

'Not everything in life goes to form,' I respond. 'Sometimes famous institutions are more fragile than they look.'

Ravel says that we need to sit down and eat or we'll miss kick-off.

'I've taken the liberty of ordering a bottle of Sancerre,' he says. 'The one they serve here is not at all bad. Will you join me?'

I don't like drinking before six, but it's the weekend, and maybe he'll be more expansive if I do. When I started in journalism in the late eighties, literally the only way to land a story was to get rat-arsed with a contact. The police were the heaviest drinkers. They wouldn't reveal anything until I was almost unconscious; if I didn't write it all down instantly there was no way I'd remember anything.

'A glass would be nice.'

We are seated next to the plate-glass window. Ravel explains the hierarchy and anthropology of a sixty-thousand-capacity stadium, where a typical season ticket costs at least a thousand pounds, and often a multiple of that. Almost every seat has been sold for the entire season, and they could have sold those tickets many times over. In the bottom and top tiers are 'our traditional fans', who still have to find an unconscionable amount of money to be here every fortnight. In the middle are the corporate boxes and so-called 'Club Level', where the hedge funders, corporate lawyers and investment bankers have their own restaurants and the best view of the game, for a premium price. This is not the armament workers' Woolwich Arsenal of 1886. The immaculate and blindingly green turf, framed by steep slopes of red seats, is a private club for oligarchs, private equity titans, the super-rich and their hangers-on from the banks and law firms. They are internationally mobile, fair-weather fans, with their accounts in Switzerland and the Dutch Antilles. If they could relocate the turf and players to Dubai, they probably would.

'I suppose the logical next step for you is to take a leaf out of Chelsea's book, and sell yourselves to a fully fledged Russian oligarch, like Abramovich,' I say.

'We've had a few approaches.'

'I imagine someone like Petr Primakov would be interested.'

If Ravel knows I'm fishing, he's far too urbane to show it. 'Ah yes, Primakov. Johnny's friend. He has been sniffing around. These oligarchs feed in similar troughs. We've indicated we're not terribly interested, although he does seem to have a bottomless purse.'

Primakov is close to Todd, so I should have guessed.

'What's the connection with our former prime minister?'

'The Russian funds one of Todd's many charitable foundations.' Ravel says 'charitable foundations' with disdain.

'I take it you are not very impressed with Todd's not-for-profit endeavours.'

'"Not-for-profit" and Johnny Todd are not natural bedfellows.'

'If Primakov offered a stupid price to the club's owners, surely they wouldn't say no?'

'I wouldn't be so sure. After all, we are Her Majesty's Arsenal. She's not going to associate with a club owned by a dubious Russian. These things matter to the board.'

'That connection between the Palace and the Arsenal, I always thought it was a joke, a myth.'

'I couldn't possibly say.'

Lunch is a buffet. Smoked salmon, Dublin Bay prawns, assorted cold cuts, salads. It's all so different from my life at Tottenham's White Hart Lane, where it's still boiled mushy hotdogs, hard seats and obstructed views. My relationship with Spurs is too much like my relationship with my family, love and hate in equal measure. In fact Spurs was at the heart of the least problematic part of being my father's son. When I was a child, the two of us went to the Lane every fortnight. It was the Spurs of Chivers, Gilzean and Ralph Coates. The swansong of the great Bill Nicholson's management years was followed by the remade Tottenham of Glenn Hoddle, and the magnificent Argentines Villa and Ardiles.

So much hope, so much style, so much disappointment. We failed gloriously. Dad and Spurs taught me the importance of believing, often against the odds and evidence. But although we lost too often, they didn't teach me how to lose graciously. I hate losing.

I spear a prawn, dip it into Rose Marie sauce, and relish it. For Proust it may have been the madeleine: for me, it's the prawn cocktail. Not kosher, of course, but a symbol from the seventies of how North London Jews had made it. I can't scorn everything about the Arsenal.

Ravel interrupts my internal conversation. 'What did you make of this morning's *Globe* front page?'

I wouldn't normally expect to chat about the UK's leading tabloid with a former cabinet secretary, but today is different. 'Breitner switching from Labour to the Tories is not a trivial event,' I say. 'Breitner's backing, or at least the absence of conspicuous opposition from him and his papers, allowed Todd – and Tudor – to govern with the confidence that they'd probably stay in power more than a single term. Breitner was part of the foundations of Modern Labour. It's a massive blow to Tudor that Breitner is back with the Tories.'

'Why has he ditched your friend Tudor?'

My friend Tudor. I don't rise to it.

'Part of it's personal. Todd and Breitner liked each other. There's never been the same warmth between Tudor and Breitner. Also, don't forget this is a different Tory Party from the one Todd faced in 1997. I assume you've come across Alex Elliott, Breitner's former director of comms. He's the most powerful PR in London. Used to work for Breitner. He's the bridge between him and Stella and Munis.'

'The big question is whether this blows up Tudor's plan – which you so elegantly teased out of him – to hold an early general election.'

'It depends on how the polls move. The Tories are desperate to prevent an early election, and Breitner is sending a message to Tudor that there are risks if he goes for it.'

*

On the pitch, it's a depressing afternoon for us. We struggle to contain Fabregas and Adebayor, though our new signing Bale works hard and looks promising. Maybe he'll turn into something. Berbatov is a genius, though too capricious. We lose. I'm not going to mention the margin.

'Sorry about that, old chap,' says Ravel. 'If it's any consolation, I don't quite see this team repeating our triumphs of a few years ago. Cup of tea, or something stronger?'

'Tea would be great.'

We return to our table, and for the first time I risk asking what he knows is my reason for being here.

'I wondered if you had any more intelligence on what happened to NewGate's servers the night of my story, why the website crashed.'

'Between us girls, my friends at GCHQ have taken a look. And they are pretty sure there was a denial-of-service attack on the bank.'

'So the crash wasn't just inadequate server capacity at a time when customer demand was through the roof?' This ought to be sensational, but I expected it. 'Any sense of where the attack originated?'

'Hard to be sure. These criminals cover their tracks, if they are any good. And this was certainly a professional operation. There is some kind of Russian link.'

Russian? My mind leaps straight to Primakov. But why would Primakov want to sink NewGate? It makes no sense. He was working with Jackson to buy NewGate, and it was the run on the bank that stopped them.

'When you say "some kind of Russian connection", are you saying the attack *originated* from Russia?'

Ravel gives me an appraising look. 'As I said, these criminals cover their tracks. But my friends in GCHQ believe that although the attack was routed through Russia, in fact it was being directed from the Middle East.'

I think of the most technically advanced country in the Middle East. 'Israel?'

'Not on this occasion. As far as we can tell, it came from Syria.'

Syria. Another, more plausible, connection suggests itself. I'm talking to a Ravel, and it's not a great leap of imagination to assume a link to his son – who has made an unspecified but colossal sum from NewGate's collapse and who was a passionate Arabist at Oxford. Always tricky asking someone about family, but here goes.

'I knew your son at Oxford. He was always incredibly bright.'

Ravel sighs. 'I wondered when you'd get round to Christopher, although I'm probably the worst person to ask. He was at prep school when I left his mother. He never forgave me.'

'Never?'

'I wasn't very nice. Things fell apart with Caroline, his mum. I thought it was for the best to rip off the plaster, make a clean break. I sent him a postcard telling him we were divorcing. Sensitive young man. Completely the wrong thing to do.'

By postcard? Jesus. I resist the temptation to ask how he could have been such a moron.

Instead: 'You presumably know he was part of the ultra-left scene at Oxford in the early eighties. He supported the PLO, hated Israel. Tricky for a North London Jew like me.'

'Tricky for his dad.'

'To be blunt, then: when you say you think the attack on NewGate's servers had a Middle Eastern connection, are you trying to tell me that your son had something to do with it?'

'I'm not saying anything. I am sharing the facts as I know them, and you can draw your own conclusions. I believe another fact, however, is that a number of hedge funds bet against NewGate and made a lot of money. One of those, I understand, was my son's fund, Lulworth.'

'I have the same understanding. Do you suspect your son of illegal market manipulation?'

'Goodness, no. How could you possibly suggest that?'

But he is amused, rather than angry. There is mischief in his brown eyes.

'As *you* know, a good deal of what happens in the City is illegal, though it is almost always impossible to prove. If I were you, I'd write one of your brilliant blogs about all this, and see what you flush out. Sprat to catch a mackerel, and all that.'

*

The only good thing about today's match is I can walk home. I don't want to be recognised: I am pretty well-known as a Spurs supporter, and I know from long and painful experience that Arsenal supporters can be merciless after victory. So I keep my head down, eyes locked to the pavement. As I walk along Hornsey Road, past the salt beef concession and the stalls selling unofficial scarves and T-shirts, I am assaulted by the shouted refrain: 'What do you think of Tottenham? Shit. What do you think of shit? Tottenham. Thank you. That's all right.' Followed, in song, by, 'We hate Tottenham and we hate Tottenham, We hate Tottenham and we hate Tottenham ...' This is not my home.

Truthfully it's less offensive than going to Stamford Bridge, home of Chelsea FC, where Spurs' fans' dubious self-identification as 'Yids' has prompted disgusting antisemitism. Last season, I took my nephew Luke to an away game. Going home on the District Line afterwards, we were surrounded by drunk white Chelsea supporters who started singing about how Chelsea would finish Hitler's job. I wanted to confront them, but didn't want to put Luke in harm's way. The humiliation of turning a blind eye haunts me.

I manage to remain anonymous as I turn left into the Holloway Road. But when I do another left into Fieldway Crescent, I let my guard drop. I'm close to home and I think I can relax. A young man walks towards me. He looks like a student. He stops and says, 'You're Gil Peck, aren't you?'

I smile.

'That's amazing. I'd heard you live round here.' He chatters on, excitedly. 'I read your book on the policies of Modern Labour. It's why I'm planning to study economics at uni, if my grades are good enough.'

I make an inane comment about how pleased I am he enjoyed the book.

'Can I have your autograph?'

He reaches into his backpack for a notebook, and I scribble on it something about how it's impossible to understand politics without understanding how the economy works. So engrossed am I in my own pretentiousness that I fail to notice a group of five young men in sharp suits have joined us. They are rowdy and drunk.

One shouts: 'You're that arsehole from the BBC who's always talking down Britain. Why are you trying to kill the City?'

'It's Peck, innit,' says another.

'You just been at the game, have you, Peck? You're a fucking Yid, aren't you?'

I ignore them, and after saying goodbye to the teenager I walk up the hill. But one of the men circles around and comes so close that I can smell his beery breath. His chest is almost pressing on mine. I am pushed backwards, and stumble as a leg thwacks my calf. I cushion my fall with my arms, as an overpolished black pointy-toed lace-up stamps on my left hand. Then an imitation Gucci slip-on kicks me in the ribs, as its wearer shouts, 'This is from Peter. If you know what's good for you, you'll stop trying to wreck the country.'

I'm in serious trouble. I curl into a foetal position, arms wrapped around my face and head – when there's an 'Oy' from a front door, and 'I've called the police, you arseholes.'

'Piss off, you lezzer,' says one of my assailants.

Another says, 'I think he's got the message.'

They start to walk, there's a sound of a siren and they run. The lady comes over, helps me up. She's short. Cropped grey hair, kind eyes; wearing a red sweatshirt and jeans.

'You OK?'

'Shaken, a bit bruised. Nothing broken, I think. Did you call the police?'

'Didn't have time. Told them that to scare them off. But you should call them now. I'm happy to give a witness statement. Do you want to come inside?'

My hand is sore, and my back is bruised. I need a bath.

'I only live round the corner. I think I'll go home and change.'

'OK. Hang on a minute, I'm just going to write down my name and number for you.'

She gives me a yellow Post-it note with her details. 'At least we have a name,' she says.

'What do you mean?'

'He said, "This is from Peter."'

'Oh yes.'

I take her number and walk with slow and raw purpose up the hill. *Peter. Or was it Petr?*

Chapter 18

J ESS IS GRUMPY. WITH ME. I don't like it.

'Of course I didn't bother to ring the police,' I say. 'They're not going to find those idiots.'

'You're the idiot. Have you never heard of CCTV?'

'The cameras are never switched on.'

'How do you know that?'

'Everyone knows that.'

She looks at me with contempt. I am topless in my kitchen, and Jess has just arrived with a tube of arnica.

'This is going to hurt,' she says.

'You don't have to sound as though you'll enjoy it.'

She squeezes a glob of the ointment onto the sore patch on my back. 'You'll have quite a bruise.'

She smooths the cream and tenderly strokes it into my skin. I register the softness of her fingertips, and almost forget that I am supposed to be in agony.

'I'm just going to check the damage,' she says, before gently prodding around my torso. I wince. But it's not excruciating.

'Does it hurt when you breathe in?'

I shake my head.

'That probably means the ribs are intact. You're lucky.'

'I don't feel lucky.'

Physical courage has never been my strong point. When I was forced to play rugby at school, my technique was to run as far away from the ball as possible.

'If it's so awful, you should call the flipping police. Even if it's just a random bunch of pissed Arsenal supporters, they shouldn't get away with it. Though the truth is you and I know this wasn't random.'

'Maybe.'

Jess loses patience and massages my lower back with a force she wants me to notice.

'Ow!'

'Serves you right. For God's sake, just take stock for a second. You've been robbed. You've had the shit kicked out of you. Two people you've known for years, both of whom are connected to the biggest story of your life, are dead. In theory, it could all be coincidence. But honestly, do you think it is?'

'Some. Some not. We don't know, do we?'

Jess puffs out her cheeks and breathes out in an exaggerated way. 'It doesn't matter whether it's all the same plot to silence you, you have to bring in the police.'

She gives my back a harsh squeeze. I grimace. She's obviously right. And as the shock of the attack subsides, I am able to see and feel the reality of the intimidation.

'Let's say you're right,' I say. 'What would I tell the police that would get them to investigate in any useful way? We haven't a clue who's behind all this.'

'Yes we do.'

'What do you mean?'

'It must be Primakov.'

'Why?'

'Because the morons who attacked you said they were doing it for "Petr", and because Primakov is a card-carrying member of the Russian mafia.'

'Jess, it's a theory. We have no proof.'

'Well, our investigation into him shows he does not let anyone get in his way. There's talk that someone has a film of him from years ago, back when he was just getting going, shooting a competitor in the head.'

'Do you think it's real?'

She shrugs. 'All I know is people are frightened of him.'

'What can you write?'

'Very little. Like most oligarchs, he's lawyered up to the eyeballs. Uses a Magic Circle firm, Hoylet Jinx, as you'd expect. Our in-house lawyers have palpitations if we even mention his name.'

The Magic Circle are London's most expensive solicitors. Employing them is a status symbol for a billionaire. The same as buying a Bentley or a Jermyn Street shirt. They can normally ensure that nothing appears in the press that a wealthy client hasn't authorised, thanks to libel laws and the power of money in the courts.

I screw up my eyes and try to work out whether it's worth talking to Jansen about all this. Before I can ask Jess, the borrowed mobile phone, which is on the table, vibrates. Jess goes over to it and recognises the number.

'It's Downing Street. You'd better take it.'

She passes it and I press the green button.

'Switch here. Is that Gilbert Peck?'

'Speaking.'

'The prime minister would like a word.'

'Sure. Thanks.'

'Putting you through.'

There's the click-click of the call being transferred, then Neville Tudor's lugubrious voice. 'Gil. Have you seen the *Globe* today?'

''Fraid so.'

'Breitner is a cunt, pardon my French. After everything we've done for him.'

I am not surprised that a single hostile tabloid front page has unnerved him so much. The *Globe*'s conversion to Johnny Todd's Modern Labour in 1997, after fifteen years of supporting the Tories, was perhaps the most potent symbol that Labour had emerged from the wilderness – because Breitner notoriously puts access to power above ideology or dogma. He backed Todd because Todd was a winner. His withdrawal of support is shattering for Tudor.

'Presumably you'll play the election long now?'

'Draw your own conclusions, Gil. It was you who fucked me on this in the first place. If it hadn't been for your story ...' He trails off.

'But I didn't ring to give you a bollocking.'

Again silence. 'So why did you ring?'

'Can we talk totally off the record?'

'Sure.'

'And when I say off the record, I mean we're not having this conversation. OK?'

'Got it.'

'Well, as you surmised, I am working on the assumption we'll have to take formal ownership of NewGate, if we're going to stabilise the banking system. It's the most direct demonstration to depositors in other banks that the government will stand behind them, that if the worst happens we'll be the owner of last resort, as it were.'

'That is the argument.'

'But I suppose you also understand my anxiety. It's important, if we were to nationalise, that we would not be seen as reverting to type, that no one could accuse us of still being the traditional Labour Party which wanted common ownership of the commanding heights of the economy.'

I hear the frustration of the trapped politician, who fears he'll be damned whatever he does. 'Do you think we will be accused of returning to traditional socialism?' he says.

'The Tories are bound to do that. And some right-wing commentators will claim Labour will never understand Darwinian capitalism. That doesn't mean voters will care. Does it matter to you if the *Mail* and the *Telegraph* claim you've abandoned free enterprise?'

'It would have mattered to Johnny. He always preferred being attacked from the left than from the right. And it won him three elections.'

'Sure. But times change. The pendulum swings.'

'Has it?'

'Yes. I know for an absolute fact that if the Tories were in office, they would nationalise.'

Before he responds, I have a sense that I also have Jess's rapt attention. I turn to her and she mouths, *'What the fuck?'* She looks pissed off.

'How do you know that?' says Tudor.

'You're just going to have to trust me.'

'You're close to Munis, aren't you?'

'As I said, you'll have to trust me.'

He goes quiet and I see my opening.

'Look, I know we agreed off the record. But it must be in your interest for me to write this. You'll want to condition the market.'

'Write what?'

'That you're going to nationalise.'

He sighs. 'You're a piece of work.'

I take that as consent for me to publish the story. But there are a couple of loose ends.

'How will you value NewGate? Is it worth anything?'

'As you have pointed out very publicly, the bank is bust. The shares are worthless. We'll pay a token penny for all the assets and liabilities.'

Wow. If Primakov's loss has been, in his words, 'very significant,' it'll now be irreversibly humungous.

'You are going to upset a few people by doing this. You know that, I assume.'

'I presume you mean Harvey Jackson? Tough titty. He's rich enough.'

'Todd works with him. Surely Johnny will attempt to talk you out of nationalising?'

'Johnny can piss off.'

He ends the call. I put the phone in my trouser pocket. The adrenaline rush of the scoop anaesthetises the aches and bruises.

'You heard?' I ask Jess.

'Most of it.'

Her voice is staccato, and she looks at me disapprovingly. I can't think why. It must be my imagination.

'A penny for the whole bank,' I say. 'You know what that means? Anyone who bought NewGate shares will have their investment wiped out.'

'Thank you. You don't need to explain.'

'I assume Jackson's consortium bought NewGate stock as the price fell over the summer,' I continue, thinking out loud. 'Nationalisation means every penny he put in will be gone forever. That's a tough pill for him and Johnny to swallow. They'll thrash and scream to stop it. As for Primakov ...'

Jess says nothing. She's fixed me with a scornful look, though I still don't understand.

'What have I done?'

'Aren't you going to ask me what I was trying to communicate to you when you were on the phone?'

There's anger in her voice. 'What?'

'You crossed the line. You should not be advising the PM on likely political and media reaction, or informing him what the opposition will do. It's just not on, not if you still think of yourself as a journalist.'

'But I was trying to get the story.' I am defensive. 'And I got the story.'

'No, you became the story. Which is not what we do. Your biggest weakness is that you are seduced by proximity to power. It flatters your ego. What do you think the BBC's viewers would say if they heard you advising the prime minister on something as important as the future of the banks?'

'They'd think I was doing my job.' I'm losing patience. I need to put out the imminent nationalisation of NewGate in my Peckonomics blog. *Government to buy NewGate.* A Peck scoop will lead the *Ten O'Clock News.* Again.

'Can we talk about it later?'

Jess can tell my focus is not on her. 'You're really not bothered, are you?'

'I respect what you say.'

'Bog off. You just want to get the story out.'

I raise my eyebrows, but don't deny it.

'I'm glad I was able to patch you up.'

'Jess, I'm sorry.' She knows I don't really mean it.

'I've got to go. Amy needs collecting from a birthday party.' She picks up her rucksack, and takes out a packet of Nurofen. 'Take a couple of these. We'll talk later. Maybe.'

After she's gone, I have an annoying thought: what if she is really fed up with me? No more Jess hugs? I dismiss the horrible notion as soon as it registers, and open the laptop, to tap out my story.

After self-publishing on the BBC's website, I call Emma.

'Yeah, I just saw it,' she says. 'They're bound to want a live on the *Ten.*'

'Phono?' I ask if I can broadcast over the phone from home, just audio, with a still photo of me on screen.

'Nah, boss,' she says. 'You've got hours yet. They'll want you in the studio. On yer bike.'

She laughs and rings off. I check the time. I've got time to kill. I'll go to the gym and work out, to stop my bruised muscles seizing up. And to displace any annoying thoughts that I've let Jess down.

*

My gym is a huge, echoey former warehouse, by the edge of the Barbican on Aldersgate Street, with an indoor track and row after row of running and climbing machines. Banks of televisions face the machines, all switched to the BBC News Channel and CNBC, so that City traders can keep an eye out for news that could wreck the books they're running.

I've been coming here for fifteen years. The endorphins are another addiction, in my life's list – as is the need to retain the definition of my show muscles. They are useless for anything practical, like scaring off gangster oligarchs, and they haven't been tested in a fight since I was nine in my school playground. That last scrap was a frenetic slapping contest that little boys confuse with actual fighting, a lot of sweat and energy. Since you ask, I won on points, against Danny Goldsmith, who went on to become a GP.

There's hardly anyone in the gym so late on a Saturday after-noon. A quarter of an hour in, I'm speed walking on a sharp incline on a running machine and am drenched with sweat. My bruises are a rumbling ache, and I've successfully displaced any nagging anxiety about my quarrel with Jess.

I've got my headphones on, so it takes me a while to register that the girl from the front desk is in front of me, trying to flag me down, as it were.

'Do you want me?'

'There's a man in reception asking for you. Says it's important.'

'Did he give a name?'

'Prikov. Something like that.'

I miss my step on the machine and almost get spat off the end of it. 'Primakov?'

'Think so.'

What the hell does he want? Since I haven't finished my workout – and since it seems unwise to keep an oligarch waiting – I go with her in my damp sports gear. When I get to reception it's not Primakov, but a flunky, in a narrow-fitting black suit.

'Mr Primakov is outside. He would like you to join him in his motor car.'

It's not an invitation. It's an instruction. Should I tell him to piss off? No: he's given his name to the receptionist. If I disappear, even Kim Jansen would be able to work out who to pursue. Probably.

I follow the minder. Outside, with hazard lights flashing, is a gleaming black Bentley. It must have cost the same as a decent-size house in the suburbs. The flunky opens the back door, revealing the square-faced, shaven head of Petr Primakov.

He takes in my dishevelled state and roars with laughter. 'Come in, come in. The seats are leather. Yuri can wipe them down when you leave.'

The Bentley has been converted into a stretch format. I didn't even know that was possible. I sit on a bench with my back to the driver, opposite Primakov. The driver is behind a glass screen in the front, and the flunky has been left on the pavement.

Primakov presses an intercom button and speaks to the driver in Russian. The car pulls away from the kerb. 'I would be grateful if you would indulge me for a few minutes, Mr Peck. I won't keep you long.'

'Are we going far? I'd like to finish my workout.'

'Just far enough so that we can talk sufficiently to understand each other.'

The blood that's pumping through me owes nothing to the running machine. I have been naive in getting into his limo. Jess would go nuts if she knew. If Primakov shoots me here, I already know Yuri would wipe down the seats. The girl in the gym would be paid off or would be 'disappeared'. I haven't even got my phone with me.

'What do you want to know?'

Primakov leans back in the leather seat. 'I understand that your friend from the *Financial Chronicle*, Ms Neeskens, has been making enquiries about me.'

Shit. How does he know about Jess? I should have listened to her and called the police immediately.

'I am not a complicated man, Mr Peck. You have questions, you ask me.'

There's menace even in an anodyne invitation. 'I understand one of my Russian colleagues asked questions and he ended up at the bottom of a lake.'

'Children's stories, Mr Peck. But you'll understand that it suits me for people to think I am the wrong person to cross.'

He smiles. Although he has the physique of a martial arts black belt, his lopsided grin and wide blue eyes are disconcertingly charming. His voice is resinous syrup.

'Is there something about me that worries you, Mr Peck?'

I gather my thoughts. I am locked in and could not get out even if I wanted to. I have nothing to lose from simply doing what I always do, which is to ask the questions that may yield a story.

'I am pretty sure you wouldn't want this car at the bottom of a lake,' I say.

He laughs. 'I like your Jewish humour.'

He knows more about me than I do about him. I need to correct the imbalance.

'Were you involved with Jackson in the bid for NewGate?'

He fiddles with the watch on his wrist, something slim, Swiss and probably worth more than I will earn in a lifetime. 'Mr Elliott said you were brighter than most journalists and that I should be careful what I say to you. But I see no reason why I should not talk to you about this. Yes, I am working with Mr Jackson.'

'Why?'

'I like Johnny. He introduced me.'

Ah, Johnny Todd. Of course. 'So what is your arrangement?'

'Well, as you presumably know, I have access to capital, quite a lot of it. I smoothed the path to acquisition by buying substantial quantities of NewGate shares.'

'You're not on the share register.'

'There are ways to disguise ownership, as I'm sure you know.'

Should I point out that buying shares to help a takeover by a third party, without declaring the purchases, is an illegal concert party? Maybe later. 'How much have you invested on his behalf? Tens of millions of pounds? Hundreds of millions?'

'Enough.'

'Oh dear.'

'Yes. Oh dear.'

'So you realise you're set to lose the lot, when the government nationalises?'

'I am aware.' He reaches deliberately into his jacket pocket and extracts a blinged-up BlackBerry. 'I read the blog you just put out.'

He sees me gawping at what looks like diamonds studded around the screen.

'A gift,' he says. 'Too much?'

I shrug. 'I was thinking about my BlackBerries. They were stolen. Yesterday.'

He lays it on the seat. 'Everyone talks about lawlessness in Russia. The only place I've ever been robbed is here.'

'Are we still talking about NewGate?'

He looks at me. It's unnerving, but I press on. 'What are you going to do?'

'I do not blame you for what happened to NewGate. You were just the messenger, or more accurately the puppet.'

I think about arguing that it was in the public interest for me to reveal NewGate's plight, but reckon he's not really interested in journalistic integrity.

'My interest,' he says, 'is in who tipped you off and why.'

It's my turn to stare and say nothing. I do my best to hold the gaze of eyes that seem permanently amused by the frailties of man.

'We understand each other now, Mr Peck. Is there anything else I can help you with?'

There is. I think of the photo of Marilyn and her urgent scribbled message to find her.

'Two of my friends have died. Both were involved in what's happened to NewGate.'

Primakov tilts his head. It could be sympathy. Or predatory. 'My condolences.'

'One is Robin Muller.' No reaction. 'A partner at Schon. Someone else who sank to the bottom of a lake.'

Still no hint of recognition or emotion. 'Lawyers, accountants, bankers ...' He gives a dismissive wave of his hand. 'I know many. I pay their bonuses.'

'Did you know Marilyn Krol?'

'That poor woman from the Bank of England who took her own life. I have been told you were close to her. Mr Elliott informed me.'

Of course he did.

'Marilyn was blackmailed shortly before she died. I wonder if you have any insight to offer?'

He smiles. This time, not in a friendly way. 'You ask me because I am the Russian thug, so obviously I must be the blackmailer.'

238

I wince. The smoothness of the Bentley had lulled me into reckless overconfidence.

'Look, I take you at your word that I should not believe the gossip about you.' Nothing registers on his face. 'But she was a close friend. I need to know why she killed herself. It was in the interest of Mr Jackson and Mr Todd to put pressure on her.'

'OK. We are being frank with each other. I don't know if there was an attempt to, shall we say, influence her, but Mr Jackson said she was friendly to us, in favour of our plan to buy NewGate. They were relieved she was on our side; they said it was crucial. In the end, they seem to have been wrong about that, as about so much.'

The car is back where we started, outside the gym. Yuri is by the door, ready to let me out. I hope.

'It would be good to keep in touch,' I say.

'If I find out anything relevant, you will hear from me.'

Primakov presses the button to open the window and nods at Yuri. 'Back to your workout.' I shuffle to the door. I can feel my bruises again. 'Mr Peck, you and I know how important it is to stay fit and healthy.'

Chapter 19

DESPITE THE BENTLEY'S VELVET SUSPENSION, I feel queasy and on edge. In the gym, I charge up the running machine's mountain, but I've misjudged. Rather than purging my stress, I am ready to throw up. I need to call Jess. As soon as I get to the changing room, I try her. Her mobile rings once and then cuts me off. Is she blocking me? I try again. Same response. She *is* blocking me. I've messed up.

I shower, change and head home. Walking through the grim concrete tunnel under the Barbican, empty of people on a Saturday evening, I am exposed. There is nowhere to run if Primakov or one of his employees were to pull up beside me. I hear footsteps accelerating towards me, but when I turn there's no one. I breathe in to the count of three, out through pursed lips, and from the back of my throat, to the count of five. My equanimity returns, gradually. I am in such a self-obsessed trance that I hear ringing and don't instantly recognise it.

My Nokia. Thank goodness. Except it's not Jess.

'Gil?'

'Who is this?'

'Susan, from the press office.' The BBC press office. 'Pete Law would love a quick word.'

'What about?'

A lorry rattles past, drowning her out. All I hear is '... quite a big story.'

'I didn't get that. Say again?'

'It's best if Pete talks you through it.'

As I walk, my anxiety level rises. Why on earth would Pete Law need to talk to me late on a Saturday? After what feels like an eternity, but is probably five minutes, Pete calls.

'What's up, Pete?'

'Never a dull moment with you, old cock.'

'What do you mean?'

'We've been contacted by the *Globe on Sunday*. They've got a story about you, about your relationship with Marilyn.'

'Oh,' is all I can muster. 'What story?'

'They say they have proof of your affair with Marilyn.'

'What does "proof" mean?'

'They're not saying.'

They don't have to. They've obviously got the stolen BlackBerries.

'Pete, there's a chance they've got my BlackBerries. They were nicked.'

'Sorry to hear it. Presumably they contain messages you'd rather the world and his wife didn't see?'

'We were both single. Why is there a story?'

He scoffs. 'Don't be an idiot.'

'Should I say something to the *Globe*. Will the BBC make a statement?'

'It all depends on what you think they're going to print. What's your guess?'

Think, think. There's so much on those phones I wouldn't want anyone to read. There's my fling with Tracy, from the Downing Street press office. What if they print the abuse she sent me after she dumped me? This is a nightmare. I assume the BBC will feel obliged to sack me. I had a good run, while it lasted.

'Can I have a few minutes to think about it?' I say.

'Sure. Call me back. But don't take too long about it. The reporter was giving me grief about how close he is to deadline.'

I've used that precise line so many times when trying to pressurise an unwilling source to cough: I know the game. 'He's had all day to ring us. He can fuck himself.'

I need advice. Not from Mum and Dad. Can you imagine? What will they say when friends and relations ask them about 'that story in the *Globe*'? *Jesus.* I have to talk to Jess.

I text: *Something bad has happened. Please please ring?*

Surely she can't read that and keep me dangling. She's my best mate. And of course she was right that I bent the rules in counselling Tudor. She said I am too easily seduced by proximity to power. Is that why I had the fling with Tracy, why I was so obsessed with Marilyn? I text again:

You were right about my unhealthy relationship with power. I get it.

The phone stays silent.

I send another text. *Jess, I wouldn't ask if it wasn't important. You know that.*

Nothing.

The phone rings. Pete. *Damn.* 'We need a plan now, old cock.'

'I know.'

'So?'

'Can this be strictly between us? As mates. We go back a long way.'

'Of course it can't. We may go back a long way, but the BBC comes first. Everyone gets sacrificed on the altar of the corporation. The public good and all that. You know it. I've got to brief Janice, and she'll brief the DG.'

This is humiliating. But I have nothing left to lose. 'It will look bad, but I don't think they can prove I crossed an editorial line. As you know, Marilyn and I were sort of together, on and off, for well over a decade. But we were respectful of the rules of each other's worlds, if you know what I mean.'

'You're talking to me, not your fucking rabbi. I presume you and Marilyn fucked each other up the arse while off your heads on coke and sharing state secrets. You and I went to the same parties in the nineties. I know the score. If your relationship was shipshape and Bristol fashion, you wouldn't have lied about it for so long. The whole of the *Globe*'s story is that they are revealing something that you concealed. It will look terrible for both of you, except she's in no state to complain.'

'I'd forgotten quite what a cunt you are.'

'I'm the only cunt you've got, and you should thank your lucky stars I'm working for you, not against you. Now stop pussying around and tell me everything.'

I've never really thought about this. Or at least not properly. When Marilyn and I first started sleeping together all those years ago, we had to keep it quiet. The *FC*'s political editor in a relationship with the Labour Party leader's closest advisor: a clear breach of propriety. Our respective bosses would have been horrified. But why didn't we normalise it as the years rolled by?

'It seemed simpler to hide from the world,' I venture. 'We're both commitment-phobes. She *was*,' I correct myself. 'I am.'

The line is deathly quiet. Has he hung up?

'Pete? What should we do?'

'My instinct, but I'll have to run this past Janice and the DG, is that we should say something like, "The BBC does not believe Gil Peck breached impartiality rules, but it will be talking to him to receive assurances that is the case."'

Talking to me. I'm on probation. 'How bad is this?'

'Depends what they print. It's obvious they've got chapter and verse. As you say, presumably from your BlackBerries.'

'But if they've taken private messages and correspondence from a stolen BlackBerry, aren't they breaking the law by publishing information obtained through a criminal act?'

'They'd claim a public interest defence. You work for the licence-payer-funded BBC, and Marilyn Krol was an official whose salary was paid by taxpayers. They'll argue your relationship created

244

a conflict of interest that the public has a right to know about. I'll run it past our lawyers in case there's the possibility of an injunction, but I doubt the lawyers will think it's worth it. Also, it's not a great look for us to be using the courts to restrict the freedom of the press. The DG would ask me for advice and I'd caution against.'

What friends are for.

When the tabloids turn over a celebrity, normally my instinct is that if you live by publicity, if you make money by being in the public eye, you have to be prepared to die by publicity. Rough with the smooth. Today I can see the merits of tougher privacy laws.

'They are shits.'

'Agreed. Do you want to provide them with a statement?'

I've played it over in my mind. 'Honestly. I can't think what to say that would help. Not until I've at least read the story.'

'You could confirm you're an arsehole.'

'I assume their readers will draw that conclusion anyway.'

*

There's nothing for me to do except go home. Janice has messaged me to say that they don't think it's appropriate for me to appear on the *Ten* this evening 'under the circumstances,' which is both ominous and annoying: it means someone else will be presenting *my* NewGate nationalisation scoop.

Have I been suspended? I text back.

She doesn't answer. I think about drinking a glass of wine, maybe an entire bottle. But I need my wits. Instead I curl up on the sofa with Dog, and try in vain to find something worth watching on the television. Finally we settle on a repeat of the whimsical BBC1 cop show *New Tricks*, about two retired officers who specialise in solving unsolved cases. Comfort viewing.

Or it would be, if I could stop thinking about the mayhem in my life. Every time the retired cops on screen make another deduction, I am reminded how far I am from understanding my own mess.

Something Primakov said feels significant: *I am the Russian thug, and therefore obviously I must be the blackmailer.*

It's vital I don't jump to wrong conclusions because of prejudice and easy stereotyping. Look at Jimmy Breitner. The world fetes him as a business genius, but he once had one of his security people try to push me off Hammersmith Bridge. As for Todd, he's done worse. Much worse.

I like Johnny

That was Primakov, but Marilyn also worshipped Todd. Till the end, as far as I know. We'd stopped talking about him. It was too difficult. I wonder what there is about him in the diaries. *The diaries!* The physical threats to my person started after Jess and I went to her flat, and took the diaries. But no one knows for sure we have them, except my nephew Luke.

Luke could be in danger. I snatch the phone and ring him, almost breathless with fear.

He's chilled, when he answers. 'Sorry Uncs, I haven't made much progress. Bogged down in mocks. Nothing really to report. Most of what I've read so far is teenage girl stuff. About fancying boys and whatnot.'

'Don't worry. But could you do me a favour: could you skip the early diaries and move on to when she's grown up?' I feel like an idiot not asking him to do that in the first place.

'Will do.'

'And Luke?'

'Yeah?'

'Don't tell anyone you're doing this.'

He must hear the anxiety in my voice. 'Would I be in trouble?'

'No. Nothing like that.' *Not the way you think.* 'It's just …
confidential.'

I can't explain more than that. The less he knows, the less at risk he'll be. I hope. 'Please get it done as quick as you can, though obviously school *is* more important.'

'Obviously. Love you.'

'Love you too.'

*

At ten o'clock, just around the time I should be going on air, Pete telephones. The first editions of tomorrow's papers have landed.

'It could be worse,' he says.

I'm doing my thing of squeezing my right earlobe while holding my phone in my left. The pain is an important distraction. 'Tell me.'

'The headline is *Sex in the City* and the strap is *Tragic affair between BBC man and dead Bank of England lover.*'

I feel as though I am about to throw up.

'I've skimmed the article and I don't think there's too much to worry about, to be honest. They've done it as a sort of tragic love story, the long romance ended by Marilyn's premature death. It's a sort of beyond-the-grave kiss-and-tell.'

'So they're not accusing me or her of behaving improperly in a professional sense, of sharing our employers' secrets, or doing improper favours for each other?'

'Not that I can see. They seem to have ignored precisely the story you'd have done, if the tables were turned.'

I am worried about revealing too much to Pete. But I need to know. 'Is that because you think they haven't got all the texts, or because they chose not to use all of them?'

Pete is thinking. 'I honestly don't know. But what I do know is that if all they're going to print is in tonight's paper, we should be able to ride this out.' He says 'we', not 'you'. He means BBC first, and me a long way second.

I've been pacing the room while talking, and now I slump back on my wide and deep art-deco-style Matthew Hilton red sofa. Why hasn't Jess been in touch? She's been my best friend for the best part of my adult life. She's not just the *most* important person in my life, she may be the *only* important person in my life, apart from my needy and dysfunctional parents. Can she really drop me, just like that? Dog looks at me mournfully, reading my thoughts.

The Nokia buzzes. It's Jess, a one-word text: *tosser*.

*

I sleep badly, and wake to the predictable buzzing of the useless Nokia. I don't want to get out of bed. Too much has gone wrong. Too much is happening that I can't control. Dog empathises. He's lying at the end of the bed, paws parallel lines in front of him.

'At least you still like me,' I say.

He gets off the bed and pads to the kitchen.

Every flippin' newspaper is ringing for a comment. Feature writers I've met over the years are asking if I'll do an interview. The booker for Channel 4's *Richard & Judy* show invites me on, as does the producer of Jeremy Vine's show on Radio 2. ITV's political editor, Tom Bradby, wonders whether I'll do a clip for their bulletins. I ignore them all.

Safety first. I ring Pete in the press office, to ask if he can handle all media enquiries and requests for interviews – and to say that my instinct is to do none of them. 'That was going to be my advice,' he says. 'You might have to give one interview after the dust has settled, just to clear the air. But let's play it by ear. By the way, have you heard yet from the director of news?'

I haven't.

'She's going to ring you.'

Oh.

*

I'm not going to sit in my flat waiting for Janice to patronise me. I pull on jeans and a jumper – I don't care what I look like – and whistle to Dog. We're going round the corner to Waitrose on the Holloway Road to buy the bloody paper.

As soon as I open the door, I realise my mistake. There are perhaps a dozen paps – paparazzi photographers – outside. The whir of shutters clicking is machine-gun fire. There's no point going back inside: the damage is done. 'Gil, over here,' shouts one snapper. 'Oi Gil, mate.' Best to look down the lens, rather than guiltily at the floor. I wish I wasn't such a mess, in tracksuit bottoms and fraying Converse trainers. I didn't even run my hand through my hair.

One of my neighbours is behind me. 'All this is slightly annoying,' she says, as she passes me on the pavement.

'I'm sorry.'

Dog and I walk on purposefully. *Ring me Jess.* The phone buzzes. It's Dad.

'Your uncle Jake told me about the *Globe*. Are you OK?'

'I'm fine, Dad. These things happen. I was going to ring you.'

'What about the BBC? Are they standing by you?'

Of course, Mum and Dad would immediately worry I'd be out of a job, and about the impact on my establishment respectability. They're that generation. 'Honestly, Dad, don't worry. I'll ring you later.'

'We do worry Gil. When will you be over?'

'Soon Dad.'

Picking up the *Globe on Sunday* in Waitrose and walking to the cash register is an excruciating experience. I add a bottle of Sauvignon Blanc, a baguette and a bag of peanuts as a sort of camouflage for the paper – as if I am a fourteen-year-old buying a dirty mag – though it's an unnecessary precaution. The oblivious checkout boy doesn't bother to raise his eyes from the conveyor belt as he scans through the items.

I make myself walk all the way back to the flat before I look at the paper. I'm not going to let some pap photograph me reading about my own humiliation. But when I finally open it, I am reassured. Pete was right: it could have been much worse. There are a few suggestive texts, but it turns out Marilyn and I were restrained in our messaging, repressed even. The tabloid makes the most of 'that was amazing last night' and 'twice in 45 minutes!' If Marilyn wasn't dead, I assume the paper's front-page headline would have been the '45 minutes' line. As it is, Breitner's hacks presumably followed some kind of code of respect for the lately departed by toning it down. I still feel ashamed. And since Janice is not calling, my assumption is that she's simply finishing the paperwork prior to dismissing me.

If it's going to happen, I might as well know. I ring her.

'Hang on a second,' she says. 'I'm with my mum.' She puts her hand over the receiver, mutters something inaudibly to her mother and then closes a door behind her. 'As I've said to you many times, you are supposed to report the story, not be the story.' She sighs.

'I know. I'll respect whatever you think is the appropriate course of action.'

Her voice is stern. 'You've been an idiot. You should have told me about your relationship when you joined the BBC.'

'It wasn't really a relationship. It was an on-off thing, that had been part of our lives for a number of years. I'm not quite sure what I would have said to you, how I would have described it. I still don't, really.'

'All right.' Intake of breath. 'I have an important question to ask you. Do you think there is evidence of you behaving improperly in a professional sense, that is in a work sense – anything that would lead the Trust to believe that you had breached impartiality rules, the Charter or the law?'

The BBC Trust is the semi-arm's-length regulator and guardian of the BBC. I note that Janice has, characteristically, chosen her words carefully. She's asked me if there is *evidence* of wrongdoing, not whether it actually happened. Obviously Marilyn and I had loads of conversations that, if they were ever made public, would be an embarrassment to us and to our employers. I assume Janice has guessed that. But I am hopeful we never committed anything too incriminating to text or email. Is this the moment to tell Janice about Tracy? Probably not.

'Because the phones were nicked, it's hard to check,' I say cautiously. 'But we were careful. If I texted about a work thing, it would have been to set up a conversation.' I also think, though don't tell her, that whoever stole the phones may not want to start hares running about Marilyn's involvement in the NewGate debacle.

There's a deafening pause. My career flashes before my eyes.

'Here's what I propose,' Janice rejoins at last. 'Take the rest of the day off. Let's wait for the fallout. And whatever you do, don't talk to the media. Direct all enquiries to Pete. For what it's worth, I think this is similar to the *Mail*'s attack on you, jealousy and sour grapes from the *Globe* and Breitner.'

'Thank you.'

'You may be on the front page of the *Globe on Sunday*, but every other paper is leading with the NewGate nationalisation story that you broke. You're getting the biggest stories of the day, for us. They're desperate to finish you off.'

There are other reasons beyond professional jealousy for someone trying to close me down, but I'll keep those to myself.

'Thanks, Janice.' I try to sound humble.

'Unless there's more to come out that you're not sharing with me, we'll stand behind you.'

*

I go for another workout, then return home. I am in a bunker. I get the odd text, my thoughtful colleagues checking I'm OK and a couple of my less sensitive male acquaintances teasing me about the twice-in-forty-five-minutes. Nothing from Jess.

251

Anxiety rinses my torso, my chest and upper arms. I ruined my only proper friendship.

The intercom in the hall buzzes. My assumption is it's a tabloid hack trying their luck. I'm about to say 'Go away' when I recognise the 'It's me.' Jess.

After waiting so long for her, now she's here I don't know what to do. The only thing I can think to say is, 'Who's looking after Amy?'

'Mum's babysitting.'

I am frozen in the hall. Jess takes charge. She looks me straight in the eyes and says, 'You're a fucking idiot. Come here.'

I do as she says. She puts her arms around me, and I burst into tears, great gasping convulsions.

'Please forgive me. I've been such an idiot.' It comes out raspingly, between gasps for air.

'Yes you have. But we're a team, aren't we?'

She steers me into my living room and we sit on the sofa. I can feel her thigh pressing against mine. Is that on purpose? Is it an accident? All I know is that I like it, and I'd like her not to move her leg away.

Another text buzzes through, this time from a number I don't recognise.

Such gripping stuff on your phones. The Globe *has only the half of it. Yours aye, Quasimodo*

'What the hell is this?' I hand it to Jess.

'Quasimodo. The hunchback of Notre Dame. What's he got to do with anything?'

'Someone's idea of a joke?' After everything that's happened, jumping at shadows and wondering if I'm going mad, it's almost a relief to see such crude intimidation.

'*Is* there more on the phones that they can use against you?' Jess asks.

'I've obviously been thinking about that.' The honest truth is I can't be sure. 'You know as well as I do, newspapers usually put the juiciest stuff first. But equally, any text out of context can be misconstrued.' I don't add that I've never felt so close to the edge. Again I don't want to mention Tracy.

Jess squeezes my hand. 'It's going to be all right. The way they're trying to silence you, it shows we're on to something important. That's what we do, you and me. We do big stories. We'll crack it.'

I feel shattered. The crying, the stress, has exhausted me.

'Quasimodo?' I croak. I think of the photographs I found in the Filofax. 'The note that was sent to Marilyn, it was signed "Q". Could that be Quasimodo?'

'Maybe.'

'So whoever was blackmailing Marilyn is trying to warn me off.'

'Which is the dumbest thing they could do.'

'Why do you say that?'

'Because when we're a team, we win.'

Then Jess does something that is incredible and what I want most in the whole universe. She gently puts her hands on either side of my face and pulls me towards her. Her lips are on mine, closed and then wide. We breathe each other in. I don't know how long we will enfold each other, but whenever we stop it will be too soon.

Chapter 20

SOMETHING IS DIFFERENT THIS MORNING, when Dog whimpers by the side of the bed to wake me rather than jumping on it. *Who's the stranger next to me?* he asks. It's Jess, warm and soft. Jess! In her knickers, and my Ramones T-shirt.

'Morning,' she says. And smiles.

What do I think about this?

'How do you feel about last night?' she asks.

I turn onto my back and stare at the ceiling. 'It was incredible.'

'Be serious.'

'I am.'

'What do you mean by incredible?'

'That it's hard to believe, that something so nice has happened.' I look at her.

She smiles. I smile.

'So what was best? That we slept in the same bed? The talking? The sex?'

I'm embarrassed. 'All of it.'

I have a flashback of tasting her, smelling her, hearing her moan, losing myself in her. 'The sex was the best ever, amazing.'

'Was it just about the sex?'

Is there an edge there?

'Is it bad that the sex was good?'

'Of course not.'

I reach out and take her hand, summoning up the courage to meet her gaze.

'It was about feeling safe with you. Like coming home.'

I panic. That sounded desperate. Mad. I've blown it.

'I feel the same,' she says. *Thank you God.*

'Maybe we'd been frozen,' she continues, 'paralysed, both of us, for years.'

I add something that takes me by surprise. 'I feel happy.'

'Same.'

She rolls towards me, on top of me, and plants generous kisses all over my face. At this Dog gets overexcited, jumps on the bed and on top of Jess. She laughs and pushes him off.

'I'd better check in with Mum and Amy.' Somewhere in between the living room and the bedroom last night, Jess rang her mum to make sure she didn't mind sleeping over with Amy.

I haul her back to me. 'A kiss first please.'

*

'What now?' Jess asks, over black coffee.

'For us, or the banking crash?'

'The crash.'

She's in work mode. Already. Fine by me. My middle names are 'compartmentalise' and 'displacement'. There'll be plenty of time later to assess and discuss where we're going.

'I've been thinking,' I say. Hiding here in the bunker, away from the paps, has not been wasted. 'What if we got it the wrong way round? What if Marilyn didn't do what the blackmailer wanted?'

Jess's eyes narrow, slightly. Does she mind me talking about Marilyn? I dismiss the thought.

'What do you mean?'

'We assumed Marilyn was being bullied into supporting Jackson's and Primakov's bid for NewGate. But what if it was

256

actually the other way round? The big money to be made was from the collapse of NewGate. What if those blackmailing her wanted her to let NewGate fail, and she was resisting by trying to facilitate the Jackson rescue?'

Jess reflects. 'In a way, that makes more sense, of the leaks to you, and everything else. And for her, whoever was threatening to shame her, it would have made no difference. Living with the imminent threat of such public humiliation would have been awful.'

Would that be reason enough for her to hang herself? Did reputation and career mean that much to Marilyn? Was it really everything?

'The note from Q doesn't say what she was supposed to do, it just threatens to send the photos to Breitner,' I say.

Jess winces. 'It's brutal, sadistic. Marilyn knew what Q wanted. And from what you've told me, she would have refused to give in to blackmail. It makes sense that her backing for Jackson's takeover was the opposite of what the blackmailer wanted.'

'We don't have to guess, do we? The diaries, the confirmation will be in them.'

Giving them to Luke was so dumb. I'll text him and make a plan to retrieve them. He'll be at school, so it may take a few hours.

I pour myself another cup of coffee. 'The photographs were taken at Elliott's place. It must be Elliott's picture. I assume he took them,' I say.

'Probably right – but if he didn't, he would know who did. We can ask him tonight.'

'What's happening tonight?'

She smirks. 'Oh yes. When I was cross with you, I didn't tell you.'

'Tell me what?'

'We're going to a party, at Elliott's place in the Cotswolds.'

257

'We are?'

'Well, me and a plus one.'

I'm trying to work out why I haven't got my own invitation. Elliott and his mind games.

'What's the party in aid of?'

'Primakov. He's introducing Primakov to people who matter.'

'Which presumably means Primakov's paying for the party. But how do you know it's for him?'

'How do you think I know? When we were sniffing around the Russian, investigating him, word got back to Elliott and he rang me. Told me I should meet him, suggested I come to the party.'

It's classic Elliott. Charm first, coerce later.

Jess stands up, leans down and kisses me. 'Be my date tonight, honeybun?'

*

We leave London on the M40, and arrive at Elliott's Worcestershire mansion in Jess's VW Golf at 8.30. Large real-flame torches light the long drive. We are signposted to a field where hessian matting has been laid as a barrier against clagging mud. Pretty much every other car is a Range Rover, a Bentley or a Merc. I notice a couple of Ferraris and a Lamborghini. Show-offs. I am wearing Christian Lacroix, a double-breasted slightly rough-weave browny grey suit. The ostentatious lining is pinkish and blue floral. It's what I love most about this suit, though only I know it's there. It matches the flamboyant pink of my shirt. Jess is even more gorgeous than normal, in a red Marc Jacobs mini dress with a low neckline and laced leather boots. Maybe I *am* in love.

'I think I should take these boots off before we get to the house,' she says. 'I don't want them ruined in the mud. Will you help me?' With the car door open, she swivels in the driver's seat towards me. She ostentatiously hitches up her skirt so I can see she's not wearing knickers. Am I supposed to say anything? 'Bit of motivation for you,' she smiles. Energised, I grip the foot of her boot and pull. 'Grab my trainers from the back seat, will you?'

As we walk to the portico, she links her arm through mine. This is new. I like it. When we're at the door, Elliott's employees check our names against those on their clipboards.

'Good to see you, Ms Neeskens, Gil,' says one, a brunette in a short beige skirt that shows off her spectacular legs.

Jess digs an elbow in my ribs. 'Stop gawping,' she whispers.

'She probably has a first in psychology and philosophy from Oxford,' I whisper back.

'That's not what's caught your attention' she says.

Elliott hires the brightest, most attractive Oxbridge gradu-ates, and persuades them to behave like hostesses. It's so hideous.

As soon as we enter, waiters offer us Krug or a Sazerac, a cocktail of absinthe and cognac. I need to keep a clear head, so I take the champagne.

'Where will I find Elliott?' I mutter to Jess.

There must be three hundred people here. Cabinet ministers mix with ageing pop idols, British movie stars and feline Russian models. Like Elliott's London parties, the drink – especially the first-growth claret – is painfully expensive, and the caviar flows like bitumen being ladled onto a road. I can't see the host.

'We should split up.'

'OK, sweet cheeks.'

I walk to a heaving ground-floor reception room. At the door, a woman I can't place says 'Gil Peck' warmly, and kisses me on each cheek. 'I always watch you on the BBC. I especially like it that you enrage my husband.'

259

Heavens. It's Lydia, Alex Elliott's Russian wife. Wearing clothes. Did she notice I was in the audience for her recent performance? I blush.

'Alex says you are the most important journalist,' she carries on. 'The only one who matters.'

She puts her hand against my chest to emphasise the point. Her wrist is garlanded with diamonds and emeralds, as is her neck – all Harry Winston, I assume. 'Some of his friends say you hate rich people, but I tell him, no, Mr Peck hates only arseholes.'

I smile, despite myself. 'Does he often discuss me?'

Either she doesn't hear me, or she ignores the question. 'I read in the newspaper that you were friends with the bank lady who died. So sad.'

'Alex knew her too.' I'm trying to remember how long Elliott and Lydia have been married. I have a flashback to Lydia's bed, only this time she's fucking Marilyn. I fight the image, try to kill it.

She doesn't bat her sumptuous mascaraed eyes. 'Alex has many friends.'

'I noticed. Where is he, by the way?'

'Oh somewhere, doing his business.' There's contempt in her voice.

And then, without even the pretence of an 'Excuse me', she detaches herself. Her antennae have detected someone more interesting. Meathead. I can't be arsed to be berated by him again. I go in the opposite direction.

*

The party spills between opulent reception rooms and a parkland warmed by braziers. Through one of the picture windows, I notice Jess is chatting up Jackson on the terrace. I want to eavesdrop, but spot a banker lost in a corner. I stroll over.

'Not my scene,' Sir Stan Blackwell says, looking unexpectedly pleased to see me. 'But everyone's here, so I guess I have to be.'

'How's it going?' I ask inanely.

He shrugs, 'Our share price still hasn't recovered. The hunt is on for the next banking basket case, thanks to you. Everyone's a short seller these days. It's not easy.'

'Ravel's the most aggressive of the lot,' I observe.

'He is and he isn't. As I told you at that bloody conference, he isn't shorting us. Owes us too much.'

I remember what Patrick Munis told me over lunch. 'I heard a rumour Ravel might be in the market to buy a bank. When they're cheap enough.'

At that, Blackwell's Calvinist face cracks a smile. 'He'll not be buying PTBG.'

'Why do you say that?'

'Trust me.'

Trust you? Give me a break. I change the subject.

'Do you fancy a glass of Elliott's extraordinary claret?'

'Does he have a fancy cellar here too?'

'Oh yes.'

I lead him to the climate-controlled wine room. In this gaff it is a barrel-ceilinged room in the basement, five times the size of the one in London. Michael, the sommelier, serves Blackwell, gives me a wink, and then discreetly pours mine from a different magnum. I look at the label: Château Haut-Brion. I would guess the price as two thousand pounds. I smell it. Just the aroma compensates for the journey here and the need to suck up to some of the worst people in the country.

I still haven't found Elliott, though, and Jess hasn't messaged me. Who here are most useful to him? He'll be with them.

'Do you like the drink?' says a deep, accented voice behind me.

I turn around. Primakov.

'Whatever else I think about Alex, I can't fault his hospitality.' I take a gulp.

'Actually, Mr Peck, I think you'll find it's my generosity you are enjoying.'

'Of course. Thank you.'

'This is *my* party. Tell me, why is making friends in Britain such an expensive business?'

'Good question. Do you think it's worse here than in other countries?'

'Yes. Even when you say you are doing something for free, you send a bill the next day. You obviously need the money.'

'In what way?'

'I have never seen such shoddily built houses as those in your country. Walls made of paper, windows that don't fit the frames, draughts, damp. And with a price of ten million pounds.'

'You don't *have* to live here, you know.'

'There are compensations.'

I take another sip of the liquid gold and brace myself. 'Did you have any thoughts about what we discussed?'

'Mr Jackson said the wrong man drowned. Should have been you.' He is deadpan.

'Oh dear,' is all I can muster. What's the etiquette? Am I supposed to laugh?

'Don't worry, Mr Peck. I am sure he was joking. By the way, it wasn't him putting pressure on your girlfriend.'

My first instinct is to explain she wasn't really my girlfriend. That Marilyn and I had an unusual relationship. And then I realise quite how nuts that would be, even by my standards. In that instant of reflection, Primakov pats my upper arm and walks purposefully away. I don't know what to think about it. Some of what he says is patently untrue. Also he is dangerous. But I believe what he says about Marilyn and Jackson. It's consistent with our view that she was psychologically tortured by the short seller.

So where is Elliott?

This is a house of corridors. I walk along one, away from the hubbub. At the end is a shut door. I knock, no answer, so I turn the handle and enter. It's a family sitting room. There's a baby grand piano in one corner covered with photographs. Let's see what memories Elliott wishes to preserve. Most are studies in vanity, snaps of him with assorted world leaders and notables. Elliott with Paul McCartney, Elliott with Bill Clinton, Elliott with Nelson Mandela. One's different. It's Elliott as a student at Oxford, with nine others, all in double-breasted, velvet-collared, three-quarter-length frock coats, the boys in grey-striped spongebag trousers, the girls in miniskirts. They are leering, waving open bottles of Bollinger and conspicuously pissed. One girl's breast is almost completely exposed, another is flaunting suspenders.

I know this mob. It's the Malmsey, one of Oxford's clubs for the spoiled and entitled, historically just for boys but latterly allowing in girls who didn't object to rampant sexism or being wanked over by sexually dysfunctional Old Etonians. I wasn't a member – their contempt for an oik like me would have been almost as much as my contempt for them – but their exploits were notorious.

I'm still staring at the photo when I hear voices at the door. *Shit.* How do I explain my snooping? I don't want to try, so I hide behind the floor-to-ceiling rose damask curtain, just as the door swings open.

Two people – so far as I can tell – come in. I hear the click as the door closes, then the wheeze of upholstery as they sit.

'I've spoken again to our Saudi friends,' says a voice I recognise. Ravel. 'They're prepared to provide twenty-five billion in the form of a convertible pref, with an eight per cent coupon.'

'That's expensive money.' Elliott's voice, nearer to me.

'Not if it's the difference between life and death.'

'I thought these guys were your friends.'

'They are. Known them for years. But they are not morons.'

As silently as I can, I fish my little Olympus recorder from my jacket pocket and switch it on. The button makes a terrifyingly loud click, but Ravel's voice drowns it out.

'Do you think Stan will bite?'

Stan Blackwell. That's why he's here.

'I bloody well hope so,' says Elliott. 'You can ask him yourself. He'll join us in a minute.'

On cue, I hear the sound of the door opening and then Blackwell's unmistakable Glaswegian. 'Gentlemen. I understand you have news.'

'The Saudis are willing to provide twenty-five billion pounds of capital,' says Ravel. 'Enough to tide you over.' He repeats what he told Elliott earlier, which in essence means that the Saudis will provide enough money to prevent PTBG from collapsing, but at a steep price.

'That's prohibitive,' Blackwell says. 'There'll be nothing left over for our other shareholders.'

'Don't be an arsehole, Stan,' says Ravel. 'If you go kaput, there'll be nothing for anyone. You are up shit creek. You're bust. The shares are effectively worthless. Your choice is between our Saudi friends, and the socialists in 10 Downing Street. Say the word, and I'll tell the Saudis their money isn't needed.'

Jesus. Ravel says the choice is between a Saudi rescue and nationalisation. Of Britain's biggest bank.

'Don't be a cunt, Chris,' says Blackwell. 'You want to keep the government out just as much as I do. Neither of us needs government-appointed auditors looking at our books.'

'Stan, calm down. We're on the same page.'

'I'm not sure you hyperactively short selling the banks puts us on the same page,' says Blackwell tartly.

'Maybe you and the others shouldn't have stuffed your balance sheets with toxic shit.'

'Ladies, ladies, behave yourselves,' Elliott pacifies. 'And by the way, neither of you should count your chickens. The Sheikh says there'll be no cash unless and until we deliver Athena.'

'I am well aware,' says Ravel. 'It's being sorted.'

There's a shuffling of chairs and feet as they stand up. 'Let me know how you get on,' says Elliott. 'Stan, the Sheikh is upstairs being entertained by two of Lydia's friends. Try not to piss him off.'

Blackwell grunts. I hear the sound of the door open and close as they head back to the party. I stay behind the curtains long enough to be sure they're all out and well clear of the room.

Blackwell didn't lie to me about one thing. Chris Ravel isn't trying to destroy PTBG; he wants to rescue it. But Stan has been lying to everyone about the financial health of PTBG: it's in dire straits. Maybe that's why he and Ravel are so desperate for the bank's books to be kept away from government auditors, but my hunch is there's something else. And what's 'Athena'?

I take the risk and emerge from behind the curtain. There is something I want before I leave. At the piano, I remove the Malmsey Club photo from its frame and put it in my inside jacket pocket. After hiding the empty frame under a sofa, I gingerly open the door and exit.

When I'm halfway along the corridor, heading towards the party, Elliott comes out of a loo on the left. He's not pleased to see me.

'What are you doing here?' There's aggression in his voice.

'Just looking for a loo.'

'You've found one. Congratulations.'

He holds open the door for me with an ironic bow. But I don't go in, because I'm paralysed by what he's wearing. Under a black baggy silk jacket – maybe Yamamoto – is a black T-shirt. The picture on the T-shirt is Charles Laughton in his classic 1939 performance as the Hunchback of Notre Dame.

Quasimodo.

'You're taking the piss.'

His eyes are wide and mocking. 'What on earth do you mean?'

'You're Quasimodo. *You* sent me the message warning me off. You paid someone to nick my phones, and you gave my texts to the *Globe*.'

He puts a condescending arm around my shoulders. 'Oh dear. You've enjoyed too much of my wine again. Maybe have a glass of water and a sit-down.'

I brush him off. 'What is your game?'

'You're nuts. Shall I find someone to look for Jess? Maybe it's time for you to go home.'

'Don't patronise me. You know what I'm talking about.'

Without me registering, Elliott's been shepherding me back to the main party room. But if he thinks the presence of his poncy guests will make me shut up, he's misjudged.

'You sent those pictures to Marilyn, you scumbag.' He just smirks. I rarely feel tempted to physical violence, but right now I want to smash his face in. 'Why were you blackmailing her? Whose interest were you serving? Ravel's?'

'"Blackmail" is an ugly word. I'd be careful what you say in front of witnesses. You wouldn't want to find yourself in court facing a suit for slander, would you?' And then he leans in and whispers in my ear. 'You're out of your depth, Gil. I hope you can swim.'

Before I can react, there's a shout of, 'Fireworks. On the lawn now.'

The crowd surges through the French windows. Elliott uses it to break away from me. I'll find him later. Now I need Jess.

The room has emptied. She must be in the park. A waiter loitering by the doors thrusts a Sazerac at me as I step outside. I take a huge mouthful, as the first rockets fizz up into the night sky.

Among the flickering torches and the flashes from the fireworks, it's impossible to find anyone in this crowd. I meander aimlessly, until I spot the glamorous, long-legged woman from the entrance.

'Have you seen Jess Neeskens?'

Overhead there's a shower of gunpowder stars that bathes the woman's face in gold. Her lips and cheeks glisten with the moisture in the air.

'I think I saw Jess down by the lake. I'll show you.'

The grass is slick with autumn dew. I am a little groggy – *wow, this cocktail is strong* – and I almost slip twice. The second time, the woman slides her arm under my jacket to steady me.

'It's cold,' she says. She's wearing a thin blouse. Her silk camisole is visible underneath. She guides me, her arm still wrapped around me.

Shit. I hope Jess can't see us. She might misinterpret. We're nearly at the lake, its black glassy surface lit up with reflected rockets and starbursts.

'I can't see Jess,' I say.

'This way.' The woman steers me around the lake, away from the crowds. I am confused. Why are we going away from everyone? It feels bad, but I don't know why. We're heading towards the water. *Water.* My head is trying to show me something, something important I've forgotten, but there's a fog in my brain and I can't see it.

Above us there's a kaleidoscope of a thousand colours. These are the most beautiful pyrotechnics of my life. I want to share the preciousness of this moment with this woman, but I am struggling to find words. I'm woozy, wobbly. I want to go back, I want to go home. I can't.

'Where are we going?' I mumble.

'Don't worry, darling. This is what you want.'

I feel planks under my feet. I'm on a pontoon dock. It's familiar. Why?

Hampstead Heath, Highgate Ponds. Muller.

I need to leave. I turn and try to walk back to the house, but my legs won't do what I'm telling them. The woman is no longer at my side. She's in front of me. Facing me. I look to left and right. Water on both sides. We've come a long way down the pontoon.

Should I shout? Or wave? I look to the shore and we're hidden by willows around the edge of the lake.

She moves closer towards me, circling her arms around me. I can feel her warm breath on my face. Her breasts are now pressed against me. *This is wrong.* 'Don't worry, darling,' she whispers again, close to my ear. 'It'll all soon be over.'

The fireworks above are exploding in a concatenation of fire and thunder. I look up and then down at the angelic face so close to mine, lips slightly parted, eyes fiery and wide.

Please let me go.

There are hands on my chest. Pushing gently, firmly. I shuffle back, and then there's nothing beneath my feet. And I am tumbling. Falling backwards. Down. Into cold and darkness.

Chapter 21

Have you ever had one of those nights where you want to wake up but you have lost all power to move your limbs? This happened to me a lot when I was a child. It was terrifying. I was paralysed, and I knew for certain I would die if I couldn't shake myself out of it. It took the most monumental effort of will to thrash about and force myself awake. That's how I feel now, except I'm not clammy under the blankets but colder than I've ever been. And I have this inescapable fear that if I do what I am desperate to do, which is breathe in, I am finished.

Kick, Gil, kick. There's a voice in my head. It's familiar. It's not mine. It's a woman's voice. Who? It's Mum. It's Jess. It's Marilyn. *Whatever you do, don't breathe in.*

Despite myself I am still sinking. Nothing works. *Nothing works!* Down I go. Deeper and deeper. I seem to be falling forever. Perhaps I want to die. I couldn't save my sister Clare, I couldn't save Marilyn, I abandoned them. I don't deserve to live.

Now I'm back in the chemotherapy room with Mum. She's grey. Something very bad has happened. What? I try to say to her, *It's all right Mum. You'll be all right.* And I see Jess on the bench of the playground in Queen's Park. Amy plunges head first down the slide. But Jess just stares blankly into nowhere.

Fuck it. Elliott's not going to win. I can see Alex Elliott's face, transformed into Charles Laughton's leering Quasimodo, brandishing a photograph. *Fuck you, Elliott. Fuck you.* From somewhere, a shot of adrenaline is injected into my system. I can barely hold my breath. Water is seeping into my lungs, despite myself.

Then it happens. The miracle. I will myself to kick and the neurons spark a reaction. Kick. Again. Kick. Again. My arms, too. They are pushing me higher. I have the power: to move, to save myself. *Fuck you, Elliott.* My head breaks the surface.

I gulp in great lungfuls of air. It's not enough. More. I need more. Where's the pontoon? I panic. Have I drifted out? The fireworks are over. It's too dark. Where's land? I flail, and my left hand hits the wood of the landing. Hard, though it's not really pain I feel because the icy water has anaesthetised my nerves.

I need to haul myself up somehow. I'm weak, too weak. I've swum a hundred miles. First I pull desperately with fingers on the edge of the pontoon. Then swivel from fingers to palms. Push. Push. Push. One more. Then slither. And wriggle. Like a fat walrus. *I am the walrus.* I laugh at my joke. The walrus has landed. I'm on my side, on the pontoon.

I'm freezing. I'm not sure I've ever been so cold. Safe now. But I'll have a quick sleep, a quick *schloof* and then I'll go back. Just a little nap. I curl up and drift into sleep. It's a nice sleep. Because someone I really like is here. *Gil,* I hear. It's that voice again, the one who saved me when I was in the water. *Gil, for God's sake wake up.* I don't want to wake up. It's nice in my dreams. I am safe here. *Gil. It's me, Jess. Please wake up.* Jess? I remember now. My girlfriend. What a nice thought. I have a girlfriend. She's brainy, and pretty, and we like each other.

What on earth?!!! Someone's hurting me. Pushing down hard on my chest. I seem to be on my back now. There are hands on

270

my thorax. Pressing. Pressing. Pressing. I open my eyes. 'What's going on?' I splutter. 'Stop that, please. It hurts.'

'Gil, you're OK.'

I push myself up into a sitting position. Jess is on her knees just in front of me.

'What were you doing?'

'I panicked. I thought your heart had stopped. I was trying to give you CPR.'

'CPR?'

'Well what I thought was CPR. I had first-aid training ages ago. But truthfully, I've forgotten how to do it.'

I laugh. She laughs. And then she sits down beside me and throws her arms around me. Just for a minute, we hold each other, till I start to shiver uncontrollably.

'You're soaked through,' she says. She takes off her jacket and wraps it around me.

I sit back on my haunches, legs tucked under me, and start rocking and crying. I seem to be crying all the time at the moment. What's got into me?

'I've got water all over your beautiful dress. I'm so sorry.'

She snorts. 'Don't be an idiot. Who cares. Are you OK?'

'I don't know. I think so.'

'How did you end up in the water?'

I try to piece it together. 'I was looking for you. That girl we saw at reception brought me here.'

'The girl with the legs?'

'Yes. Sorry.'

Jess sighs.

'She said you'd be here. She tried to kiss me. And the next thing I remember is that I was in the water.'

Jess is frowning. 'So you made a pass and she pushed you in?'

'No, I promise. That's not what happened. It was like I was really stoned, but I didn't take anything. I was totally

271

out of it. I had no interest in her. I swear. She had some game, some plan.' I'm spluttering incoherently, but it's the best I can do.

'We can talk about this later. Now we need to get you dry.'

'You are the best thing that has happened to me for years, maybe forever. I'm not going to risk losing you. Please believe me.'

'You're good with words, Gil.'

But she hauls me to my feet and wraps herself around me again.

'I think somebody wants to kill me.'

'I think you may be right. But how much did you have to drink?'

'You think I'm pissed and fell in.'

'I don't think that. But it's what other people will think, and it's what Elliott will say.'

We're walking slowly back to the lights of the house. Jess has her arm around my back, just like the long-legged angel of death. I'm still shaking.

'I had a glass of Krug when I arrived, then a glass of wine, and then a slurp of a Sazerac as I came out. Normally that would not be enough to knock me out.'

Jess shrugs. She's not convinced, and nor am I.

Every few steps, I stumble.

'You do seem pretty drunk.'

'I swear I'm not. There's something else in my system.'

There are people milling on the terrace. I have a horror of being seen like this. 'Can we go straight to the car park, please?'

'Isn't it better if we get you dry first?'

'Please Jess.'

'OK. But we need to find the girl.'

I never want to see her again.

'No.' I am thinking rationally again. 'If I make a complaint, she'll just say I made a pass. Elliott will spin it, and after what's been in the *Globe*, everyone will take her side. I'll be a laughing stock. A sex pest. Finished.'

Janice would never stand by me after a second such scandal. That would be a risk too far for the corporation.

Jess gives me a squeeze. We skirt around the front of the house. Although I calculate it's well after midnight, few guests are leaving the party, and the only observers of our eccentric retreat are a couple of car park stewards and a security guard. I am terrified they will offer to help, but none does. We're just another pair of entitled rich bastards off their heads.

Jess puts me in the VW, turns on the engine and puts the heater on full blast. 'Take off your clothes.'

'I'm not in the mood.'

'You're always in the mood.' She pecks me on the cheek. 'I'm going back to the terrace,' she says. 'Elliott put out blankets for smokers and anyone who wanted to sit outside. I'll grab a couple.' She turns and takes something from the back seat, a North Face anorak. 'Drape this over you till I'm back.'

I wriggle out of my trousers in Jess's front seat, mourning the wretched state of my beautiful suit. I assume the crappy Nokia is dead. It takes all my strength to get the horrible, clinging clothes off. By the time I've finally dumped all the wet things on the back seat, Jess has come back with three blankets. She wraps them around me, then clips the seatbelt over them. They are surprisingly soft.

I'm so exhausted, my eyes keep closing. I try to keep awake by turning to look at her. She is sombre, angry.

'I'm sorry,' I mumble.

'It's not you. It's that everyone denied any knowledge of your leggy temptress. The girls at the front said they didn't know what I was talking about. I ran into Elliott, so I made up some bullshit about her telling me she wanted to get into journalism. He said he didn't have the faintest idea who I was talking about. It's as though she never existed. They are such liars.'

I'm relieved. I'd feared she'd be wheeled out by Elliott to allege that I made a fool of myself coming on too strong. I assume at some point he'll ramp up his campaign against me, the way he did with Marilyn. But I am too tired to talk about it. I close my eyes.

Some time later, I'm woken by the stirring refrain of 'Lilliburlero'. Jess has put on the World Service. We've come into London, on the A40 flyover, passing White City on the right-hand side.

'Welcome back,' she says.

'Thanks.'

'How are you feeling?'

I think about it. 'Surprisingly OK.'

'Headache?'

'Funnily enough, nothing.'

On the radio, there's a report about the contest between Hillary Clinton and Barack Obama to be the Democrat candidate in the forthcoming presidential election.

'Do you think the lake water was clean?' I ask. 'Do I need a tetanus injection?'

'Play it safe and go to your GP in the morning.'

On the radio, the reporter is saying that the nomination is Clinton's to lose, but that the relatively unknown Obama is picking up momentum.

'I'll take you back to mine,' says Jess. I'm grateful. I'm scared of being alone tonight. 'You'll have to sleep in the spare room: I haven't had a chance to talk to Amy about the two of us yet.'

'Of course. Thank you for looking after me.'

'You'd do the same for me.'

'I worry that in practice it's always you rescuing me.'

She smiles. I feel warm, for the first time in hours.

*

I thrash around in the bed all night. I'm back in the lake, frantically trying to swim to the surface, but someone is holding my feet, trying to pull me down. At 7.15, I am roused by Amy, who comes in with a cup of black coffee.

'Are you moving in?' she asks.

I don't know the right answer. Before I make a fool of myself, Jess appears at the door. 'Is that what Mum wants, Amy?'

'Yes Mummy, I think you do.'

'What Mum wants is for you to find your school rucksack and put on your coat.'

'OK grumpy Mummy.'

After Amy runs out, Jess comes over to kiss me, checking immediately afterwards that we've not been observed.

'How are you this morning?'

'Probably better than I deserve to be.'

'You need a shower: you pong of stagnant water. We've got a lot to discuss, so get a move on.'

'Have you got anything I can wear?'

An hour later, we're in Jess's airy front room. I've just rung my neighbour on Jess's phone to ask her to feed Dog and take him out the front. I look absurd in leisurewear that's several sizes too small. Jess is in jeans and a clingy black cashmere polo neck. I can't take my eyes off her. It's embarrassing. We're next to each other on the sofa, and I still can't believe that it's OK for her body to be in contact with mine.

'Did you tell Elliott I fell in the lake, when you saw him?' I ask.

'No. You said you didn't want anyone to know.'

'So if he organised it, won't he think I'm dead?' I'm wondering if that could be used to our advantage.

'Seems unlikely. Won't he work out why I was looking for the brunette?'

'Yeah probably.' I'm feeling a bit let down. Being dead briefly felt glamorous. 'Where are my trousers?' I ask.

'Utility room at the end of the kitchen. They're still unwear-able.'

I find them and rummage through pockets until I locate the photo I stole and the Olympus recorder. The recorder won't switch on: the water killed it. But the recording is on a smart media card, which should be intact.

'Do you have an Olympus recorder, or some way of playing this media card?' I ask Jess.

'I've got a gizmo that will allow me to play it through the laptop.' She fiddles around with a box that plugs into her computer. 'What's this?'

'I eavesdropped on a conversation last night. I recorded it.'

The recording is muffled by the thick curtain I was behind, but we can make out most of it. Jess listens intently to Ravel, Blackwell and Elliott discussing their plan to save PTBG by extracting £25 billion from the Saudis. We then play it again, and Jess makes notes.

'So PTBG is almost bust and looking to the Saudis for a rescue, to avoid being nationalised by Tudor,' Jess says, and then sucks on the end of her Pilot pen. 'But why would Blackwell and Ravel prefer a takeover by the Saudis? Why does it matter so much to keep out the British government?'

'Presumably the Saudis would leave Blackwell at the helm. He'd keep his multi-million-pound salary. He'd avoid public humiliation. That wouldn't happen if Neville Tudor was in charge. Tudor would sack him and pillory him. And under Saudi control, there'd be the illusion for the board that the bank was still an independent operation.'

'But with that much money going in, it would effectively be nationalisation by Saudi Arabia. Why's that better than UK nationalisation?'

'Never underestimate the importance of appearances to these people. They live and die by self-delusion,' I say.

'But why should Ravel care about any of it?' Jess always wants all the answers at once. Uncertainty induces almost physical discomfort in her. 'If he was being consistent, he'd take the view that PTBG had been incompetent, like NewGate, and ought to be allowed to go bust.'

'Play the recording back again. There is half an answer.'

She does. Midway through we hear Blackwell's strong Glaswegian accent: *You want to keep the government out just as much as I do. Neither of us needs government-appointed auditors looking at our books.*

She presses pause. 'Blackwell implies there are transactions in PTBG's ledgers that could embarrass Ravel.'

'Now listen to the next bit.'

The Sheikh says there'll be no cash unless and until we deliver Athena.

'What's Athena?' I ask.

'I think I know.' Jess opens up her browser on the laptop, and Googles. 'I'm right. Athena Tech, based just outside of Cambridge.'

'What do they do?'

'Privately owned. There's a limit to what's in the public domain. The paper's been interested in them for a while. They're reputed to have cutting-edge military technology, something to do with missile defence systems.' She clicks on a link to the *FC* website. 'There's been talk they're about to sell themselves, for a lot of money.'

'Another great British intellectual-property success that'll be flogged off to the highest foreign bidder. Presumably to the Saudis.'

Jess is still reading. 'Guess who is close to Athena?'

'Ravel?'

'In a way. It's actually Johnny Todd. His peace institute is sponsored by Athena.'

The Johnny Todd Institute for Peace and Global Justice is a think tank set up by our erstwhile prime minister. Ostensibly it researches and promotes solutions to conflicts in the Middle East and Asia. Or – as his critics say – it provides a cover so that Todd can extract massive fees from billionaire sheikhs for commercially valuable introductions.

'I'll email Athena and ask for an off-the-record chat about its plans.'

While Jess taps away, I get up from the sofa to stretch my legs. Looking at the photos lining the mantelpiece reminds me of the second thing I learned last night.

'There's something else.' Gingerly, I unfold the photo of the Malmsey Club I nicked from Elliott's living room. Immersion in the lake has left it blurred, but recognisable.

Jess studies it. 'Sion Evans,' is all she says.

'Who?'

'A brilliant photographer. Sion Evans. As a student in the 1980s he made his name recording the antics of Oxford's gilded youth. Got him gigs with smart mags like *Tatler* and *GQ*. He's still around; very successful. We sometimes use him at the *FC*.'

'Do you think he's got the negatives? It would be useful to see who else Elliott was connected to.'

'What's a drinking club for privileged wankers from twenty years ago got to do with anything?'

'The Malmsey is more interesting than you think.' Jess didn't go to Oxford: she's too brainy for that. She got a first in maths at Imperial, and a doctorate in monetary economics at Chicago. 'New members of the Malmsey pledge allegiance to Richard, Duke of Gloucester, later Richard III, the Plantagenet who put the accretion of power above all else.

They would say that's a joke, but the joke may be on us. You wouldn't believe how many senior politicians and CEOs were in the Malmsey.'

'Isn't that because the establishment is dominated by Oxford graduates? Surely that's the correlation. The Malmsey is just incidental.'

'I'm not so sure. The club's name is a reference to the apocryphal death by drowning – reputedly on Gloucester's instructions – of Gloucester's brother George, Duke of Clarence, in a butt of Malmsey.

'The initiation ceremony, known as a "Clarencing", involves the novitiate downing a yard of Malmsey. Almost everyone pukes immediately afterwards. But the club was about more than just getting off your tits on drugs and booze and smashing things up. They were sort of Oxford freemasons, with only one rule, namely that members were supposed to promote each other's interests, till death them do part.'

'Are you sure? Isn't that just the conspiracy theory of a state-school oik who would never have been invited to join?'

'You're right that they wouldn't touch a lefty Jew like me with a bargepole. It was mostly Etonians, very occasionally someone from Westminster or Winchester. They'd have taken Harrovians, if any had been bright enough to get into Oxford.'

Jess lifts her eyes to the ceiling. 'You're in your forties, you have one of the best jobs in the media, and you're still pissed off that the Etonian boys didn't ask you to join their club.'

'Actually I'm not. But you take privilege for granted, because you went to Roedean, or Cheltenham Ladies' or St Trinian's or somewhere.'

I regret my sarcasm as soon as it's out of my mouth. Jess doesn't seem fussed, however.

'Very funny.'

'I didn't have a lot of time to look at the picture last night – but a couple of the people in it are familiar.' I stare at it now, but the lake water has muddied the faces too much. 'It would be useful to ask Sion what he remembers, if he'll speak to me.'

She laughs. 'Sion is a terrible snob. He'll love being courted by television's Gilbert Peck.'

Chapter 22

I USE JESS'S MOBILE TO RING Sion Evans and arrange to go to his studio that evening. I also ring my GP, Dr Hyde, who says he can see me if I can get to him in an hour. Jess offers to drive me. We put all my wet things in a Sainsbury's plastic bag. Before leaving, I receive a text from Luke. *I'm around tonight if you want to collect the diaries.*

An hour later, I'm sitting in a small Georgian reception room, net curtains drawn, probably originally built to be a back-of-house pantry. It's been a place of counsel and reassurance since I was a child. When I neurotically assumed I must have contracted venereal disease the first time I had sex, aged fifteen, it was Dr Hyde – white-haired even then – who told me not to be so silly.

I hope for similar reassurance today. 'I'm only seeing you out of loyalty to your mother,' he lectures me, his Viennese accent faintly audible. 'How is my precious Ginger? She's responding well to the treatment, according to reports the Marsden has sent me.'

'That's what Dad says. The Marsden has been amazing.' I cover up my failure to ring Mum for days. I haven't seen my parents since my last trip to the hospital.

'But why are *you* here?'

I am not sure how much to tell him, though sometimes I think he knows me better than I know myself.

'I had a strange experience last night. I was at a party and I suddenly became drowsy. In fact I almost lost consciousness. Believe it or not, I fell in a lake.'

He gives me the same 'foolish boy' look he would routinely give me when Mum brought me in to patch me up after the latest of my schoolboy scrapes – which was normally a head injury caused by my hyperactive fidgeting and tipping back on chairs.

'Oh dear,' he says.

He asks me to unbutton my shirt, and he listens to my lungs and heart. Then he wraps the blood-pressure cuff around my arm. 'All tickety-boo, though your blood pressure is a little higher than is ideal for someone of your age. I suspect you may be working too hard.' There's a twinkle in his eye as he speaks.

'There's a lot going on.'

'Try not to overdo it. Even at your age, there is such a thing as taking on too much.'

He takes out his pad and scribbles something, presumably that I am a classic Jewish hypochondriac.

'But what about last night? Do you think I could have been drugged?' I ask.

'It's possible. But why on earth would anyone do that?'

I am not sure what to tell him.

'I don't know. It's just that I felt so terrible, so fast.'

'I'll ask the nurse to do a blood test. Maybe something will show up. She'll also give you a tetanus booster, as a precaution.'

I get up to go. 'Do me a favour, Gil. Don't fall in any more ponds. And maybe keep out of the tabloids.' I wince. 'Try not to give your parents *tsuris*. I've known your family for the best part of half a century and they've had enough heartache.'

His implicit reference to the death of my sister overwhelms me with adolescent insecurity. 'I'll do my best,' is all I can muster.

'If I see anything to the contrary, you will be hearing from me.'

'Thank you Dr Hyde.'

*

A cab takes me to TVC, where I explain to the BBC's tech woman what happened to the Nokia. She laughs. 'Gil, you really take the biscuit.'

She extracts the SIM from the waterlogged phone and slots it into an identical one. A buzzing queue of missed texts is instantaneously unlocked.

'The BlackBerries are due to arrive tomorrow,' she reassures me.

Thank goodness. I feel like an alcoholic who has just been told he can swim in a lake of single malt.

'Can I ask a favour?' I say. 'Would you have a small digital camera I could borrow? And a voice recorder?'

'Only if you don't take them into the swimming pool with you.'

I take the gadgets to my office and read the backlog of phone messages. Elliott's is designed to wind me up: *Sorry you got damp. Mind how you go with the Sazeracs next time.*

I mustn't let him think he controls the narrative. I text back: *I've consulted a lawyer, and I am suing you for inadequate health and safety precautions at your party. :-)*

When I delete his message, one drops from Charles, the husband of my late sister, Luke's dad.

I need to see you as soon as possible.

*

I unfold my Brompton and pedal east in a frenzy. After ignoring my seventh or eighth red light, and travelling the wrong way down a one-way street where Kentish Town elides into Chalk

Farm, a policeman waves me down. I grovel an apology, and plead a family emergency. 'You'll be no use to your family in A&E,' he lectures.

I wheel the bike till I am out of his sight, and then resume my law-breaking dash. After forty minutes, I arrive sweaty and expectant. Charles opens the door. He is biting on his lower lip, and his face is drawn. We go into the front room, and sit in armchairs facing the mantelpiece. We're watched by my nephews, Mum and Dad, Clare, all in wood and gilt frames, lined up on the marble top. There are also photos of Charles with Yasmin, his Iranian new wife, and their toddler twins. It took Charles five years to start dating and then marry again. I've admired how he helped my nephews Luke and Sam adjust to the new family set-up. The eldest, Sam, has just gone to Cambridge, to study economics, like his mum.

On the glass coffee table between us are Marilyn's diaries.

'No Luke?' I say.

'He's upstairs doing his homework. I needed to talk to you alone.'

I have a feeling I have wounded Charles. It would not be the first time. 'Have I done something wrong?'

He squeezes the end of his nose. 'I'm sure you didn't mean it. I assume you didn't know what was in those diaries. But it wasn't appropriate to give them to Luke, given the risk there would be references to his mum.'

His articulation of my stupidity and insensitivity is an almighty blow. 'Oh no. What did they say?'

'Luke has been translating the one for 1997. 1997, Gil.'

The year of Clare's murder. The year she was impregnated by Johnny Todd.

'There's stuff Luke should never have been exposed to.'

Shit shit shit. I was so obsessed with how the diaries could help me, it never occurred to me they could harm Luke. I am such an arsehole.

'I should have thought it through.' I resist the temptation to explain how much pressure I've been under. 'I'm afraid to ask what he read.'

'In June, there's a long letter to you, that Marilyn never sent, I assume. It's an apology for misleading you about Clare. She admits she knew that man was having an affair with Clare. She doesn't quite say so, but she hints that she suspects he was behind her death.'

Charles cannot say the name of the former prime minister.

'Is it proof of what happened?'

'No. She wanted to believe he's innocent.'

I am processing the full horror of what I've done: I immersed Luke in the nightmare of his mum betraying his dad.

'I just wanted to give Luke the opportunity to make some cash.' As I say it, I realise how pathetic I am being. 'There's no excuse. This is the worst thing I've ever done. I am an idiot.'

Charles looks hard at me.

'Don't overdramatise and make it about you.' He softens. 'He had to know one day; I just would have liked to have controlled the timing. The good thing is Luke and I have now had an important conversation. But that's not everything.'

Charles hands me a sheaf of A4 paper that Luke used for decoding the diaries.

'Read that while I make some tea.'

He goes into the kitchen and I start. The 1997 and 1998 diaries are Marilyn's descent into self-loathing and self-harm after her initial break-up with me. She drank too much, snorted too much coke, started experimenting with heroin. She talks about her fling with Alex Elliott, who had recently left his post as director of communications at Media Corp. She writes about how damaged he is, but that she went along with his destructive games: sleeping with his friends, male and female, while he watched; being beaten up by him during sex. It is a chronicle of abuse.

Charles returns with two mugs of tea.

'Have you had a chance to speak to Luke about how abnormal and fucked up all this is?' I ask.

'I have,' he adds dryly, 'Maybe it's good he learns that such disturbed people exist.'

The translation ends when Marilyn meets me again, at one of Elliott's parties, and we end up in bed, having what by Elliott's standards would be classed as conventional sex. Reconnecting with me seemed to give her the strength to break things off with Elliott, and start to repair her life. It is a small consolation. I could and should have done so much more to help her. I feel ashamed that I wasn't faithful, that I colluded in the convenient fiction of the open relationship.

'Do you want me to talk to Luke about any of this?' I offer.

'Maybe one day. Not now. But please get the fucking things out of my house.'

*

I stuff the diaries into my rucksack and leave. I have a too-familiar feeling of shame. *Why do I always get it so wrong with my family?*

I'm standing outside the house with my bike when Jess rings.

'I've had a reply from Athena,' she says, before I can fill her in. 'It's confusing. I'll send it to you.'

'I haven't got my BlackBerries back yet,' I remind her. 'Can you read it?'

'The message itself is just a standard brush-off. The director of public affairs says Athena has a policy of not speaking to the media, but if that changes, he'll be in touch. What's weird is that he's added a stroppy sentence at the end to say he's already explained all this to me before.'

286

'Have you ever contacted them in connection with anything else?'

'No. Unless ...' I hear the tap of keys in the background. 'Actually, you remember I told you the paper's done a couple of stories on Athena? They're by our defence editor. She's another Jess. Jess Upton.'

'You think they could have confused you?'

'Come to the office. I'll see if I can get hold of her.'

*

The *FC*'s offices are a 1990s steel and glass cuboid on the south side of the Thames, just along from the post-war converted power station that houses Tate Modern. Jess's office is on the tenth floor, with floor-to-ceiling windows that offer a panorama of South London. She's waiting for me there with a woman in a pinstriped trouser suit whose short hair is fire red. She thrusts a powerful hand. 'Jessica Upton,' she says, in rhythm to a confident shake. We sit like supplicants opposite Jess, who is on the other side of her desk.

'What can you tell us about Athena Tech?' asks Jess.

Jessica grimaces. 'Not as much as I'd like. They publish almost nothing and are obsessively secretive. It's clear though that they are a rarity in the UK, a world leader in advanced technology. According to my defence sources, they've developed an unmanned remote-controlled aerial vehicle, a UAV, that can scan for booby traps and improvised explosive devices with astonishing accuracy.'

'Wow. That sounds important,' I say. Especially for the thousands of soldiers the UK has fighting insurgencies in Iraq and Afghanistan, who are there in part thanks to choices made by the eponymous founder of the Johnny Todd Institute for Peace and Global Justice.

'Athena also have missile detection systems,' Jessica continues. 'They sell themselves as offering cutting-edge, turnkey defence solutions. I've been wanting to get inside the company, to write a serious profile of them, but they won't cooperate.'

'Have you contacted them recently?' Jess asks.

'Yeah. You know the investment company MHH, Jackson's thing that's been rumoured as a bidder for NewGate?' Jessica glances at me. 'Believe it or not, I got a tip they're close to buying Athena, for a colossal sum.'

'Are you sure?' says Jess. Her tone is crisp.

'I'm not going to name my source,' she says defensively, 'but it was a banker very plugged in to the defence world. And when I put it to the MoD, they did not deny it. Refused to comment.'

'That's fascinating,' Jess reassures her. 'If I sounded surprised, it's only because I thought Jackson had his hands full with the NewGate debacle.'

'It's an interesting story,' I say.

'An important story,' Jess picks up. 'You should write it.'

Jessica looks relieved. 'Yes, boss.'

When she's left, Jess and I stare at each other. 'Is this some kind of weird tit-for-tat between Ravel and Jackson?' she asks. 'Ravel tried to kill Jackson on the NewGate deal, now Jackson's got wind that he's interested in Athena and is trying to snatch it from under him?'

I spell out the potential ramifications. 'Athena is part of what the Saudis want in return for rescuing PTBG. If Ravel can't deliver Athena, and the Saudis withdraw their potential funding, then the government will either have to nationalise PTBG or let it go bust.'

Jess starts to tap her biro on the desk. 'This is totally nuts,' she says. 'PTBG is at the heart of the financial system. If it fails, there's no bank in the country that could survive. There'd be queues outside every branch on every high street.'

'Businesses wouldn't be able to borrow. People's savings would be wiped out. It would be economic Armageddon.'

'Worse than the thirties.'

'They are playing such a dangerous game,' I say. 'Ravel, Jackson, Elliott, Blackwell, Todd. Their greed is off the charts. They'll blow up the whole system to suit their own vanity.'

We sit in silence.

'What next?' Jess asks.

I review the options in my mind. From behind the damask curtain, I witnessed Ravel, Blackwell and Elliott working in concert. On the basis that my enemy's enemy could be a useful source, it is obvious to whom I need to speak. Plus, Harvey Jackson also has the virtue that he hasn't tried to bump me off.

I think.

*

Outside Television Centre, demonstrators are announcing the End of Days. With the financial system on the brink, it doesn't seem outlandish. There's one man in a kilt, wearing a sandwich board whose front panel says: 'The devil is about to throw some of you into prison, that you may be tested'. The back declaims: 'I am the Alpha and the Omega, the beginning and the end'. He drags a large loudspeaker on wheels, and he's playing Scottish reels, to which he is doing a surprisingly deft Highland jig. When I walk past he shouts, 'Gil Peck. You are the prophet. Tell the people that Jesus Christ the shepherd is gathering in his sheep.'

'You can count on me,' I say.

I decide not to wait for the unbearably slow elevators. While I walk up the stairs, I text Jackson, asking if he'll do another interview, now that NewGate's been privatised. *It's pretty obvious Tudor won't want to own it for long, if there's an alternative. Would you be interested in taking it off his hands?*

289

Around ten minutes later, his in-house PR rings back. 'Harvey is up for it, when would suit?'

'This afternoon?'

'He's in meetings. Tomorrow?'

'That should work.'

I go straight to the producers' desk to brief Emma. 'Aren't we all a bit bored with NewGate?' is her reaction.

'Talk to the *Ten*, please. I bet they'll bite your hand off.'

Jackson is always an easy sell to editors, and sure enough the one rostered for the *Ten O'Clock News* tomorrow says yes. 'If we can get him to slag off Tudor, it'll lead the programme,' Emma says.

*

From TVC, I cycle to Sion Evans's studio, an old commercial property in Tabard Street just off Borough High Street. Sion owns the whole building: one floor is his studio, and he lives in the rest. The living area is open-plan, with industrial lighting and big windows. The walls are covered with photographs of celebrities: Princess Diana covering her face coming out of that Chelsea gym, Michael Jackson looking wistful in front of his personal funfair at Neverland, Johnny Todd grinning from ear to ear on the Southbank on the night Modern Labour won the landslide in 1997.

Sion's young assistant asks me to wait and offers me tea. 'Sion won't be long. He's shooting Pete Doherty, for *GQ*. It's chaotic.'

While I wait, I rehearse my patter. When Sion arrives, twenty minutes later, I tell him I am preparing short films on the party leaders and their senior colleagues, to run whenever the general election is called.

'You've probably noticed that the people at the top of both main parties are the vintage of Oxford graduates you chronicled. Stella Barnsbury, Munis, David Cameron, the Milibands. I love that series you shot in the eighties and I wondered if it would be possible to flick through them.'

Sion is wearing a white Jermyn Street shirt, top two buttons undone, narrow-leg blue jeans and brown suede loafers. He flops on a scuffed brown leather armchair.

'I'm not sure whether I want them on telly,' he says. He has a South Wales accent that is as soft as chamois. 'But you're welcome to take a peek.'

The assistant retrieves two cardboard box files, one marked 1985, the other 1986. They contain contact sheets and enlargements. I turn them slowly, making appreciative noises about the composition and marvelling at the spectacularly poor choices of hairstyle. It turns out that back in the day, most of our future leaders were wannabe members of Duran Duran and Spandau Ballet.

'It was quite the scene for a poor boy from the Valleys,' says Sion.

He watches me for a bit, then nips out for 'a quick wee'. As soon as he's disappeared, I race through the boxes. It's halfway down the second container. I haven't time to examine in detail – the imperative is to copy it before he returns – so I take out the digital camera and photograph it, along with a contact sheet, which I capture in four quarters.

I hear the loo flush and slip the camera back in my pocket.

'Do you remember Stella, Munis and the rest?' I ask Sion on his return. 'I'd love to interview you for the film.'

He shakes his head. 'I wasn't in any sense part of their group. I was a scholarship boy from the Rhondda who couldn't believe how the other 0.1% lives and wanted to record it. They were so in love with themselves, they were flattered and let me follow them. I had this idea that one day they could be running this place.'

'You were right.' God help us. 'What do you think about publishing the pictures now?'

'I'm not sure.' He straightens the photos so that none poke out and closes the file. 'There's a lot to think about. These are powerful people. I am not sure if the photos are more useful to me published or unpublished.'

Sion is nobody's fool.

*

Home again, I connect the camera to my laptop and download the images. I text Jess that I am about to email them to her. *One of them is dynamite.*

The snap that grabbed me is from the same set as the one on Elliott's piano. In it, Elliott is crouched over, apparently with a cushion up the back of his jacket. Maybe he is paying tribute to Richard III, the royal crookback. But the leer is a hackneyed version of Charles Laughton, in the role he played in *The Hunchback of Notre Dame*. Quasimodo.

I also spot a pink-faced, boyish Patrick Munis, and Frankie Crowther, the ex-City editor of the *Telegraph*, now making a mint in private equity. He's glassy-eyed.

'Cocaine Crowther,' I whisper to myself.

Of the others, one is also an MP, another a FTSE-100 chief executive. There are a couple of sneering young men I don't recognise. Of the two women, the one in a slit skirt, St Trinian's tart chic, is familiar, but I can't place her. She is draping herself on a pouting boy who has a fabulous mullet and is wearing velvet slippers. Jackson.

Jess rings. 'Do you think the club has some kind of role in the lives of its members after they leave Oxford?' she asks.

'It does for Elliott. He's still the hunchback.'

'He's such a wanker.'

'It's the connection with Jackson that we need to look into. Let's make the assumption that once a Crookback, always a Crookback. That they look after each other. Even now. If that were the case, Jackson would not be buying Athena to spite Elliott and Ravel. He would be doing it *for* them, as a front for the Saudis?'

'Is that plausible?'

'To an extent. Jackson would provide the ideal cover. There'd be a stink if Athena and its precious intellectual property was sold abroad, especially to interests linked to an Arab government. That would change the balance of power in the region. MPs on both sides of the house would go mad, and the Israelis would hit the roof. I don't think any British government could allow it.'

Jess pursues up the logical thread. 'MHH is seen as a model UK business,' she says. 'Jackson is a modern-day saint. And the corporate structure of MHH is so opaque that it would probably be easy to make it look as though Athena was remaining in British hands, when in fact control was being passed to Saudi.'

I have to do something to shatter the public's love of Jackson. When I have time.

'There is one aspect that doesn't quite add up,' I say. 'If Jackson is buying Athena for the Saudis, he's facilitating the Saudi rescue of PTBG. Which means he's helping Chris Ravel, even after Ravel in effect blew up his takeover of NewGate. I can't see how that works.'

I stare at the picture on my computer screen again. 'Elliott, Munis and Jackson are so powerful today, and they've been mates for so long. They run Britain, or in the case of Munis are close to doing so, and they've been getting pissed together for more than twenty years.'

'Was Ravel part of the club?'

'Nah. He was too left-wing and pious for any of that.'

'We should put this picture in the public domain,' says Jess. 'Did you ask his permission?'

'I copied it while Sion went for a wee.'

She sighs. 'That's basically theft. Neither of us can publish it.'

'But couldn't we just pass it to a mate? Public interest, and all that. The *Sentinel* would love it.'

'Maybe,' she prevaricates. 'But it feels wrong. Sion Evans isn't a bad man, and they're his property. Can we sleep on it?'

'OK.' I very much doubt I will think differently in the morning.

I am still staring at the picture when I retrieve the missing file in my brain. 'Look at the girl on the right.'

'I am.'

'Don't you recognise her?'

'No.'

The girl in question was clearly going through a Goth phase at the time. Her hair is cut asymmetrically, punky and spiky short on the right, long and covering an eye on the left. It's dyed jet black in the picture, though now it's reverted to a more natural brunette. There's a dog collar around her neck, and a pair of handcuffs dangling from her belt.

Maybe it's the handcuffs that connected the relevant neural pathways.

'It's our friend the Metropolitan Police assistant commissioner. Kim Jansen.'

'Shit.' I think Jess is actually shocked, for once. 'We've got politics, public relations, big money and the law all in the same student picture. These are the pillars of the modern state.'

'They're also linked to Marilyn's death. Elliott blackmailed her. And Kim Jansen investigated.'

'What are you implying?' Jess says. 'There was no murder for Jansen to cover up. We know Marilyn committed suicide.'

'Yes. But blackmail is a crime in itself. Especially when the blackmail victim kills herself. Elliott would never want that coming out, would he? Having Kim on the case was very convenient.'

'The night we went to Marilyn's flat,' Jess recalls, 'you'd spoken to Kim and asked her if she'd found the diaries. And when we got there, those men turned up.'

I suddenly feel sick. 'I thought Primakov sent them.' I see myself in the billionaire's Bentley. *You ask me because I am the Russian thug, and therefore obviously I must be the villain.* It wasn't the oligarch, it was a very British mafia, the alumni of an absurd Oxford club.

'Where are the diaries now?' Jess asks.

'I got them back from Luke.' I tell her about my excruciating encounter with my brother-in-law. 'I need to decipher them.'

'It'll be quicker if we work on them together,' Jess says.

'Shall I come over?'

'Hang on a second.' She shouts 'Amy,' and I hear her asking her daughter if she wants to see me. 'Tell the big fat stinky to be as fast as he can,' I hear Amy say.

Jess comes back on the line: 'I assume you heard that.'

I shut the laptop, put out fresh food for Dog, and place the diaries with some overnight things into my rucksack. I'm about to leave the flat when the Nokia rings. I'm tempted to ignore it – I already have so much to process – but habit wins.

'This is Dr Hyde's surgery. Do you have a moment to speak to him?'

It's after eight: what can be that urgent?

'Gilbert,' says Dr Hyde. 'How are you feeling?'

Is that a leading question? 'Fine, I think.'

'Delighted to hear it.' He sounds flustered, which is not reassuring.

'Is everything OK?' I ask.

He takes a deep breath. 'Look, when you told me about how you suddenly felt so woozy at the party last night, I asked the lab to test your blood for a variety of substances. It turns out there was enough Rohypnol in you to tranquillise a bull elephant.' He lets it sink in. 'You know what Rohypnol is?'

'The date-rape drug.' No wonder I passed out and fell in the lake.

'Exactly. It makes the user almost entirely passive, and afterwards they struggle to remember what happened. I take it you didn't self-administer it?'

'Of course not.'

'It's one of those drugs that flushes out really fast, leaving no trace,' he adds. 'If you hadn't come to see me when you did, no one would ever have known.'

Chapter 23

'**T**HAT FUCKER ELLIOTT DRUGGED ME, and then he had his girl push me in the lake.'

I'm in Jess's kitchen. I barely remember cycling here, my head being so full of shock and fury. She pours me a glass of wine. Did Elliott put the Rohypnol in the Sazerac, or did he know I'd go for the vintage claret? It must have been the cocktail, because I would have noticed it in the wine. I assume.

'He's a psycho,' I rage. 'If I'd died he'd have had a second party to celebrate my life, and found it fucking hilarious.'

'Not so loud,' says Jess. 'Amy's asleep.'

'No I'm not.' Amy is at the kitchen door.

'Oh God. I shouldn't have sworn. Sorry Jess. Sorry Amy.'

Amy sees her opening. 'Will you read me a story?'

I look at Jess who nods. 'I'd love to. Which one?'

'*Hobbit.*'

I look at Jess. 'Just a few pages, Amy.'

The few are around thirty. Tolkien's soporific virtues don't take hold till ten. I creep back, whispering, 'Night Bilbo, night Amy.'

There's a faint whisper from the bed. 'Night stinky.'

A short stay in Middle Earth has been a restorative, and I feel much calmer when I'm back in the kitchen.

'I'll have that glass of wine now,' I say, retrieving it from the kitchen worktop. 'Let's get on with the diaries.'

We settle down at the kitchen table with them, and start with the pages that are still in the Filofax for the months leading up to Marilyn's suicide. Jess and I agree a system. Despite our best endeavours, it's laborious and slow. I translate each letter, shout it out, and Jess writes it down. Every time something feels relevant, Jess stops me and reads aloud.

She tells me that in February, Marilyn writes, 'AE reminded me he has the photos.'

'AE? Oh yes, Alex Elliott,' I say.

Deciphering the code feels like important work. We were stupid not to do this days ago. It's also a distraction from the dangers we face. Once again, I am grateful for my superhuman ability to compartmentalise.

'Interesting he reminded her about the photos as early as February,' I add. 'That was a long time before NewGate was in trouble. Presumably he was pre-emptively reminding her, because in her position at the Bank of England she could be useful to him in so many different ways.'

'The stress on her must have been unbearable.'

I continue calling out letters. There's a lot to process. As we move through the months, familiar names crop up. Marilyn records a tip-off to the Bank of England from Palatine, the quintessentially establishment corporate broker. Palatine told Marilyn that Jackson and MHH are sitting on massive losses made from investments in CDOs. Jackson tried to maximise his returns by using borrowed money to buy the CDOs, what's known as leveraging up, and he now has £5 billion of debt due for repayment in eighteen months.

Jess reads: "'Jackson is bust. There's no chance he'll be able to roll over his debts. He's frantically searching for ways to hide his losses. I need to inform my colleagues, but AE says if I do it will be the end of me.'"

She turns to me. 'We have to assume Jackson is still in dire straits. So on your theory that he's now helping Ravel with the

298

Athena takeover, maybe Ravel has offered to help him avoid collapse in some way.'

'That could square the circle,' I say. But it's Elliott's threats and the unbearable stress that Marilyn must have been under that haunts me. 'Why didn't Marilyn tell me about any of this?' I blurt. 'I could have helped.'

Jess gives me a sceptical look. 'What would you have done? Doing the right thing would have destroyed her reputation and her career.'

'I would have told her that careers aren't that important. She could have rebuilt.'

'Says the work addict.'

*

As midnight approaches, Marilyn tells us that Jackson identified NewGate as the solution to his looming crisis. If he could get hold of it, he could channel its depositors' cash to repay his own creditors and hide his subprime losses. That would have been illegal. But within the corporate labyrinth of MHH, the flows of funds could have been moved through assorted shell companies, relabelled and disguised. Marilyn notes that Todd is extracting huge fees from Jackson to put pressure on the Bank and the PM to wave the deal through. 'Classic Johnny,' she writes.

Jess reads a line that exposes how Elliott thought he had trapped Marilyn. 'AE says if the deal goes through he'll shred the pictures.'

Jess puts down her pen and stares at me, biting her lip. I look right back. 'You don't have to say it, Jess. When I exposed NewGate's insolvency, when I blew up the MHH rescue, I destroyed her one chance of escape.'

We look at the pages in stunned silence for what feels an eternity – until Jess sits up sharply. 'That's narcissism, and bollocks. Marilyn, if she was thinking straight, when she was thinking straight, knew that. There's no way Elliott would have surrendered his hold on her. His need to control was pathological. He was lying when he said he'd destroy the photographs.'

I want to believe Jess is right. The idea that my scoop exploded Marilyn's tunnel to freedom is unbearable.

'Stop making this all about you,' she reinforces. 'What's important here is that the blackmail was on behalf of Jackson, and presumably Primakov too. Our theory that she was being punished by Ravel, or someone who wanted the takeover to fail, was wrong.'

'My instinct is to believe Primakov when he says he didn't know about it. But who knows?'

I try to force myself to carry on with the transcription. I can't focus; the grids blur in front of my eyes. I am falling into a pit of self-loathing and blame.

Jess reads my mind. 'You can blame yourself if you want. But that would be self-indulgent. You would be letting the culprits off the hook. I assume Ravel instructed Muller to give you the NewGate story. Do you think there is any chance he would have kept quiet if you hadn't put it out? If you'd gone mad and not told the world what was happening, he'd have made sure the information was given to another journalist.'

'You're right. It's just I can't forgive myself for having so little inkling of the agony Marilyn was going through.' I suppress an urge to cry.

Jess tries to distract me: 'I don't understand what Elliott thought he was doing. He was working for Jackson and for Ravel, who wanted totally different outcomes for NewGate. What's that all about?'

Having known Elliott for years, this is the least complicated part of the puzzle, for me. 'Alex has no loyalty to anyone, except himself, and to the next huge fee. In elections to the Oxford Union, he sold his own vote to every candidate, and even persuaded two of them he was working to bring in more votes for each of them. Somehow he got away with it. He gets his kicks from pulling everyone's strings, being the puppet master.'

'But why didn't Ravel and Jackson see through his double dealing?'

'Elliott would have convinced Jackson he was working for him. Which in fact he was. And Ravel couldn't have cared less. Remember Ravel is always thinking three steps ahead of everyone else. He'll have seen what Jackson and Elliott were doing, and would have been confident he could blow them up at any point. Which indeed he did. I feel a bit sorry for Jackson.'

'But not for Elliott?'

'Of course not. He never loses. Everyone knows he has no conscience and is the most treacherous person in Britain. But when he locks on to someone, he persuades them that they are more important to him than anyone, that there's nothing he won't do for them. It is an extraordinary skill. That's why they pay him the big money. I can't imagine how much Jackson will have paid him. And truthfully he will do whatever it takes for a client, with no fingerprints and no trail back to them.'

From destroying a reputation with smears placed in a tabloid to pushing a drugged hack in a lake. 'It's the laundry he operates after the dirty tricks that's perhaps most impressive,' I say. 'If I had gone to sleep with his ornamental koi carp, he'd have held another spectacular in memoriam party in his Notting Hill mansion.' I can't help wondering whether the PM would have turned up.

Jess jolts me back. 'We need to get moving. We've got tons more pages to do.'

I call out the letters 'AE' again, when there's a heavy knock on the front door.

'What the hell?' I say. 'It's well after midnight. Who can that be?'

'Should we answer it? In a minute they'll wake Amy.'

Loud male voices are instructing us to open the door.

'Metropolitan Police,' one shouts, while pressing the doorbell insistently.

'Oh fuck,' I say.

The banging stops. My mobile buzzes. It's a text, from Kim Jansen. *Please open the door. I'm here with a couple of colleagues.*

I show it to Jess. 'What does that cow want?' she hisses.

We frantically put the diaries in my rucksack, and I run with it to Jess's bedroom, where I try to hide it behind shoe boxes at the bottom of a wardrobe. I go into the kitchen, where Jess is putting our translations in a deep drawer, under saucepans.

'I'll get the door,' she says. 'You go back to the living room.'

Kim, in full ceremonial uniform, all silver brocade and epaulette badges, walks ahead of Jess, with two officers trailing behind.

'Sorry for the late visit.' She seems uncomfortable, with her gaze drifting between her regulation black shoes and the two of us. 'I'm not going to beat about the bush,' she continues. I spot she's clutching an A4-size brown envelope. 'I have a warrant to search these premises.'

'You're joking,' Jess interjects. 'This is outrageous.' She looks at me. 'We need to call a lawyer.'

'Honestly, I wouldn't waste your time,' says Kim. 'We have CCTV of you unlawfully entering the home of Marilyn Krol. We have reason to believe you removed property relevant to our investigation.'

I think about spluttering a denial, but it's pointless.

Kim looks first at me, and then at Jess. 'You would save yourself an awful lot of bother if you just give me the diaries. My colleagues will obviously take great care not to cause too much mess if you insist on them conducting a search, but it will take hours, and no one will get any sleep.'

A bleary-eyed Amy comes in, rubbing her eyes. 'What's going on, Mum?' she asks. 'Why's the police lady here?'

'For fuck's sake, Kim,' says Jess. 'Is this really necessary?' She scoops up Amy. 'Back to bed, young lady. Nothing to worry about.'

Jansen and her two colleagues seem to fill all the space in the room. I have to get out. 'Kim, I'm just going to have a private word with Jess.'

I follow Jess to Amy's bedroom and loiter outside. When Jess emerges, she says, 'If you are about to say we shouldn't expose Amy to a police search, forget it. She'll love it.'

I smile. 'I believe you. But they are bound to find the rucksack. Let's just hand them over.'

I interpret Jess's silence as agreement and go to the bedroom to retrieve the diaries. Back in the living room, I give them to Kim, who instructs her colleagues to put them carefully into evidence bags.

Kim turns back to us. 'Thank you for your cooperation.' She fixes her gaze on me. 'I should charge you with interfering in a police investigation. But I understand how upset you've been by Ms Krol's death. I will make an exception on the basis of extenuating circumstances. But you should consider yourselves on warning. If you cross the line again, I won't hesitate to arrest you.'

If she's expecting me to be grateful, she's misjudged. I'm fuming. 'There was no bloody crime,' I say. 'Marilyn committed suicide. So how could we be interfering with a crime scene?'

Kim dispenses with the formalities. 'Don't be so bloody stupid. It is a crime scene until I say it isn't. Second, I could arrest you on a charge of theft and burglary. Thank your lucky stars I'm giving you the benefit of the doubt that your grief has damaged your judgement.'

The idea that I should feel lucky is absurd. She's killed any chance we have of exposing the fraud and blackmail. The diaries will be consigned to an evidence storage facility, never to be seen again.

'Are you working for Elliott too?' I sneer.

Kim's gaze shifts to the ceiling. 'I haven't the faintest idea what you are talking about,' she says.

'Once a Crookback, always a Crookback, eh?'

The officers with her exchange a glance. Kim does not want me to explain in front of them. She struggles to keep her composure.

'I am very happy to talk about this at the station, if you prefer. But there's a chance the tabloids would somehow get wind of your arrest. A photo of the BBC's business editor getting out of one of our cars would make an interesting front page for the *Globe*.'

Jess looks at me and mouths 'Bitch.' She turns to Jansen: 'We understand the legal position, assistant commissioner. But as you are aware, when a serious crime has been committed, there is a public interest defence for obtaining documents in the way we did. You can expect we will be talking to our lawyers about everything that has happened tonight.'

'By all means do that,' says Jansen. She turns to her uniformed colleagues. 'Gentlemen, we should leave Mr Peck and Ms Neeskens to their beauty sleep.'

As soon as they've gone, I screw up my face, put my clenched fists to my forehead. 'Fuck, fuck, fuck, fuck, fuck,' is my whispered, tortured scream.

Jess comes over and puts an arm around me. 'We're not done. Let's sleep, and regroup in the morning.'

'I mustn't stay here,' I croak. The magnitude of what happened is sinking in. 'I've put you and Amy in harm's way. They knew we had the diaries, and they knew I would be here.'

I feel a huge weight pressing down on the top of my head. I am back in the lake.

'Stop being a drama queen. It's the least attractive thing about you. Now come to bed.'

By the bedroom door I say, 'We have to get that Malmsey picture on a front page. Jansen needs to know we see her and what she's doing.'

Jess does not argue. 'Do you want me to handle it?'

'No. I'll ring Alan Scott. The *Sentinel* will eat it up.' The *Sentinel* is a broadsheet edited and written by the same Oxbridge types that populate all the broadsheets, but their conceit is that they are left rather than right, on the side of the poor and under-privileged rather than free market. Their schtick is sanctimony rather than vindictiveness. Scott is their senior investigative reporter. I've done business with him in the past. He won't dump us in it as his source.

I head to the spare room, but Jess grabs my arm.

'Wrong room.'

Our eyes meet. 'You sure?'

'Oh yes. Bilbo Baggins won it for you.'

*

The alarm wakes us at seven. Before Jess has silenced it, Amy's already at the bedroom door.

'Mummy?'

'Morning Amy, darling,' says Jess.

'Hi Amy,' I say.

Amy clambers on the end of the bed. She starts jumping and shouting, 'Mummy's got a boyfriend, Mummy's got a boyfriend.' I suppose Mummy does have a boyfriend.

'Uniform on, please,' says Jess.

When Amy's left the room, I roll in Jess's direction and kiss her. 'Morning.'

'Morning.'

Amy sticks her head back in. 'No funny business, you guys.' She giggles and runs off.

'Where does she get these ideas?' I ask.

'God knows.'

I press the full length of my body against Jess's back and bottom. She can feel I am aroused and screws her head towards me. 'No time for that now, lover boy,' she says. I stick out my bottom lip in disappointment. Being in her flat, in her bed, is an escape to a new life, one I never thought would be mine. I have been a teenager since our first kiss.

'At least we know what we're up against.' She is talking about the seizure of the diaries.

On their side is the Met, a former PM, a Russian gangster, huge money. 'We can't win,' I say.

'I wouldn't be so sure.' Jess gets out of bed and walks to the bathroom. She leaves the door open while she pees. 'Everything they're doing – getting their thugs to beat you up, drugging you, Kim taking the diaries – it's a sign we're worrying them.'

'Maybe. What are they frightened of?'

She looks at me as though I'm mad. 'That we'll expose them. It's what we do.'

Perhaps for the first time, I realise quite how lucky I am not to be alone, to have Jess in my life. Without her, I might have capitulated. Somehow I have to prove I am worthy of her.

'We need more undeniable evidence,' I say.

'Which is why we need the Malmsey photo out there. It's bait.'

Jess flushes, and picks up her phone, which is on the cistern behind her. She clocks the time. 'We've got to get a move on. Pull your trousers on. You're coming with us.'

We walk Amy the three streets to her primary school, Our Lady of Queen's Park. Amy gives me a hug goodbye. The trust she shows in me is like putting on armour. For the second time today, as Jess and I walk back to her home, I feel very fortunate.

'RC?' I query.

'It's the best local school.'

'Are you Catholic?'

'I was brought up as one. I'm not really a believer, though when I'm stressed I find myself drawn to the ritual. I've been known to whisper the odd Hail Mary. It's the best school around here by a mile. And Amy's bright enough to make up her own mind about all the nonsense they feed her.'

'OK.' This connection between Marilyn and Jess, both brought up as Catholics, strikes me. Do I have a type? Do they have other things in common? The thought is unnerving.

'I need to go to the office,' says Jess. 'I'll find out if Jessica's heard anything more about Athena, and I'll talk to the banking team about PTBG, see if they've got an idea of the size of the hole in its balance sheet.'

I remember that my new BlackBerries should have arrived at Television Centre. 'I'm interviewing Jackson this afternoon,' I remind Jess. When I set up the interview, it was because I thought Jackson's interests were diametrically opposed to those of Elliott, Ravel and Blackwell. And I'd begun to think Ravel was more responsible for Marilyn's death than him. Now that I've read some of the diaries and seen Jackson in the Malmsey photo, I realise they're all in the same conspiracy.

Jess pecks me on the cheek. I won't let her get away with that. 'Come here, you.' We stand outside her front door and I kiss her on the mouth for a full minute.

'What on earth will the neighbours think?' she whispers.

*

At 2.30, Emma, Petra and I are back in Jackson's office at the Adelphi. Before I got in the lift, I went to the men's room, switched on my Olympus recorder and attached its mic to my lapel. Now that we're upstairs, and the office is being rigged for a two-camera shoot, Petra gives me a radio pack and a second lapel mic, which I clip on my jacket.

Harvey swaggers in. 'Gil. Great to see you, man. How've you been? Alex made a huge splash with that party, didn't he?'

He's baiting me. Either Elliott told him about the lake, or Jackson was in on the plan. I guess I know for sure that Jackson is not going to be an ally if I want to bring down Elliott.

He winks at me and sits down. I do the sync clap and ask the first question.

'How disappointed are you that NewGate has been nationalised?'

He clasps his hands and leans forward. 'I'm afraid to say that I think the prime minister has made a serious mistake.' Bingo. Britain's favourite businessman has attacked the prime minister for taking NewGate into public ownership. The *Ten O'Clock News* have their headline.

'Could you elaborate?'

'History shows that businesses in public ownership stagnate at best, and quite often sink. They lose their dynamism. The dead hand of Whitehall stifles all enterprise and innovation.' Jackson then repeats the pitch he made last time, that his ambition to buy NewGate is all about community banking, returning a bank to the marvellous Geordies so he can be their servant.

'This is not about profit.' *That again.* He gives me his habitual smile of blue-eyed sincerity. 'I have plenty of other opportunities to make money. This is about doing the right thing for a community in the north-east that has too often been neglected by those who run this country from Westminster and London. Not all banks need to be about maximising bonuses for their executives. Some are about creating jobs and opportunities in parts of the country that have been left behind. That's why Meathead is with me. That's why the great city of Newcastle is supporting us.'

God he can be smug and self-righteous. 'You say it's not about profit. But I'm hearing you are sitting on huge subprime losses, that you made a spectacularly unwise bet on CDOs.'

There's a pause, longer than would look natural if this were live television. His lightly tanned forehead furrows. I can see the cogs whirring.

Less naturally and more deliberately than usual, he says: 'I have no idea where you heard that? I assume it's the normal nonsense from the City rumour mill. Sadly we're used to our jealous competitors spreading misinformation. I can categorically assure you it's untrue. MHH is in great shape. And as I said, we're always looking at a spread of acquisitions to become even stronger, so that we can generate the income that will lift more people out of poverty in Africa.'

He gives me another opening that he may regret. 'You say MHH is looking at plenty of opportunities. I hear you are in talks to acquire the advanced defence systems manufacturer, Athena Tech?'

'Where did you hear that?'

'You're not denying it.'

'I'm not confirming it either. As I said, at any given moment we are assessing a significant number of value-enhancing deals. But today we're here to talk about NewGate. You shouldn't read anything into my reticence.'

Obviously I'll read a world into his reticence.

'Back to NewGate then. Is the Russian billionaire Petr Primakov supporting your bid?'

Jackson is struggling to retain his habitual and jovial equanimity. 'A lot of people want to invest with MHH, because they know they'll make great returns. Obviously I can't comment on individual partners and clients. That would be to breach confidentiality.'

'But you'd acknowledge that a Russian oligarch trying to buy a stake in a British bank would be controversial.'

Jackson manufactures a laugh. 'Gil, Gil, you need to get out of your Cold War bunker. We're not in the 1980s anymore. The Berlin Wall has gone. Russia is modernising fast under Vladimir Putin. These are our friends and allies.'

I change tack. 'You've always presented yourself as an outsider, shaking up the stuffy world of British business.'

'I'm a disruptor.' He has relaxed, but not much. He shifts in his chair, unsure whether I am laying a trap. 'All my career I've come up against vested interests who don't welcome our pioneering way of operating.'

'Really? Aren't you as much part of the establishment as all the other bankers and private equity investors? Since university, you've been in the same *society* as prominent politicians, bankers, top civil servants and so on. In fact, at university you were a member of a notorious club filled with the privileged people you now claim to be challenging.'

His eyes move from mine, looking for an aide who can give him a clue how and whether to terminate the interview. But there's no one in sight. He draws breath, puts on a rigid smile and leans back. 'I always say, don't judge a man by his friends. Judge him by the people who stand against him.'

*

When we finish, Jackson leads me to a small adjacent meeting room, while my team packs up our kit. 'What were you doing in there?' he hisses. 'You asked for an interview about NewGate. What was all that stuff about our alleged losses and Athena Tech? Someone set you up.'

I stay calm. I need to normalise the conversation. 'Relax. I'm just asking the questions that have to be asked. Athena's an important business, and someone I trust tells me you *are* close to buying it.'

'Who?'

'I never reveal sources.' I wait a beat, then deliver the prepared lie. 'But you and I are friends, so I think it's OK to tell you Elliott suggested the question. He said Athena was playing hard to get, and that if we outed them there'd be pressure from the shareholders to sell.'

Has Jackson bought the line? His blue eyes are calculating. 'Alex didn't mention it.'

I shrug. 'Odd. But I assume it's true, about the takeover.'

Jackson's guard is down. 'Between you and me, and totally off the record, yes we'd love to own it. The politics aren't easy, though.'

'Fixable?'

'Johnny thinks so.'

Of course Johnny Todd thinks so.

'But if you're doing Athena, how on earth would you finance a second bite at NewGate?'

'Still off the record, right?'

'Yes. Of course.'

'Raising the cash is the least of our worries.'

'Even with your CDO losses? I wasn't speculating when I asked you about them, as you know.'

Silence. He walks over to the window and stares at the hundreds of little people hurrying through their lives on each side of the river.

'It's a timing and cash flow issue. Obviously there'd be a problem if we had to mark the bonds to market. But we're confident we'll get a hundred cents on the dollar if we hold them to maturity. And I've secured an important line of credit that will allow us to do that.'

He's telling me he's a victim of market mispricing. I resist the temptation to tell him he's a fool if he really believes that, because he's given me an important piece of the puzzle.

'A loan from PTBG,' I say.

He jerks his head round.

'Yes. But don't reveal that. It's highly sensitive.'

'I assume Chris Ravel arranged it for you.'

'How do you find out this stuff?'

'As I said, I can't disclose sources. There's one other thing. You may be able to ride out the CDO losses, but the nationalisation of NewGate must have crystallised a real loss for you, on the NewGate shares you bought.'

311

At this he relaxes. And laughs.

'I'm not that thick. We didn't use our own funds.'

'None?'

'None whatsoever.'

'But what about your friend Primakov? He bought a ton of stock, to give you leverage, to help you. He'll have lost hundreds of millions, maybe a billion. Didn't you indemnify him?'

'Of course not. He knew this was caveat emptor.'

'Won't he feel wounded? No way he'll support you again.'

Jackson grins. 'Petr? He's not going to miss a billion or so. He stole it all in the first place. Just another greedy Russian Jew. He can afford it. If he doesn't want to help us, who gives a fuck? We can manage perfectly well without him.'

*

Back on the Strand, I turn on my wonderful new BlackBerries. I've missed a call from home: normally, I wouldn't ring back immediately, but something nags at me. My mum picks up immediately, and I can hear something's wrong.

'What's happened?'

'It's Dad,' she says. 'He's not been feeling well all day.'

'Not feeling well how?'

'Pains in his arms and chest. I wanted him to call a doctor, but he refused.'

I squeeze my earlobe. 'Is he better now?'

'Well, no.' She's stammering, anxious. I sense she's close to panic. 'He got out of his armchair to walk to the kitchen to get a cup of tea, and fainted. He's on the floor of the sitting room. He's breathing and mumbling, but I can't get him up.'

Kill me now, kill me now, kill me now. 'When did all this happen?'

'About forty-five minutes ago.'

'Oh Mum. Have you called an ambulance?'

312

'Is that what I should do? Maybe he's just a bit tired.' She tails off. 'I wanted to speak to you first.'

What is the matter with my parents? Why when there's a crisis do they lose the capacity to function?

'I'll ring an ambulance and I'll come straight round.'

'Your dad has been under a lot of strain. He's been worried about me.'

I flag down a black cab and tell the driver 'Mecklenburgh Square.' It's probably only fifteen minutes away, even in traffic, but it feels a lifetime. *Don't die Dad, don't die Dad, don't die Dad. Kill me, kill me, kill me.*

Outside the house, I see a paramedic's motorbike but no ambulance. In the sitting room, the paramedic is with Dad, performing CPR, zapping him with the pads, then pumping hard on his chest. Mum is on the sofa, ashen, mumbling something to herself.

'How is Dad doing?' I ask.

The paramedic doesn't answer directly. 'We need to get him to hospital.'

There's a ring on the door. I let in the ambulance crew, and rush back to Dad. I kneel beside him. Against a lifetime of not showing emotion within the family, I take his hand. 'You'll be OK,' I insist. 'I'm here with Mum. We love you, Dad.'

Mum sobs. 'He'll be fine, won't he?'

'We're taking you to University College Hospital, Dad,' I say. 'Just down the road. They'll make you better.'

He opens his eyes and tries to say something, but it's too hard. He's gasping for air. I see a terrified child. I want to make him better.

The paramedic and two ambulance men gently lift him onto a stretcher, which they wheel cautiously to the ambulance.

'Mum, you go in the ambulance. I'll see you there. Make sure your phone is switched on.'

UCLH is close, maybe a twenty-minute walk. I run all the way and get there in ten minutes, panting and sweaty. I ring

Mum and ask where they are. She says they are only now taking Dad off the stretcher. She asks a paramedic what I should do. He says to wait in A&E and then ring Mum in ten minutes.

I sit down by the crying babies and injured drunks in the waiting room. I try to call Mum, but it takes half an hour to get through. When I do, she tells me to come round the front and follow signs to the cardiac department. When I get there, Mum is in a corner, her head slumped.

Dad has been pronounced dead, she says. At 16.42.

Chapter 24

THERE'S A MOMENT WHEN I wonder whether Alex Elliott had my father murdered. I don't, however, share this theory with Jess. I speak to the doctors and they say he'd probably ignored the warning signs of clogged arteries. Lots of men, one says, prefer to live in denial than see a GP. That sounds like my dad. I mention that he'd been living with the stress of Mum's cancer for months. The doctor nods wearily, as though she hears these stories too often.

I'm angry I was too wrapped up in myself to hear him. When he rang me and I sensed something was wrong, I should have gone to see him there and then. Jess tells me it's not my fault, that I can't protect everyone, but I can't be comforted. I lose track of time, with all the admin at the hospital and the contacting relatives. Back at their house, at 10.30, Ginger pulls a different rug from under me.

'We're going to have to sit shiva, you know.'

'What are you saying, Mum?' I am flabbergasted. Dad was militantly atheist. He called all religious rituals hocus-pocus. 'Remember how he refused to sit shiva for Clare?'

Mum sighs. 'So much changed over the past year. Maybe it had something to do with me getting ill. But he went back to the faith.'

I am dumbstruck. When I was growing up, Dad would make fun of Uncle Jake and our relatives who kept up the traditions.

'You might as well say "Abracadabra", and wish to win the football pools,' was his verdict on prayer.

'He started going to *shul* every Saturday morning. He had earnest discussions with the rabbi. I had to start keeping a kosher kitchen. If you'd come over more often, you'd have seen him doing Friday night prayers.'

Fuck fuck fuck. The fucking family guilt trip. Fuck. I am struggling to know what to say. Mum is describing a Dad I didn't know. How is it that those I love can have so much going on that I don't see? I am overwhelmed. I need to talk to Jess.

'Why didn't you tell me, Mum? Why didn't *he* tell me?'

'He asked me not to. He wanted to tell you himself, when the time was right. I suppose he thought you'd disapprove.'

Secrets. Always secrets.

'What about the funeral, then?'

'Don't worry, it's all arranged.'

'What do you mean?'

'After I got ill, he bought a plot – well, two, one for each of us – at Rainham. From the Federation of Synagogues.'

Properly Orthodox? It makes so little sense. I've been to Rainham many times to say goodbye to extended family. That he chose it as his burial place is as bizarre as everything else. It's like going through a time slip to the *shtetls* of the nineteenth century.

'Has anyone contacted Rainham?' I ask in a sort of daze.

'Uncle Jake. He's sorted it all. The funeral's at two thirty tomorrow.'

*

I have no idea what it is about Rainham, but even in high summer it feels like midwinter on the Russian steppes. As you stand on a plain that seems to go on for miles, with row after

316

row of marble tombs, the wind is always icy. It's a cold like none I've ever felt. Whenever I'm there, I expect the Cossacks to gallop through and scythe us down.

This time, I've taken precautions. I'm wearing my Jasper Conran deep brown wool coat, sombre apart from a blue velvet collar, and a navy blue John Smedley lambswool cardigan under my Paul Smith suit. I've even got an M&S vest beneath my Turnbull & Asser shirt. I'm wearing a knitted plain blue Charvet tie, and on my head is the koppel I always wear, white and blue silk in the colours of Israel. Stamped inside is '*Bahmitzvah of Ronnie Pearlstein, November 1977*'. I borrowed a hairclip from Mum to stop it slipping off, which it still tries to do.

We are standing in a dark, unadorned wood-panelled chapel. As if by magic, the men and women are in separate groups. On either side of me are my nephews, Luke and Sam. They know less about this stuff than I do. They're both several inches taller than me. Luke puts an arm around my shoulder, and I encircle his waist.

'You OK, Uncs?'

'Thanks. You?'

This isn't the time to apologise for what I exposed him to with the diaries, but I give him an extra squeeze as I look for my mum. She's holding the hand of her younger sister, Sheila, and is crying quietly. We each have a prayer book, with Hebrew on the right and English on the left. It's easy to get in a muddle with the reverse, right-to-left, order of pages in Hebrew. I spend quite a lot of the service scrambling to find the correct prayer.

The officiating rabbi starts the service. His eulogy is a long list of Bernard Peck's academic and uxorial achievements. Top of his class at a grammar school in the East End, where his dad was a tailor of ladies' garments. First-class degree at University College, London, and doctorate at Yale. Professor of Sociology and Politics at the London School of Economics, fellow of the British Academy, advisor to successive Labour governments.

Influential books on what in the 1970s was the New Left, and is now 'old Labour'. He met Ginger in 1958 at a Labour Party meeting in Hackney, and the rest was history. They battled together in the 1960s against grammar schools, against the war in Vietnam, as innocent firebrand believers in a better world. The achievements of their children, the late Clare, and Gilbert, are testament to the devotion of their parents. It's all formal, the ritual honouring of a great man.

Dad had a full life. The death of his daughter was a desperate sadness that never left him, but he achieved so much in the public realm. His contributions to the politics of the left from the 1970s to the 1990s are out of fashion, but they'll come back. His passion for egalitarianism didn't mean frugality or asceticism in the way he lived. While the rabbi memorialises, I remember what Dad and Mum shared with me when I was growing up: Pinter and Stoppard plays with Mum as a teenager, the Michelin-starred restaurants adored by Dad. One imprint on me is Dad devouring a vast bouillabaisse, starched white napkin tucked into his collar, grunting and sighing at each fishy and peppery delight.

I've agreed to say a prayer, which I've been practising. I don't read Hebrew so I've had to learn it phonetically. It was only when I looked it up in the King James Bible translation that I realised it was sung as a hymn at Marilyn's funeral. The walls between compartments in my life are crumbling. Is this a beginning or an end?

The Lord is my shepherd ... Yea, though I walk through the valley of the shadow of death, I will fear no evil: for thou art with me; thy rod and thy staff they comfort me. Thou preparest a table before me in the presence of mine enemies.

Then the plain, closed coffin is lifted onto the cart and wheeled several hundred yards to the grave. I walk slowly with Mum. Rain begins to spit. Absolutely bloody typical. When we get there, the rabbi says more prayers. The coffin is lowered. All around is the brown and black earth that's just been excavated. We're invited to take turns in shovelling it back in. It's my duty to begin.

I let go of Mum's hand, but she becomes terrified. 'No, Gil.' She rushes forward, as if to throw herself into the grave. I stand on the mound by the grave and catch her. I hug her and guide her back. My brother-in-law Charles puts his arm and coat around her. I pick up the shovel and start returning the earth to where it came. The effort of shovelling is catharsis. I am only supposed to do two or three loads, but I don't want to stop, and I pick up speed.

I am embarrassing my relatives. We are all supposed to take turns. Uncle Jake comes up to me, and gently eases the shovel from my hands. As I walk back to Mum, my feet feel heavier: the clagging clay has enveloped my Jeffery-West brogued winklepickers.

When it's over, I make my way towards the car park with Mum. The words of the psalm are in my head. 'Thou preparest a table before me in the presence of mine enemies; Thou hast anointed my head with oil; my cup runneth over.' If only. It's my enemies who are feasting, and taunting me.

They're winning, Dad. The bad guys. They're beating me. What am I going to do?

Dad's favourite movies were westerns, which we often watched together. *High Noon; Shane.* The conceit was always the same. A solitary man, usually someone who'd seen too much killing and had tried to forswear the life of the gun, felt compelled one last time to conscript the tools of violence when the bad guys threatened those he loved. More in sorrow than anger. The little man against the corporation, truth standing up to the big lie.

Never let the bastards grind you down, Gil. Live by the Kennedy motto: 'Don't get mad, get even.'

I remember a particular conversation with Dad, in his study, after a teacher humiliated me in front of the class for the messiness of my handwriting. 'I know you think you deserve an A plus, Gilbert Peck. But I couldn't understand a word. "F" for you.' It was a project about the English civil war which I had been working on for weeks. I cried in front of my classmates, and was instructed to 'stop snivelling'. I was still feeling sorry for myself when I went to see Dad.

He said, 'Gil, son, it's not always such a bad thing to be underestimated. It's not what others think of you that matters. It's what you think of yourself.'

*

Back at Mecklenburgh Square, the mourning period known as 'sitting shiva' has begun. Kaddish, the prayers, will be said. Uncle Jake has volunteered to lead them, since I don't have a clue what to say or do. Jake has also brought the requisite tiny stools and chairs.

'Why've we got the Oompa Loompa furniture?' asks Luke, and I laugh, despite myself. That's exactly what his grandpa would have said, in the old days.

To say kaddish we need a minyan of ten men: that is, ten men over the age of thirteen. There are twelve, including cousins and Dad's former colleagues. At least half of us, including Luke, Sam, Charles and me, are cyphers in all this, Jews by birth, lifestyle and culture, ignorant of religious practice. I have already decided I am not going to sit shiva for the full seven days, no matter how much I loved my dad and want to honour him. He did too good a job of robbing me of any sense of awe for the faith. But I will show respect tonight.

When I tell Jake, I am surprised by his response. 'I get it, Gil. It is important to know ourselves. Even though your dad and I had many arguments, I learned that from him. He was a great man.'

An hour later, I am wolfing down a smoked salmon beigel. Auntie Sheila has persuaded Mum to stay with her for the next

320

few days, at least for as long as the period of mourning. 'She's insisting she wants to come back here afterwards, to live on her own,' Sheila frets. 'She'll be lonely.'

'Mum's very self-sufficient,' I counter. 'She still does her screen prints. She's got her friends. But it's early days. Let's see how it goes.' I stoop down to spoon chopped herring onto a piece of matzah. 'Sheila, this is delicious. Thank you so much for bringing it.' Food is the glue in our family.

The BlackBerry buzzes. It's a text from Jess. *Don't go home. I told Amy your dad died. She says you've got to come and stay with us.*

I reply: *Thank you. And please say big thanks to Amy.*

Jess: *I want to fuck your brains out.*

Me: *Sadly we can't have sex. I looked it up and intimate relations are banned during the seven days of shiva, as is the wearing of makeup.*

Jess: *Screw that. Apostasy is the best aphrodisiac.*

Me: *I'll ask Jackie to look after Dog.*

I love Jess, I realise. I love her. I'm smiling, even though I want to burst into tears.

I put the phone in my jacket pocket, and feel the crinkle of the paper that has the words of my reading, the psalm that is a bridge between Dad's and Marilyn's respective funerals. Two people I loved, two different religions, one message at both.

Thou preparest a table before me in the presence of mine enemies.

I think back to the service for Marilyn, the people who were there, the exquisite buffet that Marilyn's aunt, the Countess Woolard, laid on. I was feasting in the presence of mine enemies that day.

It's not always such a bad thing to be underestimated.

Dad's life was devoted to making society fairer and more equal. Looking at the world I inhabit, of bankers and billionaires, it's hard to argue he succeeded. Men like Stan Blackwell earn millions running their banks into the ground, and are bailed out by taxpayers. Harvey Jackson is adored like a rock star and hailed as a business genius, even though he's a fraud. Prime ministers gulp exorbitantly priced claret in Alex Elliott's drawing room like cringing hangers-on. Chris Ravel has accumulated enough wealth to buy anything and anyone.

It dawns on me which part of the puzzle I am missing. I temporarily leave the mourners and go into the hall to make a call.

'Could I leave a message for Lord Ravel? It's Gil Peck. Yes, he knows me. Could you tell him that it would be a good idea for us to meet, as a matter of some urgency?'

Chapter 25

LORD RAVEL SUGGESTS WE CHAT at his club, the Garrick. 'I assume you know, but you'll need to wear a tie,' he tells me over the phone. 'And we don't allow trainers.'

'Really? In which case, let's not bother.'

A pause. 'You're joking.'

'I'm joking.'

'When you get there, tell the porters you're meeting me.'

The dining room is crimson, with a long table down the middle for members – all men – who simply want to turn up and chat with other random members. When I enter, Ravel is seated at one of the smaller tables by a sash window. He pours me a glass of tap water from a jug.

'My condolences about your father. I came across him as a junior official during the Callaghan government. A great man.'

Of course Ravel knew him, though I'm not sure what Dad would have made of Ravel. Dad wanted to change the world; men like Ravel are the bastions of the status quo.

'Thanks. It's been quite upsetting.' With Ravel I default to understatement.

Ravel hands me the menu and suggests I play it safe in my choices. I choose smoked salmon and jugged hare.

'You are taking a risk with the hare, but so long as you like living dangerously.' He orders the smoked salmon, and the saddle of lamb from the trolley.

'Thanks for coming here. I imagine our gender rule is not your thing.' I give a peremptory nod. 'I have become more wary with age, and I am pretty sure this is one place where Mr Putin won't be eavesdropping.'

'Putin? I thought he was our friend.'

'That is the fashionable view, but not mine. Now what was so urgent?'

I'm fed up with all the euphemisms and evasions of the mandarin class. I plough straight in. 'Your son, Chris. I need to know about his friendship with Islamist terrorists.'

Ravel is about to take a sip of water, but my question stays his hand. *Good. He's human after all.* He holds the glass just in front of his mouth, his breath misting the rim.

'Ah, that.'

'Yes. That.'

He puts the glass down. 'My son is a man of contradictions. As I think I told you, we were estranged. But I did become aware, as I assume you did too, that he joined a number of left-wing sects at university.'

'Various revolutionary communist groups, from memory.'

'Quite. Now, like many lefties of the era, he spent his vacations in the Middle East. I don't suppose you did, or if so it would have been in a different country.'

Wow. The predictability of these bigots. It must be genetic. The British establishment is endlessly inventive in its needling antisemitism.

'By contrast, Chris felt, and there is a case for this, that a terrible injustice had been done to the Palestinians in the creation of the state of Israel. I hope you don't mind me saying that.'

'It's complicated. But yes, having sympathy for the Palestinians is neither unusual nor unreasonable.'

'Christopher's allegiances were more than sympathy. I was in a position to keep an eye on him, and over time I became concerned.'

'You could keep an eye because you were inside MI6 at the time?'

'You will draw your own conclusions.' *My God, he was spying on his own son.* 'Christopher became fanatical in his commitment to the Palestinian cause. They could do no wrong. Any atrocity they committed against the Jews of Israel was justified.'

'That was a fashionable view on the left.'

'Yes, well, Christopher took it further than that. He effectively joined Fatah. Went to their training camps. Learned how to use their assault weapons, to construct an improvised bomb.'

'You're joking, of course.'

He takes a sip of water.

'I wish I was. We had eyes and ears in the camps – I saw the footage myself. I became so concerned that when he returned to Oxford, I visited him in his rooms. It did not go well. We haven't spoken since.'

'Have you really not spoken once in more than twenty years?' I feel a surge of gratitude that at least dad and I talked, even if it was rarely about what matters.

'Not in any way you would recognise as a conversation. We run into each other at family events. Births, marriages, deaths. But we don't linger to chat.'

The hare arrives. It's better than I feared: a bit too bony, but the pepperiness of the juniper berries works a treat with the gaminess of the meat.

Ravel notes my relish. 'You may have gambled and won,' he says. 'Let it be an omen. Where was I?'

'Your son and Palestine.'

'Oh yes. I assume this is the bit you want to know about. Not long after Oxford, he graduated from the PLO to those who fund it. He got to know some immensely wealthy Saudis, the sheikh class, as it were. One of their businesses was supplying arms to unsavoury characters in Syria, Lebanon and Gaza. Colossally remunerative.'

'And you were still tracking all this through the Secret Intelligence Service?'

Ravel ignores the question. 'Christopher fell in with these Saudis. He became a sort of intermediary between the manufacturers of the weapons, and those who needed them.'

'Presumably you mean "terrorists".'

'Christopher was the perfect go-between. Which western arms manufacturer could question the bona fides of an Oxford graduate whose papa was something senior in the Foreign Office?'

Jesus. Ravel junior was supplying arms to terrorists and paramilitaries, all of them avowed enemies of the West, while Ravel senior was watching from his eyrie in MI6. So British.

'Is that how he got the cash to seed his hedge-fund business?' I ask.

'It was very much a mutually beneficial arrangement. The fund was the perfect vehicle to launder the Saudis' cash, especially since it turned out Christopher had a talent for making the money grow.'

My leg is shaking, as it does when I'm on edge. I calm it. 'If the intelligence services knew all this, why on earth didn't you shut him down?'

Ravel gives me the kind of withering look that mandarins of a certain seniority and class must be taught somewhere. 'The view was taken that if Christopher wasn't doing it, someone else would be. At least, once we worked out what was happening, we could keep an eye on him – and his customers. You'd be surprised the useful things we learned.'

The waiter clears our plates. 'Tea, coffee?'

'Black coffee, please.'

Ravel makes a face. 'Undrinkable muck. Worst coffee in London.' He turns back to the waiter. 'Two black coffees.'

There's so much more I need to know. 'Tell me about the Athena deal.'

Ravel arches against the straight back of the mahogany chair. 'You know about that, do you?'

'It's the quid pro quo for a Saudi rescue of PTBG. Jackson and MHH are fronting for the beneficial owners.'

He frowns. For once, just possibly, I know a little more than he does. Then his face relaxes back into its normal resting position of effortless superiority. 'That makes sense. Christopher would be desperate to prevent PTBG falling into the hands of the government and would presumably do almost anything to stop it.'

I remember Blackwell at Elliott's party: *Neither of us needs government-appointed auditors looking at the books.* And earlier, when I spoke to Blackwell at the Brewery: *We've been prime broker to Lulworth forever. And as his prime broker, I of course know his bets.*

I am not sure which nauseates me more: that Blackwell was completely oblivious to the toxic risk of the CDOs and CDSs his bank was piling high, or that he was cognisant of and complicit in Ravel's illegal trade with paramilitaries. Where there was a return to be made, scruple was pushed aside.

'If this came out, it would be an establishment scandal like none other.' I don't know how much of this Marilyn knew, but I more properly understand the meaning of her warning. *This is much bigger than you know.*

'It would be ugly,' Ravel concurs.

'It would be pretty bad for you too, wouldn't it, given that you've known about it all these years?'

'A secondary consideration.'

Which presumably means no one would be able to prove that MI6 tacitly sanctioned the illicit arms deals and the laundering of the proceeds through Lulworth and PTBG. I can't prove it, and stupidly I didn't bring my Olympus. Ravel's tentacles make him a one-man Malmsey.

The coffee arrives. It is as stewed and bitter as Ravel suggested. 'Why are you being so frank?'

'Whatever you think of me, Mr Peck, I have served my country for forty years. I am a patriot. And I take the view that Athena should not be sold abroad, and most certainly not to the Saudis. It would upset the fragile balance of power in the region, and lead to goodness knows what kind of disaster. The sale must be stopped.'

'Surely the government can just ban the technology transfer and prohibit the deal?'

Ravel peers down his aquiline beak. 'This is Modern Labour, Mr Peck. One of Todd's founding principles is that everything is for sale. It's not my normal style to engage with the media' – he pronounces it 'meeja', to signal his disdain – 'but it would be a service to the public if you could get all of this in the public domain in your inimitable way as soon as humanly possible. It's possible you'll create enough of a stink to shame Tudor into action.'

My phone buzzes and I instinctively pull it out to answer it. A waiter appears within a millisecond and informs me telephones are not permitted in the dining room.

'You're on your toes when it suits you, aren't you?' Ravel joshes.

'Sorry sir. Club's rules.'

'Quite right too. Anyway, Mr Peck and I were just finishing. Gil, why don't you ring back your interlocutor in the lobby downstairs? I'll pick this up.'

'Are you sure? It was my idea to meet, so surely I should pay.'

'Your money isn't any good here, I'm afraid.'

As I go to the lobby, I note that the call was from Jess's landline at home. She picks up the second I ring her back.

328

'Everything OK?'

'It's Amy.'

Dread rolls over me as I hear the anxiety in her tone. 'What about her?'

'She's disappeared.'

Chapter 26

'WHAT DO YOU MEAN, DISAPPEARED?'

'The school telephoned. She left the playground at lunch break. No one knows how. She didn't go back inside for registration. I'm about to go to the school.'

'I'm sure there's an innocent explanation and she'll turn up soon.' The words come out automatically, reassuring her in the way I always reassure my parents, though as soon as they're out I realise I'm being patronising and stupid. 'We should ring the police, though.'

'If there's an innocent explanation, why would we contact the police?'

'Sorry. I wasn't trying to minimise. I'll see you at the school in twenty minutes.'

I don't think I've ever cycled so fast. I ignore the red light and cross the Euston Road at Tottenham Court Road and narrowly miss being turned to pulp by an ambulance at the junction on the north side. When I get to the gates of Our Lady of Queen's Park, Jess is pulling up in her car. I notice there's a CCTV camera at the entrance, and the gate is locked.

'The security seems to be good,' I say, and then again regret my inanity. If Amy's missing, it wasn't good enough.

Jess buzzes the intercom, and we walk in together to see the headteacher, Ms Ditton. She offers us a couple of those plastic stacking chairs that every school owns. We sit facing her across her paper-strewn desk. Ms Ditton is trying to be calm, but concern is etched in her every self-conscious gesture.

'I talked to Amy's classmates. They say a young couple came into the playground at lunchtime. They went up to Amy as though they knew her, as though they were family or close friends.'

'Do Amy's friends have any idea who these people were and why Amy felt minded to leave with them?' Jess asks.

'Apparently one of them said they worked with your new boyfriend, and he'd arranged for Amy to have a treat.'

I reach out to Jess and squeeze her hand. 'That would be me, I suppose.'

'They told her you'd asked them to pick her up. Apparently, she said she wanted to speak to you, and they called you on the phone.'

Jess looks hard at me. 'They didn't ring me,' I say. 'Someone must have impersonated me.'

I daren't look at Jess. It's obvious she's going to think that knowing me is too dangerous. All those hopes I've been building of making a family with Jess and Amy – of escaping to something normal and healthy from my obsessively compulsive, solipsistic bubble – is just so much dry sand escaping through my fingers.

I turn to the headteacher and dispense with tact. 'How did they get in? Aren't the gates locked when the children are in the playground?'

'Yes, they are, normally. We are looking into it.'

'What about CCTV? I saw the camera outside.'

'Yes. We have it. But it broke last year. Money is tight and we haven't been able to fix it. We do have one possible lead, though. One of the boys who saw Amy leave is obsessed with cars. He says they all got into a Bentley, and he said it was bigger than a normal one.'

Jess's eyes go wide, and there's no need for us to articulate what we're both thinking. *Primakov.*

'Do you have an idea who took her?' the headteacher asks.

A Russian billionaire whose enemies drown in lakes or get bullets in their heads. I'm wondering how I can possibly explain the insanity of our life to the headteacher when my phone buzzes. I recognise the number and step outside for two minutes.

On my return, I say, 'That was Kim Jansen.'

'Jesus,' says Jess. 'She's the last person we need.'

'She says she's pulling up outside.'

'Who is she?' asks the head.

'The assistant commissioner of the Met.' Jess rounds on me. 'Did you call her?'

'No. Of course not. Presumably the school contacted the police?' I look at Ms Ditton, who nods. 'And someone must have informed Kim, I suppose.'

'Well it's odd. And I want you to tell her to fuck right off.'

'But isn't it a good thing the police are taking this seriously?' Ms Ditton is bewildered.

'I'll go and see what she's doing here,' I say. 'I'll encourage her to leave, but I can't be sure she'll listen to me.'

Outside the gates, there's a navy blue official Jaguar, and a Vauxhall estate dressed in the luminescent yellow and blue Met livery. Kim is sitting next to the driver in the Jag. She winds down the window, and signals to me to wait, while she finishes a call. I walk up and down, increasingly agitated. I can see she's actually laughing as she winds up on the phone. It is a struggle to suppress my rage.

She steps onto the pavement. 'Jess must be frantic.'

I'm not in the mood for her phoney sympathy. 'Why are *you* here.'

'Your names were live on our database of open cases, because of your involvement in the Marilyn Krol suicide. Control room alerted me and I came straight over. We'll obviously do everything we can to find Amy.'

The officers in the other car are getting out to join us. 'Don't give me that sanctimonious bollocks,' I snarl. 'I don't believe your internal systems are anywhere near as efficient as that. You knew this was going to happen. You're here because you're in on it.'

Jansen looks around to see if we've been overheard. 'Calm down.' She shoots her colleagues a look and they instantly withdraw from earshot. 'What you've just said is wrong and totally out of order. I'm here to help. If you have any sense, you'll tell me everything you know. You can trust me.'

She's the last person I trust. But however much she's been corrupted by Elliott, she seems genuinely anxious.

'Amy has been taken away by a couple who were using a car – an oversized Bentley – owned by a Russian billionaire called Primakov. I imagine his name is familiar, because he's in business with your Malmsey friends Elliott and Jackson. Jess and I have been investigating their criminal activities, which include blackmailing a Bank of England director, fraudulently hiding massive losses in the MHH fund from creditors and investors, and failing to disclose substantial purchases of NewGate shares. And just to avoid any doubt in your mind about what I think about your culpability, if there is so much as a scratch on Amy, I will make it my life's mission to destroy you.'

Kim's jaw tightens. 'Pipe down, before you say something you'll regret. I can only imagine how upset Ms Neeskens feels. But don't confuse conspiracy fantasies with the real world. You can rest assured I take the disappearance of a child very seriously. We will move heaven and earth to find her. First of all, though, it's best if we go inside and talk with the head.'

'Jess doesn't want you here,' I say.

'It's not her call. As I said, the disappearance of a seven-year-old is extremely serious.'

'Did Elliott give you that script?'

Without responding, she strides into the school, the officers trailing behind. A moment later, Jess comes out.

'I told you to get rid of her.'

I shrug. 'I told her she wasn't wanted, but she wouldn't listen. Why have you left the office?'

'She said she needed to talk to the head alone.'

Jess looks around the playground, presumably hoping for a miracle and that Amy will pop out from behind the climbing frame or the sparse trees. 'Gil, what did you say to the Russian? What does he want from us?'

'I don't know. Maybe he's in on the Athena deal and knows that if we expose it then it probably won't happen.'

'Oh don't be so stupid,' she hisses. I feel as though I've been slapped. 'Take responsibility for once in your life. It's all because you prevented the initial takeover of NewGate and then you told Tudor to nationalise. You cost Primakov a fortune. It's his revenge.'

Kill me now, kill me now, kill me now.

'What are you mumbling now?' I've never seen her eyes so ablaze with anger. Fury. At me. I've ruined everything.

'I'm sorry, Jess,' I say. 'Honestly, if I'd known . . .'

It *is* my fault. She's right. There is nothing and no one I won't put at risk, as the price of a scoop that will lead the news bulletins.

'I'll put it right. I swear.'

'How can you possibly give that assurance?' Jess is raving. 'We don't know where she is, what they're doing to her, whether we're too late.'

'They won't hurt her.'

'Stop with the platitudes. I'm not your child.'

'I'm pretty sure Kim won't allow it.'

'Are you mad? She's up to her neck.'

'We don't know that. She was obviously willing to help Elliott by seizing the diaries, but I don't believe she would sanction harm to a child.'

'You have no idea what Elliott can make people do.' Jess turns away from me and stares at a woman escorting her son across the playground. 'Anyway, if she's not part of the kidnapping, as you seem to think, then she won't have a clue where Amy is.'

The head's office has a window overlooking us. Ms Ditton is deep in conversation with Kim. 'That woman is evil,' says Jess. 'I'm going back inside.'

Jess doesn't invite me to go with her. 'I'll make some calls,' I say. She doesn't acknowledge me.

I am alone in the rubberised playground, next to the faded lines of a hopscotch grid and the pirate-ship climbing frame.

Who would know anything about what happened? I ring Primakov and it goes straight to voicemail. I leave a message saying he needs to ring urgently without specifying why. I try to work out if there is anything I can promise him in exchange for Amy's safe return.

Almost immediately there's a text from Quasimodo's number, the one he used to threaten me with further leaks to the tabloids of messages stored on my stolen BlackBerries.

You've mislaid something important. If you want it back, come now. PTBG Building, South Colonnade, Canary Wharf. Top floor. Go to reception and ask for New Minerva LLC.

The signature is 'QED'. So witty. I run back to the school's reception and grab the Brompton. Before mounting, I text Jess. *I have a lead. Don't mention to ANYONE. X*

*

The PTBG building in Canary Wharf is huge enough to be a small city in itself. From the main foyer, I can see down escalators leading to an underground shopping centre, while banks of elevators wait to whisk employees up the fifty storeys. It is an arrogant, hubristic citadel for a banking empire that is intent on global domination.

At the front desk, I say I have an appointment with New Minerva. They direct me to a security guard sitting at the end. I give him my name and he doesn't bother issuing me with a pass. Instead he ushers me through the glass gates to a lift reserved for access to the top floor. Alone in the high-speed lift, I realise he didn't even bother to note down my name. There's no record of me entering the building.

The lift doors open on a building site, an echoey empty shell waiting to be fitted and kitted out. There are no partitions or rooms yet, but at the far end a piece of translucent plastic hangs from the ceiling like a curtain. Behind it, I can see the silhouettes of a group of men, five of them. I leave my Brompton by the lift and walk towards the sheet.

I'm spotted. A stocky double act in blazers and chinos, the uniform of ex-special forces who've privatised themselves, tell me to wait where I am. They come over, one stands behind me, while the other pats me down. He takes my BlackBerries and the Olympus. 'Good gear,' he says. And grins.

A third man comes out from behind the plastic sheeting. Elliott.

'Where's Primakov?' I ask.

Elliott laughs. 'Primakov? I thought you were brighter than that. Bill, be a love and demonstrate to our friend Gil that he has to stop asking impertinent questions.'

'I'm sorry about this, Mr Peck,' says the man who patted me down. Before I know what's happened, I'm doubled up in excruciating pain, struggling to breathe, barely able to speak. He hit me expertly in the solar plexus.

'Take it easy, Mr Peck,' he says. 'Don't panic. Small breaths. You'll be all right in a moment.'

My eyes are watering. I'm wondering if I will ever be able to breathe normally again. Gradually my composure returns, and I am able to push myself back up to standing. Elliott is staring at me intently, as though committing the image of my humiliation to memory.

337

'Such fun,' he says. 'Wish I'd filmed it. I'd wank over it later.'
He nods to Bill. 'Bring him through.'

Bill takes a firm grip on my arm and steers me around the
plastic sheeting. One day, when the building is finished, this will
be a palatial corner office for some master-of-the-universe chief
executive. At the moment, the only thing that's ready is the view.
Through the floor-to-ceiling windows, you can see the world
like a god. The lesser buildings of Canary Wharf stand like
acolytes around the PTBG building, while the glistening ribbon
of the Thames winds into the distance.

Two men are by the window. I had an idea who I was going
to find here, but it turns out I was only sixty-six per cent correct.

Chris Ravel, of course. The billions he's made from arms sales
has given him control over Britain's biggest bank, PTBG, and
one of the biggest investment funds, MHH. He's writing on his
BlackBerry, and barely looks up when I nod at him.

I should have anticipated the other participant, and now feel
stupid that I didn't. He's been omnipresent from the moment
NewGate went down: at Marilyn's funeral, in the melee of
Elliott's parties, on the walls of Jackson's office, making introductions for Primakov, taking funds from Athena.

'Hello, Gil,' he says, with that dazzling smile that lit up a
thousand party rallies and political broadcasts.

'Hi, Johnny.'

The former prime minister is the glue between everyone:
Ravel, Jackson, Primakov, Elliott, Blackwell, Breitner, the Saudis.
He is the only one of them who can access any government,
any boardroom, any bank. Tudor is still scared of him. Jackson
needs him to give legitimacy to the spurious philanthropy that
cloaks his asset stripping. Ravel worships him as some kind of
role model of unsentimental ruthlessness, the father he never
had. Elliott's fortune was built on his proximity to him. And
Marilyn devoted too much of her short life to winning him
that election from which all his power subsequently flowed.

Even my sister Clare was seduced and manipulated by him, until she saw him for the rapacious monster he is, and he arranged her murder.

Seeing him, I realise by coming here I've almost certainly signed my own death warrant. I should run, but Bill is inches to my left. I wouldn't get two yards. Todd comes over and puts his mouth two inches from mine. His breath is warm and odourless.

'I told you to take care, that sad day at Marilyn's funeral. You've never taken my advice. Just like Marilyn, you don't know when someone's trying to help you.'

I refuse to be intimidated. If I'm done, I'm done. But I won't acknowledge his victory.

'Go fuck yourself, Johnny.'

'This isn't ideal, I agree, but we couldn't ignore you any longer, not after you made the mistake of revealing to Harvey how much you know. That was a schoolboy error. I was disappointed.' He walks back a couple of paces and nods at Elliott.

'I imagine you've worked out why we invited you here,' says Elliott.

'Enlighten me.'

'It's important that Harvey buys that brilliant little defence business you've been nosing around,' he says. 'In case you hadn't guessed, it'll be renamed New Minerva, once we own it. The deal will be between two private institutions, of no interest to BBC viewers, or indeed to anyone. You will forget everything about why it's happening that you think you know. And if anyone were to ask about it, you will sing its praises as unlocking capital for investment in further high-tech ventures in the UK.'

Todd nods at Bill, for reasons I don't understand, who walks to the side of the room and opens a black attaché case. I can't see what he removes.

'Are you listening to me? Don't worry about Bill.'

'OK.'

'This is important. On the other hand, you are *not* to ignore our Saudi friends' investment in PTBG. You will report it on the news as a brilliantly creative partnership that goes with the grain of globalisation. You will say it cements an important relationship between a great British bank and one of the powerful emerging economies.'

I take a deep breath. It's time I told Elliott quite how much he has miscalculated.

'Fuck you, Alex,' I rasp. 'I'll tell you what I am going to do. As soon as I leave here, I will file a blog that tells the world about your and your friend's illegal profits from arming terrorists' – I point at Ravel – 'and how all the proceeds are laundered through Chris's hedge fund and PTBG accounts. I'll tell them how MHH and PTBG are sitting on huge losses, and how you blackmailed a director of the Bank of England to try and cover it all up. You are toast.'

Alex smirks, and Todd beckons to Bill. I brace myself for being walloped again. But instead Bill puts me in an armlock while his associate grabs my right hand. Before I know what's happened there's a lightning strike of pain in my hand. I look down. My little finger is on the floor. When I look up, Elliott has walked to the window and is throwing up. Todd is actually smiling.

The former prime minister says to Bill: 'Probably an idea to wrap the finger in a tissue, and put it in his jacket pocket. You never know, if he gets out of here, they may be able to sew it back. It's marvellous what they can do these days.'

Through shock, pain and tears, I hiss, 'Fuck all of you.'

Ravel looks up from his phone. 'Take a deep breath, Gil. This doesn't have to end badly for you. Analyse your situation and evaluate how you can profit.' He carries a grey plastic, stackable chair to me. 'If I were you, I'd sit down. And before you pass out you can write a short blog, one of your great scoops. You can reveal that the up-and-coming Saudi invest-ment firm, Asclepius, is making an inspired investment in the

UK's most important bank, PTBG. Just think of the personal glory, another Gil Peck world exclusive. You may even win another award.'

The pain is oddly less acute than I expected, but the blood is pouring out of the wound. They sliced it off just below the knuckle. Bill goes back to his suitcase and gets a gauze pad and some surgical tape, which he wraps deftly around my injured finger. He has done this before.

I look into Todd's famous green eyes, heavily lidded and under-pinned by dark, fleshy half-moons. The boyish innocence that propelled him to power in 1997 has long since been dissipated.

'Gil, we've known each other a long time,' Todd says. I won't acknowledge him. 'I know how fond you are of that lovely little girl and her mum. You may not care about your own life, but if you want them reunited, it's a good idea to write the blog suggested by Chris. We all have your interest at heart.'

'Give him his BlackBerry,' says Ravel. He looks at me. 'Go to your inbox. At the top there's a suggested version written by one of Alex's colleagues. Cut and paste it into a new message, sprinkle a bit of your magic dust on it, and Bob's your uncle.'

Bill whispers in my ear: 'Sit down.' I'm not being offered a choice. He hands me one of the BlackBerries. I think of dialling 999, but he's standing directly behind me. I won't get past the first '9'.

It's over. I've lost.

'You will return Amy to Jess?' I say.

'Just as soon as we see the blog on the BBC website, Amy will arrive home in Queen's Park after a lovely day out,' says Ravel. 'She will remember this day all her life.'

I open the dummy blog drafted by Elliott's firm. 'This is shite,' I say. 'No one's going to think I wrote this. I need more information. How much capital is being invested by the Saudis? Will they get a seat on the board? Are any of you joining the board?'

Ravel bursts out laughing. 'I knew that in the end your desperation for one more story would save you.'

I start writing and editing, holding the phone with my good hand while I tap out the letters with the index finger of my bandaged hand. My head is dizzy, my eyes are watering with the pain, and blood is seeping out of the bandage. No one offers to help. Ravel is back on his own BlackBerry, and Elliott gazes out the window at the reconstruction of East London. Todd says goodbye to them, ignores me, and walks to the lift. The sunset turns the windows of the adjacent buildings into burning copper.

It doesn't take long. Just a few minutes. Ravel insists I read it to him. *PTBG, the UK's largest bank, has secured a $25 billion investment from investors connected to the Saudi state, I have learned. The deal will secure PTBG's future, in these turbulent market and economic conditions ...*

He nods and I press send.

Ravel addresses Bill and his friend. 'We're late for a meeting. Alex will text you when the blog is up on the BBC website. When you get the message, take our friend down to the ground floor and put him in the black cab that's waiting there. There'll be his name on a card in the window. The driver's been given the destination.'

'Cheerio old friend,' Elliott says as they leave. 'Thanks for being such a sport. You won't regret it.'

I haven't got the strength to respond. I'm delirious. Marilyn is talking to me: *It's life or death. For both of us.* If I die here, at least I've done the right thing. For once.

'Can I ring my girlfriend, check she's OK?' I ask Bill.

'Against the rules, my friend. You know that.'

'Yeah. Stupid of me.'

Time stretches on for an eternity. Or maybe only for ten minutes. A call comes through to Bill. 'OK, Mr Elliott. We'll take him to the car now.'

The two former soldiers stand on either side of me, hoik me up and carry me in standing position to the elevator. When we get to reception, Bill nods at the officials on the desk. He explains: 'He was celebrating his bonus, overdid it, needs to sleep it off. You know what it's like.'

I'm too exhausted to protest that I'm not just another spoiled, overpaid yuppie banker, and that the former prime minister of the United Kingdom has been torturing me. When Bill dumps me on the bench seat at the back of the cab, the driver barely gives me a glance. As we drive off, he says: 'UCLH Accident and Emergency. All right, mate?'

It's the last thing I hear.

Chapter 27

I AM BACK AT THE BOTTOM of that lake, frantically kicking and pushing to get to the surface. There's a bright light above me but I struggle to reach it. Through the roar of rushing water I think I can hear my name being called.

I open my eyes. Jess is leaning down, so close I can feel her warmth on my face, smell her scent.

'Gil. Thank God. You're back.'

I try to talk, but my mouth is too dry. 'Drink,' I whisper. I force myself to sit up and Jess lifts a plastic cup to my parched lips.

I am in a bed on a hospital ward, with a tube inserted in my forearm. The curtains are drawn. Jess and I are alone.

'Ow,' I say.

'Are you OK, darling?'

'My finger hurts.'

I look at my right hand. It is meticulously bandaged. As I lift it in front of my face, memory floods in, a torrent gushing through the open sluice of a dam.

'Amy?' I ask.

'At home. My mum's with her. The mysterious couple took her to Legoland. Inevitably she had the time of her life. Wants to know when Auntie Jean and Uncle Ron will be taking her out again.'

'Did they bring her home?'

'Near home. Around six, the police received an anonymous tip-off that a little girl was on her own outside the Sainsbury's on Kilburn High Road. They brought her back.'

'Thank God.' I have never felt so relieved. 'Has Amy got a description of them?'

I can see from the tightness of her jaw that Jess is suppressing vengeful fury against the kidnappers. They'd better pray she never finds them. 'I didn't want to upset Amy so I've extracted what I can, as gently as I can. The woman sounds remarkably like the leggy brunette who pushed you in Elliott's lake.'

I feel dizzy, vertiginous, a feeling of being perched perilously above the rapids on a flimsy rope bridge. I stare at my right hand, but the bandaging is so thick and dense I have no sense of what's underneath it.

'Do I still have a little finger?'

Jess's mouth tightens. 'They tried to stitch it back, but it was too late.'

I lie back, trying to absorb what it means. Despite myself, I start crying. Jess takes my left hand and starts to stroke it.

'I assume this is all connected with why they gave Amy back to us?'

I hesitate. 'Can anyone hear us?'

Jess pokes her head through the curtains. 'Bed on left, empty. Old man asleep on right.'

'Come as near as you can.'

In the quietest voice that's still audible, I tell her as much as I can remember, about the ex-military heavies, Elliott, Ravel, Todd. Every time I close my eyes, it's Todd's cold emotionless eyes I see.

'We've lost, Jess. I'm done. These are people who have no moral checks or limits. They've shown what they'll do to Amy. We can't put her in harm's way.'

Jess shuts her eyes. She's trying to control all the different conflicting feelings: fear, anger, guilt.

'I was shocked by your bizarre blog about how we should be thrilled that the Saudis are investing in PTBG. I get it now.' She squeezes my left hand again.

'Was the blog that bad?'

She laughs. 'I'm glad you're feeling better.'

'How long have I been here?'

'A few hours. It's just gone ten o'clock.'

'God.' I sit up, almost pulling over the drip bag attached to my arm. 'I'm supposed to be on the news right now. What on earth will the BBC think?'

'Stop it, you idiot. When Kim Jansen told me you were here, I contacted your producer, Emma.'

'Jansen rang you?'

'Yes. She said UCLH worked out who you are from your press card and contacted the Met.'

Maybe that's what happened. Or maybe Jansen knew where I'd be anyway. I can't be bothered to think about it.

'What did you tell Emma?'

'I said you'd fallen off your bike. That you were shaken up: bashed about but basically fine. She said she'd let Janice Oldham know.'

'Dog!' I shout. 'I need a huge favour. Jackie's been looking after him. She will be going spare. Could you bear to?' I make what I hope is a winning smile.

'Oh hell,' Jess says. 'I've been refusing to let Amy have a dog for a year. Now she's never going to let you leave.'

She goes to my suit, which is folded over the back of a chair. There are deep bloodstains all over it. I doubt any dry cleaner will be able to remove them. How many suits are going to be destroyed before the banking crisis is over? She rummages in the pockets and finds my keys.

I slump back.

'It's over,' I say again. 'I'll never get justice for Marilyn, or for Clare. These people always win.'

Jess looks me in the eye and gives me a smile. 'You're safe. Amy's safe. After the last twenty-four hours, that's enough.'

'I suppose so.' My eyes close. I can feel sleep overwhelming me. 'Is it enough?'

*

UCLH keeps me in overnight for observation. The following morning, the on-duty houseman gives me instructions about how to put my bandaged hand in a plastic bag when I bathe or shower, and to come back in a week to have the dressing changed.

'Really, a week?'

'Yes. So long as you don't damage the dressing, it's best to let it heal.'

He says that if all goes to plan, if it heals up as it should, I can go to my GP after that for future check-ups.

'When can I get back to work?'

'Take a good few days. Are you right-handed?'

'Left, actually.'

'That's a blessing. In which case, just use your own judgement. By the way, how did it happen?'

'Fell off my bike. Ripped off by a passing motorbike.'

The look he gives me says he doesn't believe a word.

'We spoke to the police when you came in. It looked to us like a brutal attack. They'll want to talk to you about it.'

'I very much doubt that.'

*

I take three weeks away from the BBC. Everyone buys the bike-accident lie, and is solicitous. Janice rings to say I should take all the time I need, and that news will still be happening whenever I want to return to it.

I sleep every night in Jess's bed. Amy insisted. It would have been churlish to refuse. To my amazement, I hardly give a moment's thought to the banks, and am happy to leave the BlackBerries switched off. Maybe this will turn out to be good for me.

The day after I leave hospital, there is a ring on the bell of Jess's house. A man is holding my Brompton. 'Gil Peck?' I nod. 'This is for you.' There's a huge blue ribbon wrapped around it, with a cardboard tag attached, like a birthday present. It reads: *You forgot your bike, yours ever Q.* I don't feel like climbing on it, quite yet.

I do, however, break one promise to myself. I had said I wouldn't sit more than one night's shiva. But that night I go to Mum's. After the prayers, after everyone leaves, we hug, and cry. 'I let Dad down.'

'Don't be so silly. Dad was proud of you.'

We sit on the sofa for hours, going through the hundreds and hundreds of photos from family holidays and school plays.

'I miss Clare so much,' I say, when we look at the two of us riding donkeys at Broadstairs.

'So do I, darling.'

'I won't ever leave you, Mum.'

'You'd better not.'

*

In the late afternoons, I hang out with Amy. I play her the songs my dad used to play me when I was her age. Our favourite is 'Istanbul (Not Constantinople)' by the Four Lads. It leads to a nightly game that drives Jess mad.

'Mum?' Amy says.

'Yes, Amy.'

'Why did Constantinople get the works?'

'I don't know, Amy, why did Constantinople get the works?'

'That's nobody's business but the Turks'. Silly Mummy.' And Amy bursts into helpless laughter.

'I'm glad you two are getting on so well,' Jess says, after one of these nightly rituals. 'But you can't mope around here all day, even if the BBC doesn't seem to miss you.'

'Ha ha. Actually, Janice rang me today. They are keen to have a date for my return.'

'And?'

'Well, they want an hour-long documentary for BBC2 on where this banking mess is heading.' After the Saudi investment, PTBG is secure, for a while at least. But across the world, bank after bank is being forced by economic reality to recognise massive looming losses on recklessly made loans and investments. The dominos are about to tumble from New York, to London, to Madrid and Milan.

'I'll go to my first production meeting on Monday.'

'That's great news.'

'As for the day job, I've agreed I'll go to Davos. It'll be my formal return.'

Davos is the Swiss alpine resort where the World Economic Forum has its annual January gathering of the world's business leaders, bankers, financiers and prime ministers. It's ostensibly where the global elite comes together to show its humanitarian side, by discussing solutions to poverty, disease and climate change. In practice, it's a magnificent charade, a cover for hole-and-corner money-making deals.

Jess gives me a hard look. 'Is that a good idea? You know who'll be at Davos?'

I do. *Everyone* is always there, including presumably Jackson, Elliott, Ravel and Primakov. As for quintessential Davos man, the king of the mountain, that's Johnny Todd, the living embodiment of self-righteous do-gooding and ruthless money-making.

'We can't hide from them,' I say. 'There is a limit to the victory we allow them. Fuck 'em, Jess. We have to get on with our jobs.'

Jess looks anxious. They hacked my phone, mugged me, beat me up, tried to drown me and mutilated me. I should be running in the opposite direction. But a flashback to Todd's smirking face reinforces my determination.

'I have to get used to being around them. Davos will be immersion therapy.'

'At least we'll be together,' she says.

'It'll be fun. Our first Davos as a couple.'

She gives me her patented 'you're stark raving bonkers' look. But all I'm thinking about is the motto I inherited from Dad.

Don't get mad . . .

Chapter 28

THE JOURNEY FROM ZÜRICH TO Davos is magical. Jess and I have been making this trip for years and it doesn't pall, no matter how many times we do it. Immaculately clean double-decker trains, soiled only by melted snow off skiers' boots; travelling up mountains through a brilliantly white, icy landscape; picture-postcard chalets and farmsteads on both sides. And punctual to the second. Having grown up staring at the vast departure board in brutalist Euston station, hoping the delay won't be much more than half an hour, and then being grateful for a seat far enough away from the sulphurous stink of the loo, the Swiss train up the mountain is fantastical.

'What's your priority while you're here?' Jess asks. She's worrying about me. She keeps checking whether I'm really ready to get back on my bike, both metaphorically and literally. She knows that my survival strategy is to compartmentalise, to section off anxieties and troubling thoughts into separate hermetically sealed boxes. Understandably, she's concerned that one or all of those boxes will explode under the pressure of the attempts on my life, the suicide of a former girlfriend, and the death of Dad. Heaven knows the consequences if I do surrender control.

'Tudor is coming,' I say. 'I assume I'll get my normal interview, though Jane's being tricky, says it's not guaranteed, that it depends on the timing of other commitments he's made. Other than that, it's about picking up the gossip, working out which bank will be next to fall. How about you? What are your plans?'

'Same. There's a ton of speculation that Lehman is sitting on huge losses. We need to bottom it out. The big set piece is an interview with Doug Blank.'

Blank is the chairman of Schon. 'Gosh. That's a big deal.' I inwardly curse myself for not putting in a bid to see him. 'I can't remember the last time he did something on the record.'

'Shares in bulge bracket firms have been tanking, because of concerns over their subprime losses. I'm assuming he wants to reassure me the industry can manage through this without help from government. For banks like Schon, being forced to take dollars from the public purse would be the ultimate humiliation.'

'Not to mention that they'd be banned from taking huge bonuses, poor things.'

As we climb, it's getting darker. The clouds are glowering. More snow is coming, maybe a storm.

I touch the stump on my right hand where my little finger used to be. Three times, for luck. If I press it hard against my palm, the pain can distract me from unwelcome thoughts, and focus me on what matters.

'It's incredible how these men who've been educated at Harvard, Yale and Stanford confuse naked self-interest with the economic good,' I say. 'They actually believe that if they're banned from trousering twenty-five million dollars every year, everyone suffers.'

'The truth is precisely the other way round,' says Jess. 'In their conviction they know best, they're going to upset the entire apple cart.'

'I suspect it's too late to save the apple cart,' I say. 'I'm counting on you to sock it to Doug Blank.'

*

Davos is a small tourist town. Before Klaus Schwab, the founder of the World Economic Forum, had the eccentric idea of inviting the world's richest and most powerful people here for four days every January, it was dowdy and sleepy. Think Bournemouth, or Coney Island, on top of a mountain.

The snow is ankle-deep as we disembark at Davos Dorf station. I take detachable crampons from my rucksack and stretch them over the toes and backs of my boots. I always feel a slight sense of shame when doing this, because one year when I was interviewing the Norwegian prime minister here she looked at my feet and said in her country only grannies wear them. I felt shamed into not wearing them for a whole day, till I slipped on my bum and decided that falling over was more undignified than being teased by a Scandinavian premier. Jess is also putting them on. We can be grannies together. It's a reassuring thought.

We trudge to the accreditation office, collect our passes, and then split up – to check into our hotels and be debriefed by colleagues. As usual, I'm in a modest guest house that the BBC rents in its entirety every year. It's clean, basic and hospitable. A jovial middle-aged pair have owned and managed it for years, though they are under pressure to sell the property for a small fortune to developers. After every Davos they warn us this is probably goodbye for the last time, but it never has been.

The *Financial Chronicle*, as the house newspaper for the WEF and the assembled demigods of finance, pays for Jess to be in the lavish Steigenberger Grandhotel Belvédère, a vast neo-classical palace which is where so much of the action takes place in private functions. I have already accepted an invitation to Prince Andrew's schmoozing party, which tends to be early Thursday evening, and is largely attended by the British banking and business contingent. The Steigenberger also has the advantage of being across the road from the large, specially constructed, state-of-the-art conference centre. Its roof is a small city of broadcasters' tents, which all have one side open to the majestic Alps. It's a spectacular mountainous backdrop for televised interviews.

I arrive in the hallway of our hostel. It's early afternoon. I can smell the leek and potato soup that will have accompanied a lunch of salami-filled rolls and fruit. Emma, Petra and the crew arrived at the weekend. They said this was necessary to make technical checks and suss out broadcasting locations, but somehow they always find a few hours to ski down the pristine slopes. Emma spies me from the dining room.

'Wotcha, Gil.'

'How was the skiing?'

'Amazing.' She gives me a concerned look, which makes me bristle, though it's kindly meant. 'How are you doing?'

'Pretty much back to normal, thanks.' I don't want to discuss my missing finger. 'What's going on?'

'Jane Walters has been in touch. Tudor wants to do the interview late this afternoon, five o'clock on the roof of the conference centre. Is that OK?'

'It's fine. I'll get there by four thirty.'

She knows me too well to believe me. 'Just make sure you're there before five. And put your thermals on. It's bitter.'

I dump my bag in my bedroom and make my way to the members' room in the conference centre, in the hope of gathering gossip. It's a large white space, midway up the central staircase in the conference centre, filled with coffee tables and white calf leather chairs. The room is reserved for white badge holders only – which means the bankers, government members and billionaires, plus a handful of privileged hacks like me. It's here, and in assorted small meeting rooms that feed off it, that the real business of Davos gets done – the swapping of insider information, the trading of scurrilous tittle-tattle, the lubrication of multi-billion-dollar transactions.

The uniformed woman on the desk checks my badge and lets me in. I head for the counter to order a double espresso

356

and nab a small Emmental-filled roll, when a familiar Irish lilt greets me.

'Gil Peck. Talk of the charming devil. I'd just been gossiping to Alex about you. I was so shocked to hear about your accident. Have you got a second?'

'Harvey.' There's no warmth in my voice as I turn around to greet Jackson. He's wearing a charcoal cashmere rollneck, and a pair of black skinny jeans that are presumably meant to make him look like Steve Jobs. I don't know how much he knew about what Todd and Elliott did to me, or even if he understands precisely why they set him up as the front for the acquisition of Athena. Is he a player or a pawn? I wonder whether he even cares, given that MHH is bankrupt – or at least would be, if the truth ever came out about its CDO losses.

I grit my teeth and force a smile. 'For you Harvey, of course I've got time.'

We go to a table being held for him by a flunky, who promptly makes herself scarce.

'I've got some good news, which you can have as an exclusive, if you like.' Jackson smiles broadly. 'Tudor has agreed to sell us NewGate after all.'

Black coffee spills on my saucer when I put down my cup clumsily. 'Blimey. It's only just been nationalised. How can that be?'

'He finally understood that we'll manage it better than he could.'

I assume he means Tudor has finally caved in to bullying from Johnny Todd, but I can't be bothered to state the obvious. 'What are you paying for it?'

'That's the beauty of it. NewGate will come to us for what it cost the taxpayer, which as you know was a solitary penny.'

My mind is in turmoil, trying to grasp what he's saying. 'Of course you'll take responsibility for future liabilities.'

His smile widens. 'Most of them.'

'What do you mean, "most of them"?'

'We'll have an indemnity for losses over a certain level.'

No wonder Jackson is so happy. 'What about future profits? Will the taxpayer have any ability to share in them?'

'There'll be a partial profit-sharing arrangement.'

Oh. My. God. This is a scandal. Tudor is making a present to Jackson of a business where the taxpayer will continue to be on the hook for future losses, but where Jackson will get most of any future profit. It's corrupt. What on earth is Tudor thinking? I'm definitely going to ask him, in the full glare of television lights.

'Is this on the record?'

'Don't quote me, but you're welcome to put it out. Heads of agreement will be signed in a few minutes, and I'd expect the Treasury to announce it later today. I'm sure you'll agree it's good news for a change.'

'You've had a lot of good news lately,' I say. 'The Athena deal, now this. It's all working out well for you.'

Jackson clasps his hands together. 'The important thing is that every penny we earn is going towards making the world a better place for tomorrow's children.'

At that moment, both our phones buzz simultaneously. It's Elliott. He's inviting us to a private dinner tonight with the leader of the opposition, Stella Barnsbury, at the Alte Post inn down towards Davos Platz railway station.

Just a few interesting people. The wine will be spectacular.

'Sort of a celebration,' says Jackson. 'I hope we'll see you there?'

Thou preparest a table before me in the presence of my enemies. I touch my pinkie stump again, three times, and feel the cleansing stab of pain. 'I wouldn't miss it.'

Jackson leaves for a conference call with a team from the Treasury, led by Merlyn Whipplington, and to finalise the wording of the press release. I do my job and call Jane Walters, Tudor's long-standing aide, to reassure myself that Jackson isn't setting me up about NewGate.

She confirms it. 'Neville was planning to tell you in the interview. But I should have guessed you'd find out about it.'

I start the two-fingered dance on my BlackBerry to write the blog, and half an hour later I press 'send' on the scoop. Within minutes after that, the wires are ablaze with reports that follow up my NewGate revelation.

This is the kind of moment for which I used to live. So many of my competitors are here and they're all chasing my story. Just a few weeks ago I would have been high on such a coup. This time it feels grubby and pointless. As I get up to leave, I see Petr Primakov at a table on my right, talking to someone I don't recognise. He winks at me. Funny how in this convocation of bankers, I have least antipathy to the acknowledged gangster.

*

Tudor turns up to the BBC's rooftop gazebo without a coat or a scarf, and is freezing. Schoolboy mistake. 'You've been here so many times before, prime minister. Had you forgotten how cold it is?'

'Don't be such a wimp. A bit of cold air never hurt anyone.'

Jane Walters raises her eyes to the heavens. It'll be a bad look if her boss's teeth chatter during the interview. 'You've got six minutes, Gil. Do. Not. Go. Over.'

I nod mischievously at Emma. I've never in my life kept an interview to six minutes; part of the ritual of these things is Jane's invective when we bust it.'

I interview the prime minister standing up, with evening creeping in on the snowy peaks behind him. Emma does the sync clap, and I plunge in.

'Prime minister, that was the shortest privatisation in history. What on earth is going on?'

'You say "the shortest privatisation in history" as if it's a bad thing, Gil. But Modern Labour doesn't think it's appropriate for the government to keep hold of assets one minute longer than is strictly necessary. The widely respected Mr Jackson made the government a generous offer that will potentially yield taxpayers a profit in the long term.'

'But as I understand it, what you've effectively agreed is an arrangement where taxpayers will continue to take most of the risk and Mr Jackson will end up with most of the gain. Many would say that is scandalous.'

'That's a misrepresentation, if I may say so. What we've put in place is an arrangement that carefully calibrates risk and reward for both sides.'

Meaningless. Jackson has turned him over, though I'll never get him to admit that on camera. I turn to the Saudi rescue of PTBG.

'It's not a rescue,' says Tudor. 'It's a far-sighted investment by one of the world's younger growing economies, in a business central to the UK's prosperity. It's a vote for the future success of Britain, and it's good news.'

He might as well be reading straight from Elliott's press release. When I ask him how concerned he is that the woes of banks, and the squeeze on lending by them, is tipping the UK into recession, he launches into a sermon about how Modern Labour will never let down the hard-working British people. 'But you can't compel banks to lend, can you?' I ask. 'That sounds like what happens in China.'

'I am not going to give you the details here and now. But we will restore confidence, and credit will start flowing again.'

Jane has put herself in my line of sight, and is doing frantic windmill motions with her arm, meaning, *Wind up or you'll never get an interview again.*

I put on a forced smile and say, 'Sadly we've run out of time. Thank you, prime minister.'

Jane is fuming. 'I said *six* minutes. You've really pushed your luck this time, Gil.'

She barks at the prime minister that Sky are expecting them. 'You couldn't get me a warm drink, could you Jane?' he replies. He's shivering, and his lips are blue.

Before he leaves, and while Jane is instructing another aide to find a hot chocolate for the PM, I grab him for one off-the-record question. 'Prime minister, I simply don't understand why you've given NewGate to Jackson. It doesn't make sense.'

He leads me to one side, out of earshot. 'I think you probably do. NewGate. PTBG. Athena. The Saudis. If the real story came out, Labour would be out of office for a generation.'

'I get the feeling Lord Ravel's been talking to you.' He gives me a half nod, which is all I need. 'But it's nothing to do with you, prime minister. The corruption and fraud is all Johnny Todd.'

'For God's sake, Gil, I wouldn't expect you to be so naive. In the public mind, Johnny *is* Labour, whether or not he's still PM.'

*

At 8.30, Jess and I arrive at the Alte Post. I've been here before: it's old-fashioned Switzerland, verging on Disney clichés. Wooden farmhouse-style chairs, with backs in the shape of hearts and smaller hearts carved in the middle of each of them. Dark oak-panelled walls, red cloth napkins.

I pause at the front door. Jess squeezes my hand, in encouragement. If meeting Jackson was hard, seeing Elliott in his pomp will be excruciating.

'We don't have to go.'

'It's the job.'

Elliott is waiting for us as soon as we cross the threshold, all floppy-haired public schoolboy charm. He greets us as long-lost friends, not a hint that the last time we met he said he would masturbate over a mental image of me being thumped.

'Wonderful you could make it,' he enthuses. 'Britain's next prime minister was very sad to hear about the loss of your vital member.'

361

'You'll understand how traumatic it was for Gil,' says Jess, 'because his little finger is the same size as your cock.'

Elliott's comeback is prevented by the approach of Jackson. This is going to be a much better evening than I feared, thanks to Jess.

'Brilliant blog, Gil,' Jackson booms. 'Where do you get your extraordinary information?'

Patrick Munis joins in. 'I loved your interview with the PM. When he was forced to defend what you called "the fastest privatisation in history", he almost choked. Priceless.'

It's a fucking Malmsey society reunion. I can see Ravel in the background, too. It's disorientating to be surrounded by men who have no moral core and think they can get away with anything.

Todd is also here. No shame or remorse, he heads straight for me. He extends a hand, and then remembers and tries to withdraw. But I won't let him off. I grab his hand with my mutilated right and squeeze hard, adding extra force where my little finger should have been.

He winces. 'I see you've recovered from your bicycle accident.'

'Yup. I'm in the pink again.'

'Good to hear it. How did it happen?'

'The accident?'

Oh my God, he actually wants to play this stupid game.

'I was just looking in the wrong direction, didn't notice the danger.'

'After what happened to your sister, you must've been really shaken.'

Wow. He's so arrogant he's actually telling me he killed Clare. He thinks he's untouchable. Maybe he is.

'Actually I see it as good luck. I'm still here.'

'Yes. Both of us. Still here.'

Jess has been on my right, talking to Munis, but is shooting me concerned glances. She leads the shadow chancellor in our

362

direction and turns to Todd. 'Does the prime minister know you're dining with the leader of the opposition?'

Todd's smile is oleaginous. 'Oh, I don't think it would be of any interest to him, do you?'

Alex Elliott is hovering, with Chris Ravel. 'We're all friends here, aren't we?' he says. 'Including you, Gil. You've been writing such insightful things recently.'

Ravel looks at me. 'I've always said about our friend here that he's the only journalist who properly understands the system.'

A white-jacketed waiter hands me a glass of white wine. I gulp it. Is this my life from now on, colluding with these monsters?

I turn to Todd. 'Are you here for the duration?'

Todd shakes his head. 'Chris and I are leaving tomorrow morning.'

'You're missing Tudor's plenary speech in the afternoon?'

He snorts. 'I've done my duty by Neville over the years. I've just come from seeing him, in fact, to congratulate him on selling NewGate to Harvey. He finally understood that privatisation is what Modern Labour is all about.'

There's the clang of an alpine goat bell.

'They're saying we should go in for dinner,' says Elliott.

I turn to Jess. 'I need to make arrangements for tomorrow. If you go through, I'll be back in two minutes.'

I step outside, into the snowy street. The cold air pinches my nostrils, though it is thawing and a few flakes of snow drift down. As I make my call, one of the sword-length icicles hanging from the eaves falls and shatters. I do my business and return.

Elliott isn't staying for dinner. He's the organiser, but rarely does he hang around for the event itself. He doesn't have the attention span. He always needs to be in transit, in this instance to a party in his enormous rented chalet over by Davos Dorf. We're all invited. He leaves encouraging us to enjoy the wine. I note what it is: Château Palmer 1989. I feel confident I will drink too much.

I am seated next to Munis, while Jess is opposite next to Stella Barnsbury. The chair on Stella's other side is empty, but only for a moment. There's a booming South African voice behind me. I swivel to see Jimmy Breitner, founder and owner of Media Corp, which owns the *Globe* tabloid as well as the *Financial Chronicle*.

'Apologies for being late, Mrs B,' he bellows. He turns to Jess. 'And you, Miss Neeskens, are doing fantastic work covering the banking crisis. You do me proud.'

Jess thanks him with convincing sincerity, though I know she is as repulsed as I am by how he deploys his newspapers and television channels to promote the biddable politicians who pay homage to him and serve his commercial interests. Stella Barnsbury is owned by the man on her right, whether she admits it or not.

In front of us are vast pots of melting cheese, the fondue, on burners. We each have skewers to stab chunks of bread or new potatoes, to immerse in the molten Gruyere. Mrs Barnsbury taps her fork on the side of her wine glass to attract our attention.

'Before we tuck in, I wanted to thank you all for being here. And to remind our media friends that this is all strictly off the record. I don't know about you, but I think change is in the air. I read somewhere, I am not sure where, that Neville Tudor was tired and had run out of ideas. That it's time for a new team to take over. Where did I read that, Jimmy?'

Breitner roars with laughter and makes a thumbs up. 'The *Globe* was one hundred per cent right on Tudor. He's turning profit into a dirty word, crushing enterprise, stealing our precious freedoms.' He looks directly at Johnny Todd. 'He's not even a pale imitation of his predecessor. He can't be turfed out soon enough.'

There are cries of 'Well said,' and 'Hear hear.' I'm dying with embarrassment; Jess is stony-faced. I turn to my right to see

Patrick Munis mouthing 'Thank you' at Breitner. As for Todd, he's grinning from ear to ear. Why am I putting myself through this torture?

Munis spends most of dinner trying to extract as much information from me as he can about how Tudor operates and what's happening inside the banks. I say as little as possible while getting him to open up about his plans for government. It's what mathematicians would call a zero-sum game, in which it's impossible for each of us to end up on the credit side of the balance sheet. When it's time to go, Munis is scratchy. Maybe I won, this time.

Jess scoops me up and we head for the door. 'We could skip Elliott's party,' she says.

'Nah. It's the only point of coming to this terrible place.'

Munis is already in the minivan that has been laid on to whisk us there. He's about to shut the sliding door when I wave at him and we climb in. 'I'm not going to stay late,' says Munis. 'I'm talking at a Schon breakfast in the morning.'

'Pull the other one, Patrick,' I laugh. 'You're always the last to leave. I wish I had your stamina.'

Elliott's party is filled with politicians, hacks and bankers, who turn up to mingle with the film stars and ageing rock gods who are clients of his celebrity PR operation. They come to Davos to urge world leaders to end poverty, stem climate change and educate young girls in developing countries. It is a giant washing machine for the consciences of the overpaid and the entitled.

The chalet door is patrolled by half a dozen women with East European accents in skimpy black dresses.

'Does Elliott lay on the escorts for the theatre of it, or do you think they provide personal services?' Jess asks.

'I've always been too squeamish to investigate.'

'Hmmm.'

Although we're here to schmooze, we can't be bothered. I want to dance, and Jess humours me. It's an appalling playlist: Davos

Man has pedestrian tastes, early Rolling Stones, late Fleetwood Mac and mid-period Bowie. But we don't care. We're pretty much on our own till the DJ makes a concession to the year we're in, and plays 'Low' by Flo Rida. The floor is suddenly heaving with men whose dancing prowess is in inverse relationship to their net worth.

I lean close into Jess and shout, 'What are apple bottom jeans, and who's shawty?'

'Stop being so fucking OCD and hold me tight.'

I pull her close and this time whisper, 'Sorry for everything.'

'What do you mean?'

'Sorry for involving you and Amy in my nightmare. It's not fair.'

'She's OK. We're OK.'

'I love you, Jess.'

'I know, stupid.'

She puts her hands behind my head and pulls my mouth towards hers. She kisses me full on the lips. In front of everyone.

Chapter 29

'I S IT WORTH RINGING ROOM service for a cup of coffee?'
I am naked in Jess's bed in the Steigenberger. When
we're together, everything in my life feels more hopeful.
I roll over and kiss her cheek.

'You can try,' she yawns. As she stretches, I can see her breasts
through her T-shirt. It's all too good to be true. 'It'll take hours,
though.'

'OK. Let's dress and get a free coffee from the conference
centre.'

She wags a finger at me. 'I can't believe you said that. Nothing
is free here. There's a price on everything.'

I stoop down and kiss her. 'On everything?' I ask.

'Oh lord, Gil. You'll never change.'

We jump in the shower and then head to the lobby. As we
exit the lift, my world of Jess-infused happiness dissipates, when
Jackson sees us and summons us.

'Can I have a word?' He is talking to Jess.

I'm worried. The kidnapping of Amy was as appalling a trauma
for her as anything that has happened to me. Can she keep her
composure with Jackson?

I shouldn't have doubted her professionalism. 'I thought
you'd already given Gil all the scoops,' she quips.

'There's so much more to our takeover of NewGate,' he says.
'Gil gets the headlines, but it's you and the FC who get all the

important nitty gritty.' He's laying it on. 'Shall we grab a coffee? Now, if you're free.'

He means without me.

'I'll head over to the conference centre,' I say. I turn to Jess. 'Text when you're done.'

I head out and down the treacherous stone steps to the Promenade, and then left through the thick snow to the big white blocks of the main conference building. Later today, Angela Merkel, the German chancellor, will be the main event in the central auditorium, along with Henry Kissinger, Mick Jackson, Angelina Jolie – and Neville Tudor. I leave my Conran overcoat in the cloakroom and head through to the members' room.

Before I reach the staircase, I run into Stan Blackwell. He looks genuinely pleased to see me.

'I heard about your crash. Are you OK?'

Perhaps I am being naive, but my sense is he doesn't know the truth of it. 'I seem to be. I was pretty shaken. How is it with your new Saudi owners?'

'Early days.' He glances over his shoulder. 'I can't pretend it's easy, though. Big cultural differences.'

'With the Saudis?'

'They've appointed Chris Ravel to the board to look after their interests. Between you and me, he's a nightmare. He wants to micromanage everything.'

I suppress a smile. Blackwell is notorious for being a control freak who can't delegate, so to have another control freak as – in effect – his boss is a recipe for stress. They deserve each other.

'Thanks for what you wrote when you got wind of the deal,' he continues. 'Made a huge difference. Without it I think we'd have struggled to get approval from the government.'

Not the plaudit I would choose.

'Quite all right,' I say. 'I just write as I see.' The problem with lies is they inevitably breed new lies.

The marble-floored hall is buzzing with the self-regarding chatter of people who know they matter. Over Blackwell's right shoulder I see Elliott, Todd and Ravel forging towards us I press hard on my stump. The plan was to inure myself to them, like taking small doses of poison, but whenever I see them I find myself back in their torture chamber at the top of the Canary Wharf tower.

'I thought you'd gone,' I say, abruptly.

'Just leaving now,' says Todd. 'Primakov is lending us his helicopter, to take us down the mountain.'

I look directly into his green eyes. 'What's your relationship with Primakov?'

'He's a client, and a friend.'

'Don't you feel bad about all that money he lost backing the initial NewGate bid?'

Todd shrugs. 'Rough with the smooth. Petr understands that. Why else would he be giving us a lift in his chopper?'

He ostentatiously checks the time on his Patek Philippe, as if to say, *If you were more like me, you could afford one of these too.* 'We should go.'

'Just the three of you?' I ask.

'Harvey's joining us,' says Todd.

Ravel sighs. 'You mean I have to sit in a confined space with that fuckwit?'

'Relax, Chris. It's only a short ride.'

'I'll catch you at Prince Andrew's soirée,' I say to Blackwell. The event only ever serves cheap white wine and stale crisps, but it is always heaving. There's a view among the British businessmen here that it would be unpatriotic to stay away.

'Stan will be there if by some miracle he's managed to get the data I need by then,' says Ravel. He looks directly at the PTBG boss. 'Those numbers you sent me last night were a joke.'

If it were anyone but Blackwell, I'd be sympathetic. But it's still tedious to be a witness to Ravel's bullying, so I wish them a pleasant journey home and head for the members' room – where I grab my coffee. Sorting through my emails, the senior partner of a Silicon Valley venture capital fund is introduced by his PR minder and starts evangelising about all the amazing digital services that are coming down the track. I've heard it all before. I need another coffee.

I'm leaning on the bar, waiting for the barista, when my BlackBerry vibrates.

It's Jess. I smile in anticipation.

Hi darling. Jackson is going to give me an interview, on both Athena and NewGate. It's too good an opportunity to miss. So I'll travel with him in Primakov's helicopter down to Zurich, then take the train back up the mountain. Miss you. Love you. xxx

I read it twice. The second time in blind panic. *This can't be happening. Please God. This must not happen.* I ring her, but I'm sent straight to voicemail: no signal, or the phone is switched off.

I send a text. *Don't get on the helicopter. I'll explain when I see you. YOU MUST NOT LEAVE DAVOS.*

Without stopping to get my coat, I run to her hotel. Maybe she hasn't left yet. In my rush, I almost fall on the icy stairs up to the Steigenberger. When I get there I have to queue to go through the security scanners. It's intolerable. I grind my teeth. Every second standing in line is agonising. I try to ring: again, and again, and again. Nothing. I am flapping and talking aloud attracting quizzical looks. I must calm down.

I'll call Primakov. Tell him not to give Jess a ride. He'll understand; he'll stop it. But he's not picking up. I text him.

When I finally get through the scanners to the hotel lobby, there's no sign of Jess.

The heliport. I should have gone there straightaway.

I go back to the Promenade. *Where on earth are the taxis?*

370

'Hey, Gil,' says the woman waiting next to me at the cab rank. It's Irena Levin, a Bloomberg journalist who used to work for me at the *FC* in the 1990s.

'Hi.'

'You OK? You look stressed.'

'I—'

I'm interrupted by a dull thud, maybe from a mile or so away. Irena cocks her head. 'Is that an explosion?'

Every part of me turns to ice. I can't move or think.

'You OK, Gil?' says Irena. 'You've gone white as a sheet. Probably just avalanche control at the ski resort.'

'Will you excuse me?' I walk away. Where should I go, what should I do? My mind is having terrifying, uncontrollable thoughts. This is hell. *What have I done?*

My phone buzzes. I snatch it out of my pocket as if pulling it out of a fire. *Please be Jess. Please be Jess. Please be Jess.*

It's Primakov. *Come up the mountain and we'll talk.*

He's rented the landmark chalet at the top of Thomas Mann's *Magic Mountain,* on the far side of the Schatzalp, the former tuberculosis sanatorium. I run along Obere Strasse to the funicular station, then endure an unbearable ten-minute wait for the Schatzalp-Bahn carriages to be cranked down the mountainside. A minor British royal engages me in conversation. Is this my first World Economic Forum? What do I think of it? She's here to highlight the scandal of illiteracy among young girls in developing countries. She seems well-intentioned and nice. But I can't concentrate. All my tics have been triggered. If anyone's watching closely they'll see a lunatic rocking and muttering spells to ward off demons.

We chug up the mountain in the cable car. Once at the top, I head up the path, through some kind of citadel, into the former sanatorium, which has been turned into a dowdy, vast hotel. I spring up the stairs, out the other side, over a moat, and then left down a path to a long two-storey house.

The door opens before I arrive. A blonde woman, in a figure-hugging jersey dress, says Mr Primakov is having drinks in the front room. Would I care to join him? I rush through.

Primakov is sitting on a vast brown leather sofa, in front of full-length windows that give spectacular views over the Alps. Next to him is Lydia, Elliott's wife. A bottle of Krug is open on the glass table in front of them. They are celebrating. It's unbearable.

'I thought we had an understanding,' I stutter. 'I thought ...' I can't bring myself to say Jess's name.

Primakov gestures to a servant, who brings over a third champagne glass and fills it. 'If we had an understanding, Mr Peck, you may rest assured I would honour it. Sit down and join us?'

Is he really so heartless, so ruthless? Does life not mean anything to him? The person I care about most in the whole world has just smashed into the mountain, and he is offering me champagne.

I feel dizzy and clasp the back of an armchair. I try to compose the question I have to ask, when someone circles their arms around my waist.

'Hello, my love.'

Jess. Jess!

Thank you God, thank you God, thank you God.

I turn and hug her harder than I've hugged anyone. 'Darling! I thought you'd ...'

I'm overwhelmed. I can barely talk. It's the same rush of redemption as breaking the surface of Elliott's lake. My life was over and now it's begun again. I have to keep staring at her, holding her, making sure this is not a dream.

She gives me a bemused look. 'Are you all right?'

'I ... just ... didn't expect to see you.'

'Mr Primakov rang the heliport. The officials there gave me a message that you needed me urgently and I wasn't to take the trip. So I told Jackson I'd contact him in London.'

'Thank God,' is all I can say.

Over her shoulder, I hear the buzz of Primakov's phone, and then his clipped voice speaking to someone. 'Yes ... Yes ... All of them? You are sure? That is terrible.'

He clears his throat to get our attention. 'Shocking news. My helicopter crashed soon after take-off. Everyone on board is dead.'

Now it's my turn to hold up Jess as she goes limp in my arms. 'What?'

'You are very lucky to be alive, Ms Neeskens.'

She pulls back from me, face taut with shock. But her logical brain is already making the connections that will be difficult for me.

'Did you know?'

'I heard the explosion from down the hill. I worried.' I can see she is unconvinced. 'You know me. I fear the worst, especially when it comes to those I love.'

She pulls back from me. And turns to Primakov. 'Johnny Todd was on that flight. And Jackson, and Ravel.'

Primakov nods.

'And Elliott,' I add.

I'd forgotten that Lydia, Alex's now-widow, is on the sofa with Primakov. I turn to her to apologise for my lack of tact, but she seems unconcerned. Perhaps in shock. She takes another sip of her champagne. Condensation frosts the icy glass.

Jess is shaking her head. 'Elliott wasn't on board.'

Lydia and I stare at her.

'Lucky escape,' says a voice behind me.

I turn. It's Elliott. 'Alex drove me back,' says Jess. She explains that he'd decided to stay after receiving a distressed call from one of his clients, a Hollywood actor, who was snapped with a Russian escort at Elliott's party – and whose wife took exception when she saw the photo in the *New York Post*.

'Luck of the devil,' says Alex. He crosses to his wife and wraps his hands around both her wrists. 'I hope you weren't worried about me.'

'Of course not, darling,' she says. 'Nothing hurts you.' Her face is dry, her makeup flawless. Not a speck of mascara dislodged.

'I should get back to my chalet,' Elliott says. 'I need to organise how we contextualise this terrible tragedy for the media.'

He'll be spinning for Johnny Todd. It's all about curating the legacy.

I look at Primakov, who is busy refilling his champagne glass. He winks at me.

'Such a tragedy,' I say.

'What tragedy?' he replies. 'The stupid greedy Jew has lost a helicopter. I can afford it.'

Chapter 30

DEATH IS AN END. BUT not for those left behind. I thought the crash – the deaths of Todd, Jackson and Ravel – would be justice for Clare and for Marilyn. But the justice is shallow. It is too private. Todd should have been tried, condemned and executed in the court of public opinion.

Instead, he's being lionised. The media coverage of the deaths goes on day after day. The prime minister puts out a statement about how Johnny Todd will be seen alongside Churchill and Thatcher as one of the great prime ministers of our age, and how the country is less for the deaths of him, Ravel and Jackson. The press lauds Jackson and Ravel as business geniuses, the cream of a younger generation of British entrepreneurs. As he said he would, Elliott is managing their respective images. Even in death, they're still winning.

For the first time, there's a shadow over my relationship with Jess. She doesn't say anything, but she's too smart to believe they died by pure chance. She's waiting for me to tell her how I knew to keep her off the helicopter – and she wonders why the only corpse not to be discovered was that of the pilot, the sole individual employed by Primakov. She doesn't believe in luck, intuition or foresight. There's never been a big secret separating us before, and I know I'll have to find a way to dispel it. Or our love will wither and die in this dark shadow.

*

It's a week after Davos, and I am in the prime minister's office on a white sofa. There's a pot of tea and a jug of coffee between us, plain digestives on a plate.

'I ask for chocolate. Every day,' Tudor complains. 'You'd think the prime minister could have any biscuit he wanted, but chocolate is not on the approved list. Nothing I can do about it.'

'There are worse privations. Are we here to talk about biscuits?'

He shakes his head. He's aged in the last week. When I saw him on TV delivering the eulogy at Johnny Todd's funeral, I was struck by how grey and washed-out he was. Despite all the rivalry between the two men, they were partners through almost twenty years of brutal politics. Without Johnny, he's smaller.

'PTBG,' he says.

'What about it?'

'The Saudis have pulled out.'

I don't hide my surprise. 'I didn't know they could.'

'Only heads of agreement were signed. No money was handed over. Apparently the death of Ravel counts as force majeure. He was supposed to run the thing for them.'

'Are you giving me this as a story?' It would make the NewGate scoop look like small potatoes.

'I'm asking you what to do. As I am sure you know, though we've tried to keep it quiet, the bank is bust without the Saudi capital.'

'Yes. I was aware.' I pretend to think for a moment, though he's surely worked out the answer already. 'Seems to me it's all pretty straightforward. You have to buy the bank. You have to take it into public ownership.'

'It's huge, though. Balance sheet pretty much the same size as the national debt. Quite a liability. A whole different ball game to NewGate – which, by the way, is ours again, now that Jackson's popped his clogs.'

I top up my black coffee, giving a wide berth to the digestives. 'Yes, there's a potential cost. But there's also an opportunity. The City, the banks, they were out of control. You can be the new sheriff in town. You can clean them up. And, by the way, this banking debacle is not a uniquely British phenomenon. Banks are going to tumble like Skittles all over the world. You can be a pioneer, set an example, show the world how to protect citizens' hard-won savings and ensure credit continues to be extended to the businesses that provide jobs.'

'Maybe.' He glances at the wall, where a framed photograph of Todd has been hastily hung, edged in black. 'What do you think Johnny would do?'

I put down my coffee cup, careful not to spill any. 'Fuck Johnny. He's dead.'

*

From Downing Street, I go to Television Centre. I write the predictable blog about the looming government rescue of PTBG, and do the first of what will be twenty-odd live broadcasts on the biggest nationalisation in British history: from the *PM* programme with Eddie Mair, to the *18.00* Radio Four news half hour and the *Six O'Clock News* on television, to endless two-ways on the News Channel, and on and on and on. Against my better judgement, I finish with *Newsnight*. Way too late: I'll be exhausted tomorrow.

Somewhere in between being mic-ed up, made-up, telling the presenters about core capital and credit derivatives, I find a few precious seconds of time to think. And as I bicycle back to Queen's Park, I've made my decision.

When I arrive, I head for the kitchen. Jess is sitting at the table, answering emails. No need for a preamble.

'We have to talk about what happened in Davos.' I search her face for encouragement, terrified of what I'm about to say next. If I get this wrong, I'll lose everything.

She closes the laptop. 'I know what you're going to say.'

'I knew Primakov was going to assassinate them. In fact, I organised it.'

She nods. 'How?'

I sit down and play her the recording that I made on my Olympus, Jackson's antisemitic rant when he thought the microphones were off after our interview. *He's not going to miss a billion or so. He stole it all in the first place. Just another greedy Russian Jew. He can afford it. If he doesn't want to help us, who gives a fuck? We can manage perfectly well without him.*

'Primakov didn't care about the money. I don't think he even minded that I put out stories that damaged his interests. But he wouldn't be played for a fool. Not by Jackson and Todd. Not by anyone.'

'You gave him the recording?'

'After I was mutilated by Elliott, I had a lot of time to think. I couldn't let them get away with what they did. They'd only do it again. The world is better off without them. As Dad used to say, "Don't get mad, get even."'

I tell her about a long conversation I had with Primakov when I was convalescing in her bed, and the phone call I made outside the Alte Post restaurant, after I found out precisely when Todd would be leaving.

I'm under no illusions about Primakov. He may well be responsible for Robin Muller's murder. I haven't asked him. Maybe I should care.

'Have I done the wrong thing?'

'Yes.' Jess scratches at a knot in the wood of the kitchen table, refusing to meet my eye. I feel myself shrivelling into my chair. I've lost her. I go over and over in my mind what a fool I've been, that my life is over, that I should never have been so stupid and reckless.

But when she looks up, her eyes are bright and her face is calm. 'Sooner or later, doing what we do, we'd have come up against Todd and his people again. And if we had gone against their interests in any way, they would have had no compunction in killing you, killing me, killing Amy.'

I look deep into the darkness of her pupils. They tell me it's going to be OK.

'It's just a bit of a disappointment that Elliott dodged it.'

The air I didn't know I was holding in pours out. I slump forward, reach forward across the table and take her hands.

'I should have told you. But I didn't want to implicate you.'

'I had a right to know,' she says. 'Next time you're thinking of doing something quite so – well – radical, would you mind discussing it with me first? If we're a team, I get a vote.'

'You do. I am an idiot. I wasn't myself.'

That gets a laugh. 'You were completely yourself. You're a lone wolf. But now you have to learn to hunt in a pack.'

'Of two?'

'It's a start.'

I take a bottle of wine from the rack and start to wind in the corkscrew. 'I still don't feel that justice has been done.'

'Agreed. Todd is a martyr, Jackson's a saint, Ravel's a genius and Elliott is still alive.'

The cork comes out with a pop. 'I have a plan.'

'You normally do.'

*

Three days later, we're walking along the Embankment with Kim Jansen. I'm mildly surprised she agreed to see us so readily: it could be residual guilt, but more likely it's the legitimate fear of what we have on her. It's a grey, dark day in early February, when the wind coming off the Thames is damp and feels colder than the Swiss Alps.

'I've been reflecting on the well-known fact that the dead can't sue,' I say.

Kim darts a glance at me. 'They can't be charged with a crime, either, if that's what you want.'

'Not in a court of law. But there are other forums where people are judged.'

She stops and turns towards me.

'Jess and I are going to publish and broadcast everything we know, about the deaths of Clare and Marilyn, about Chris Ravel's illegal arms sales to terrorists, about how he sabotaged NewGate's servers, about Jackson's blackmailing of Marilyn. About how a recent prime minister was up to his neck in all of it.'

'You can print that?'

'As I said, the dead can't sue. And we have detailed notes, we have copies we made of some of the diaries, we have photographic evidence.'

Kim digs her hands in her pockets and starts walking again. 'Why are you telling me this?'

'Maybe you can understand how I felt when they took my daughter. As a mother I can never forget, or forgive.'

'I told you, I was not involved—'

Jess cuts her off. 'We know you collaborated with Elliott and Ravel in trying to intimidate us. I can only guess why you did. Maybe Elliott has compromising pictures of you too, from your Malmsey days, pictures that would destroy your chances of becoming the first female commissioner of the Met, if they were ever printed in the *Globe*.'

Kim continues to walk. Bolt upright, staring forward, almost as though she daren't acknowledge our presence.

I pick up the thread. 'I don't know if you intended us harm. You certainly did us harm. We can, however, forget it happened, in return for something.'

'What do you want?' Kim sighs.

'This is our offer,' says Jess. 'You give us back Marilyn's diaries. All of them. They are more properly Gil's than yours, in any case. The BBC and *FC* will shortly publish our joint investigation into the deaths of Clare and Marilyn, and the rottenness at the heart of PTBG, MHH and Lulworth. You will respond in a press release, that we will pre-agree, promising a formal Met investigation.'

'And if I don't cooperate?'

'We'll publish everything anyway. But we will include your name in every article, every chapter, every broadcast. Which is not hard, because you were in the thick of it – turning a blind eye, stupidly negligent, actively working against justice.'

Jansen stops and turns to Jess. 'You must believe me that I had no idea they were going to take Amy.'

I laugh, which is completely inappropriate, but she sounds just like the bankers. *We had no idea what we were doing was toxic. We pocketed our bonuses in good faith. No one was supposed to get hurt.*

'It's easy not to know something if you don't want to,' I tell her. 'The question is, are you going to take responsibility?'

*

A week later, I am back in Rainham, on that vast icy plain, and walking past row after row of Star-of-David- and menorah-inscribed headstones. I've never known a week like it. Two days after we saw Jansen, and after extensive negotiations with Janice Oldham and the DG, the BBC and the *FC* pressed the button on what we called the Marilyn Files. It's the biggest story of our careers. Jansen kept her word and launched a police enquiry. There are at least three investigations by parliamentary select committees, and the prime minister is under pressure from the Tories to launch a judge-led public enquiry. Alex Elliott's reputation and tactics are under scrutiny, at last. It turns out there are a lot of celebrities who have stories to tell about the way he sold them out to the tabloids, now that they don't fear retribution. I've had one text from him, which I intend to treasure forever. A single word: *cunt*.

Down the long gravel path, in the biting wind, I retrace my steps to Dad's grave, which will not get its headstone for another nine months. I'm alone. There are no mourners or gardeners or caretakers anywhere in view. I wouldn't have cared if there were. I am not self-conscious. I don't care who witnesses me. All that matters is that I do and say the right thing.

'Hi, Dad. I didn't hear you when you needed me. No excuse. I was too up my own backside to understand, as usual. I know now you always believed in me, even though I used to think Clare was your favourite and I was the big disappointment. But if you hadn't believed in me, I would never have been able to secure justice for Clare. I would have lacked the courage.

'Did you notice, Dad? They underestimated me. It was useful that they didn't have my measure, as you said it would be. I didn't get mad. I got even.'

I pause. If he was here, alive, there's so much more I would tell him, the truth of what men like Elliott and Todd and Ravel do. Dad always told me the system stinks. I only half believed him and made too many compromises for too long. I've repented.

I know that he knows. But, there's one thing I need to tell him, which used to be impossible to say. 'I love you, Dad.'

I take out a tatty sheet of A4. I've been carrying it around for days, trying to memorise it. It's a Kaddish prayer, written out phonetically. I am aware it's blasphemy at worst, and pretty useless at best, because there's no minyan, no caucus of adult Jews with me. But Dad will get it. And as I sing, I try to channel the cantors who – Mum says – were my forebears.

Y'hei sh'mei raba m'varach l'alam u-l'almei almaya.

'May God's great name be praised throughout all eternity.'

Oseh shalom bi-m'romav, hu ya'aseh shalom aleinu v'al kol yisrael, v'imru amen.

'May the One who brings peace to the universe bring peace to us and to all the people of Israel. And let us say: Amen.'

Then I place a pebble at the end of the marble tomb. *I love you Dad, I love you Dad, I love you Dad.*

It starts to rain. Of course. It's Rainham.

Who cares? I certainly don't. I'm going home. To Amy and Jess.

If you enjoyed *The Crash*, why not join the

ROBERT PESTON READERS' CLUB?

When you sign up, you'll receive news about books, giveaways, events, and exclusive material from Robert Peston straight to your inbox

To join, simply visit:
geni.us/PestonReadersClub

Hello!

Thank you for getting hold of *The Crash*. I hope it's as much fun to read as it was to write. *The Crash* is the sequel to *The Whistleblower*, my thriller about the politics and business skullduggery of the late 1990s. A decade later, in the autumn of 2007, the hero, or perhaps anti-hero, Gil Peck has moved out of newspapers and is now a broadcaster. He is delivering the bad news to the nation that it's on the brink of economic collapse, because of the greed and recklessness of banks, when his lover – who works at the Bank of England – is found hanged. His ensuing obsessive pursuit of the truth of what happened to her, and his determination to bring her persecutors to justice, takes place against the backdrop of high politics, base greed and the extreme profligacy of that era's party culture. It's a parable of the big economic and political shifts in the form of edge-of-the seat entertainment. Or at least that was my plan.

What I've tried to do with this book, as I did with *The Whistleblower*, is to draw on my personal experience of big events to create a plausible alternative reality, that informs as much as it should give pleasure. Every character is both a figment of my imagination and an amalgam of people I've encountered and know. Every event is invented but – I hope – plausible, albeit often at the extreme edge of plausibility.

If you would like to hear more about my books, you can visit **geni.us/PestonReadersClub** where you can become part of the Robert Peston Readers' Club. It only takes a few moments to sign up, there are no catches or costs. Bonnier Books UK will keep your data private and confidential, and it will never be passed on to a third party. We won't spam you with loads of emails, just get in touch now and again with news about my books, and you can unsubscribe any time you want. And if you would like to get involved in a wider conversation about my books, please do review *The Crash* on Amazon, on GoodReads, on any other e-store, on your own blog and social media accounts, or talk about it with friends, family or reader groups! Sharing your thoughts helps other readers, and I always enjoy hearing about what people experience from my writing. Thank you again for reading *The Crash*.

Best wishes

Robert Peston

Don't miss out on Gil Peck's first case . . .

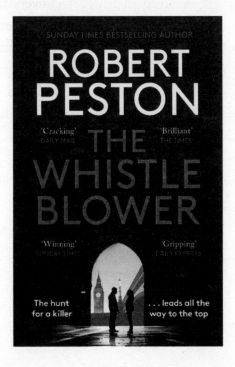

1997. A desperate government clings to power; a hungry opposition will do anything to win. And journalist Gil Peck watches from the sidelines, a respected commentator on the sport of power politics. He thinks he knows how things work. He thinks he knows the rules.

But when Gil's estranged sister Clare dies in a hit-and-run, he begins to believe it was no accident. Clare knew some of the most sensitive secrets in government. One of them might have got her killed.

As election day approaches, Gil follows the story into the dark web of interests that link politics, finance and the media. And the deeper he goes, the more he realises how wrong he has been.

Power isn't sport: it's war. And if Gil doesn't stop digging, he might be the next casualty.

AVAILABLE NOW